Martyn Whittock was   degree in Politics at Bristol University. After graduating he taught History in Dorset and in Buckinghamshire, and has since become Head of Humanities and Senior Teacher at another school in Dorset. He has published a number of scholarly articles and is the author of two textbooks, *The Origins of England, AD 410–600* and *The Roman Empire*. He has acted as a historical consultant to both the National Trust and BBC Radio. *The Dice in Flight* is his first novel and he has recently completed his second, also set in medieval England, *The Moon in the Morning*. Martyn Whittock lives in Dorchester with his wife and daughter.

Also by Martyn Whittock

The Moon in the Morning

The Dice in Flight

Martyn Whittock

HEADLINE

Copyright © 1991 Martyn Whittock

The right of Martyn Whittock to be identified as the Author of the Work has been asserted by him in accordance with the Copyright, Designs and Patents Act 1988.

First published in 1991
by Barrie & Jenkins Ltd

First published in paperback in 1992
by HEADLINE BOOK PUBLISHING PLC

10 9 8 7 6 5 4 3 2 1

All rights reserved. No part of this publication may be reproduced, stored in a retrieval system, or transmitted, in any form or by any means without the prior written permission of the publisher, nor be otherwise circulated in any form of binding or cover other than that in which it is published and without a similar condition being imposed on the subsequent purchaser.

All characters in this publication are fictitious and any resemblance to real persons, living or dead, is purely coincidental.

ISBN 0 7472 3837 5

Printed and bound in Great Britain by
HarperCollins Manufacturing, Glasgow

HEADLINE BOOK PUBLISHING PLC
Headline House
79 Great Titchfield Street
London W1P 7FN

*To Hannah Elizabeth Whittock,
with love*

CONTENTS

Acknowledgements ix

Part One: A Game of Chess, 1377-8   1

Part Two: Hoodman Blind, 1378-9   77

Part Three: A Game of Fox and Goose, 1379-80   149

Part Four: Nine Men's Morris, 1380-81   249

Afterword   345

Acknowledgements

Whilst the Mentmore family are a fictitious creation, the background to their story is not. They can stand for a host of senior guild families whose lives were intertwined with national events in the 1370s and 1380s. The framework on which their story hangs is a factual one. London was divided by bitter guild rivalries in the 1370s; the shift of the cloth industry to a rural setting was a major economic and social event in the fourteenth and fifteenth centuries; there was enormous unrest in the countryside when landlords tried to enforce their rights on a more confident peasantry, or turn vacated land over to sheep. Families like the Compworths fished in the troubled waters of their neighbours' estates; hedge priests were a noted social phenomenon to be loathed or loved depending on your social station.

Other details, too, are well attested in the contemporary records. Gaunt did steal the show at Sheen with his theatrical forgiveness of the Londoners; Buckingham did face defeat when the French sallied forth from the St Nicholas gate at Nantes and it was Knollys who stopped the breakout; Knollys's town house was an armed camp in 1381 in preparation for another Breton adventure. Many other fragments of real events also appear within this story.

Some historical areas are a little more complex and ambiguous and allow for more licence. The two squires *were* seized at Westminster *and* Kirkby was executed for the killing of a Genoese merchant. I have chosen to link these two incidents. Whether Gaunt was actually at the Savoy when the squires were seized is open to question. There is some contemporary evidence to suggest that he may have been abroad. However, he *was* behind the plot and I have underscored that by making him present in London on the night in question. Concerning the real-life role of Horne in the events of June 1381, there is some ambiguity. Contemporary accounts disagree as to the extent of his culpability. I have used the hints given in the medieval sources to develop his role as the enemy of the Mentmores. This is not without historical foundation since he clearly played a significant part in the entry of the peasants into London and the bloody consequences. I have fleshed out his motives which are only touched on in the surviving fourteenth-century chronicles.

For the details of the revolt, there are a number of near contemporary sources: *Froissart's Chronicle*, the *Anonimalle Chronicle* of York and Malverne's continuation of the *Polychronicon*. There is also a London account quoted by H. T. Rily in *Memorials of London and London Life II* (1868) and other fragments contained in Walsingham's *Historia Anglicana*. From these witnesses it is possible to gain intimate insights into the events of the revolt. These include vignettes concerning Ball writing letters to sympathisers with his 'Great Society', the shops destroyed on Fleet Street because they spoilt the scenery and Walworth wearing armour under his robe. Other details from them are also woven into the fiction.

There is still debate over exactly what happened at Smithfield on Saturday 15 June 1381. I have made Tyler's death the result of a preconceived gamble by Walworth and Knollys. The chronicles allow for this interpretation, even if they do not state it explicitly.

I have been greatly assisted by the Bucks Library Service who chased up numerous books for me, and the staff of the Museum of London who answered by queries with patience. I am very grateful to Sandra Jacobs, who typed the manuscript with care and enthusiasm.

I would like to thank my wife and family for their support and suggestions; Sarah Molloy and Jane Hill, my editors, who have been the source of so much valuable and constructive advice. Last but not least I must thank my baby daughter Hannah. Though only a week old, she managed to stay asleep long enough for me to finish the last chapter!

Winslow
St Thomas' Day

The Dice in Flight

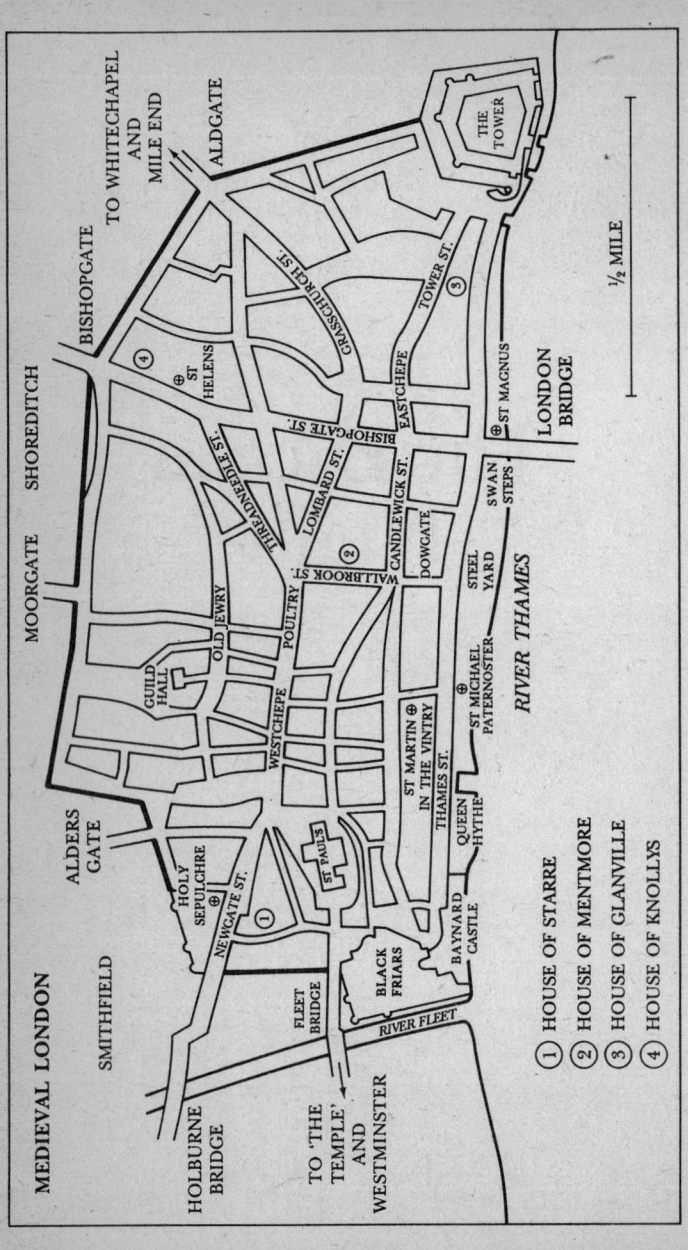

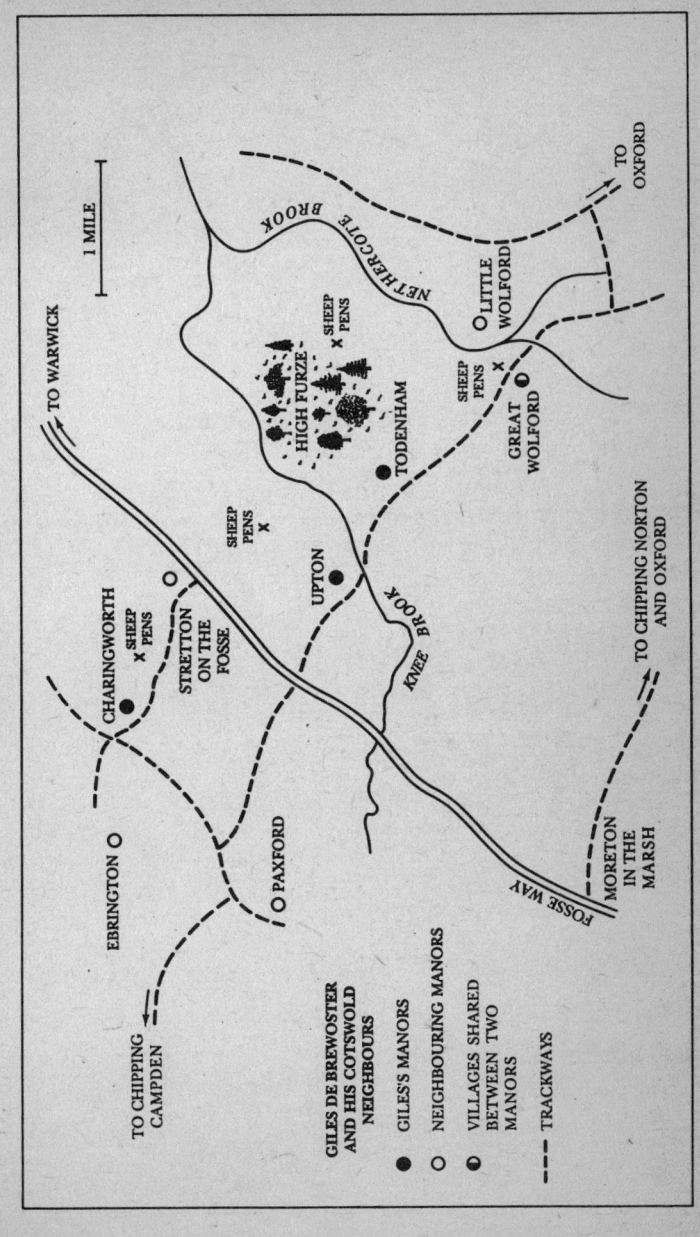

PART ONE

*A Game of Chess
1377-8*

Chapter One

A wet, cold night gave way to a hesitant dove-grey dawn. Across the shining roofs the light fluttered, pale-winged. It slowly penetrated dripping alleyways and brushed the glistening eaves of overhung buildings. At last it spread its wing beats far and wide across the city. Towers, steeples, yards and roadways found that night had succumbed. Day had arrived. Sparrows chirped nervously. Pigeons shocked the air with the sharp clap of their rising flight.

London was awake. A teeming and tumultuous city of thirty-five thousand souls had shaken off its sleep. At all points men and women were abroad and busy. With first light the city gates were open and soon the narrow entrances were hectic with rumbling and clattering carts. Each cart was heavy with merchandise. Along the streets of the city flowed a nation's wealth, like blood through veins.

Agnes Bakwell had risen at dawn. By first light she was fussing and bartering along the market stalls of West Chepe. Pinching the well-endowed breast of a strung pullet she seemed unaware of the familiar gaze of the stall holder.

'Does it suit you, my lady?' the jovial fellow enquired. His false formality caused her to smile.

'At half the price it might, John Toghull.'

'By St John, Agnes, it's the finest pullet you'll find this morning.'

The plump woman, in her well-worn grey gown, shrugged. She had already tested dozens of fowls along the wide street called 'The Poultry'. She knew the best were on this stall, but knew better than to reveal her approval.

'Only the best will suit my young master,' she added simply, 'and neither he nor his father will thank me for throwing good silver away.'

'So it's for John Mentmore's wedding, is it? You'll not do better than here, Agnes. I've pullets enough – and fresh – to suit a wedding as grand as that of a Mentmore.'

'Perhaps, perhaps,' the silver-haired cook agreed. 'But at half the price!'

'Two pennies for the twelve,' retorted the butcher.

'One penny for nine.'

'Huh, huh – you'll ruin me. One penny for eight.'

'For nine, John Toghull. For nine!'

'Very well.'

Both were secretly pleased at their compromise. Money flashed and the pullets were piled into the arms of a wispy scullery lad.

John Toghull touched the arm of the old matron. 'Shop quickly this morning, Agnes. Don't tarry about West Chepe.'

Agnes laughed. It was a full and sensuous burst of merriment. 'Oh, I don't fear the soldiers, you fool!'

The leather-faced butcher shook his head. He glanced at a passing gang of brightly jerkined soldiery. On their surcoats they wore the double 'S' badge of John of Gaunt, Duke of Lancaster.

'I'm not a fool, Agnes.' There was a real note of tenderness in his voice. 'But the bishop has summoned John Wyclif to St Paul's and John of Gaunt will not stand by and see his man destroyed.'

'Good luck to Wyclif,' Agnes retorted. 'We can all see the rich princes of the church dine well on our tithes and they could take a lesson.'

'Yes, yes,' the butcher chipped in, 'but the bishop's soldiers and Gaunt's soldiers will take little notice of the views of you or I.'

'Well thank you, John, anyway,' she said. 'I'll keep myself safe and never you mind.'

Leaving him, she finished her shopping more swiftly than usual. Despite her merriment she had seen the worry on the butcher's face. Towards Threadneedle Street the stall holders were already packing away. Here and there a shop window was covered with rough planks. The crowds along Chepeside were tense and rumours were passing of trouble brewing.

Agnes and her boy attendant hurriedly bought their spices

and fluttering bunches of dried herbs. Without further delay she steered for home.

In St Paul's churchyard Gaunt's men and the troops of Percy, Lord Marshall of the realm, were gathering in a clear attempt to overawe the bishop. Gaunt's threat was written in pike, sword and dagger. Amongst the watching crowd, sympathy for Wyclif's opinions was drowning beneath a rising current of resentment. Gaunt's entry into the city seemed an open insult to its freedoms and its liberties. Already the word was passing from house to house. Along streets and alleyways whispers of anger seethed and soon the idle, the lazy and the criminal were on the move. Good and bad, sincere and rogue, gravitated towards the cathedral. Slowly but surely the ingredients of a riot were being blended.

If Philippa Starre was aware of any of this, she did not show it. She had arisen very early that morning and dressed with particular care in a cotte of deep blue. Its full, layered skirt contrasted with the close-fitting bodice. Clinging to her figure it emphasised the firm, pointed pyramids of her breasts. Since the morning was cold she wore a thick woollen surcoat with a low neck and large armholes and long ornamental sleeves.

She had stood silently while a serving girl made up her hair in plaits turned up on either side of her face. Chattering like a jay, the girl had fussed about her, catching up loose strands of hair and drawing her auburn tresses close to her head with a jewelled band that resembled a small crown. The room was full of fiddling attendants, cousins and maiden aunts. They had arrived with the first light. Their presence slowed down every aspect of the proceedings, yet each was assured of her right to be there and each was convinced that she was making a vital contribution to the preparations for the wedding day.

Murmuring to each other they stroked and fondled the deep-blue silks and ruffled the furs and gave unwanted but unstoppable advice.

'Now, now, my dear, you should not wear your hair so,' one matriarch advised.

'No, it should *not* change,' another contradicted. 'She wears it as I did upon my own wedding day.'

The two aunts faced each other in taut-cheeked indignation.

Their argument rose in tone and volume.

Philippa stood, cool and silent, amidst the noise and fuss. She gazed at herself in the mirror. The graceful swan's neck curve of her throat was like polished ivory in the light of the fine wax candles. Turning her head this way and that she caught sight of the firm line of her jaw. Gazing back at her was a slim oval face. Large, dark-brown eyes were set above high cheekbones and skin that warmed to palest rose. Usually those eyes shone with a quiet, proud confidence. Today she could not fail to notice the nervousness that played in their depths.

'Madam, you are as lovely as Our Lady,' the serving girl whispered. Then she bit her lip at her outspokenness.

Philippa smiled. The expression was but a gloss on her set features. 'Thank you, Emma,' she said, her voice a little distant. 'But I should not express such a view to my father's chaplain.'

'No, my lady, not to him – only to yourself.' The quarrelling aunts seemed unaware of the quiet intimacy between mistress and maid. The two of them occupied the eye of a turbulent storm.

Despite the noise and clatter Philippa was apparently tranquil. She kept her thoughts to herself. As if she were alone, she moved about the chamber.

The room was adequately furnished but by no means full. Apart from the wooden box bed, a chest stood in one corner beside a chair. A copper washbasin was on top of the chest. It reflected back the candle flame with a dancing red glow. Within the bowl the water was cool. Absent-mindedly Philippa crossed to it. Dipping her long fingers she marvelled at its coldness. Raising a glistening hand she stroked her face with the freshening water then, restless, she returned to the bed. Outside the shuttered window the street noises rose and fell. Light fell through gaps in the wooden slats and traced a filigree pattern on the knots and warps in the floorboards. Despite the clucking crowd, Philippa was the prisoner of her own thoughts.

This had been the last morning she would ever wake up in this room. This was the last time she would splash water from that bowl; throw aside the heaps of bedding. It had been so familiar for so long. It was only now when she was leaving it that she truly saw it for the first time. Her eyes passed over every wooden beam and heap of rushes on the floor. She had seen it all before, but only now was she so intensely aware that it was hers. Only now, as she felt it slip through her fingers, did she truly appreciate the security of its mundane familiarity. Something like a panic rose in her throat and it was with difficulty that she mastered it. She wondered if this was how every woman felt on the morning of her wedding.

She also wondered if all brides felt so unsettled at the thought of the identity of the groom. John Mentmore was a kind and considerate young man. A marriage to a Mentmore was no distress. Such an alliance between two great merchant families was no surprise to anyone.

Yet her mind kept trailing back to another young man. Ralph Horne had been such a dashing and heart-stirring creature. The son of the Fishmonger Alderman of Billingsgate, he had almost become her fiancé. But then her father had decided against the match. Merchants and fishmongers bickered. A proposed marriage had been set aside.

Despite this, her thoughts would not let Ralph Horne aside. Try as she might, she could not remove his dark looks and firm chin from her mind.

'Philippa, my dear,' one of her aunts interrupted her thoughts. 'What do you think of your hair?'

Philippa gazed at her questioner without comprehension. So lost had she been in her thoughts that she had scarcely been aware of the latest alterations to her coiffure.

'Your hair, my dear. Your hair!'

Shaking off her mental chains Philippa pondered the mirror image of her face. Her hair was coiled in shining loops above her ears and the jewelled headband glittered.

'Yes, it is fine,' she said flatly.

There was a flutter at the door of the chamber. Emma, the servant girl, had returned from an errand to the ground floor.

'Beg your pardon, mistress, but your father requests your presence in the hall.' Emma bit her lip again. 'He grows a *little* impatient mistress . . .' For the first time that morning Philippa smiled warmly. She could imagine her father was impatient. A stocky, red-faced man, he was a product of impatience. Driven by a restless energy he had built up a strong business enterprise. A dealer in fine goods and luxury cloths, his stone cellars and outhouses were piled high with his merchandise. An army of clerks scurried about his courtyard and attended to clients in the hall of the house. Roger Starre was a man well aware of his wealth and power.

Donning a long, midnight-blue coat, or pelisse, cut full to go over cotte and surcoat, Philippa Starre – only daughter of Roger Starre, merchant – descended to the hall.

Pacing up and down beside the open fire in the centre of the hall was her father. He was dressed for out of doors. A richly brocaded scarlet surcoat was fastened to his chin. Lined with fur, it hung like an embroidered tent around his stocky frame. Long, pointed sleeves hung almost to his knees. On his head he wore a capuchon, or hood, twisted up like a turban. It was of a rich red colour. One scalloped end stuck out from the top of the turban like the raised comb of a fighting cock.

As Philippa descended he was indeed like an agitated bantam. 'By the mass, girl,' he exploded, 'do you think Thomas Mentmore will wait for ever?'

Philippa bowed her head demurely. 'I am sorry, Father,' she replied quietly. 'I did not know I kept you waiting.' She noted her father had mentioned the name of her bridegroom's father. Clearly the groom's situation was of small concern to Roger Starre.

'Pah! – ' he exclaimed with irritation. 'Come now, girl, before we are too late.'

Philippa's two brothers – lean and pale where their patriarch was short and ruddy – nodded in masculine solidarity.

As the family processed from the hall, followed by retainers, Philippa composed herself mentally. Out in the street eyes turned to see the passing of the bride. Clerks and servants of Roger Starre wore the mauve livery of the household and embroidered on each surcoat was a silver star – the badge of the family.

Aunts and uncles, cousins and servants jostled in a kaleidoscope of colour and fur. Silks, satins and fine woollen cloth trumpeted the wealth and influence of the Starre clan. Here it was written in every imaginable shade of blue, red and green. The morning sun picked out the embroidered threads of gold and silver.

'Good luck to yer, girl,' a voice cried from the crowd of onlookers.

'Aye, and don't she look a picture of innocence!' a neighbour cried in deliberate praise.

Roger Starre, strutting out in front, nodded magnanimously to the appreciative crowd.

'Watch out for the soldiers,' a serious-minded tailor called out to Roger. 'They're mustering at St Paul's and are in an ugly mood.'

Roger frowned at the thought of any external force threatening his day. He dismissed the comment with an irritated wave of the hand.

From the Starre house the party processed towards Newgate Street and the Church of the Holy Sepulchre. It was nine o'clock and the watery winter sun was well up. Walking northward the party resembled Thames salmon swimming against the tide for all other pedestrian traffic seemed to be moving south. Here and there shopkeepers were closing their doors. One cutler, on the corner of Newgate Street, was boarding up his ground-floor windows. This was not the usual halt for dinner and attendance at morning mass. Trouble was in the air. Trouble mixed with a curious anticipation.

Within ten minutes the wedding party had reached the church. At the carved stone doorway stood a small group resplendent in fine clothing. They seemed relieved at the approach of Roger Starre and his entourage. To one side stood another richly adorned group of wedding guests. City merchants and guild members, they were business associates and social equals of both Mentmores and Starres.

Philippa looked for Ralph Horne but he was not there. She did not know if she felt pain or relief. Her fate was sealed.

Thomas Mentmore and Roger Starre greeted each other. Thomas, at fifty-four years of age, stood nearly a head taller than Roger. Unlike Starre he was bare-headed and thin grey hair scarcely covered his balding dome. His quick blue eyes flicked over the Starres. John, his son, similarly appraised the newcomers. His eyes flashed and for a brief moment they fixed on Philippa.

She glanced downwards before the steady gaze of the groom. In the few moments since she had arrived she had taken in her husband-to-be. He was well dressed. His tight-fitting doublet was embroidered with yellow fleur-de-lys which were all but covered by a brocaded blue tunic and a long cloak with the fashionable pointed sleeves. He held himself with a confident angle to his chin. His thick thatch of hair was fair and bobbed under at the sides, like a page.

A priest stood at the doorway. This brief ceremony of marriage would take place in the open air. Roger Starre hustled Philippa forward. John Mentmore stood waiting for her.

'Do you freely consent to be wed?' the priest enquired. John Mentmore's reply of 'yes' was clear and firm. Philippa liked his voice. The priest turned to Roger Starre. 'Does the bride give her consent?'

'Yes, yes,' he muttered impatiently. 'My daughter is in full consent.'

Philippa felt his hand tighten on her arm. It was like a pudgy vice. She nodded and the priest seemed satisfied.

Philippa's father gave her away more swiftly than he had given away anything in his entire life. He snapped his fingers sharply. A clerk – a scurrier taken from his ledgers – hurried forward. He was carrying a shoe. It was an old one with a patched instep.

'She goes from my authority to your authority,' Roger stentoriously declared.

John Mentmore reached out and took the shoe. Suddenly Philippa recognised it. It was the one her father had used to spank her with as a child. Then John stepped backwards and handed the shoe to his brother Edmund.

Now bride and groom faced one another. For a moment the focus of the occasion shifted. Roger Starre was reading out the details of the dowry which he had seized from the hands of a clerk who stood fish-mouthed in surprise. All eyes were on Roger, except for the grey-blue ones of John Mentmore. Those were on Philippa.

'My daughter shall take to her husband's house her oaken chest, the pewter candle holders from her chamber, two silver goblets, six rolls of pure blue silk, seven rolls of the finest green wool cloth . . .' Roger Starre paused for breath as he neared the end of the dowry list. Content that he held everyone's attention he concluded with a flourish: 'And in addition to these items she takes to her husband twenty pounds in silver shillings.'

There was an intake of breath from some of the onlookers.

Roger Starre was more than satisfied with the effect that the dowry had had on his family and neighbours. Before those assembled he had declared his wealth.

Philippa scarcely heard a word of the list. She was thinking of her husband. He is a fine-looking man, she told herself. And a good man so they say. A fair and a firm man. Not given to drink and to violence. But what she did not admit, even to herself, was that he did not cause the sap to rise in her. Here then was marriage as she had been rigidly taught to expect it. It was not the romances of Troilus and Criseyde, or Lancelot and Guinevere, as the stories told them. That was love, love and romance. This was marriage. Suddenly she thought of the flashing smile and the winning ways of Ralph, John Horne's son, and blushed to think of such a thing. Guilty, lest her sin should be apparent, she glanced up. John, catching the summer dawn flush on her cheeks, smiled. She glanced down again. If only he knew why she had blushed. Touched by her demure avoidance of his frank gaze, John smiled once more.

The dowry having been agreed, the priest blessed the ring held out by John. 'In the name of the Father and of the Son and of the Holy Spirit,' he intoned softly over the band of yellow metal. The groom placed it on her left hand and, as a sign of his prosperity and a token of his joy, he gave her two silver coins; two others he offered to her father.

The priest then blessed them. His voice echoed in the porch. 'The Lord bless you and keep you. The Lord lift up His face to shine upon you and be gracious unto you. The Lord lift up His countenance upon you and give you peace.'

Taking lighted candles, brought by servants, the newly married couple and their respective families followed the priest into the dark, cold interior of the church. Having paused to make an offering, the couple processed to the front of the church. Stopping well short of the altar, the priest turned to give them a second blessing. One of Philippa's brothers placed a veil over her head. John's brother Edmund spread the long, loose folds of the veil over the shoulder of his brother.

The nuptial blessing completed, the priest retreated to the altar and alone before the crucifix he prepared to enact the glorious mystery of the eucharist. The others in the church knelt in silence. Each was occupied with his or her own devotions.

With all the words in Latin, private prayer was now the occupation of the laity.

Philippa's mind was racing. This was it. It had been done. She was married. No longer a Starre but a Mentmore. Behind her knelt a family that was now her own and one which was no longer hers. There was Edmund Mentmore. As she gazed fixedly forward she could catch a glimpse of his ultra-fashionable tight doublet buttoned to the chin. Its red silk, bordered with white and embroidered with gold, burnt like an Easter candle. He was John's younger brother at twenty-five years. Dashing, handsome and aware of both he was the adopted heir of his uncle Giles de Brewoster. That elderly knight, scarred from the French wars, knelt further back. Edmund was his uncle's esquire and moved in the court circles. Philippa had watched him joust at Smithfield. He was like a breath of spring air from one of the romances.

Philippa blushed for the second time and her thoughts passed on to William. Kneeling beside Edmund he was a serious, mouse-haired young man of twenty-three. Down from his studies at Oxford he was an ardent disciple of Wyclif. His enthusiasm for his master's new patron won him few friends. Despite this, William maintained his commitment with an undying zeal – much to the chagrin of his family.

And then there was Margaret Mentmore. Margaret with her shock of red hair and her appealingly freckled face. Where Philippa had developed the virtues of submissiveness – preferring to conduct her campaigns by quiet attrition – Margaret was a creature of full frontal siege and scaling ladders. At Smithfield tournaments she accompanied her brother Edmund like a queen. When Thomas Mentmore feasted his friends she was mistress of the preparations and scourge of lazy servants. Here was a formidable force indeed!

Aged nineteen, Margaret was three years Philippa's junior but like her new sister-in-law she was the baby of the family. Both had lost their mothers in the pestilence year of 1361 and in one fell swoop they had both been elevated to the role of mistress of their father's house. Margaret had been only three years old; Philippa aged six. It was a role they had grown into, knowing no other. The difference lay in their fathers. Roger Starre was a hard taskmaster to sons, daughter and servants alike. By comparison it was common knowledge that Thomas Mentmore doted on his daughter and almost encouraged her practised wilfulness. Yet that was over. In a few moments, at the church door, all had changed. Now Philippa Mentmore, née Starre, was the wife of Thomas Mentmore's heir. Margaret was no longer mistress of the Mentmore house. Kneeling in devotional posture Philippa could almost feel the cold eyes of Margaret boring into her back like a torturer's tools.

For the second time that day Philippa felt the panic rise in her throat. The candles on the altar seemed to bob and move and her throat tightened. The flesh felt drawn over her fine cheekbones. Her mouth was dry like cold ashes. She felt cold, clammy and faint. With an immense act of the will she mastered the panic attack. Her knuckles showed white where her hands were clasped, vice-like, in the act of prayer.

Throwing aside her thoughts, Philippa concentrated on the priest who stood before the high altar. She allowed herself to become drawn into and lost within the rich ritual and mystery of the eucharistic celebration. Every pause and movement of the robed celebrant was steeped in history; marinated in a mystic significance. Like a dancer he moved through the steps of a complex reel as he declared the drama of Christ's passion.

Then he elevated the Host. The most sacred part of the service. All eyes were fixed on his upheld hand. Philippa felt a deep release within herself. This was a blessing for her, a blessing on her marriage. All would be well. Yes, all would be well.

As the couple, and then their families, took communion even the most devout could not fail to hear the running feet and raised voices in the street outside. 'Come on, come on, we'll show that bastard,' a rough voice shouted. The voice seemed to come from another, cruder world.

The marriage was over. John took his new wife by the arm and led her to the door of the church. Outside the thin sunshine was almost mild in the shelter of the building. Edmund and William followed their father in kissing the bride. Edmund winked at her in a conspiratorial way and Margaret came to her and kissed her cheek. 'Welcome to our family, sister,' she said meekly. Her eyes flashed ice fire and belied her humility. 'Thank you, sister,' Philippa replied, composed. The duel had begun.

From the Church of the Holy Sepulchre the way to the Mentmore house led along Newgate Street and West Chepe. Thomas

Mentmore had laid on a great wedding breakfast as befitted his position. His chief clerk, Adam Yonge, was even now supervising its presentation and display.

Before they had reached the corner of Newgate Street and Aldersgate Street the sound of a great commotion reached their ears. It came from the direction of the cathedral. John Mentmore smiled reassuringly at his wife and Thomas and Roger exchanged glances. Philippa read concern in Thomas's face and her father's face was blackening with annoyance. Clearly he anticipated some disturbance of their stately procession. He snapped his fingers and sent a servant running down to St Paul's. The wedding party halted. For minutes they exchanged banalities in pleasantly forced conversation. Philippa and John stood in silence. Roger Starre paced to and fro like an agitated hen.

Soon the servant was back, panting and rose-cheeked from his exertions. He was a mere boy and took a moment to compose his thoughts. Evidently he had a message of some importance.

'Come on, come on,' Roger Starre clucked angrily. His red coxcomb waved in a belligerent fashion.

The boy panted, 'Gaunt, sir . . . Gaunt has . . .'

'The Duke of Lancaster, boy. The king's son and a prince,' William Mentmore interrupted in an outraged tone. Roger glared at him.

'Yes, sir. Your pardon, sir. The Duke of Lancaster, sir. The king's son, sir . . .'

'By God's blood, get to the point, fool!' Roger Starre was beside himself.

The boy, caught between the two millstones of William Mentmore and Roger Starre evidently decided that Starre would grind smaller and for longer and gave up his attempt to placate William. In addition, Thomas Mentmore had silenced his pro-Lancastrian son with a dismissive wave of his hand.

'The Duke of Lancaster has attacked the Lord Bishop, sir. There is fighting in the cathedral, sir.'

Outraged gasps and growls rose on all sides. William looked thoughtful.

The boy continued: 'He has insulted the bishop and the meeting has broken up, sir.'

'And what of Wyclif and the duke?' Thomas queried.

'They are gone, sir,' the boy answered lamely.

'Where? Where, boy?' Roger interjected.

'The duke's men-at-arms are escorting them along Fleet Street toward Temple Gate, sir.'

'That's predictable,' Edmund commented. 'He has bitten off more than he can chew in the city. By the sound of it the whole populace is up in riot, but his men-at-arms will carry him safely out of harm's way to his Palace of the Savoy.' The boy nodded. That was just what he had been trying to say.

Thomas and Roger had a hurried consultation. They could not remain where they were indefinitely, but they did not want to walk into a riot. From the boy's report and Edmund's observations it seemed Gaunt was moving away west of St Paul's. That would be where the focus of the violence was. The noise of hoarse cries, and even the ringing of steel on steel, came from that direction. Since the wedding party, some fifty strong, was now due north of the cathedral they should be out of danger. To continue along Chepeside seemed the best course of action, for this should put them travelling east while the riot moved west. More to the point, neither man wished to see the carefully laid plans for the day disrupted. The quicker they could get to Mentmore's house the better.

Once the decision had been made, progress was resumed. This time, though, the pace was far from stately and when they reached Chepeside the street was full of milling people. There was much pushing and shoving. All the city's rough seemed to have descended on the market. From behind came the brutal sound of splintering wood followed by great oaths. Philippa turned her head and saw a stall holder's stand in ruins. Rolls of cloth and hose lay in a rainbow confusion and a fight was taking place amongst the multicoloured chaos. John propelled her forward. Now the oaths were punctuated with screams and the whole of West Chepe seemed in chaos. Far from being a safe route it had become the focus of its own disturbance. The wedding guests were being separated in the crowd.

A group of Gaunt's men-at-arms had become detached from the main body of his force. Once splintered off, they had been driven north-eastwards by the howling mob. Retreating along the thoroughfare of Chepeside, they had become further fragmented. Heavily outnumbered by the crowd, they were fighting desperately. Their long pikes were unwieldy and ineffective amongst the stalls and under the eaves of overhanging timber and plaster buildings. Many had thrown down their weapons and were relying on swords and daggers to defend themselves. Chepeside was a seething mass of struggling, cursing humanity.

Edmund took charge. He hustled the party into the side alley of Bread Street and, catching a confused group of wedding guests, he increased the size of his flock to twenty. They sheltered for perhaps an hour in the shop of a baker known to the family. At intervals Edmund and John made forays out on to Chepeside. Each time they returned they were accompanied by at least one confused and dishevelled guest.

On one reconnaissance Edmund could not fail but notice a tussle going on beside a goldsmith's shop. He and John had just rescued a portly old draper and were guiding him back to the safe haven of the baker's in Bread Street. A woman appeared to be in distress. Her men-at-arms were pinned down some distance from her and, backed into a corner, she was striking out at a raucous gang of youths. One of the young men had caught a corner of her embroidered yellow sleeve and would not be shaken off. His tenacity was that of a terrier in sudden possession of a rare joint. He hung on tightly. Only this rare joint was a lady, and this 'terrier' was slowly hauling her in as he wrapped the cloth round about his clenched fist.

Edmund signalled to John. 'Go on, brother. I can best handle this.'

John looked doubtfully at the gang of youths and then at his rotund charge.

'Go on ... go on,' Edmund insisted. 'It will take but a moment.'

Reluctantly John hurried his lost sheep back to the flock.

Edmund sprinted up the street. In his experience of the free-for-all tournament, termed 'the mêlée', he had noted the devastating effect caused by a determined warrior bursting into an otherwise occupied group. What appeared foolhardy to any onlooker was a practised tactic.

Edmund exploded into the fracas. Round the heads turned. Cries of alarm. A curse. An oath. In passing Edmund clubbed the terrier. The pommel of his dagger struck the bone above the man's left eye. It was a hammer blow. A strike of earth-bound lightning.

The man dropped where he stood. His hand still gripped the sleeve and he dragged the woman down. She fell into Edmund's arms with a cry of alarm. Edmund caught her. Her long flowing hair swirled across his cheek. Twisting, he hacked at her sleeve. She was free! With his left hand he thrust her behind him. He glimpsed two serving women. He pushed the dark-haired woman back to where they cowered. Just in time. As he turned, one of the terrier's companions, recovering, was moving in.

Edmund struck him on the bridge of his nose with his dagger pommel. A side step and the dagger flickered to the right. It sliced through a coarse cloth doublet and drew blood. Stabbed below the ribs, another attacker squealed and made off. Still, things could have turned out badly for Edmund. The remaining thugs were now brandishing broken planks of wood. One spat at him and missed. Just then a snarling group of liveried men broke out of a nearby brawl and fell upon the wood-wielding attackers.

'My father's men, sir knight. Do not destroy *these*, my lord.'

Edmund turned. The woman who stood behind him caused him to gasp. He had scarcely noted her good looks as he rescued her. She had skin like alabaster. Her hair was like a fall of night. Free of its jewelled braids, one shadow of it fell across her cheek and shoulders. She shook it back with a proud toss of her head. Her eyes were deep and black; great jet jewels set in her perfect face. Her nose was long and slim and her mouth full and sensuously curved in a smile. Behind her the serving women wept hysterically. Not so this one. She was formed from a more resilient substance.

Convinced she was now safe, Edmund knelt before her and kissed her hand. 'Your servant, my lady.' He was breathless. She was beautiful! Then he rose and turned away from her.

'Sir knight,' she cried. 'Whom shall I thank for my rescue?'

'My name is Edmund Mentmore,' he replied simply. He turned and retraced his steps through the turmoil.

Waving away her worried servants, Anne Glanville watched him go.

Reunited at the baker's shop, the brothers concluded that the Chepeside riot could go on for hours and decided that the safest way home was to avoid that area altogether. In the crisis,

Thomas and Roger were strangely silent. It was as if all authority had devolved on to the eldest Mentmore sons.

Leaving the baker's shop they passed on down Bread Street. From here it was but ten minutes' walk to the Mentmore's house. Despite the noise of riot emanating from the north, this way was almost deserted. Clearly they had left the excitement behind them. There was general relief when, at last, the Mentmore household was reached.

It was a fine building indeed. Constructed on three storeys, each level jutted out further over the street than the one below. Its timbers were solid and reassuring. Its plasterwork was white and reflected Thomas Mentmore's civic pride. A heavy, iron-girded oak door led into a long, wide passageway. To the left lay the pantry and the buttery, or wine store. To the right, behind tapestry screens, was the great hall. Ahead the passageway crossed the width of the house to where another doorway gave access on to a good sized courtyard. Along the passageway and within the hall, guests were grouped in whispering knots. Servants hung back in corners. The hall was hung with the richest tapestries of Arras, and along the two longest sides of the room trestle tables bent under the pewter plates of cold roast meats and delicacies.

On a raised dais at the far end of the hall stood the bridal table. Thomas Mentmore led the way past the iron firedogs and their blazing logs. The guests clapped and cheered. Roger Starre and Thomas Mentmore acknowledged the good-natured applause. At a command from Thomas Mentmore a group of musicians began to play, then the room dissolved into the happy chatter of feasting and merrymaking.

Scurrying servants brought trays of roast hog, sheep and goose. From the main body of the hall, Agnes Bakwell looked in approval at the arrival of her roast pullets.

'Will you take a little of the venison?' John Mentmore offered a steaming platter to his new wife. Philippa nodded shyly. He heaped the rich, dark meat on to her bread trencher.

'Eat up, girl. Eat up, or your guests will think I've shrunken your belly with poor food these years!'

Philippa did not have to look to know the voice belonged to her father. He was tearing apart one of Agnes's pullets.

'Eat up, eat up.' He gestured to a pile of meat fritters and turned back to his host. 'Fine food, Thomas, fine food I must say.'

Thomas Mentmore, in appreciation of a rare compliment from Starre, signalled for a servant to fill the man's silver goblet with more Gascon wine.

Philippa picked at her food under the dutiful gaze of her husband. How nervous each was of the other! When she had finished one course, he introduced her to another. No one else seemed to need such encouragement. Edmund and William had their trenchers piled high with meat. Throughout the hall the food was vanishing at an astonishing rate. Still the musicians played; and their melody seemed lost within the tumult.

There was, however, one other present who also picked at her food. Margaret Mentmore seemed to have no appetite whatsoever.

Between courses an elaborate table decoration was carried to the dais. It was a confectionery creation which portrayed Gabriel saluting the Virgin. Worked in sugar and paper it produced thunderous applause from the guests. Roger Starre was impressed, Thomas Mentmore pleased and Agnes the cook relieved.

The decoration was presented to Philippa. Blushing, she rose and bowed in gratitude to her new father-in-law. In a moment of inspiration she also bowed to the assembled guests. Her meek acknowledgement of the crowd prompted a tidal wave of clapping.

As she sat, John leaned towards her. 'The purity and beauty of the decoration is in honour of your purity and beauty.' It was a rather self-conscious comment. John frowned slightly. Perhaps he was aware of how stiff and nervous he had sounded.

For the first time since her wedding Philippa smiled openly. The thought that her husband felt as awkward as herself was a welcome one. She looked at him fully. His grey-blue eyes suddenly took on a sparkling life of their own. He flushed. She thought how boyish he looked and smiled again.

'The sweetmeats!' he exclaimed. 'You will love the sweetmeats.' His own confident self again, he snapped his fingers at a servant. From the offered tray of ginger, spice and nut pastes John took a spoonful of the sticky mixture. Smearing it on soft white bread he offered it to his wife.

'Thank you, John.' Philippa took the little gift. It was the first time she had used his Christian name. It pleased him.

The attentive groom was shaken from his activity by his father. Thomas Mentmore had risen from his place at the table. Storm clouds of anger scudded across his features. At his elbow stood a pale-faced clerk. The man swayed a little and seemed drawn and faint.

'My son, your wedding day has been desecrated.'

John looked at his father without comprehension.

'What's that, Thomas?' the bantam figure of Roger Starre asked with a note of irritation.

Thomas did not seem to have heard Starre. Instead he fixed a furious eye on his son. 'Adam Yonge . . . Adam Yonge,' was all he could say. His voice was choked with anger.

John heard the name of the household's chief clerk with puzzlement. Only then did it occur to him that he had not seen the man in the hall. In the excitement of the wedding breakfast it had not occurred to him. With terse instructions Thomas signalled to John, Edmund, William and Starre to follow him. Accompanied by the clerk they descended from the dais. Expecting some new diversion a ripple of applause arose from the guests. It died away as they caught sight of the look on Thomas's face.

The head of the Mentmore household led the way out of the hall. Swiftly he strode down the narrow corridor which led to the rear courtyard. Crossing the yard they entered one of the flanking sheds which acted as a warehouse. Bales of fine cloth lined the walls of the dark, timber building. Inside the door an accountant's desk was covered with a profusion of tally sticks and vellum sheets. Ink spread a dark pool on the flagstone floor. A quill pen lay snapped in the middle of the pool. Bales were scattered about. It was as if some wild hunt had ended in this shadowy storeroom.

Stepping over the confusion, Thomas led them deeper into the shed. Against one wall the hunt had ended. Adam Yonge lay broken in a heap. A thin man of perhaps forty years he stared, with glazed eyes, at the beamed roof. Even in the shadows it was plain to see that he was twisted up in a pool of his own blood.

Chapter Two

John Mentmore lay back on his pillow. The sun dappled the bed with a gold filigree. Beside him his wife was stirring.

In these few moments of stillness he took stock of his thoughts. Reaching out a hesitant finger he stroked one of Philippa's tumbled tresses. He was beginning to feel a real affection for this pretty and shy stranger. In all things she was gentle and feminine.

Hearing the noise of work from the yard, he reluctantly flung back the covers and swung his legs out of the bed. For a few moments he sat yawning. Then, with an effort, he was up. Philippa was awake now. John pulled on his clothes, still yawning.

'John?' It was Philippa's voice.

He turned a warm smile on her. 'Yes, my heart?'

'Where are you working today?'

'I shall stay within the yard this morning, checking in the new stocks. Why?'

'I wanted to ask you something,' she said, her voice hesitant.

John laughed good-naturedly. 'The sun's up and I am late to my work! Is it a quick request?'

He had only meant to jest but now she was flustered.

'No . . . yes . . . well . . .' she faltered. 'Perhaps I can talk of it later.'

John grinned. He would never fathom women. 'Very well, my heart, ask me later.'

Pulling on a jacket he left the bedchamber and descended to the courtyard. From down below came the bustle of a busy guild household.

When Thomas Mentmore's grandfather, Robert, had become a master craftsman of the clothmaker's guild in the 1290s, he had entered a world that was rightly described as 'mysterious'. Within the city there had been (and still were) a whole host of guilds. Each guild, a company of master craftsmen and apprentices, had jealously guarded its manufacturing skills or 'mysteries'. When each young apprentice finally graduated to the role of fully fledged craftsman he did so because he was adept at these mysteries. Made powerful by his knowledge, he and his fellow craftsmen hedged themselves round with privileges, monopolies and protections.

Of such mysteries London had many. Some were great and powerful: Mercers (Merchants), Drapers, Goldsmiths, Tailors, Salters, Grocers, Fishmongers, Skinners, Haberdashers, Ironmongers, Vintners and Clothmakers. Others held less power and included such diverse trades as Brewers, Apothecaries, Dyers, Saddlers, Cutlers, Bakers, Leather-workers and Candlemakers. Some guilds worked closely with each other, such as the Clothworkers and Tailors and Drapers. Others competed in petty rivalries as when Pepperers and Spicers bickered over the sale of drugs. Yet others could become locked in rivalries ranging from sharp practice and political intrigue to arson and even murder.

John Mentmore was pondering this last point as he watched servants stacking bales of cloth in the warehouse. A clerk stood at his desk marking off the bales on a tally stick. He stood at the place where Adam Yonge should have been. John frowned at that thought. He hissed an intake of breath, a habit of his when preoccupied, and rhythmically chewed at his own cheek – a habit of his when angry or agitated. Adam Yonge had been an efficient and honest clerk. He had also been a friend.

John Mentmore, like his father Thomas, was a mercer. As a dealer in high quality merchandise and cloths he was in one of the most powerful guilds of merchant middlemen in the city. And if power brought wealth and one of the finest houses in the city, it also brought enemies . . .

When Robert Mentmore entered his mystery it was already losing its magic and he knew it. By the end of the 1290s the English cloth producers had been driven out of the international market for high quality cloth. Fierce competition from Flanders and Brabant had seen to that. In the cutthroat world of international trade there was no chivalry or gentleness.

Robert had seen this coming. As the weavers declined he

married his son Henry to the daughter of a mercer, Elizabeth Martyn. Robert had recognised the need to diversify the business and Henry had continued the policy. By the time that the other guilds, scenting weakness, had abolished the weavers' monopoly on producing cloth in 1336, he had divested himself of his weaving sheds. Many weavers saw him as a betrayer. He knew he was simply a businessman.

Henry's eldest son died in the plague year of 1349. That same year Henry had his second son, Thomas, married to Anne Wyting, the offspring of another wealthy mercer. In two generations the Mentmore dynasty was established and secure.

Robert and Henry had acted in time. From the early fourteenth century London guilds were changing. More and more of the wealthier guilds shifted from manufacturing goods to distribution. No longer did a guild master oversee all levels of production from raw material to sale; no longer did apprentices eat with their masters and rise to join him as an equal. The new guilds were exclusive. Entrance was limited by payment of huge sums of money; Thomas clothed his workers in expensive liveries carrying his colours of blue and gold and a florid 'M'. The production was done elsewhere.

Thomas employed weavers around Threadneedle Street but they were his creatures, not his men. Try as they might to organise themselves into bachelor or yeomanry guilds they could not break the new legal requirements which forced them to sell the fruit of their labour via the rich chartered livery guilds, or companies. Thomas was one of the leaders of a great power base in the city.

Yet it would be fair to say that John Mentmore, heir to this great enterprise, was troubled. For months now his father had been locked in an industrial dispute with the weavers. The small master craftsmen were not giving up their positions without a fight. Strikes and restrictive practices had become a burr under Thomas Mentmore's saddle. The weavers' guilds banned nightwork and were making a desperate attempt at lowering their hours and increasing their pay. The intermittent French wars, raging on and off since 1339, had increased the demand for English cloth once more. The weavers had not been slow to seize the opportunity. Now cloth supplies were delayed by strikes. Some mercers had even found their warehouses broken into and stocks damaged.

John did not have to look far for suspects for Adam Yonge's death. None of the servants had recognised the men who came to 'talk' to the clerk the morning of the wedding. That of course was no surprise. Who, after all, would send their leading members on such a mission? In a city like London there were always knives for hire. While the busy servants had carried food into the hall or jostled in the buttery and pantry, Adam Yonge had been hunted; hunted like a rat into a dark corner of the warehouse. Cornered at last, he had died amongst the bales of merchandise.

John hissed again and his eyes narrowed. In the week since Adam's death, they were no closer to getting satisfaction. One more death had been swallowed up in the events of the riot. John assumed it had been planned with that in mind. It had been common knowledge that Gaunt's confrontation with the Bishop of London would lead to trouble.

He was called from his private deliberations by the voice of his wife. Turning he saw her framed in the doorway. Her hair was held up in a fine golden net which the sun caught in a sparkling sheen. It seemed to make her auburn hair catch fire.

John was sorry for the way in which her wedding day had been so badly marred. In the days since that chaotic occasion he had been too busy to spend much time with her. Nevertheless she seemed to have settled into the household well and he was pleased with the way Margaret was helping her do so. He had noticed, with approval, how his sister spent a good deal of time with Philippa. As she set to organising their living quarters, familiarising herself with the routine of house and kitchen or studying the household accounts, Margaret was always there with her.

He had also been satisfied with Philippa's other wifely duties. Clearly she had, as a virgin, no understanding of the needs of a man but she had submitted to his desires in an acceptable fashion. She was an attractive woman. John recalled, with pleasure, his first sight of her nakedness on their wedding night. He was not inexperienced with women and although she had been hesitant and shy she had aroused him with her submission. He felt a spreading heat within himself as he mentally dwelt upon that first assertion of his husband's authority. For a few blissful moments the turbulent thoughts of riots, strikes and killing had been swept away by the rhythmic tide of his penetration of his virgin bride. The explosion of his climax had released the pent-up energy and tension of days. He had slept more soundly since his marriage.

'Your father desires that you meet him in the solar,' Philippa said, with her sweet smile. 'He has an important visitor.'

John was interested. 'Who is this visitor?' he queried.

'He did not tell me,' Philippa replied.

John kissed her on the cheek. He felt the upward curve of her breast against his chest. He would have lingered if the place had not been so public. Bound by duty and a sense of propriety, he brushed on past her and crossed the hall to the solar.

Philippa remained in the doorway. From the direction of the kitchen, in a corner of the yard, came the magpie chatter of scullions and the dull clatter of pewter plates. In the shelter of the yard the day was surprisingly mild. Lazily she watched the young clerk busy with his tally sticks. The light perfume of dyed cloth drifted across the yard. For a moment she took off her sweet smile and put it away. Then Margaret was calling in the passageway behind her. Philippa donned her smile once more, adjusted it and turned to meet her sister-in-law.

The solar was a first floor room which ran the depth of the house. It was reached by a stairway which went from the raised dais at the south end of the hall. Underneath the solar was a storeroom and counting house, entered by a doorway at the opposite end of the dais to the stairs. The solar was a private family area. It was linked to a parlour by a narrow passage which ran the length of the house in the thickness of the wall. Since the high-roofed hall occupied the equivalent of two levels of the house, the solar and the parlour, along with a gallery at the northern end of the hall, occupied the first floor of the building. When Thomas or his family wished to sit and talk privately they did so in the solar. When they wished to eat separately from the servants in the hall they might do so in the parlour.

The solar was a light room. Enormously expensive windows, on its southern wall, penned in the sun like a bright flock of sheep. The room, as with much of the house, was only sparsely furnished. A bench of dark oak stood at one end, beside a trestle table. A half-finished sampler lay, neatly folded, on its knotted wood.

As John entered he saw that his father and a stranger stood beside the window. Two silver wine cups were on the trestle table. Beside the cups was a wine jar of silver gilt. John raised a wondering eyebrow. The stranger was obviously of some importance.

The two men ceased their conversation and turned towards him. The stranger was tall and well built. He was large boned and did not carry excess flesh. His face was surprisingly soft and smooth for such a robustly built man. Although he was perhaps fifty he had not lost his hair. His fingers were well ringed and a ruby shone bloodily from one hand. He gave John a penetrating look. It was the gaze of a man used to summing up another in an instant. John felt uncomfortable. He was not used to being so coolly appraised in his own home. He chewed at his cheek. The watcher smiled faintly.

Even before Thomas spoke, John guessed the identity of the visitor. Six men-at-arms, without livery over their mail, were in the hall below. Only John of Gaunt would send men without an identifying livery into the city at this time.

Thomas strode forward. Taking his son by the arm, he led him to meet their guest. 'John my son, this is Hugh le Breton, secretary to his grace the Duke of Lancaster.'

Hugh le Breton, a prince amongst clerks, nodded stiffly. John repeated the salutation. So, he thought, this is indeed a deputation from Gaunt!

Thomas invited le Breton to sit beside him; John sat on his other side. 'Our honoured guest brings us gracious tidings from his grace the Duke of Lancaster,' Thomas informed his son.

John could scarcely believe his father's reverent tones. Really, he was beginning to sound as bad as William. John decided to withhold judgement until he had heard the nature of these 'gracious tidings' from the wily old fox.

Unabashed, Thomas continued: 'His grace invites us to his Palace of the Savoy to discuss . . . to discuss . . .' He paused for dramatic effect. 'To discuss a commission for a great tapestry work!'

Now John understood. The French wars had disrupted the trade in tapestries from Paris and Arras. These beautiful luxury items had graced the walls of castles, palaces and rich houses. The break in trade had frustrated many a wealthy lord and lady.

What lady wished to sit in a bare-walled solar, listening to tales of chivalry? What lord wished to entertain his guests in a hall walled only in plaster or stone blocks? The wealthy had searched high and low for these prestige items. King Edward III had even created the office of 'Tapestry Maker to the King'. Thomas Mentmore had coveted the title. To his disappointment he had not been granted it.

Nevertheless Thomas had spotted the possibility of trade and had set up a small workshop in premises next door to the family house. Tapestry manufacture was a new venture, but the increasing demand and the improvement in the home cloth industry since the 1340s had made it a good risk. Now it seemed to have paid off. Such a triumph could eclipse old enmities against the duke! Even John smiled with satisfaction. His father noted the thaw and beamed. He valued his son's support and advice. After all, one day he would inherit the Mentmore business.

'This is indeed an honour to bring a confidant of the Duke to our house . . . In these – how shall I say? – disturbed times,' he added coyly.

Hugh le Breton frowned. 'His grace, my lord, is no stranger to the machinations of evil-minded men who plot the downfall of this realm! He does not allow himself to be restricted by those who would intimidate his gracious honour with mob violence.'

Which is why you travel incognito, no doubt! John thought maliciously. 'Of course we do not have any truck with those who question the Duke of Lancaster's legitimacy,' he said aloud.

Hugh le Breton's eyes narrowed. He could not tell whether this was a display of loyalty or a wicked raising of issues designed to tease a dutiful servant of the House of Lancaster.

Thomas, quite at ease in his new-found sympathy for the much-maligned duke, said, 'It is a shameful thing that London citizens accuse the duke of being the bastard son of a Flemish butcher.' He appeared unaware of Hugh le Breton's flush. Clearly even loyalty did not benefit from rehearsing these dreadful accusations.

John half considered 'condemning' those who said that the duke whored with his children's governess Katherine Swinford, but decided better of it. Instead he shoved the conversation back on course by asking, 'Perhaps you would be good enough to explain the nature of the commission?'

Hugh seemed relieved at this change of direction. Rising to his feet, for added effect, he paced the floor. 'My lord the Duke of Lancaster is, as you know, a patron of the arts as well as a chivalrous exponent of military might. As a true knight he loves the beautiful. The duke desires to make a gift of a tapestry, but before he issues that commission he requires a smaller work for his solar.' Hugh le Breton paused for a moment, so as to choose his next words with care. A practised secretary, he did not use words as carelessly as his initial oratory might have suggested. He was prodigal with words as and when it suited him. 'The duke is, of course, familiar with the tapestry work of northern France. He is less familiar with the products of your workshops. Though', he added swiftly and smoothly, 'he has heard much of your excellent work and of your ability to meet the deadline of a major commission.'

Thomas looked thoughtful. John hissed an intake of breath as he measured up the significance of le Breton's words. Gaunt evidently had a prodigious project in mind, something so important that it was not to be divulged at this stage in the proceedings. The duke, as canny as ever, was testing the water before he jumped in. John wondered how many others had been approached in this way. The duke must have made contact with the Tapestry Makers to the King. Perhaps he had also put out feelers to other mercers who might be in a position to link the duke with craftsmen abroad.

John glanced at his father. Thomas was lost in reflection. It was likely he was mulling over the same thoughts as John.

Seeing that neither Mentmore intended to speak, le Breton concluded with a flourish: 'The duke would meet with you tomorrow before prime and his morning mass. He trusts you will be keen to keep such an appointment?'

Thomas nodded. John was too busy calculating the hour of dawn. He had no wish to be seen riding out to the Savoy in broad daylight.

Le Breton prepared to take his leave. Both Mentmores rose and escorted him down to the hall. There his escort waited and in a clinking of mail and a clatter of hoofbeats they were away.

Thomas Mentmore smiled broadly at his son. 'At last, at last the opportunity that I – we – have worked for. Think, my son, of what such a commission could mean to the Mentmores!'

That night the servants ate in the hall and Thomas and his immediate family took supper in the parlour. Using the privacy of this room, on the first floor, he outlined the main thrust of Hugh le Breton's argument. Interrupted before the close of the meal by a servant, Thomas went downstairs to receive a surprise visitor.

When he returned it was with the news that the constable and his posse had so far found no clues to the identity of Adam Yonge's murderers. No one in the parish had seen the intrusion, or would admit to having seen it. The constable concluded that the gang must have been lordless men, in the city for the much pre-publicised riot. He would continue his enquiries and the aldermen of the various city wards had been alerted. This, of course, was not news. Thomas and John had seen their own alderman the very next day and demanded justice.

All in all it was a poor business and the constable seemed convinced that the gang had got clean away. It was news designed to dampen the lightest of spirits and that night there were no stories about the fire or public reading of a romance. The servants could play their own games before they slept on their straw-filled mattresses about the hall. The Mentmore family retired to bed early and slept badly.

John and Thomas arose before dawn. It was cold in the parlour and they ate a brief breakfast by candlelight. It was still dark when a groom brought two horses from the stable beside the house. Mounting in silence the only noise was the snickering of the horses as they recognised the scent of their riders.

John and Thomas had resolved to ride to the Savoy by a roundabout route. With the state of unrest in the city it did not suit either of them to be seen going out to meet John of Gaunt. Wrapped in thick-hooded cloaks they went north up Moorgate Street. By the time they reached the gate it was first light and the city watchmen were opening up for the waiting carts. The two horsemen, hooded and silent, rode out.

They made their way due north for perhaps half a mile. On their right was the meandering Walbrook and beyond it Shoreditch. After a quarter of an hour they turned westward and rode along the edge of the suburbs. Following Fleet Street to Temple Bar they had soon left the city behind them. Ahead they could see the towers and walls of Edward the Confessor's church at

Westminster. Well before that historic edifice was Gaunt's Palace of the Savoy. Even from a distance they could make out damage to its walls and gates. It was to these very gates that a howling mob had pursued Gaunt on 19 February. So great was their fury that Gaunt had been forced to take flight across the Thames. Seeking shelter with his sister-in-law, the Princess of Wales, at Kennington, he had waited out the anger of the London crowd. At last, cheated of their prey, they had withdrawn.

As John and Thomas approached they were met by armed retainers. Each bore the double 'S' badge of Lancaster. They eyed the two horsemen critically but they seemed to be expected.

Once inside the gates they were privy to the splendours of Gaunt's huge palace. Here were the halls and chambers where Gaunt held his own court. Situated between the city and the Palace of Westminster it was a finger on the very pulse of English government. From its courtyards and shady corridors, orchards and rose gardens swept down to the Thames. The Savoy was dramatically ostentatious. Open shutters revealed panes of rare glass. The stonework was finely worked and banners hung and fluttered in the light breeze.

A clerk met them, an anonymous bobbing man. He led them, from their horses, along an imposing passageway.

'Look at the tapestry, son.'

Thomas need not have spoken. Already John's eyes were wide with amazement. The corridors and rooms had their walls richly adorned. Here hung a king's ransom in works of art. Every tapestry workshop in northern Europe was represented.

'He is truly a connoisseur ... and think, son, he calls us to himself.' Thomas could not conceal the excitement in his voice.

Despite this, John felt uneasy. John of Gaunt was a dangerous man. Why would he call them into his very presence?

Hugh le Breton was waiting for them. Once more there were the formal courtesies. It seemed to John that he was being led deeper and deeper into the viper's nest. Scurrying servants shot quick glances at the strangers.

John of Gaunt was in his solar. As with the halls through which Hugh had led them, it was richly decorated with tapestries and wall hangings. The greatest was a fabulous hanging, exquisitely decorated with coats of arms and heraldic devices.

As John surveyed its staggering display of dragons, lions and unicorns he could not help but consider the exacting standards of the man they had come to meet. This would be no easy commission, if it were to satisfy John of Lancaster.

The bear-like figure of Hugh le Breton bowed before his lord and declared: 'Your grace, I bring Thomas and John Mentmore, merchants of the city of London.' Gaunt smiled briefly and waved them forward.

At thirty-seven, John of Gaunt, Duke of the County Palatine of Lancaster was a man in his prime. He had the familiar oval face and long, finely chiselled nose of the Plantagenets. His wavy hair was bobbed in below his ears. His beard was close cut, like that of his father. Only the absence of the long, drooping moustache differentiated him from his dead brother, the fighting 'Black Prince'. His eyes were quick and active. If Hugh le Breton interrogated in a look, this son of Edward III was an inquisitor. His boldness of glance arose from one whose power was unequalled in the land.

'Welcome, my honoured guests.' His voice had a velvet smoothness betrayed, here and there, by a glimpse of steel beneath the tones.

'It is indeed we who are honoured,' Thomas replied. He bowed his balding head. John did likewise. 'Honoured by the kindness of your grace's approach to us.'

This was how Gaunt liked to see London merchants. What a contrast to the whooping beasts who had driven him from the city and hung his arms upside down! The great man was obviously pleased by their due reverence. With a gracious movement of his hand he beckoned them to join him. Caught unaware by the informality of the setting they hesitated for a moment. Then, more confident, they joined him on an available bench near the window.

At a nod from Gaunt Hugh le Breton poured wine for his master and for the Mentmores. He seemed in no way abashed at adopting this servile status. It was clear that Gaunt intended this to be a very private audience. No servants disturbed the intimacy of the scene within the solar. Besides this, le Breton was honoured to act as butler to his lord.

John savoured the fruity breath of the red Gascon wine. Gaunt seemed to be lost in some private reverie as he slowly imbibed from his silver goblet. Somehow John was sure that the scene was not as relaxed as it appeared. He had the worrying feeling that he was an actor in a carefully rehearsed play, but no one had divulged script or plot to this wary mummer. Eyeing his father, Gaunt and le Breton over the rim of his goblet, he wondered which parts had been assigned to whom. Which one was the infidel awaiting destruction at the hands of St George? Only the chief mummer could know that, and he was gazing wistfully out of the window. Watching Gaunt's relaxed pose, John had a growing suspicion that the least important prop within this play was the tapestry.

'May I congratulate you on your recent marriage?' Gaunt's voice shook him out of his contemplations and astonished him.

'Thank you, your grace,' John said, 'although I fear we were inconvenienced by the same outrages that disturbed your grace's peace.'

Hugh le Breton was staring at John but said not a word.

'Ah yes,' Gaunt murmured, as if he had trouble recalling that minor irritation. 'Ah yes . . . but you will no doubt rejoice that justice has been done to those who so insulted the king's son and the royal lineage.' He paused to let that sink in then dropped a shower of arrows into the unsuspecting circle. 'It is much to my lord the king's pleasure that the city of London recognises its duty to the realm. The decision of the Common Council of the city to remove the mayor from office will serve as a salutary reminder to others that authority must go hand in hand with loyalty.'

The arrows struck home with devastating effect. This was surprise news indeed and neither John nor Thomas was ready for it. As guild masters it was they who elected the Common Council and the aldermen who governed the turbulent capital of the realm. They, in turn, elected London's mayor. In one fell swoop Gaunt had struck off the head of his greatest critics.

John was acutely aware of the way in which his surprise must be registering on his face. It was all too obvious on his father's features. His own emotions were a curious combination of outrage and astonished admiration at the swift counterblow struck by Gaunt. He was a wily fox indeed! Thomas's face revealed a similar diversity of emotions.

The duke was sweetness and light. He enquired further about

John's new bride and professed deep regret at the disturbance done to their wedding plans. 'And how is your youngest son? His name is William, is it not?' Thomas nodded. 'I am told he is a most promising young man. He will make a useful member of a great household one day. There is always room for young men of talent. I am also told he holds John Wyclif in respect.'

The duke briefly held forth on the wisdom of the Oxford theologian's views. It was curious, though, that he seemed less interested in Wyclif than in congratulating Thomas on the allegiance of his third son. Thomas could not help but react as the proud father. John winced inwardly when he recalled how frequently he had berated William for his pro-Lancastrian views. Perhaps Thomas was aware of this, for it was noticeable how he avoided catching the eye of his eldest son.

Hugh le Breton had worked overtime giving his master a briefing on the Mentmore family. The soft-faced clerk was watching the 'show' with quiet satisfaction. Having displayed his power, Gaunt was relaxed again. It was as if the news of the mayor's removal had been cunningly designed to disarm his guests by force. Now, before their pride could rise, he was disarming them with charm. It seemed a mighty effort just to secure a tapestry.

It reminded John of an amorous pursuit. He knew all too well how a pretty face could arouse chivalric tactics. One displayed one's prowess and manly grandeur as Edmund did. One sought out information on her family. One wooed by courteous conversation. Nothing she did was too trivial to be noticed. One congratulated and praised and exalted her virtues. How often had John pursued such a goal? How often had Gaunt? More times than John! Yet now it was a family that was being wooed. The thought troubled John. What alliance, what union, did Gaunt have in mind? The crowd thought only of Gaunt the arrogant; Gaunt who according to popular belief had poisoned his first wife's sister for her inheritance and who would surely poison Richard of Bordeaux, the young heir to the throne. Here, though, was another Gaunt. Gaunt the charmer. Gaunt the accomplished courtier. Here was a Gaunt that Katherine Swinford would recognise. Why had the Mentmores become the object of his charms?

Then the talk at last turned to tapestries. The duke clicked his fingers and le Breton produced a sheet of fine vellum. On it an unknown artist had inked in a complex scene. In the centre a winged St Michael, his head crowned by a sunburst halo, drove a spear into the mouth of a dragon. The dragon's body was twisted in a heap of coils. Surrounding this scene, from the Book of Revelation, were four panels interlocked by weaving fronds. Each panel contained an angel. Each had six wings and arms outstretched in blessing. It was a well-executed sketch. Even as a simple ink drawing on sheep hide it was a dramatic representation.

'I desire a tapestry to this design,' the duke instructed. 'It is to be a relatively small work.' He indicated dimensions, neatly penned in one corner of the vellum sheet. 'But there are other works that I have planned. Before I issue a commission on a larger scale I wish to enjoy a sample.'

The duke rose to his feet. Crossing the solar he brushed past the bench on which John sat. The rustle of his rich robe was like a distant breeze. Gaunt ran one hand across the heraldic hanging which John had noticed earlier.

'This fine piece is of the size of my final commission.' He fixed Thomas Mentmore with a firm glance. 'I value the beautiful, as you can see. For this I paid a thousand marks.' He watched the effect of this little revelation. He was not disappointed.

Such a sum was astonishing. Thomas bit his lip, thinking of so much silver in one place at one time! John took an intake of breath. Gaunt smiled innocently.

'You see?' the duke continued. 'You see why I desire a trial piece when my final wish is to commission a work of such exquisite beauty? ... and worth.' He let that last word trip off his tongue as if it were of no importance. Casually he watched it explode in the mental calculations of his hearers.

Content that he had made his point he summoned food. Servants hurriedly brought in pots of preserved plums and damsons to tempt the appetites. Jovial and the perfect host, Gaunt called upon his guests to eat and refresh themselves. Those present had been up for four hours already, it being nine o'clock in the morning, and all were hungry. Soon they had cleared the preliminary fruits and were heaping their bread trenchers with courses of sliced salted beef, mutton and capon.

When at last the dinner was over, Gaunt turned once again to talking about Thomas's family. It was a most congenial occasion and one designed to impress. Thomas and John accepted the duke's invitation to hear mass at his private chapel, so it was mid-morning before the two mercers – full of food and speculation – rode out of the gates of the Palace of the Savoy.

Their caution had not entirely evaporated, however. Before they reached the Fleet, they turned north and entered the city via Holburne Bridge and Newgate. This disguised the direction from which they had come.

Philippa watched her husband and father-in-law ride up to the house. Once dismounted they went immediately to the tapestry workshop and vanished from sight. In the jetty, which carried her chamber out over the street, she had opened the shutters and from her window seat could see far down the street. Making herself comfortable against the oak beam, which supported the side of the overhanging room, she watched the carts pulling slowly up from the wharves below Thames Street and listened idly to the waggoners' conversations with their beasts.

It was good simply to sit. To sit, watch and listen. From the street below arose a cacophony of sound and a pot pourri of the most astonishing smells. Philippa had lived in the city all her life. Its sights – sacred and profane – and its sounds and its smells were part of the background embroidery against which she played out her life. It was so much part of her that often she did not even consciously recognise its existence.

That was not true of today. Today she sat and absorbed it and appreciated it as never before. Turning her gaze she watched the street sellers haggling on the corner of Candlewick Street. Armed retainers of the Hanseatic League escorted foreign merchants from the factory at the Steel Yard. Pigeons rose from the Tower of St Magnus Martyr, and Philippa imagined the salt smell of fish where Swan Steps led to the Thames by London Bridge.

Solitude was bliss. She had arisen shortly after John and begun to tackle the tasks of the day. As the wife to the heir of the Mentmore family, there were innumerable things to attend to. The provisions of the deep stone cellars of pantry and buttery needed constant checking. The running of the kitchen called for daily supervision. Servants needed scolding. The hall needed clearing of the beds and night soil of the retainers. There was always much to do.

Philippa had attended to such household duties since she was a child. Her mother's death had left all such tasks to her. A stern father and demanding brothers had allowed her no opportunity to forget that the day-to-day running of the household was in her care. It was an exhausting duty but one which gave her a real sense of satisfaction. The keys to the house jangling at her girdle were the visible signs of her womanly authority.

The problem was that Margaret Mentmore had mirrored Philippa's experience almost exactly. The Mentmore household was no badly run establishment grateful for a stranger's discerning eye and deft touch. It was quite the opposite! Margaret ran a tight ship and showed no signs of surrendering that ship to an alien boarding party; particularly when that boarding party came in the form of Philippa Mentmore, née Starre.

Wherever Philippa turned, her sister-in-law was there. If Philippa called for the household accounts from one of Thomas's clerks, Margaret was at her shoulder. 'Is there a problem, sister?' 'Can I help you, sister?' 'Is it not as it should be, sister?' Every 'helpful' question was delivered with the maximum false charm that Margaret could muster. If Philippa checked on the numbers of wine bottles in the cool, flag-floored, buttery or questioned the butler, Margaret was there to assist her. If Philippa chose to count the pewter plates, jugs and spoons in the pantry, her sister-in-law would appear from nowhere to give her assistance.

At no time was Margaret rude. Not once was she critical or offensive. She was simply there. She was simply everywhere! Wherever Philippa went, so went Margaret – to help her.

After days of this Philippa was beginning to feel like a prisoner with a personal gaoler in hourly attendance. It was clear that Margaret was checking up on everything she did. More than this, it was becoming increasingly obvious that Philippa could not exercise any personal authority whatsoever without Margaret's presence. It was as if none of Philippa's decisions possessed legitimacy without the silent, ghostlike presence of Thomas Mentmore's daughter.

Even when Philippa retired to the solar to sew she could not do so alone. At last, unable to bear it any longer, she had escaped to her chamber. She knew that when she finally re-emerged it would be to innocent questions like, 'Where have you been, sister?' Or, 'I have looked for you everywhere, sister.'

The matter was made worse by the fact that the servants continued to look to Margaret for their orders. Worse still, Margaret had made no attempt to surrender the household keys. Philippa had assumed this would happen soon after her arrival in the house. It had not. The sight and sound of those keys, swinging against Margaret's long thighs, cut deep into Philippa. They were hers now, not Margaret's. It was intolerable that she should have to ask for them. It was unbearable that she should have to make an issue out of their surrender. Secretly she knew she was frightened of the flaming-haired, fire-eyed, passionate Margaret.

How she longed to pour this out to John! Yet he was almost as much a stranger, this man who shared her bed and who nightly possessed her submissive body. A kindly stranger, but one nevertheless. What irked Philippa was the knowledge that Margaret and John were not such to each other. Their brotherly and sisterly union was of more meaning in this house than the physical one John and she shared. This truly made Philippa feel an outsider.

That night, after supper and talk and sewing by candlelight, John and Philippa lay in bed together. He had once more made love to her and was breathing in quick, shallow gasps. Now was Philippa's opportunity.

'John,' she asked him, in her softest tones, 'would you do something for me? A little thing?'

John stared at the ceiling sleepily. 'What is it?' he said absent-mindedly.

'Would you ask Margaret to give me the keys of the house? It would take a burden from her. I meant to speak of it with her, but I . . . forgot.'

John smiled. What little things concerned his wife, next to the matters that filled his thoughts. 'Of course, my dear,' he replied. Then, his passion spent and weary, he turned and slept. And he quite forgot her request.

Chapter Three

London Bridge was crowded with travellers and jostling shops. John Mentmore paused to look at the wares displayed outside each teetering building. Casually, as if in no hurry whatsoever, he examined the fine-made gloves and the high-class gold jewellery; with practised small talk he haggled with the sellers of the soft leather pouches and purses. On impulse he had stopped at this particular shop. His eye had been taken by a calfskin purse. He felt the supple leather with hands used to fabric and to texture. The front of the purse was embroidered with a flowering acanthus, a popular decoration on old manuscripts. He haggled with the seller and then bought it for a price acceptable to both. Whilst he had wanted a new purse for some time, his mind was not fully on the transaction.

John Mentmore was a worried man. He had begun his own investigations into the death of the trusted clerk, Adam Yonge. In the taverns and bawdy houses of the East End of the city he had plied questions to publicans and customers alike. He was no experienced investigator. His raw and unannounced visits were often met with sullen suspicion and noncommittal replies. Nevertheless the background noise that he identified suggested serious trouble. Amongst the weavers and the other yeoman guilds agitators were at work. Aggravation with the entrenched power of the livery guilds was deepening into something more determined, more threatening.

Only one tavern owner showed any sympathy. He also possessed a scrap of evidence. Yes, there had been strangers in the night before the riot. Yes, they had been in the company of weavers. No, he could not recall which weavers, or what they looked like.

Despite his understandable forgetfulness he did divulge two

useful items. One of the strangers bore an A-shaped birthmark on his cheek. 'Like a raspberry stain,' the innkeeper suggested. Also some of the group appeared to have come over from the Pelican Inn in Southwark.

Passing through the southern gatehouse of London Bridge, John crossed the drawbridge. A few minutes later he strolled out through the south bank gatehouse and into the teeming sprawl of Southwark.

Southwark was a thriving suburb free from the jurisdiction of London and its mayor. Here lay the houses and gardens of the Bishops of Winchester and Rochester. Along the Borough High Street jostled the inns and brothels which serviced this bridgehead on the south bank of the Thames.

The Pelican Inn was a popular haunt of travellers. It was also the gathering point for parties of pilgrims en route to the shrine of Becket at Canterbury. As such it was a gathering ground for gossip. Its landlord was a sharp, weasel-faced character with the unlikely surname of Bythebrook.

'The night before the riot,' John quizzed him over a wooden tankard of beer. 'Did you have a gang of men in, going over to the city before the shutting of the gates?'

'Which riot?' the innkeeper said.

'The riot which drove Gaunt out of the city, man!' John snapped. 'What other riot has been on everyone's lips these past months?'

John had heard too many blocking comments since his quest had begun. He was in no mood for cleverness.

The innkeeper twitched his rodent nose. 'Only asking,' he said. 'Only asking. We get a riot here most Saturday nights.'

John laughed. 'Very well, very well. I am sorry for my lack of courtesy but I have had too many people obstructing me recently.'

As soon as the words were out he regretted them. Too late, the words hung in the air like smoke. The innkeeper looked thoughtful.

'Mean a lot to you to find them?' John nodded. 'Mean a lot, young sir?'

John got the drift of the conversation and fumbled in his pocket for a silver penny. He tapped it on the trestle table. 'Yes, it means a lot to me.'

The innkeeper, without any display of shame, reached out and took the coin. 'Anything to tell them by?'

John touched his own cheek and explained about the raspberry stain. The weasel-faced man was lost in thought. Minutes passed. John began to wonder if he should ask for a refund.

At last, with another twitch of his nose, the innkeeper whispered, 'From Kent they were.' And that was all. Wiping his hands in his apron he took John's empty tankard and was off. The audience had been terminated. Pleased that his penny had secured some real information John pulled on his tunic and left. He had no idea of the significance of the clue he had purchased so expensively. Still, at least it was something.

With an exaggerated sense of satisfaction he lingered by the market stalls on the High Street, then sauntered home again. Had he been less engrossed he would not have failed to see Margaret, his sister. As it was he strode on unconscious of the figure who, aware of him, sidestepped into an alleyway.

Margaret waited for some minutes before resuming her course. Hood pulled up to extinguish her blaze of hair she hurried down Bishopgate Street towards the bridge. A few moments later and she would have walked straight into John coming in the opposite direction. She made for the church which stood at the northern end of the bridge and checked she was not being observed. Then she lifted the heavy iron latch and slipped into the building. It was the church of St Magnus Martyr, the very church whose tower Philippa had gazed upon from her chamber. Soon after a powerfully built, black-bearded man approached the same door. Like Margaret he checked for onlookers. Like her he lifted the latch and stepped inside.

The sunlight poured in through the church's southern windows. Along its northern wall the small side altars were less illuminated and here Margaret knelt in silent prayer. Soon the bearded man was beside her. He too knelt, his hands clasped. Margaret felt his presence.

'I have missed you, Robert,' she stated.

'And I have missed you, my precious heart,' the bearded man replied. At the passionate tone in his voice she turned to him.

By the combined light of tired sunbeams and more immediate candles it was clear that this man was concentrating fixedly on his female companion. He had a strong face. His eyes were deep mahogany and his cheeks were a little pale. A small scar caught at one end of his mouth. It gave him the appearance of constantly being on the brink of a wry smile. It was this feature that had first drawn Margaret's attention to him.

'It is not easy to get away,' she confided. 'And . . . and . . .' She bit her lip. 'And I do not know what will become of the household, now that woman is there.' She paused for a moment and considered her next words carefully. 'I have worked too hard, too, too hard, to let her take it away from me.'

Robert reached out and touched her arm. It was a firm touch. His hand lay, strong, across her forearm.

Margaret snorted. 'She is into everything. I can hardly turn away but she is in my place, organising my house, checking up on my administration.'

'Perhaps she means no ill,' Robert suggested. 'Surely she only seeks to become familiar with a strange place?'

Margaret flashed him a look of fire. Her hood was down. In the subdued light her hair burned like polished copper.

'I thought you would understand,' she said. Robert did not speak. Instead he merely gripped her arm. His eyes spoke his intense love for her.

'I am sorry,' she said. 'There is no call to speak that way to you, my heart.' At last she smiled. It was a thin smile, a wintry smile, which sat unseasonally on her summer features. Robert smiled back. For a few moments they knelt together in silence. In the stillness they searched the depths of each other's eyes.

'John tells us there is unrest among the weavers.' It was a solemn statement. It broke the silence like a tolling bell.

'There is little new in that news,' Robert said softly.

'No, but it seems worse.'

Margaret was painfully aware of the friction between the weaving guildsmen and the great mercers. There had been an uneasy armed truce for months, but recently the rash of strikes and disputes had spread like an epidemic. Many of the separate groups of workers were uniting to free themselves from the restricting power of the merchant guilds.

Robert did not speak. All that was left of his smile was the wry twist which never left his features. His eyes were fixed on hers.

'Does it get worse?' She repeated her question. This time it was less rhetorical. She required an answer.

'It gets worse,' he said. 'How can it not? The craftsman guilds are fighting for their lives.' Then, because she was who she was, he toned down his speech. 'We require more pay; a right to negotiate our wages, to be consulted, to improve our lot. Until we gain a fragment of the old independence we are lost. We are just the dumb creatures of others. Your father must know this. He is a proud man, an independent man. His family were weavers once. It is not so long since a Mentmore plied a shuttle and made the cloth he sells. The mercers forget the practice of the mystery which gave them birth. When amongst their richest merchandise, amongst their finest silks, they come upon *our* cloth – they come upon the way by which so many of them rose. It is a great trade, the cloth trade. It was and is a worthy mystery. It is an ancient mystery and not to be scorned.'

Now it was her turn to look at him in silence. The fire in her eyes had died down. Now it glowed like embers. Like a fire banked down for the night.

'What will become of us?' she asked simply.

'I do not know. By the mass and by St John I do not know.'

Outside the traffic rumbled and the air was full of noise. Inside the church it was still. For now just being together was enough. Even though it was a dangerous thing, to be hushed up, to be kept locked away. A secret thing.

Margaret remembered how she had met this man she loved and who loved her. Two years before the trouble between mercer and weaver, between livery company and craftsman yeoman guild, had seemed far away. Then Robert Newton had come often to the house. He had carried cloth and accepted Mentmore prices. Once Thomas had even given a feast for the small guild members and Robert had been an honoured guest. Now the frost of disputation had settled on all that. It had frozen that sweet rose of memory. It had frozen and blighted it. Now Robert was a minor guild master in his own right. He was a guild master, in company with others, fighting for his independence and locked in conflict with her father. Margaret Mentmore and Robert Newton stared into each other's eyes and almost despaired.

Had Thomas Mentmore known of the secret meetings between his daughter and the articulate young weaver it would have only added one more intolerable worry to a mind already well burdened. As it was, he and John were engrossed with other concerns.

On 21 June 1377 King Edward III died at Sheen. Two days later the Mentmores – father and son – attended a meeting of the Common Council. It was a tense occasion.

When they arrived John Philipot, a wealthy guild master, was speaking. It did not take long to pick up the thread of his argument.

'... Our only hope is that the young King Richard will act as a mediator between the city and his uncle.'

'And what if he does not? What if Gaunt does not wish for peace with the city?' The speaker was a goldsmith. As he looked about him he saw that his words had struck home. 'What reason have we got to trust Gaunt? His troops are all over the city again. At our own cost we have had to put up his coat of arms on West Chepe. Let no one be deceived. He means to crush us since we have opposed him.'

'Hasty talk, friend. Hasty talk. The Duke of Lancaster is surely as keen as we are to resolve our differences.' The optimistic tones belonged to Richard Lyons, a wealthy Londoner and Gaunt's man through and through. His comments brought sneers from a number of quarters. Gaunt had few friends at this meeting.

At this point Thomas Mentmore himself stood up. He was respected amongst the guild masters and when he signalled to be heard a hush quickly fell.

'My friends, I know how troubled you are. The death of the old king concerns us all. The rift between the city and the Duke of Lancaster is a source of great unhappiness to each one of us. But somehow we must try to settle our differences with Gaunt.'

John Mentmore cast a quizzical glance at his father. Before the tapestry commission it would have been difficult to imagine such conciliatory words flowing from Thomas. A number of others were surprised too. Richard Lyons was watching Thomas intently.

'We must trust the young king,' Thomas continued. 'We must look to him to settle the conflict between us. Our friend John Philipot is right. We must start the moves ourself. Only then will Gaunt learn to trust us.'

There was consternation in parts of the room. Many felt it was Gaunt who needed to show proof of his trustworthiness. At that point the meeting was interrupted. An excited servant flew into the room. Rushing up to Philipot he whispered some urgent message. Philipot looked startled for a moment. Composing himself he addressed the anxious meeting.

'My friends, we have an emissary from King Richard.'

When the royal messenger stalked in, he produced scowls on many of the watching faces. Lord Latimer was one of Gaunt's right-hand men. Few in the city trusted him.

'His Grace King Richard summons to himself at Sheen the representatives of the great and loyal city of London. He commands that they should join him in the mourning of his beloved grandfather. He summons them to talk with him concerning matters close to the heart of himself as king.'

Latimer's words produced a stunned silence.

'I am sure your lordship will allow us some moments to consider our response to this royal command,' Philipot said finally. Latimer nodded but did not move. 'As a council of the city, your lordship . . . in private if you would so graciously allow it.'

Philipot's words were quiet but had iron in them. Latimer's face was a mask. He made no comment. He stalked from the room. A turmoil of voices rose in consternation.

'It's a trap!'

'Gaunt means to draw us to Sheen and finish us!'

'The duke will destroy us and the young king together!'

Then Thomas Mentmore spoke again. 'My friends, we must trust the young king. And more than this, our city's trade can only flourish in an atmosphere of peace. Surely the king offers our only hope of such reconciliation. We must go to Sheen and accept the judgement of Richard.'

It could not be said that Thomas had convinced all of his hearers but none could deny the desperate need for peace. Had Lyons put forward such an argument it would have been rejected immediately by many present. Thomas Mentmore was a more neutral figure. Heads nodded at his advice – if reluctantly.

Latimer was brought back and given the council's reply. He smiled a thin smile when Philipot suggested that Gaunt himself should also submit himself to the king's will. The council agreed that the very next day they would send their representatives to the royal court. That deputation was to include Thomas Mentmore and his heir.

The royal manor of Sheen lay at Richmond, on the south bank of the Thames. Richard II, his mother Joan the Princess of Wales and the surviving sons of the old king had gathered there to mourn his passing.

It was to Sheen that the deputation of Londoners rode. They crossed London Bridge to Southwark and then turned their horses westward to where Richmond occupied a wide bend of the Thames.

Sheen was alive with pageantry. The royal household was camped in and about the manor. Courtiers and men-at-arms were in profusion. It was warily and carefully that the Londoners approached this great gathering. Along the way there had been much talk concerning the wisest tactics to adopt. Many in the party still harboured a deep distrust of the Duke of Lancaster.

On arrival the deputation first went to pay their respects to the dead monarch. His body had been laid in the chapel under armed guard and one by one the citizens filed past his corpse and gazed down on the frozen face of their king.

John had never been so close to the monarch before. Had he dared, he could have reached out and touched his smooth grey face. Death had eased out some of the lines and wrinkles. Prominent still, though, was the distorted, drooping mouth from the stroke that finally felled him.

When the deputation had paid their respects they were taken to see the new king. They went with mounting trepidation and in a tense silence. Richard II was but a boy of ten. With him were his mother and his powerful uncles. Here was the familiar face of John, Duke of Lancaster. Here also were the courtiers and great men of the realm. As the citizens entered the room, silence fell. All eyes were on them. The sense of tension was extreme. Here, face to face, was the royal party and those who had despoiled the royal arms. Here was the Duke of Lancaster and those who had delighted to name him as a Flemish butcher's bastard. The feeling was akin to the heaviness before a thunderstorm. Many in the delegation began to doubt the wisdom of their coming.

Then the lightning fell. But not as anyone in the awestruck party had expected. John of Gaunt fell at the feet of his royal nephew. Clasping his hands together, he begged him to settle the dispute once and for all.

'Your grace knows of the wrongs done to me, to my lineage and yours. You know too well of acts of violence and of treason. You have heard the defamations of your house and family.' The duke's eyes were sharp and active as he spoke.

This seemed the prelude to some terrible revenge. The Londoners were frozen. John felt his own mouth twitch. His throat was dry. He bit at his cheek relentlessly.

'Your grace knows these things,' the duke continued, 'and yet, I beg you, pardon those who have so offended you. Pardon them, I pray you, as I have pardoned them. I who have suffered the worst of wrongs have searched my heart and found forgiveness there.'

The sigh of relief within the room was audible. In one action Gaunt had seized the initiative and dumbfounded his enemies. The fears and suspicions of the Londoners were, in that moment, allayed. A dangerous division between Crown and people had been bridged. Reconciliation was the day's theme. Yet the credit was given to the new king.

John added his relief to that of his companions. Never, ever would he underestimate Gaunt. The man was a manipulator of real skill. Now all was plain. The duke had master-minded the whole reconciliation but used it as a means to enhance the prestige of the boy king. This was both manipulation and political wisdom. John could not but admire the man, despite his distrust!

So the meeting was an unqualified success. Honour was satisfied and peace established. The London delegation rode home satisfied. It had been an auspicious day. It had also added to the prestige of the Mentmores. Men recalled that it was Thomas who had counselled acceptance of the royal summons and the day had proved him right. Thomas, more than most, was satisfied with the events at Sheen.

A week after the momentous visit a royal order arrived for the Mentmores to supervise the provision of black cloth for the funeral procession of the dead king.

'His grace, our liege King Richard, is advised by his royal uncle that the house of Mentmore can fulfil such a request with care and with sobriety.'

The royal messenger had recited his lines with care. John wondered whether they had come direct from Richard, or from Gaunt.

Thomas was little concerned about the ultimate origins of the messenger. He set to work with a will. The order would deplete his stock of black cloth and he hurriedly despatched an order for five hundred ells of thick, black woollen finespun to his weaving shops.

Philippa and John rode down to Sheen with the packhorses carrying the bound black rolls.

'It's a tremendous honour, you know,' John commented as they rode. 'Tongues are wagging as to how we secured such a tremendous contract.'

Philippa pushed a handful of hair back under her pale blue silk hood. She was glad to be out of the house. When John had suggested that she went with him to Sheen she had almost cried aloud with joy, but her husband seemed unaware of the lightness in his wife's step since he had made the suggestion.

'We shall stand to do well from the coronation, too. Father has ordered bales of silk and rolls of finespun without number. You must look through the new rolls yourself and choose the best for your own dress. I have spoken to father. You may take whatever pleases you.'

Philippa smiled. The thought of a free rein in the cloth store sheds revived her spirits. 'I shall wear blue,' she said, 'and have it decorated with silver stars and a border of embroidered Ms.' Already she could see the tight-fitting bodice, the sweeping skirt and the richly trailing sleeves.

As she rode and planned it, the morning air seemed fresher and sweeter. How she loved it to be out of the house! How free she felt away from the haunting presence of Margaret! Looking at the blond locks of her husband, she felt that soon she would no longer even think of Ralph Horne.

John urged his horse forward to avoid a cart slowly clattering down the dusty highway. 'I spoke to Margaret,' he called back to his wife. 'She thanks you for your concern but says that the household duties are no worry to her. She knows how busy you are. She would not burden you with the small matters that she attends to. She is happy to keep the keys and to spare you the work. You are not to worry about her; though she thanks you kindly.'

John was more than pleased by Margaret's response to her new sister's concerns. Riding ahead of Philippa he could not see her face. If he had, he would have been astonished at the storm of dismay which darkened her previously sunny countenance.

Spurring on his mount John led the pack train forward.

For the Mentmores, the funeral contract was an unexpected coup. Twice John rode down to the royal manor with his sombre cargo. Only when the final cloth was delivered could the cortège make its way to London.

It took three days for Edward's body to be transported to Westminster from Sheen. It was a grand and solemn procession. The coffin was accompanied by poor men dressed in black. The black was Mentmore cloth. Each carried a flaming torch.

Thomas and John were at the abbey to see the king arrive. With them were Philippa and Margaret. Edmund and Giles de Brewoster were there also, having ridden from Giles's Cotswold estates for the funeral and the coronation. For Giles, as for Edmund, it was an opportunity to strengthen relationships with the new court. Giles's Lord, Thomas of Woodstock, the new king's uncle, was using the occasion to display his own retinue and knightly following. For this magnate, as for Giles and Edmund, the funeral and coronation were opportunities to make an impact on the boy king and his court.

Philippa was pleased that Edmund was home again. There was a lightness in his spirit which lifted the whole household even though everyone was dressed in black. At the abbey she could feel a prickling of excitement at the thought of the impending coronation. Her mind was far away as the cortège passed.

In silence Edward Plantagenet was carried to his final resting place. His wooden death mask perfectly represented the blank eyes and the distorted, drooping mouth that had so moved John Mentmore at Sheen.

With the funeral over, the city could turn its attentions to the coronation itself. Here was an opportunity for wild displays of pageantry and joy. It was an explosion of relief after months of tension.

The Mentmore hall was busy and the store sheds full. True to his promise, John escorted Philippa through the sheds to pick out her cloth. Here were profusions of weights and shades and qualities. Philippa took hours to make up her mind. She fondled and stroked the linens and the watermarked silks; she caressed the broadcloths and held up the finespun to the light; she mused over the Lincoln greens and the Bristol reds.

'Do you think me better in this blue or that green?' she asked her husband, lifting each roll in turn and holding it across her breast.

'You'll look lovely in either,' John replied, grinning.

The clerks had stopped their business for a moment and were watching the whole proceedings.

'No, no John,' she pleaded, 'I know that one will look better than the other. You choose. You tell me.' She desperately wanted to please him.

John pondered for a moment. 'The blue,' he decided. And so the blue was chosen; a rare and costly blue silk that had crossed the world from China.

In the hall Thomas had laid out trestle tables. These were the same boards which had carried John and Philippa's wedding breakfast, and were now rainbow laden with rolls of cloth. All the wealthy of the city seemed to be passing through the rush-strewn hall. Clerks and servants hurried to and fro. Cloth was stretched, compared and haggled over. Silver exchanged hands in astonishing amounts. Shears sliced through the weave.

Thomas Mentmore watched with silent satisfaction. In the solar upstairs Philippa's maidservant, Emma, was busily sewing her mistress's new dress. Her light fingers darted to and fro across the smooth surface of the silk. Tiny seed pearls and strips of brocade lay beside her needles and thread. With deft and practised movements she caught and tucked the precious material.

For hours at a time Philippa would hover in the room. Anxiously she watched the dress take shape. In those seed pearls and in that silk sheen seemed to lie her status as wife to the heir of Thomas Mentmore. She watched the birth of the dress with close attention to detail. She could scarcely contain her excitement at the thought of the king's crowning and the promise of the public celebrations.

A few days before his coronation the king kept his promise to visit the city. He was met with jubilant scenes. Cheering crowds lined the evening streets. At West Chepe a pageant was performed before him. At its height, flaring torches revealed a young boy and a beautiful young girl seemingly floating in the air high above the king. Robed in spotless white and golden-haired, they appeared like visions of angels.

Philippa, in the crowd with John, gazed with delight. She gripped his arm and he smiled at his wife. He was gratified by her appreciation of the spectacle. Even the more worldly-wise Margaret, on Edmund's arm, looked impressed. The king was clearly enthralled.

John and other sons of the guilds had supervised the construction of this Chepeside marvel. Fine ropes running from wooden frames and worked by pulleys held the 'angels' in the air and allowed them to descend and ascend. By night, and in the grip of the festive excitement, this contraption was all but invisible.

Slowly, gently, the two 'angels' floated down to the king. To his delight the boy presented him with a leather bag full of gold coins. The girl held out a silver goblet, soon filled with wine by an eager attendant. The crowd roared its approval.

The night was magical. As Richard of Bordeaux paraded through the streets, John and Philippa strolled arm in arm through the crowds. For the first time in weeks Philippa felt carefree.

John splashed wine from the rippling conduit into his cupped hands. 'Here, a toast to you and the new king.'

Philippa sipped the splashing liquid. The wine was sweet on her tongue. She felt the warmth of her husband's hand as she drank. His sweat, against her tongue, was salty and somehow strong. Giggling, she wiped the wine from her lips. John brushed splashes from her woollen dress. The wine turned the green an autumnal hue.

Philippa took his arm. 'Come, John, let's follow the king!'

She felt that this night he was eager to please her. No thoughts of business took his mind away. Tonight he was her husband. She would not let such a moment slip away. No – she would enjoy it to the full.

'Yes, John. Let's follow the king!'

Behind them, equally relaxed, sauntered Edmund and his redhead sister. She was always more relaxed when he was at home. Of all Thomas's children these two were the closest. Edmund, alone, dared to tease the fiery Margaret and to him she was always 'Meg'. Margaret, who would have felt intensely patronised if so treated by anybody else, would take it from Edmund with a freckled grin.

Thus by a combination of coronation and Edmund's homecoming, the Mentmore household was infinitely less explosive than of late. For the time being it was peacefully united. Even Thomas noted the change of atmosphere. John, previously preoccupied with his many concerns, had been far less aware of the combustible atmosphere in the house. It was also noticeable how fond Edmund seemed of Philippa. He would always find time to speak with her. She responded less openly to his characteristic teasing but took it good-naturedly. John noted this and was pleased. If Margaret was aware of it, she gave no obvious sign one way or the other.

On the morning of 16 July the whole household, indeed the whole city, was up at dawn. This was the day of the coronation. By prime the streets were thronged with excited citizens. Tapestries hung from buildings. Flowers were strewn over the roads. Vendors hawked sweetmeats along the teeming streets. Pickpockets prepared for a field day.

Emma rose early and laid out her mistress's dress. While John was giving orders for the day to the servants, she came to her mistress's chamber to dress her.

Philippa had woken with John but had lain in bed, awaiting the light knock on the door. Soon Emma was fussing about her mistress. Already the morning was warm and Philippa was relieved she had chosen the light silk. With Emma's help she slipped on a thin cotton shift. Her firm breasts lifted the material in white pyramids.

'My lady, this makes me think of your wedding day,' Emma remarked cheerily as she fastened the bodice.

That thought had also been on Philippa's mind. Emma's innocent comment drove it home. For a moment Philippa felt a stab of pain. Few of the anxieties of that day had been resolved. Margaret was quiet now but for how long? Her own place within the house was far from defined. Even John, whom she had come to be very fond of, spent little time with her and lacked that intimate knowledge of her, or sufficient intuition, to understand her concerns.

'My, that was such an exciting day, my lady. I think I shall never forget it. And then there was that poor man . . .' Suddenly Emma checked herself, realising such a memory was quite out of place. The poor teenager stammered: 'I beg your pardon, mistress. I am so sorry. I did not mean to . . . I did not think . . .'

The girl's instant misery swept away Philippa's self-pity. She patted Emma's arm. 'You meant no harm, Emma. You meant no hurt and none has been taken. Fret not, girl. We've too much work to do.'

Emma was Philippa's only real link with her old life. She valued the girl despite her careless chatter. In truth, Emma would willingly have died for her mistress. Philippa was aware of this. To experience such love made up for a hundred little errors.

Emma smoothed out the full dress. Over the pale blue silk Philippa put on a draping pelisse, or over-robe, of thin blue wool. It was a deep blue. Emma's nimble fingers lifted Philippa's hair up into a fine gold net, kept in place with a jewelled band. Garnet glinted in the subdued light of the chamber. Only two long curls deliberately escaped the net. They framed Philippa's oval face in an appealingly girlish fashion.

Emma stepped back. 'You are beautiful, my lady.'

'Indeed she is.'

John had silently lifted the latch. He was in the doorway. Both women jumped. Emma giggled, gathered up her bits and pieces and, curtseying, slipped out of the room. Philippa blushed pale rose.

'Thank you, John.' She felt strangely shy again. John sat beside her.

'Truly I love you, my heart. Truly you do look beautiful today.' Then he laid one warm hand upon her breast and kissed her full on the mouth. 'And if I do not change,' he whispered, after the kiss, 'we shall miss the king and Edmund and all!'

In ebullient mood he pulled on his finery and soon the Mentmore household, in their peacock best, were out on the streets to watch the triumphal spectacle.

As steward of England, John of Lancaster rode at the head of the gorgeous procession which wound its way from the Tower to Westminster. Beside him rode the Marshal, Lord Percy. Here were the two men who had been driven in humiliation from St Paul's. Today all was different. All was holiday. All was joy. The crowds cheered them warmly. Soon the route was alive with fabulous costumes and the heavy standards of England. Golden lions and fleur-de-lys were everywhere in flapping profusion. Philippa and John threw flowers with the rest. Margaret too tossed petals and seemed in a holiday mood.

John called over a boy and brought sweetmeats for his wife and sister and even serious William, fresh from Oxford, picked at the sticky delights. Thomas Mentmore was at Westminster itself with a delegation from the London guilds.

The crowd jostled and pushed for the best places. Constables of the local alderman recognised John and pushed apart the crowd to let them through.

'I think every woman is wearing Mentmore silk,' Philippa whispered to John.

'And every poor man is wearing Mentmore broadcloth,' John whispered back. 'From rich to poor we've dressed half the city.' Philippa laughed.

It was true that all the best of London was on display. Jewels and fine cloth dazzled in profusion. Liveried retainers held back the gawping multitude from their richly dressed masters and mistresses.

Other guild masters smiled and nodded at John. Their wives smiled and nodded at Philippa. Their experienced eyes took in her slim body, rich silk and jewels at a practised glance. Clearly more than the king was on display.

'They are jealous of you, my dear,' John muttered conspiratorially.

'Jealous of what?' But Philippa knew full well what he meant! 'Jealous that you are lovely and they are not.'

Before this nodding, smiling multitude of London rode the splendid chivalry of the land. Amongst the hundreds of knights and warriors rode Giles de Brewoster, Lord of Woodlands and Knolton. Beside him rode his esquire and adopted heir Edmund Mentmore. Both were superbly apparelled in exuberantly embroidered doublet and tunic. As they passed a wave of cheering in a great ocean of cheering rose from the Mentmore household.

The procession left the city and rode out along the Strand and the shouting crowds closed in and followed them. Laughing and in high spirits John, Philippa, Margaret and William were with them.

At Westminster the young monarch processed from the palace to the abbey for his crowning. It seemed an age since a wooden-faced king had passed that way by the light of black-draped torches. Now all was colour and light.

The coronation was followed by days of celebrations. The coronation feast itself lasted a week and caused the demise of some four hundred oxen and as many sheep, pigs and wild boar. On Chepeside the water conduits ran with wine, courtesy of the vintners guild. The Mentmores ate and danced and made merry in company with thousands of their fellow citizens.

In the midst of one of the many feasts, given by the Common Council, Edmund caught sight of a strangely familiar face. The raven's wing hair and the alabaster skin were not easily forgotten. Anne Glanville was a woman who made an impression on the memory of many a man. Whilst Edmund had been away on Giles's estates his thoughts had turned, more than once, to the beautiful young woman whom he had rescued in West Chepe.

Sitting between her father and brother she seemed unassailable. Turning to John, Edmund whispered urgently, 'Who is that woman? The one with the jet-black hair?'

John followed his gaze. 'Ah yes, the pale-skinned beauty pretending to ignore you.' Edmund laughed. 'That is the daughter of Lionel Glanville. She is, they say, obliquely descended from the justiciar who was Sheriff of Yorkshire in the days of King Henry the Second.'

'Yes, yes,' Edmund said, impatient at the history lesson, 'but who is Lionel Glanville, man?'

'Her father,' John replied impishly, but when he caught the look on Edmund's face added, 'he has estates in Middlesex and Wiltshire. He is related through his late wife to a guild master of the fishmongers.'

Edmund seemed satisfied with the answer. Then the feast gave way to dancing and John lost sight of Edmund as he danced with his wife. When he next saw his brother he noted that he was talking casually to the white-skinned Anne. Somehow Edmund had run the gauntlet of father and brother and slipped through their defences. John smiled. Edmund had a habit of doing that!

Anne Glanville was not a woman to ignore the attentions of a handsome young man. Neither was she one openly to advertise her appreciation.

'I am glad I have an opportunity to thank you more properly, sir,' she said coolly. 'Were it not for your action, my serving women would have been in some danger.'

'You are too kind, madam,' Edmund said with a guarded formality. 'But I had hoped I might have been of some service to *you* also.'

A smile betrayed the ice queen. Edmund was quick to press home his advantage.

'But, of course, I am glad to have been of use to your servants at least.' Then he added, 'It was a good job for that rogue that I rescued him from you. By Our Lady, a moment longer and you would have quite ensnared him.'

Anne laughed. Her laughter was rich and musical. Her father and brother looked at her with furrowed brows. They had not wished to bar the way to her rescuer but were disconcerted by his clear success with their charge.

'This is only the second time we have met, my lady. Does your father bring you to London often?'

'My father brings me often enough.' She was playing with him again. 'But I am well able to come here by myself. I am not a child, sir knight!'

'No, my lady,' Edmund said with a rich grin. 'You are no child.' He paused then said: 'I wondered if I should have the honour of your conversation again.'

There followed a full and heavy silence. Anne Glanville's dark eyes were studying the forward young hero. 'I am surprised,' she said at last, 'that the son of a mercer should wish conversation with the daughter of a fishmonger's child.'

'It is with beauty that I converse, madam, not with occupation.' Edmund trod warily once more.

'Then it would not matter were I . . . were I even a weaver's daughter?'

Even Edmund was caught off guard by such acute awareness of politics. Anne Glanville was a force to be reckoned with.

'My lady, beauty stands as its own champion.'

'Pity, sir knight, that I should, as you say, have such a champion. For if you are right I shall not need another.'

Edmund was floored. Never in any joust had he been so deftly struck from his saddle.

Anne glanced at her father. 'Pray excuse me, sir knight. My father would have me join him.' With a sweep of her dark hair she was gone.

Edmund watched her go, astonished. A wry smile finally lit his lips. When all these celebrations were completed he would keep an eye open for Anne Glanville. But next time he would be better armed in readiness!

When the week's festivities were over, the Mentmore clan gathered in the wood-beamed parlour of their house. Soon Edmund and Giles would return to the Cotswolds and William would go back up to Oxford. John had things he wanted to say before the family dispersed. He had chosen this night to reveal his plans. The coronation had put everyone in a good mood. As the servants brought in food and wine the atmosphere was genial.

John's plans hinged on his careful observation of the economy and on Giles. Giles de Brewoster was a country knight. Born on one of the Dorset manors of his father, he was Lord of Woodlands and Knolton in the north-east of the county. As a young knight he had fought with Edward III. He had married Margaret Mentmore, Thomas's sister, and obtained a substantial dowry. This money had helped him recruit and arm a company for the Black Prince's French campaign of 1356.

It was the 1356 campaign that had been the making of Giles. At thirty-five he had fought in the thick of it at Poitiers. More importantly he had won a fortune in ransoms. Returning home he found his elder brother dead, without issue, and himself the inheritor of the family's Cotswold estates. Two years earlier his wife, whom he had come to cherish, had died. On his return from Poitiers Giles had adopted young Edmund Mentmore, his four-year-old nephew, as his heir.

Giles was sitting close to John at table. The old warhorse was drinking his wine with great enthusiasm.

'Did I ever tell you,' he quizzed Margaret Mentmore, 'of how I saw the French king captured at Poitiers?'

Margaret recollected that he had. The news did not prevent Giles from telling her again.

In the centre of the table more serious conversation was involving John, William, Thomas and Edmund. It was a conversation which John had started.

'The business is going well. The cloth trade is buoyant and the tapestry side of the business is, as you know, most encouraging.' There were grunts of agreement from his listeners. They were now aware of Gaunt's commission to the Mentmores. John continued: 'The family finances are in the best shape they have ever been in. Because of this, I now believe we can afford the expansion that the state of the market in cloth is offering us.'

Giles had finished the introduction to his tale of martial glory. Margaret was spared more by the old knight's interest being taken by John's sermon.

'Think carefully about how we operate the sale of cloth. Although we are proud of our power and independence we are tied to the yeoman guilds. Yes I know', he added quickly to counter any rising objection, 'that we keep power to fix prices and retail the cloth but we rely on their craft skills to produce the basic cloth itself.'

Philippa was lightly picking meat from her bread trencher. The food only occupied part of her concentration. Most of her mind was focussed on John. She could recognise the earnestness in his face and voice. Without making it obvious, she followed the line of his argument.

John studied the faces of his male hearers. They had listened carefully to his words so far, and he waited in case any present wished to challenge his assertions. He knew no one would. He was less sure, however, of what their reactions would be to what was coming next.

'If we are to triumph over these limitations,' he went on, 'we must disentangle ourselves from the whole guild system in weaving. Imagine a situation in which we controlled the entire process of cloth production. Such a situation would free us, once and for all, from the yeoman guilds. All it needs is capital. We have the money . . .'

He picked up a chicken wing. Calmly, disguising the intensity of his feelings, he began to strip the bone.

'But we've been through this before. You're surely not asking us to become weavers again?' The voice belonged to William.

Edmund winked at John. 'No, William,' he intervened. 'That's not what he means. Just let him finish and you'll see.'

'Edmund's right, William, that's not what I mean. We will not be involved in any part of the process of producing the cloth. We shall organise and control it – '

'But the weavers' guilds will never allow it! You could never get the yeoman guilds in London to surrender such power to you!' Once again the interruption came from William. Thomas was silent and made no comment.

Margaret called to one of the servants to replenish the empty wine goblets. William drained his and looked at his brother, waiting for his answer.

'Quite true,' John conceded. 'They would never let us do such a thing. They would recognise it for what it was: the final end of their existence. But we will bypass them. We will totally discard them. We will turn to the growing rural cloth industry. They have no guilds. They work in their homes and their numbers are growing. They are ripe for being organised – by us! This is the way the trend is going – out of the city. You know how fulling mills have sprung up in the Cotswolds. For years now even the yeoman guilds have had to send their cloth *out* of the city for fulling. They've resisted it, by St John, but they can't stop it. And around the fulling mills a cloth industry is growing. It's small but it's there. They have no guilds. They are poorly organised. They take low wages.'

There was a stir of comment in the room. Both Margaret and Philippa gave up pretence of eating. This was radical stuff! Thomas looked sceptical. Edmund and Giles seemed in agreement with John. William was thoughtful.

At last Thomas spoke. 'You forget the tapestry work. That is our way forward.'

'No, my father, I do not forget it,' John said. 'I know the tremendous work that has gone into it. Indeed it has arisen from similar needs. It has made us less reliant on the weavers. What I'm suggesting will build on that foundation. It will take it further. The time is right for this move. Others are beginning to go this way and soon it will be obvious to all. We need to get there before the others. We need to take the high ground first.' Edmund nodded at this military metaphor.

'You move too fast, my son,' Thomas commented. 'You push too far too fast. You would risk all on this venture. You would gamble everything that we have built so far. It is a dangerous game.'

'It would not be all changed, father,' John retorted. 'The royalty and nobility would buy our fine cloth, just as now. What we would have done is to capture the sale of domestic cloth. That would not even have to come to London. It can be sold in inns and chambers. It is a hard thing to tax when sold that way . . .'

There were chuckles around the room.

'That's good news, father,' Edmund suggested in conciliatory fashion. 'A method of selling which avoids the cloth tax entirely.'

'There's much in favour of the scheme,' John concluded. 'It's been forty years since we saw to it that the weaving guilds lost their monopoly, yet we still choose to rely on them. Now is the chance to remove them totally. The way forward is clear. Giles has an abundance of sheep. His manor at Upton is sheep pasture and many of his Cotswold neighbours go that way. In Dorset his lands run cheek by jowl with the Glastonbury Abbey sheep runs at Damerham. If we move into the Cotswold market we can seize the domestic cloth production of middle England. We can even ship out of Bristol for the Gascon trade. My own contacts indicate that the same expansion is possible in Suffolk. Think of it: the Mentmores a great dynasty of merchant clothiers.'

'No!' It was Thomas who spoke. His tone was quite emphatic. 'No. You move too far too fast.' He was angry. It was clear that John had already discussed the matter, at length, with Giles and Edmund. Thomas was not only conservative. He was offended. 'No! I will not gamble on this, this . . . flight of the dice. I shall not do so. Good night, gentlemen.'

With Thomas's exit the party broke up. Giles shook his head but reserved comment. The ladies retired discreetly.

Edmund consoled his brother. 'He will see, John. He will see it in time.'

John shrugged and blew out the flickering candle.

Chapter Four

The night was very dark indeed. An autumnal rain squall had swept over the city at dusk. Behind it bank on bank of cloud had been marshalled in by the rising wind. By the time the city gates had closed all stars had been snuffed out. No moon broke through the heavy blanket of night. The rain had stopped but the wet streets were plunged into deep darkness.

Edmund Mentmore cursed himself as a fool. He was wet and cold and had little to show for his discomfort. He had ridden into the city just before the gates closed and his journey from Gloucestershire had been long, muddy and lacking in any pleasant diversions. He had left Giles de Brewoster's manor the previous afternoon and spent the evening with William at Oxford. It had been a tedious social call. His clerical brother was possessed of only one subject of conversation. Soon Edmund had tired of talk of Wyclif and of theology. Using his journey as an excuse, he had retired to bed early and risen late.

The ride from Oxford to London had been memorable only for the October mud on the road and the carriers' carts which blocked the highway. When he arrived home he was in some need of light relief.

The family, unwarned of his arrival, were not at home. To his exasperated enquiry he received the information that they were attending a guild function, a gathering to celebrate the feast of St Simon and St Jude. Annoyed at having missed such a feast, Edmund resolved on a little night-time adventure.

The adventure had gone as badly awry as his journey. Before he had left London, following the coronation, he had made enquiries regarding Anne Glanville. Interrogation of servants and a judicial use of silver pennies had produced the information that the lady in question would be in town for the autumn. Further investigation had turned up the stimulating intelligence that she would not be accompanied by her father or brother. Clearly, the raven-headed beauty was an independent-minded young woman.

Edmund was well practised at slipping past serving women and chaperons. Anne's cool intelligence had had quite an impact on the young Mentmore. His early return to London had good reasons behind it as far as Giles or his family were concerned. The more pressing reason, unknown to them, was Anne and for this reason Edmund had been considerably vague in his estimated time of arrival. As a military man he knew the advantages which could accrue from the element of surprise.

Everything had gone wrong. When he eventually reached the Tower Street town house of the Glanvilles he had found it dark and shut up. Repeated knocking had aroused an elderly servant. Aggrieved at being disturbed he had shown some malicious delight in declaring the absence of his mistress. No, she was not here; no, she had not been here; no, he knew not when she would come to the city. 'And when she does come,' he commented drily, 'she will surely warn her house servants and will not send out a general proclamation to casual callers.'

To all of this even the ebullient Edmund had no reply. Considerably disappointed and deflated the young warrior had beat a hasty, tactical retreat.

He had drowned some of his sorrows at a tavern opposite the Thames-side Customs House. He had even toyed with the idea of expending some of his pent-up energies in one of the bawdy houses near Billingsgate Market. Instead, in a moment of rare self-denial, he had pocketed his silver and made for home.

The rutted surface of Thames Street was oozing with mud – and worse. Seeking to avoid it, Edmund kept close to the dripping, overhanging buildings. The city was remarkably quiet now and he trudged along deep in thought. As he passed St Magnus Martyr and the entrance to London Bridge he was almost the only traveller out and about. Almost the only one – but not quite. To the west of the bridge Swan Steps ran down to the banked-up waters of the river. Here, in a well of shadows, a knot of deeper darkness shifted and moved. Edmund did not see the group of four or five men emerge from the slippery steps. Even had he seen them, he would no doubt have ignored them.

By the time he was approaching the Steel Yard of the Hanseatic traders, the fellow travellers were close to him. Whatever their business, they appeared to be in somewhat of a hurry. Despite the state of the street their pace increased.

Edmund turned right into a side alley. It was a short cut. The fellow travellers did likewise. Their pace quickened. The alley was overhung by rearing jetties. Drip, drip, the loose water sang. Edmund tugged at his cloak. Drip, drip. He heard footsteps close behind. Boots splashed into the gutter and its filth. Edmund quickened his own pace. Drip, drip. The alley narrowed. The jetties almost joined. He was in a dark tunnel.

For the first time it dawned on Edmund that he was in a dangerous situation. Rarely was he caught off guard. Now, almost too late, he awoke to reality. All thoughts of Anne Glanville dissolved.

The boots behind were running. Edmund turned. A ghost band of shadows leapt towards him. He fumbled with his cloak. The shadows were almost on him. His long, thin dagger slipped free from his cloak. The shadows enveloped him.

For a split second there was chaos. The leading footpad ran onto Edmund's outstretched dagger. It was no credit to Mentmore. The night was dark for attacker as well as for attacked.

'God's blood, God's blood.' The shadow found voice. It reeled away. 'Curse you, damn you.'

A fist caught Edmund on the temple. The edge of a ring sliced along the side of his head. Edmund stumbled under the blow. He jerked up his blade – and sliced the air. As he did so a knife plunged at his chest, missed its mark. The steel, thin and wickedly sharp, cut a deep, clean furrow along a rib and under his arm. Edmund fell. A rough boot kicked him. More blades sliced at him. They bored through cloak and linen shirt.

Edmund felt death leering in his face. His dagger was lost. Helplessly he used his arms as a shield. Without any sensation of pain he felt the jabbing blades slash and cut his forearms.

Suddenly he was alone. The alley was full of splashing, echoing footsteps. Rough hands pulled him up and drew aside his arms. He was defenceless. He could not think who this new wave of attackers could be. Weakly he struggled.

'Vor the sick of Gott man, holt yourself still. Holt, man . . . Holt. Ve bee frenz, by Gott. Frenz, by Gott . . .'

Edmund felt a hot breath on his face. It stank of ale. Laughing weakly he recognised the gutteral tones of German guards from the Steel Yard.

'Ve bee frenz, by Gott . . .'

Edmund shook with hysterical laughter. Then he passed out.

By the next morning the clouds had cleared. A golden autumn day replaced the previous run of wet days without any seeming incongruity.

For Edmund, patched up and reclining in the solar, the previous night's adventure seemed like a bad dream. The only things that persuaded him of its reality were the bandages round his chest and arms, the stiffness of his wounds and the hectoring tones of his brother.

John Mentmore chewed his cheek. One hand pushed back his blond hair. He was very angry indeed.

'By St Peter, John, do not go on so.' Edmund was his cheerful self again. 'By the way you speak you would think I was the footpad and not their victim. I am not to blame, man. Save your lecturing for them – as they hang.'

'You not to blame? You not to blame?' John queried savagely. 'You come home unannounced. You wander the streets at midnight. We do not know where you are, or if you are alive or dead. And you are not to blame? Why were you in an alley at midnight, man?'

Edmund too was angry now. 'I will not be lectured so, John. I was there because I chose to be there; that is why.'

'Some woman, I suggest. Some whore on East Chepe?'

'And what if it was? I do not answer to you, John Mentmore. I do not question you and will not be treated so myself. I am not your servant, or your child.' Edmund was particularly nettled by John's assertion. All too readily he recalled his sexual self-control at Billingsgate.

John was not impressed.

'And I can protect myself, my elder brother!'

'Ha!' John exclaimed. 'Look after yourself? You should thank God for the Hanser guards and their sharp ears. Were it not for them you would be a matter for a chantry priest this morning.' John paused. 'How do you think we felt last night – father, Philippa, Margaret and me? We return to find you in a pool of blood and the hall overrun with damn Hanser guards. Looking the place over. Poking about and bullying the servants.'

'So it is because I spoilt your evening that you are angry? I apologise, John. I am deeply sorry I was so inconsiderate. When next I am subject to murder, I shall arrange it to avoid your social needs – brother.' Edmund's tone was deeply mocking. 'And do not damn the Hansers. God knows I shall never curse them or their presence in the city again. They saved my life, foreigners or no! As God is my judge, I shall not forget them.' Grasping another line of argument, Edmund added, 'And if I am to blame, why is it you and not father here lecturing me? If I am so much in the wrong, why is he not here?'

This was a clever move and it caught John on the raw. He was aware that Thomas would not rail against his son. The elderly mercer was furious, but his anger was directed at the criminals who had sought the life of a Mentmore.

'He has to increase the profit of the business, Edmund. That is why he is not here. If we are to purchase a chantry priest to pray for your murdered soul some of us will have to work for a living.'

The two brothers faced each other. There was silence. Then Edmund grinned.

John shook his head in despair and laughed. 'Edmund Mentmore, the French will never kill you. You will fall to a chamberpot wielded by an outraged woman or . . .' They were both laughing now. 'Or . . . or to the fury of a cuckold husband!'

John embraced his brother. Edmund winced. When the laughing was over, John was serious again. He sat down and frowned.

'What's wrong John? There's more to this lecture than you're telling.'

'Aye,' John said heavily, 'things are not as they might be. The weavers' guilds are full of unrest again. We've had strikes and even assaults on the servants.'

Edmund flushed angrily. 'How long has this been going on? What punishment has been handed out to these scum?'

'We begin the second week of a strike. We have had no fresh broadcloth for six days now. As to the punishment, there has been none. Like your assailants of last night, these night birds stalk in darkness and are gone. A servant with a cracked head remembers little, and how can we prove it is the work of the yeoman guilds?'

Edmund spoke pensively. 'You mentioned last night's attack.' John nodded, lost in thought. 'So you think that was no chance waylaying of an innocent in a dark alley?'

John shook his head. 'No, I am sure it is part of the pattern. God's blood but I would like to put a noose around a few necks!'

'But you have no proof? No proof to take before the constable, or an alderman?'

'That's just it, Edmund. We cannot prove anything. Agnes Bakwell is struck from behind, a clerk is pushed into the Fleet, a groom is beaten in an alley.'

'You say these scoundrels laid hands on Agnes? She is not . . . not . . .?'

'No, she's not dead. Agnes Bakwell has a kick like a mule and a skull built of Purbeck stone! She took fright for a time, but is now as spirited as a fighting cock. You know Agnes!'

'But she saw nothing? She caught no glimpse of . . .'

'I told you: these brave assailants strike at night and from behind. No one sees a thing. We can as little prove who struck Agnes as we can prove who murdered Adam Yonge.'

Edmund gave a long, low whistle. 'So you think Adam's death and my near murder are part of one strategy?' He fixed his brother with an interrogatory stare.

'I do. And before you can ask, I have not told father. Like the alderman he would ask for proof.' John grimaced. 'I see murder and assault and know it has a common cause, yet I cannot find one sworn witness who will uphold my belief before a court. Any sergeant-at-law would dismiss my accusations against the weavers, and laugh as he did it.'

John was thinking of the Pelican Inn at Southwark and the raspberry-stained man. All his assembled clues either led out of the city or dissolved away into guesswork. He was deeply frustrated. Frustrated and angry. He noticed Thomas's ivory chess set. A piece had fallen. He carefully set it upright. It was a pawn. John wondered who was moving the pieces in his own deadly game. Who were kings; who were pawns?

At that moment the two brothers were interrupted in their discussions. Emma, Philippa's maidservant, stood at the door of the solar.

'I beg your pardon, masters. The mistress Philippa asks that you would come down to the hall. She says a company of men have come to see you, sirs.'

John and Edmund exchanged glances. 'Thank you, Emma,' John said. 'I shall be there immediately.' As the girl left, he turned to his brother. 'Now, who would come in a company? In a company and unbidden?' He looked as if he knew the answer to his own question.

As John descended the stair to the raised dais in the hall, he could make out a group of men in the main body of the room. There was an air of defiance about them. They stared about the hall without respect or civility.

Philippa and Margaret were there. The red-haired Mentmore daughter was uncharacteristically pale and worried. Before John could ponder on this unusual demeanour, his wife had reached him.

'Weavers, John. They come to speak with the Mentmores. They demand, John. They demand – '

'Aye, my heart, I guessed they were weavers. And as to demand – well, we shall see about that!' John faced the deputation. 'Who comes unbidden to the house of Mentmore and who demands . . . demands to see the master of a livery guild?'

A bearded man stepped forward. His brown eyes flashed. A scar pulled at his mouth. 'We do not demand. We ask, as civil men, to state our grievances.'

'But we may yet demand and make no mistake!' The interruption came from a tall, jaundiced-looking man in his late forties. His jaw was stuck out in defiance. His black eyes blazed.

'Enough, Nicholas, enough.' The bearded weaver half turned. 'I speak for those present – as agreed.'

'Then speak not so weakly to a Mentmore,' came the calculated reply. The jaw jerked back.

Face tight with anger, the bearded man turned once again to John. 'We do not demand. We request,' he stated with a note of finality.

'Thank you, Robert,' John replied civilly. He had recognised Robert Newton. 'But my father is not here and *he* is guild master of the house of Mentmore. I cannot speak without his leave.'

'Then when may we see him?'

'I will tell him of your visit and he may send a servant to you in due time.' John lingered over the word 'may'.

The hall was filling up with liveried Mentmore retainers. Some of the confidence seemed to be going out of the weavers.

'Tell your father, tell Thomas Mentmore, that we would speak about the price of a roll of cloth and of how much more we should receive for our labours. We shall accept no less than eight pence a day for our work.'

The accompanying weavers nodded vigorously. John looked grim. The price was high. 'I shall tell my father,' was his only reply.

Robert Newton hesitated for a moment, then he nodded and strode off. The gaggle of weavers followed him. When they were gone John turned to face Edmund, who had descended from the solar.

'You heard that? Not content with killing our clerk and murdering you, these dogs would rob us as well.'

'John, dear, you do not really think they could have . . .?' Philippa's shocked voice trailed away.

'I do. I do,' John said emphatically. Why should he keep his thoughts a secret? Taking his wife by one arm he led her from the dais. Concern was etched on her oval face.

Edmund followed them and the liveried servants dispersed. Soon only Margaret was left in the room. Her hands were clenched. She was as pale as a corpse. Leaving the hall, she spent an agitated day walking the busy markets. John's allegations had stunned her. She needed time to think. Within the jostling crowds she could lose herself and gather her thoughts together. Along Poultry and West Chepe she wandered in a dreamlike state. She was hardly aware of the overburdened stalls and their haggling owners.

Filled with a bitter curiosity, she slowly drifted down towards the river. She paused to watch the elevation of the Host in St Michael Paternoster Royal. She hung back amongst the crowd of others, who had dropped into the church to watch this height of the liturgy. Satisfied with a blessing by merely watching the elevation the crowd drifted away as the more devout moved forward to receive communion. Margaret hesitated for a moment, then left the church also. She felt less than at peace with herself. Perhaps she would partake of mass tomorrow, she thought, when a pressing question had at last been answered.

Passing the Steel Yard she noticed the German guards on duty with their heavy quilted leather jerkins and long swords. The day, begun with so much promise, had turned damp again. She turned up her hood against a passing shower. For a long time she stood in the lane where Edmund had been assaulted. Even in daylight it was dark and dirty. She shivered to think of the place by night. Passing on, she came to Grasschurch Street and spent an idle hour in the herb market. Handling the dried rosemary and camomile, she breathed in the rising perfume of the place.

When it was time, she made her way furtively to the church of St Magnus Martyr.

Robert was already there. As usual the quiet sanctuary was quite deserted. He kissed her hand. She was not diverted from her purpose, however. Her eyes were afire.

'Did your people do it? Did your people try to murder Edmund?'

Once spoken, the question hung naked and terrible in the air. It was so awful that she almost shrank from it. 'Did they? Did they do it, Robert?'

Newton was aghast. The natural horror of his look was like a cleansing to her. She knew at once he knew nothing of the crime.

'Murder? Murder Edmund? What are you saying, Margaret?'

'You do not know?'

He shook his head. 'I do not know what you are talking about, my heart,' he replied with real passion.

She collapsed into his arms. Such vulnerability was rarely seen in Margaret. Robert folded his strength around her and drew her to his chest in a great hug. Her flaming hair lay like cold fire against his bearded cheek.

'Oh my heart, my own dear heart,' she sobbed. 'You do not know how I have been torn apart.'

Gently, carefully, Robert took her to one side. He sat her down upon an oak box and when she had composed herself he questioned her concerning her accusation.

Still fragile she poured out the news. It tumbled from her as a winter river in wild spate: the attacks on the servants, the assault on Edmund, John's belief in the complicity of the weavers.

'I swear I know nothing of any act against Edmund. More than that, I would do nothing to hurt your family. I would hang first. Aye, and see those who did the hurt hanged themselves.'

Margaret nodded. She believed him.

Robert continued: 'Things are difficult between us now. There is hard bargaining and ill feeling on both sides. A jostle in the market, even a hot-headed blow struck, but never talk of murder or attempted murder. I know nothing of it and if I know nothing there is nothing to know.'

'Then you think John misreads these actions?'

'I do not say that the weavers are blameless, but your brother attempts too much when he lays all at our door. This matter of Edmund. Does it not sound likely to be a chance attack by murderous ruffians taking advantage of a lone man? Dear heart, it happens many a night in this city.'

Margaret shivered, then said, 'Do all weavers think as you? Are there not others more angry?' She was remembering the altercation in the Mentmores' hall.

Robert cleared his throat. 'Aye,' he said flatly. Then he added, 'Nick Smalecombe thinks I tread too delicately on Mentmore toes. You heard a sample of Nicholas's wares in your own hall, did you not?' Margaret nodded again. 'And Dick Appulby and his friends accuse me of over-gentleness, but none of them would murder. They are guild leaders as myself. They love their mystery and fear to see it driven down so, but they would never knife a man in a dark alley. None of them would do so wicked and cowardly a thing. None of them.'

Margaret squeezed his hand. 'Will you work for peace between the Mentmores and the weavers?' she asked. 'Will you, Rob? For me?'

'It is not easy, my love. We have just demands, and I am not my own spokesman; I speak for many. I speak for my mystery. Your father must meet us halfway if there is to be peace. The angry ones – Smalecombe, Appulby and others – they fear betrayal. They feel that the Mentmores despise us. Your father must make concessions if there is to be peace.'

'But if he does? If he does meet you – and make concessions – will you work for peace?'

'I swear it.'

She rose and kissed him. 'And now,' she said, 'I must go. They will wonder where I am, as it is. If I am gone much longer they will fear that I am kidnapped. Kidnapped by weavers!' She laughed. The life had come back into her once more. Then she was gone.

Robert Newton watched her go. He had a lot on his mind. So much so that he did not notice a slight movement near a shadowy side door. Quiet as the church had been, they had not been alone.

Margaret Mentmore walked home feeling something like her old self. There was still moisture in the air but she flung back her hood. With her red locks streaming, she strode on like a queen. The paleness had gone from her cheeks.

When she returned to the hall she dismissed the anxious questions of her brothers and Philippa. 'I have been busy,' she said tartly. 'This house is not run by sitting at home. One must be up and about.'

Philippa flinched at the barbed comment. She had been at home but had scarcely been sitting about.

John was relieved at his sister's reappearance but it was clear that other thoughts dominated his mind. That evening he and Thomas retired to the parlour and talked for hours. Philippa, Margaret and Edmund were left to occupy the table on the raised dais. Edmund did his best to entertain, but John and Thomas's preoccupations were dampening everyone's spirits. Even the household clerks and apprentices were subdued.

At last Edmund too succumbed and went to join his father in the parlour. The two women retired to the solar to sew by candlelight. If Margaret had recovered, it had not made her any more genial company for Philippa. They sat in silence.

Shortly before bed, Thomas sent a servant out to the weavers. Now it was common knowledge that he would face his rebellious workers.

'Surely you cannot afford to pay what they demand?' Philippa said to her husband as they prepared for bed.

John gave a wry smile. 'No, but we may have an offer to make which will please them and be paid for by others.'

Philippa looked at him quizzically. He had the boyish air of one who had discovered a great secret and was unwilling to share it.

'What can such an offer consist of?' she queried. Philippa was no fool and had witnessed more than one trade dispute in the Starre household. She knew solutions did not come free.

John was obviously not going to display his plan until the morning. 'Wait and see,' he said.

It irritated Philippa when her husband was in such a mood. She was fully capable of grasping his strategies. More than that she desperately wished to be taken into his confidence. But she knew that there was no winning him round. His boyishness would only take it as more of a challenge to keep the strategy secret.

'Come now, wife,' he muttered. 'Come and I will show you strategies far more fitting for a wife to see.'

He slipped a hand into her thin linen shift. She could feel his fingers, hot and urgent, upon her breast. He kissed her passionately on her neck and throat. She felt little aroused and still annoyed. Taking her reticence as coyness, he kissed her more hungrily.

'Come, my wife, come now to me.'

John took her and she meekly surrendered to him. As a good wife should.

When he had spent his passion, he slept soundly. Philippa did not sleep. She lay awake in the dark and felt desperately unfulfilled. For much of the night she tossed and turned. Her sleep, when it came, was patchy and light. By dawn she felt that telltale ache in her belly and knew it was her time again. All things seemed to conspire to make her miserable.

John was up early, bright and chirpy as a sparrow. 'There's no good will come of lying in bed all day,' he quipped. 'Remember what Margaret said – we must be up and about.'

It was the worst tactic he could have chosen. Philippa flashed a furious glance at his back. What was the use of trying to tell him? He would never understand.

Still chirping cheerfully, John threw back the shutters and left the room.

The family took its usual brief breakfast of bread in wine in the parlour. Downstairs in the hall the household servants were clearing away their mattresses and soiled rushes. Liveried clerks, grooms and apprentices were moving trestles and benches.

By the time the family descended, the scene was fully set out. Just below the dais a trestle table faced the hall. On it was a pewter wine jug, fresh from the buttery, and two goblets. A bench behind the table was covered with a neatly embroidered banker. Behind the bench stood the clerks, and along the sides of the hall the grooms and carrying men; at the end of the hall were the apprentices. All wore the livery decorated with the florid 'M'.

John and Thomas too wore the rich livery associated with their guild and rank. Gold threads picked out the patterns on their flowing surcoats. They took seats on the bench. Margaret, Philippa and Edmund stood behind them. The principal actors were ready.

Conscious of the theatricality of it, John remarked to his father, 'The audience is ready. Pray bring on the jugglers!' Thomas did not smile.

One hour after dawn the weavers arrived as bidden. This time there was less insolence. They came in quietly and warily. John recognised the leading spokesmen of the craft guilds and saw the familiar face of Newton and the square chin and handsome features of Appulby; he recognised the insolent Smalecombe – now more subdued. Behind them gathered a little knot of other workers. They crossed the length of the hall and stood before the table. The scene had a curious resemblance to a trial. John and Thomas had planned it that way.

John took the pewter jug and, unhurriedly, poured Gascon wine into the two goblets. He handed one to his father. They both drank.

Robert Newton broke the silence. 'We come, sir, to hear your response to our requirements. Your son will have told you of the needs of the mystery that we represent.'

'Demands . . . demands is the word I heard was used!' Thomas was stern and his voice had a low, thunder roll in it. 'I heard you used the word 'demand' to the house of Mentmore.'

Robert flushed. With quiet dignity he said: 'I did not use such a word and shall not use it now.' There was a shuffling amongst the assembled weavers. 'We simply seek justice. Fair pay for our labours and for the fruits of our – '

'Fair pay, man? Fair pay? You call eight silver pence a day fair pay? I call it robbery, Master Newton!'

The weavers growled and muttered. They were finding their courage again.

John leaned across the table. It was a deliberately casual gesture. It looked as if he had practised it.

'We can pay you no more than six pence, my friend, and that the City Council may decide is too high.' He had already gained assurances from that quarter that five pence would be the maximum wage fixed.

Newton frowned. The weavers behind him grew very restless.

John played his full hand. 'But we can go further. We have spoken – at length – with John of Northampton.'

The weavers looked startled and Newton smiled wryly. Or was it just the scar? John could not tell.

The mention of Northampton had taken them by surprise. A draper by guild and a charismatic personality, Northampton was leading agitation for making the government of the city more answerable to the guild members. He was also the advocate of breaking the fishmongers' guilds' monopoly on their product. The promise of cheaper food, and his associated attacks on the more obviously corrupt churchmen, had won Northampton a following among the minor guilds.

'We have spoken with John of Northampton,' John continued, 'and we believe his cause is our cause. It is a great wrong that a few should deny food to the mouths of the many. We have said this before but now will go further. The family and company of Mentmore will do all in its power to press Northampton's argument with the council, and with the king in parliament . . .'

The bomb exploded in the midst of the weavers. John had learnt that much from Gaunt! His proposal had clearly caught the weavers unprepared. A real fall in the price of food would substitute for a substantial rise in pay. It would also, of course, cost the Mentmores nothing, or so John and Thomas calculated. The move had one further argument to recommend it. Northampton, whilst keeping somewhat distant, was known to favour Gaunt. Mentmore support for a friend of the duke would surely not go unnoticed at the Palace of the Savoy.

'We must retire to consider your proposal,' Newton said.

'Of course, of course,' John concurred. 'For half an hour. We shall wait for that long.'

The weavers retired in disarray. John poured his father another goblet of wine. The servants chattered excitedly. Philippa and Edmund talked. Margaret was silent.

When the weavers returned, they had the look of people who had disagreed but had been forced to accept the inevitable.

'We have spoken and considered your offer,' Robert said, without emotion. 'It is not what we have asked for, but it goes some way towards meeting our needs. We will accept six pennies a day and we look to you to honour your agreement with John of Northampton.'

John Mentmore was elated. The pact with Northampton had been his idea and he felt the thrill of triumph. He rose and first Thomas then John shook Newton's hand, and the deal was struck.

Making the best of it, the craftsmen retreated with dignity. They had, after all, gained some of what they had set out for.

John and Thomas called for more goblets. Wine was poured for the rest of the family. Margaret was quietly relieved. She knew at least one other reason why Robert Newton had met the Mentmores halfway. But that was her secret. She smiled and sipped her wine.

For John, the peace accord with the weavers was a major coup. It did much for his standing both with his father and with the other guild masters of the livery guilds. This was the more enhanced when the Common Council barred the Mentmores from paying the promised six pence and fixed the rate at five.

The new era of peace also allowed Thomas's heir more time to pursue his amateur efforts to locate the killers of Adam Yonge and the attackers of Edmund. He questioned the constables and harried the aldermen. He interrogated the carriers, who transported goods to and from the Kentish towns. To all he had one simple approach: 'Have you seen a man with a raspberry stain on his cheek?'

As he continued with his quest, word of his search – some called it his obsession – spread. And yet he came no nearer to locating his elusive quarry.

One Wednesday evening he was returning from a visit to Roger Starre's house. He scarcely warmed to that proud bantam cock, but the business between them was good. It was 30 November, the feast of St Andrew, and like the apostle John Mentmore was intent on fishing in muddy waters. He stopped at a tavern in the shadow of Baynard Castle near the Fleet Bridge where he recognised a carrier and began his routine questioning – to no avail. Finishing his interrogation, and giving the man the price of a pitcher of ale, he noticed that he was being watched.

The man nodded and came to join him at his bench. The good-looking features seemed open in what might almost have been friendship. For an instant John was caught off guard. He had not expected to see Dick Appulby in this quarter of the city.

Appulby was in a genial mood. He was also well informed concerning John's quest. That was hardly surprising. John had made no secret of his search for information.

'No luck then?' Appulby asked with a look of genuine concern. 'God's blood, but the beasts who killed a good man like Adam should not go free.' His voice was thick with indignation.

'Did you know him well?'

Appulby reflected for a moment. 'Not so well as some. Like any weaving master I saw the Mentmores' chief clerk, and a good, honest man he was. Others saw him more.'

'Who? Who saw him more?'

Appulby shrugged. 'He kept his business to himself but he was often in the weavers' quarter after Christmas.'

This was news to John. 'To see whom?' he asked. 'That was just before his death!'

'Why yes,' Dick said with sudden realisation. 'Of course it was.'

'So who did he see, man?'

'Well, there were a few who he had words with.' Appulby pondered. 'It's hard to say now, exactly . . .' A frown crossed his face. 'There was one he saw more often than the others. There seemed to be some bad blood between them. Yonge met him about a week before he died – they argued, I recall. Then he was about your house the night before the riot with Gaunt. I thought, that's good. They're patching things up.'

John flushed with excitement.

Appulby continued: 'I remember the night because of the riot the next day. That was quite a day. You know I was only – '

'His name?' John interrupted. 'The name of the man Adam saw more than others? The one he argued with? His name, man?'

Dick Appulby looked startled. 'I never meant to accuse anyone. I only know that . . .'

'His name, Appulby.'

'Why, it's no great secret. Ask Smalecombe, or some of the others. It was Robert Newton.'

75

PART TWO

*Hoodman Blind
1378-9*

Chapter Five

Edmund did not take long to recover from his injuries. The knife wounds were clean; rest and plentiful supply of ointments soon put him on his way to fitness.

John of Gaunt heard of the attack and despatched his own doctor with a treasury of frankincense, opium and a host of exotic drugs and spices. Whether Edmund's swift recovery was due to the attentions of Master William Apilton or not, Thomas was deeply touched at the duke's gesture. That was surely the motive behind the act.

Gaunt was once more in need of friends that winter. A poll tax of four pence a head had been passed in the autumn and parliament was obsessed with the thought that any of it might be siphoned off by the duke for his own ends. Their actions to prevent it added another topic of conversation to the dinner tables of the guild masters. John Philipot himself – assisted by the fishmonger William Walworth – had been appointed to oversee the manner in which the money was spent. For the Mentmores, now hovering on the fringe of Gaunt's Lancastrian party in the city, it was a time to tread very nimbly.

Edmund, however, was planning to tread anything but nimbly. He was leaving for France. The news came as something of a surprise. Edmund's official reason for his return from the Cotswolds had been to raise troops for Giles de Brewoster. The news that he was to lead them in place of Giles was not expected. Announced one suppertime with his usual aplomb, it led to a barrage of questions.

'Why not Giles?' Thomas queried. 'This will be the first campaign he has missed in twenty years.'

'Where are you going?' Margaret asked.

Not to be left out, Philippa chipped in with, 'How long will you be gone and who will you take?'

Edmund, well pleased at the reaction, laughed. 'Too many questions at one time. I can never answer them now!'

'You may start by answering mine, son,' Thomas said severely.

Edmund became serious again. 'Giles feels he is too old for the open weather on the march. More to the point this campaign will entail a siege and Giles has no wish to sit drenching in the Breton rain.'

'So it's to Brittany you are going?' Margaret challenged.

'Yes, we go to St Malo.'

'And what takes you to Brittany, Edmund?' This time the speaker was his elder brother.

'We've lost the initiative in the war. The gains of Edward have been frittered away, and what's to show for the glories of Crécy and Poitiers? We hold Calais, Brest, the area around Bordeaux and a few insignificant Breton ports. Not much to show for all the victories.'

'And the French raid Hastings, Rye and the Isle of Wight.'

'Aye, John, that they do. It's not a satisfying situation, by St Peter.'

'So you sail for St Malo to seize it?' John's question had a rhetorical ring to it.

'Just so,' Edmund replied. 'We sail to seize it and make it ours. If we hold Brest and St Malo we can drive the French out of Brittany.'

John was doubtful but said nothing.

'The king will not go,' Thomas asserted, 'so in whose name do you raise this army, Edmund?'

'The Duke of Lancaster will have the command. It's not common knowledge yet, but Richard will name him his royal deputy in France and Aquitaine. He has chosen St Alban's day, June 17th, to announce the new command. The king not leading, it will be no great host we take; the feudal host shall not be called this time. Gaunt issues contracts to the old captains of the French wars. Robert Knollys goes again as do other heroes of the wars.'

'So Knollys sails again for France.' John laughed. 'The French had best beware. They've cause enough to fear that captain.'

'Indeed they have! He's more of a terror to the French than a hundred companies of archers. They fear him like the pestilence and with good reason. They say that when he marched on Ancenis the good citizens threw themselves into the Loire at the mere terror of his approach. And now he sails again!'

'And are you part of Knollys's company this time?' John asked with a certain sense of awe. Knollys – the 'old brigand' – was a legendary mercenary soldier and captain of men.

Edmund gulped down his wine. 'I am that. Knollys is to raise a company of knights and archers and men-at-arms, and Giles has contracted to raise a company within that army. I have forty-two pounds to spend of the king's money.'

'Of our money!' Thomas interjected. 'Money from the fourpence tax. And how many men will you buy for forty-two pounds?'

Edmund did a little mental arithmetic. 'Giles has contracted to supply six knight bachelors, twenty men-at-arms and twelve mounted archers.'

'Contracted for how long?' It was Thomas again – ever the businessman.

'For forty days, and after that we are to be self-financing.'

Philippa looked puzzled and John grinned. 'He means to steal as much as he can to pay his men and turn in a profit on the enterprise. Is that not so, Edmund? Money, furs, bedclothes, hostages . . .'

'Spoils of war!' Edmund protested in mock indignation. 'Seized from the enemy.'

'There, my dear.' John turned to his wife. 'That is the meaning of "self-financing".'

Once he had fully recovered, Edmund was out and about recruiting his men. Word had gone round the exclusive club of professional soldiers that an enterprise was under way. As if by magic they gravitated to London. By the end of May, the taverns were full of bronzed, scarred faces.

Edmund was experienced at this kind of thing and had sent out messengers to likely sources of recruits before he had left the Cotswolds. The base for the preparation was Robert Knollys's London house. Soon that establishment had the appearance of an armed camp.

Knollys himself was away arranging the impounding of the

necessary shipping in Southampton and Poole. However, his agents were all over the city buying up men and weapons. The preparations were not without profit for Thomas Mentmore. An order for green and white cloth, to dress the Welsh companies, came the way of Gaunt's friendly mercer. Eyes were raised by some, but Thomas quietly counted in the silver coins and had the cloth brought from his warehouse.

At his own expense Edmund bought two new warhorses. John winced when he heard the price of the destriers, but Edmund assured him they would be more than paid for by plunder.

The excitement pushed mundane matters to the back of everybody's mind. Even John thought more of the adventure than the issues which had preoccupied him of late. Besides which he was not yet sure what to do with Appulby's information. The diversion offered by Edmund was in some ways very welcome. Besides which, more contracts for military cloth had come the way of the Mentmores. John had his work cut out supplying the welcome but urgent demand.

When Edmund finally left it was a warm and blue domed day of lark-soaring splendour. Even in the city there was a freshness to the air, despite the stinking streets.

The whole family turned out to see him leave and walked beside him to the Fleet Bridge. There were tears from Margaret and Philippa. Even Thomas looked red-eyed.

As Edmund rode out through Temple Gate at the head of his little company, who could tell if he would return again? John felt a choking in his throat as he waved. Edmund, as irrepressible as ever, waved back as if he were on his way to a joust.

The roads were dry and yet not dusty as they would be in high summer, and Edmund felt a strange exhilaration as he rode. He reckoned he should reach the embarkation port of Poole in six days if he moved at the pace of his foot soldiers. There was no rush, and the atmosphere resembled a holiday rather than a preparation for war and death.

As they travelled they fell in with other marching bands, some bound for Poole, others for Southampton. Each new encounter was an excuse for ribald comments, shouted greetings and vainglorious boasting. Country people kept a distance and locked up their wives and daughters. The 'terror of the French countryside' looked threatening enough in the English one. At night they slept out, if between inns, and the clear open skies brought no rain to unsettle their bivouacs. Edmund's knights were practised campaigners and settled to any discomfort without comment. Silent, experienced killers, these knights had ridden a long way from romance. They did not make jovial company.

Here and there in the rolling countryside ruined homesteads and grass-grown ploughland bore testimony to the ravages of the pestilence. The mouldy timbers of the deserted dwellings stuck like the grotesque ribs of a butchered carcase into the darkening evening air. Edmund and his party avoided these tragic sources of shelter. Who knew what scent of death might still lurk in these cottages of the dead? The thickening night air gave the illusion of a shifting miasma over the ruins. With studious care the soldiers bypassed the assarts, now reverting to the scrub from which a desperate population had carved them.

It was on the evening of the fourth day that Edmund led his party towards the lush, green water meadows about Salisbury. Below the great fortifications of Old Sarum's Castle, the bishop's gridiron-plan new town sprawled into the twilight. From dozens of its tenements cooking smoke rose in long columns of grey into the still air.

The next morning Edmund sent his company on ahead of him to Wimborne. It did no hurt to be parted from that brutalised, cheerless band. Besides which he had things to buy in Salisbury. A new woollen cloak was no rarity in this expanding cloth town. He shopped widely in the market and eventually satisfied his tastes at a good price. He was familiar with the city and its bright new cathedral. He had visited Salisbury several times in the company of Giles de Brewoster. Only a morning's ride south of the city lay Giles's Dorset manors. He had assiduously built up his contacts – both with his immediate neighbours, the monks who tended a sheep grange for far-off Glastonbury Abbey and with the bishop's new market centre to the north. It was these relationships which had triggered so many of John Mentmore's speculations.

It was almost noon when Edmund crossed the Harnham bridge and left the city. Riding south, he soon rose up on to the downland dotted with grazing sheep. Here and there a shepherd's cottage brought a hint of domesticity to the scene. Apart from this the land was lonely and wild under the stupendous canopy of a mackerel cloud sky. Following the drovers' road, he passed through a landscape dotted with the barrows and banks of ancient civilisations. Overhead, larks called and plummeted to their nests in the tall grass tussocks.

By late afternoon he had reached Cranborne. Stopping here he watered his horse and, despite the suspicious stares of the country folk, he stretched his legs. From the nearby abbey the bell was ringing for vespers. Edmund was in no hurry. Giles's manors of Woodlands and Knolton lay only two or three miles beyond the abbey by the river Crane. Passing through bluebell woods, which swept up to the moss-grown motte of a deserted castle, the route once again broke out on to a rolling plateau. The road, called the Harpway, was an ancient one. Its deep ruts were familiar to this rider. He forced his horse on to the greening verge and soon achieved a pleasing canter. On his left a swelling hill gave rise to a high ridge, running north to south. Soon he could see the manor house perched high on the ridge. This was the settlement called Le Knoll. Held by Hugh de Knolton, from Giles, it gazed out over the spreading valley of the Allen. Below it a small chapel crouched within the yew-fenced strangeness of an ancient earth circle – one of three such features. Totally separated from the church lay the riverside hamlets of Knolton, Brockington and Philipston.

Spurring on his horse, Edmund mounted the chalky track to Le Knoll. From the immediate flurry of activity amongst the collection of buildings it was clear he was expected.

Hugh de Knolton was there to greet him. A short, stocky, barrel of a man with weathered brown face, untidy hair and bushy grey beard, he was a dramatic contrast to his tall, pale son. Stephen de Knolton was the prime reason for Edmund's visit to this lonely manor. An earlier agreement between Hugh and Giles had stipulated that he should enter Giles's household as Edmund's squire. The occasion of Edmund's French campaign gave opportunity for the enacting of the agreement. Besides which Stephen was fourteen years old and more than capable of earning his own keep.

'Welcome, Edmund!' Hugh's greeting was effusive and genuine. A subservient land-holder but an independent man, Hugh was in no way servile towards his feudal superior. Stephen seemed altogether more cautious.

Over dinner that evening, Hugh brought Edmund up to date with regard to the manor and its finances. Edmund listened attentively. Giles would require a full and exact account of the discussion.

'The land's unsettled,' Hugh admitted, 'what with runaway villeins and tenants denying labour service on the home farms. They begin to feel they have a power in the land. Still,' he admitted with a grin, 'things have been fairly quiet on the manor. We've abandoned tenements in Knolton, of course. The village still shows signs of the pestilence. We had to put Dowdiche and Furzey down to pasture, as they'll not be tilled again.' Edmund noted the quaint names since Giles would have a perfect grasp of their topography. 'But,' Hugh continued, 'we lost little of the value of the manor over all. Tenants have agreed to take on holdings, even if they have villein status attached.'

'They'll settle for some inconvenience now for a larger stake in the village.'

'Aye, that's about the short of it. They feel that labour service owed is a fair price to pay for doubling their land.'

'And one day soon they'll look to convert that service to cash payments?'

Hugh was impressed with his guest's astuteness. 'That is what they hope, no doubt. But we shall see. That will be in Stephen's time and not mine, so, by St John, I'll not turn grey through worrying over it. Speaking of which, you'll take him to France?' Hugh spoke as if Stephen was not present. The question was more of a statement.

'That I will, lad.' Edmund addressed himself to the boy. 'We'll see some adventures there. Hard work, but a story to tell your children.' He noted that the teenager seemed doubtful. His long lashes flickered over doleful, big brown eyes.

Hugh seemed oblivious of his son's reluctance. 'You'll come back from France a man, by God! By St Peter's chains, you'll soon be a knight of the king!'

Both Edmund and Hugh laughed. Stephen nodded with the philosophical stoicism of a sacrificial lamb. His look disturbed Edmund.

The household rose early. Edmund and Stephen ate a light breakfast and soon they were horsed and riding back down the white dusted track. Stephen's belongings were packed into two panniers slung behind his saddle. There was no mother or sister in the household. Stephen must have attended to his own packing. There was a pathetic aspect to this unhappy, gangling teenager and his carefully stored possessions.

By mid-morning Edmund picked up the rest of his party at Wimborne. Crossing the Stour, the road took them over the high heathland. Below lay the vast sweep of Poole harbour. Jostling beyond its churches and tenements the assembled fleet looked a forest of masts.

If Edmund had expected an orderly embarkation he was to be sorely disappointed.

'Plague on you, man!' he exclaimed to Knollys's agent in the town, 'what do you mean you have not impounded sufficient ships?'

The agent was defensive. 'A king's commission rides well at Westminster, sir knight. Here, though, it has not sufficient power to hold a wayward captain who does not wish to see his ship seized for the king.'

'Then hang a few of them, man! Hang a few.'

The agent sighed, as one faced with explaining a complex problem to a simple but petulant child. 'Aye, sir knight, it would indeed be a lesson to hang them or confiscate their goods. But,' he added patiently, 'they are not here, sir knight. The birds have flown.'

'Plague on them!' Edmund exploded. Stephen was shocked at the vitriolic nature of his new master's outburst. His judgemental glance did nothing to calm Edmund's temper. 'Plague on them, and on their families!'

For all Edmund's anger, nothing could be done until the ships of Weymouth and of Melcombe Regis had been subjected to the king's commission and brought eastward to Poole. For two days Edmund kicked his heels with the other angry soldiers, forced to camp on an isolated spit of land between sea and marsh. It did little to add to his humour to discover that plague victims had been buried here. Leaving his men, Edmund took a room in the town and shared it with two other captains from south Wales.

On the third day sufficient ships had been mustered to embark the men and horses. Edmund's riding horse and two destriers, along with the horses of his knights and mounted archers, were embarked on the *Christmas*. Edmund's party and a company of

Welsh archers embarked on the *Gabriel*.

Cramped in the narrow deck space between the fore and aft fighting castles of the ship, Edmund's foul mood did not improve.

'Come on, boy,' he scolded Stephen. 'Fetch up my cloak!' The boy looked to be in a pit of unhappiness. Edmund's annoyance drowned his sense of pity. 'Come on, boy; by St Peter, shift yourself. I freeze to death.'

By evening the fleet was well out into the Channel. The wind rose and the sea was choppy. Pitching and rolling the *Gabriel* soon became a ship cargoed with misery. Stephen was continually sick and the rising sea swamped all aboard. The Welsh soldiers conducted their conversations in a manner unintelligible to the English soldiers. Their interpreter informed a curious Edmund that they hailed from Llantrisant, from villages with names utterly alien to Edmund's ears. From Beddau, Llanharan, Llantwit Fadre and Creigiau. They wore the familiar green and white. It was probably Mentmore cloth.

Soon, however, even this topic of conversation was lost in the sound of the howling wind. Wrapped in his Salisbury blanket, Edmund watched the slight form of Stephen de Knolton spewing endlessly over the side. Soon Edmund retired to the crowded cabin beneath the forecastle.

By morning they had made little progress. The fleet was scattered. The captain of the *Gabriel* put into Melcombe to ride out the storm. His sailors ran nimbly among the wretched soldiery and pulled at ropes and tackle in the drenching air. They jeered at the misery of the landlubbers.

Even in Melcombe harbour the *Gabriel* heaved on the passing swells. It was not until late afternoon that the wind abated and the captain nosed out into the Channel once more. From then on the progress quickened. A freshening wind pushed the fleet south-westward down the Channel.

The scattered shipping gathered again off the English-held port of Brest. The wind dropped and they sat lazily on their anchors. No troops were disembarked but, by the hour, the number of ships increased as the fleet reassembled. One of the new arrivals carried Gaunt's standard. Alone of the fleet it put into port. The rest sat it out off the coast.

At first light one vessel, richly carved and painted, moved

from ship to ship. Edmund and Stephen watched its slow progress.

'What is it doing?' Stephen asked, his brown eyes wide in curiosity. His sickness had passed.

'Am I a prophet?' Edmund grunted. 'I do not know.'

Stephen was crestfallen at the rebuff. Edmund frowned. Neither Philippa nor Margaret would have recognised this peevish young knight. The sea crossing had had as much of an effect on Edmund as on his unhappy squire.

Edmund's knights were awake now. Elbowing Stephen aside, they joined Edmund at the rail. They too were cramped and eager for action. They too hoped that the strange antics of the lone ship heralded some excitement. It was clear that the ship was not visiting every vessel. An unknown logic took it to some but caused it to bypass others. At last it homed in on the *Gabriel*.

'It's Knollys's,' Edmund said, to no one in particular. He recognised the personal banner which moved in the breeze.

There was a stir of excitement in the *Gabriel*. The rail was thronged with curious soldiers and even the bored sailors in the castles seemed interested in this departure from routine.

Knollys's ship, the *Campion*, ground up against the *Gabriel*'s planked port side. Ropes were thrown and secured. The wood groaned as the two ships rose and fell against each other and a boarding platform fell heavily over the *Gabriel*'s rail. Soon the captain of the Great Company had come aboard.

Robert Knollys was a tough, bull-necked individual with a flat Cheshire accent. Yet he had a natural air of command. Without any fuss or explanation he summoned the knights and captains to the forecastle of the ship. Rising up from the bows like a castellated turret this fighting platform lifted conversation up beyond the thronged deck. The occupying sailors made themselves scarce.

Secure in something approaching privacy Knollys turned to his captains. 'We sail for Bayonne,' he said in a matter-of-fact tone.

There was a murmur of astonishment. What had happened to the objective of St Malo?

Knollys anticipated the rather obvious question. 'A Spanish fleet is sailing north to aid the king's enemies. The Duke of Lancaster orders its destruction before it can have influence upon his plans.'

'And what of St Malo itself?' The questioner was Edmund Mentmore. He was thinking of the French countryside being left for others to plunder and of two expensive destriers aboard the *Christmas*. His aggravation must have showed on his face.

'Be not distressed, sir knight,' Knollys answered, with a slight sneer. 'The duke has sufficient men to take that place before we return. He will miss you, no doubt, but I swear he shall still achieve his goal.'

Edmund reddened but wisely held his tongue. His example had silenced any other would-be questioners. He was not alone in his sense of grievance but it was clear that any complaint would be quite useless.

'Then we sail and sink the king's enemies. Perhaps before this venture is complete so much Spanish blood shall be shed abroad that the fish themselves might speak Spanish!'

It was a rough but not a new joke. All assembled laughed loyally. Knollys, it should be noted, did not even smile.

So, for this reason, whilst most of the fleet stayed off the French coast preparing for plunder, the *Campion* (accompanied by the *Gabriel* and six sister ships) set sail across Biscay.

Edmund was grumpier than ever. His dreams of glory seemed to have faded to a tawdry rag. Everyone avoided him where possible, a difficult feat in so cramped a space. Stephen and the men-at-arms were forced to endure his temper on more than one occasion.

Two days out from Brest the lookout high atop the mast spotted the distant sails of the Spanish fleet. Suddenly the decks of the English ships were alive with activity. The Welsh bowmen produced their bowstrings – protected from damp inside their tunics – and strung the bows. Great boxes of goose-feathered arrows were hauled up into the fighting castles and even up into the crow's nest. Men-at-arms pulled on their tunics and knights their armour.

'Hurry boy, hurry,' Edmund scolded Stephen as the young squire fumbled with the knightly panoply of war. 'Hurry, or the Spanish will be on us.' Stephen's unpractised fingers fiddled with the leather straps of the breastplate as he pulled it over Edmund's quilted tunic. His fingers slipped against the armour.

'Hurry, boy! Move yourself for pity's sake!'

Then came the turn of the tight *jupon* or surcoat. With difficulty Edmund pulled it over his head. Stephen brought forward the heavy leather baldrick and helped Edmund fasten the belt's buckle. The long, two-edged sword was unwrapped and slid deftly into its wood and leather scabbard. Lastly the short, narrow-bladed dagger was slipped into the belt: the misericord. Its slim blade could work between the armoured protection of a fallen knight.

'Hold the helmet, boy. I shall not need it yet.'

Stephen clung on to the heavy bascinet, its visor gaping open. He himself wore a heavy old chainmail hauberk under a faded surcoat. Both were too big for him, having been made for a stouter man. For a moment Edmund could almost see the barrel body of Hugh de Knolton. Then the vision faded. All that was left was this gangling youth in a man's armour.

Bowmen were clambering into the fore and aft castles. Two of Edmund's men were climbing up to the crow's nest, their six-foot yew bows hanging awkwardly over their shoulders. The men-at-arms and the knights clustered at the sides of the ship. Those who had fought at sea before knew that a naval engagement lacked any degree of sophistication. It would soon develop into a colliding chaos as archers vied for targets and men-at-arms attempted to board the vessel of the enemy.

'Keep by me, Stephen,' Edmund commanded. 'As soon as we draw near enough we shall grapple the enemy and board her. Follow me across the planks and guard my back.'

Already the sailors were hauling up boarding bridges and roped grappling irons. Stephen's face was as pale as the chalk track which led down from his father's farm.

'Be of good cheer, Stephen. By God's grace we shall board them, take them, and the day will be ours.'

It was pathetic to see how Stephen's vulnerable face brightened at these brave words of encouragement.

'Are you frightened, boy?' Edmund asked.

Stephen shook his head. No, he was terrified.

'Neither am I,' his knight replied resolutely. Edmund felt a terror grip his stomach. 'Neither am I!'

The Spanish vessels were close now and the flapping standard of Castile could plainly be seen on the foremost ship. Knollys's own craft – his flag snapping – made for it. A volley of arrows flew from Knollys's vessel and a reply came from the Spanish archers.

Edmund had no time to watch the result. The range was closing with another Castilian vessel. The Welsh and English yew bows creaked. Feathered shafts lay next to stubbled cheeks. A slight wave slapped the planking. Edmund could see the scurry of activity aboard the enemy ship, but nothing else. His vision had narrowed. Now there was only the *Gabriel* and the Castilian vessel in the whole world. The sea swept them together. He could feel his pulse beating in his temples. Closer, closer. The Spanish crossbowmen were leaning towards him.

Suddenly the rising flight of the Welsh arrows seemed to shake the air. A dark cloud rose in whistling flight and streaked towards the enemy.

The air was full of arrows; a storm of arrows and crossbow bolts swept the rival decks. Edmund threw himself below the rail. Behind him animal screams accompanied the shrieking shafts. Around him dull thuds announced the incoming volley as it tore into deck and humanity.

A man-at-arms, one of Edmund's soldiers, slumped to the deck. He clawed at a crossbow bolt sunk into his chest. As Edmund watched, he died.

In horror, Edmund realised that Stephen still held his bascinet. 'The helmet, boy. Give me my helmet!' Still crouching, he half turned. Another volley shrieked over the decks. Men-at-arms huddled behind anything solid. Death whistled through the rigging.

Stephen lay twitching on the oak planking, his back to Edmund. A dark stain was spreading out over his surcoat. An arrow head protruded obscenely through the ragged material and the twisted mail.

'God's blood, boy. No!' Edmund was oblivious to the arrows now. He sprawled across Stephen's hunched body and turned him over. A feathered shaft stuck out from beneath the right shoulder.

Stephen's face was screwed up in agony. Tight fingers gripped the shaft. From a spittle-flecked mouth issued incoherent moaning sounds and confused words. One word repeated itself. Like a plaintive pleading it came again and again: 'Mother. Mother.

Mother...'

Then the two ships came together with a jarring, splintering crash. The force threw Edmund sidelong. With fierce cries the men-at-arms were up and across the decks. Grappling irons flew and engaged on timbers. The hull planking screeched and groaned.

Edmund seized the bascinet – carelessly tossed away – and pulled on its suffocating protection. An arrow glanced off its steel plate and dazed him. Visor up, he clawed his way back to the rail and clambered on to a boarding bridge. Below the two ships clung in an agonised embrace. Linking ropes strained and parted. A man fell, howling, from the bridge. Roaring with fury, Edmund teetered over the chasm and on to the enemy decks.

The Castilian ship was a shambles. The superior fire power of the Welsh archers had overwhelmed the slower crossbowmen. The deck had been swept by their shafts and already the Spanish were giving ground. Before the bowcastle a Spanish knight was rallying the dispirited men-at-arms. Beside him a squire held aloft a heavy, embroidered banner. The English soldiers were hanging back, their swords and axes idle. Two, with short lances, jabbed at the knight and his banner carrier.

Edmund drew his sword. Pushing the English soldiers aside, he faced his opposite number. The two swords met. The air rang. Hands were numb from the force of the terrible impact. Edmund panted. He struck out again. More confidently now, the English lancemen flanked him. As he advanced, they made their way forward resolutely.

A lance blade caught the banner bearer and he stumbled forward. Other English blades arced and he vanished beneath hacking blows.

Edmund was concentrating on the knight. He noticed that his opponent had suffered a wound to his sword arm. Clearly in pain, his use of the weapon was cramped. Edmund brought his sword crashing down on the enemy blade, and the knight recovered with some difficulty. Some of the Spanish men-at-arms were casting down their weapons.

'Yield, sir knight, yield,' Edmund commanded. 'Yield or I shall leave you to the soldiery to despatch.' The threat hung – real and terrible – over the blood-stained deck. The Castilian raised his visor. He looked tired. Edmund remembered Stephen's face. In anger he lunged at his opponent. This sudden, savage reminder of his own martial capabilities decided the issue.

'Yield. I yield!' the exhausted nobleman cried. He threw his sword down at Edmund's feet. He spoke in Spanish-accented French.

Turning to one of the Welsh captains, Edmund motioned for him to take the captive into custody.

Leaving his hostage, Edmund climbed the swaying ladder on to the fighting castle of the enemy ship. He was met with a scene of utter devastation. The boxlike structure was full of dying men. In one corner a badly wounded knight was desperately fending off two dagger-wielding Welshmen. They danced about him like terriers before a mortally wounded bull.

Prevented by his exalted status from surrendering to the common soldiers, he seemed doomed to extinction. Edmund's appearance was therefore a godsend. Seeing the English knight he held out his sword in surrender. One of the Welshmen slashed at him with his dagger. Edmund struck the furious soldier with the flat of his sword and put an end to that nonsense. The other Welshman was enraged at losing his prize and blurted out an incomprehensible stream of anger. Edmund raised his sword. The soldier fell silent. His eyes glowered with rage.

By now the fighting was dying down. All over the ship the Spanish survivors were laying down their arms. Edmund looked about him and saw that those Spanish ships which had not been captured were in flight.

Knollys's vessel grated alongside. 'Ho, sir knight!' he hollered. 'Who holds this ship – the King of England, or Castile?'

'Richard, King of England, holds this ship . . . and I, Edmund Mentmore,' the victor in the forecastle replied, pushing up his visor.

Knollys, even at a distance, recognised the face. 'Good work, Edmund,' he called out in his flat tones. 'Good work and worth twice the glory of St Malo.'

The victory off Bayonne brought Edmund more prestige than he was prepared for. The capture of the Castilian vessel was credited to him rather than to the Welsh archers, and as the highest-ranking Englishman present praise flowed his way.

Battered but triumphant the English fleet put in at Bordeaux for repairs and for the tending of the wounded. Knollys himself congratulated the young knight and acclaimed his victory. That was an ally not gained easily and worth many hostages. Notwithstanding this, the two knights who had yielded to Edmund Mentmore were of high blood and would be worth a weighty gold ransom. That much made up for the diversion at St Malo.

The wounding of Stephen de Knolton, however, took much off the glory. Edmund felt a deep guilt that the boy had almost died off Bayonne. When he was carried ashore at Bordeaux, no one was more attentive than this particular knight to his squire. Despite the seriousness of the wound Stephen did not die, as Edmund, for one, was sure that he would. For the best part of a week he lay close to death, while the garrison physicians plied him with bleeding and ointments. During this period Edmund sat with him. This again was the chivalrous knight whom Philippa, John and Margaret would have recognised. When it was clear that Stephen would live, a bond had been forged between the two men.

Repaired and revictualled, the fleet was ready. Knollys sailed on to St Malo with the swiftest vessel whilst the others, with their prizes, made a more stately procession behind.

By the time they reached Brest the soldiers were rested and ready for action, but it was not to be. Gaunt had squandered his opportunity. Whilst Knollys and his fleet had battled off Bayonne, he had held his forces off shore unable to finalise his strategies for the capture of St Malo.

'Spent more time with his Katherine than with his generals,' the English pilot out of Brest commented. 'He'd have gained more glory riding on St Malo than on her,' he added coarsely.

Despite the cuffing such a comment deserved, there was no denying the Duke of Lancaster had indeed squandered his opportunity. When at last he had landed, his storming of the town had been a total failure and even Robert Knollys's arrival could not rescue the venture from ignominious defeat. The troops were grumbling and little plunder had been taken. Only those who had sailed with Knollys had made a profit on the hapless venture.

Worse was to follow. As Edmund and Stephen sat inactive on the *Gabriel*, a new Spanish fleet raided Gaunt's supply ships.

Edmund was to learn that the *Christmas* was sunk – with all its horses. The waiting turned to weeks. Soldiers were billeted ashore on the reluctant Breton communities. The summer was turning wet. Grumbling rumbled on every side. The French rushed men and supplies to Brittany to prevent a breakout.

Whilst Gaunt and his senior commanders debated a way of extricating themselves from this hole a fast ship arrived at Brest. Out of Southampton, she carried the news that Scottish pirates were raiding the east coast.

Humiliated and defeated Gaunt signalled to his captains to return home.

Chapter Six

The Mentmore household was a humming hive of activity. Servants were hustling and bustling in pantry and buttery. Agnes Bakwell was hurrying to and fro between the hall and the kitchen. This excitement was in addition to the normal work of the household. Through the extra turmoil the carrying men hauled and stacked the rolls of cloth and luxury merchandise; the clerks scurried with their tally sticks and ledgers; the apprentices felt and memorised the textures and colours of a rainbow array of rolls and bales. Between the two – the everyday work and the unexpected bustle – the hall and courtyard were alive with hurrying humanity. Even the most casual onlooker would have noticed the activity. The more practised observer might even have hazarded a guess as to its cause: Thomas Mentmore was preparing for a feast!

In the solar John and Thomas were relaxing by the open shutters. Summer sunshine was pouring on to them. Having just returned from mass, they were enjoying a welcome jug of wine. Thomas was in ebullient mood. His naturally well-balanced nature was being enhanced by the sun and the wine.

'Here John, see who I have invited.' A quill and parchment lay on the trestle table beside the stoneware jug of wine. He pushed the parchment towards John. It was a sign of his increasing affluence, as well as of his good mood, that he had squandered a piece of expensive parchment on a mere list.

John glanced over the pale yellow sheet. 'William Walworth . . . yes, Philipot will appreciate his inclusion. Besides, he's more of a power within the city than ever.' John came to the next name. 'John Kirkby. There's a man who does not hide his sympathy. There can be little love lost between Gaunt and himself. Do you think Gaunt will be pleased when he hears of such a party entertained at your house? There's not a name so far but would stick in his throat like a fishbone.' His eyes travelled back up the list to the name of William Walworth. Walworth was a fishmonger.

'Gaunt's a long way from home, John. As far distant as Edmund, in fact.'

'True enough, but his eyes and ears are everywhere. Was it not only yesterday that you took dinner with Hugh le Breton?'

Thomas smiled at the memory of le Breton's praise for the sample tapestry. 'I know of the Duke's intelligence, lad! But I too have a nose for a quick move. Look at that list. Most stick in Gaunt's throat, yes?'

John nodded. Philipot and Walworth were persona non grata at the Palace of the Savoy. Both had sat as treasurers on the 1377 poll tax and Gaunt would have particular reason to resent that. They symbolised the city's distrust of the royal government — overshadowed as it was by the young king's powerful uncle.

'Well then,' Thomas continued, a twinkle in his eyes, 'who in the city will call me Gaunt's creature if I feast such men as these?'

'You're not cutting yourself free from the duke, Father? Not with another commission on the way, surely.' John raised his hands in mock horror and consternation.

'Hardly,' Thomas replied briskly, 'but it'll do the duke no harm to see that I am not his creature. More to the point it will do no harm to my credit within the city for such a fact to be noted.'

'A shrewd move.' John, as much as his father, had become all too well aware of the unpopularity as well as danger which could go with the label of 'Gaunt's man'.

'Anyway, John, read on,' his father advised.

'Richard Lyons. There's a man of Gaunt's. And a fly one, if ever I saw one. You had better not sit him beside Walworth.'

'Read on.'

'John of Northampton. Hah, now there's a shrewd man, but a mite too popular with the yeoman guilds to be the toast of such an assembly.'

'Aye perhaps, but he'd reform the clerics and the church courts and that will go down well with most. And Lyons can't fault him as he's kindly disposed towards Gaunt just now.

Besides, he would reduce the price of fish and that will win him the warm affection of all the livery guild masters.'

'But not the love of Walworth, who is a fishmonger.'

'No, but there's no one on that list loved by all. But, mark you, there are tangled webs of affection and of policy that will tie many on it together as strange bedfellows, and those who cannot agree can be sat apart. The House of Mentmore is seen to be in no one's pocket but the hub of every faction.'

'You did not invite John Horne or his son Ralph?'

Thomas shook his head. 'Walworth can represent the fishmongers. Besides which, Ralph was rejected in favour of you. I did not wish to antagonise the Hornes unnecessarily.'

John smiled wryly. He recalled watching a juggler on Chepeside who worked with half a dozen multicoloured clubs. Once he had juggled one too many. He still had vivid recollections of the ensuing chaos and the cascading clubs. The crowd, who had previously cheered the juggler, had united in jeering at his failure. There would be clubs in plenty in the air during this feast!

Down in the buttery Philippa's mind was a long way from the intricate politics being discussed by her husband and father-in-law. Nevertheless she felt like something of a juggler herself. Only her clubs were not comprised of factions but of accounts, ingredients and courses. She knew how important the meal was for the family. Both John and Thomas had impressed that upon her. She felt as if she was under inspection and always performed least well when under scrutiny. Whilst she was not privy to the guest list – yet – she was aware that it would include most of the great guildsmen of the city and their wives. She was also aware of the tremendous praise being heaped upon the guest of honour: John Philipot.

With Gaunt away at St Malo, the eastern seaboard had been plagued by Scottish pirates. Much of the trade of the city had been disrupted by the sporadic raids and many had cursed Gaunt for eating into taxes to support a drawn-out disaster in Brittany whilst England suffered foreign attacks. Then Philipot had raised money about the city and equipped a scratch fleet. It was Philipot's little navy which had finally swept the Scots off the sea and captured their pirate chief. Now London sang the praises of the energetic guild master and heaped scorn upon the absent Duke of Lancaster and his army.

This was on Philippa's mind as she counted the casks and flagons within the flag-floored coolness of the buttery. Only the best would do for such a celebration and for such an honoured guest. The pressure weighed upon her.

'You have plenty of the Gascon wine?' she asked the butler, who nodded his grizzled head. 'And what of the wines of Anjou and Auxerre?'

The butler frowned. 'Less than I would like, my lady. The war disrupts the trade.'

'But enough for the feast?'

'Oh aye, my lady, we have quite sufficient for the feast, but it pains me to see our stocks so low.' He frowned again. Philippa smiled at the deep, professional pride of the man.

'But enough for the feast is enough for now. We must see if we can get more afterwards. There are often ways.'

The butler beamed. He knew there were ways and means to trade with the king's enemies. Still, he would have liked to have seen the store better stocked.

Leaving the buttery Philippa almost collided with a breathless Agnes Bakwell. She was clutching a pile of lettuces to her ample, aproned bosom.

'Ah yes,' Philippa exclaimed, 'lettuces. See that they are boiled well, Agnes.'

The cook had a peevish look. She needed no instructions as to how to boil a lettuce! Sensing the gaff that she had just committed, Philippa switched the subject swiftly. 'What bread have we, Agnes?'

'More than enough,' the cook panted, catching at a wayward lettuce.

'Fresh wheat for the top table . . .'

'Aye, mistress. Fresh bread for the top table, one-day-old bread to the lesser guildsmen and three-day-old bread for the household, as is usual. And for the trenchers the bread from last week.' She thought quickly. 'That will be five days old. We can scrape the green from the older bread and the household can use that as trenchers . . . as usual, madam.'

Agnes was a good-natured soul but the repetitive 'as usuals' seemed to be signalling that this was just routine and there was no need for a discussion concerning it. Philippa sensed the attitude but was determined to assert her own authority. In this respect she had achieved very little since her marriage.

'I want the partridges re-hung today. I'm not satisfied they are high enough, and the woodcock also. Will you see to it this morning, please?'

Agnes nodded, grabbed at a falling lettuce and scurried off. Satisfied that things were well indoors, Philippa decided to check on the outside kitchen.

Thomas was aware of the dangers of fire and he had had his kitchen erected in the back yard and separate from the house. It was stone built for added safety. In the kitchen two servants were fixing up a spit over a great open fire in the wall. Beside them was the pink body of a young pig. Before the metal-doored oven a young woman was raking glowing ashes and at her side was a tray of sweet pies to be cooked in the cooling embers. The stonework of the oven glowed red with heat and beads of perspiration stood out on the servant's brow as she worked the long-handled rake. On a nearby trestle table were bowls of almond cream, chicken brawn and fish in amber jelly.

Philippa waited until the spitting was completed and then spoke. 'Are the swans and rabbits here yet?' She had given the order for their collection from the markets only the night before. It was still a day until the feast but she wanted everything just so.

The two servants shuffled nervously. One of them wiped her wet hands on her coarse woollen robe. 'Beg pardon, mistress, but we were told to leave the swan.'

'And the rabbits too,' the other added with a sidelong glance.

Philippa paled. 'Who told you to do so when I had given you clear instructions?' She knew full well.

'It was the mistress Mentmore . . .' the first speaker began.

Philippa exploded. 'I am the mistress Mentmore.' Her face was contorted with fury. She realised she should not display her feelings but could not control the sheer intensity of her anger. Her fists were clenched; her knuckles white.

The servant shifted from foot to foot. 'A – aye, M – Mistress Ph – Philippa. We, I . . . were meaning Mistress Margaret.'

'Fine. Fine. You have time to go and collect what I ordered *now*. If you hurry you may yet find the items available. Go.'

Without waiting to see her order executed, she turned and marched from the room. As she crossed the yard she was met by

Emma, who appeared apprehensive. Philippa was surprised to see her. Immediately after morning mass she had despatched her to the market to buy fresh fruit and vegetables. It had not taken her very long.

Emma was tearful. 'I would have got it, mistress,' she pleaded. 'It was not my fault. I would have fetched it for you.' She had the look of one who had betrayed a cause. Philippa felt a tightening in her stomach.

'What did she say to you?' she said softly.

Emma was relieved. 'Then you know, mistress?'

Philippa did not respond to this. Instead she simply repeated her question: 'What did she say to you?'

'Mistress Margaret told me not to get fresh fruit and vegetables. She said she had sufficient stewed and preserved under mutton fat. She told me she could roast what was left in the pantry and that ... that ...' Her voice trailed off.

'What did she say?' Philippa's voice was ice.

'She said to beware salad, fruit and green food for it gives a man a feeble belly.'

'Enough!' Philippa said sharply, and Emma burst into tears.

Ignoring the curious stares of the clerks in the storerooms, Philippa put her arms round the girl and comforted her. Her anger was for Margaret not for this poor child.

Philippa had had her fill of Margaret Mentmore. This was the latest in a series of such incidents. Within the last week Margaret had countermanded a host of Philippa's orders: new cutlery and cloths for the table had been cancelled; a novelty box of forks had been rejected as effete and extravagant; a list of sauces and mustards (indispensable for flavouring old meat) had been altered without explanation.

Philippa had borne each of these challenges to her authority stoically. She had mentioned the matter of the forks to John but had given it up when it became clear that he shared his sister's disparaging view of these instruments. In all these situations Philippa had kept a low profile, battened down hatches and prepared to see the storm through. Now she had come to the end of her meekness. A cold fury burst inside her fuelled by John's lack of support for her. As she comforted Emma, the girl's tears acted as a breeze upon her fire. Her anger flared.

It was past noon when Margaret put in an appearance.

Philippa was in the hall supervising the removal of the old rushes from the floor. They had lain there for weeks and grown rancid with spit, spillage and worse, and Philippa had resolved to replace them before the feast. Piles of fresh rushes, new from Grasschurch Street market, lay against one wall. Emma was sorting them into bundles and servants were getting on with the task with a will. Perhaps Philippa was not the only one to have noted the smell?

'What's this?' Margaret demanded.

Philippa had not seen her enter. She turned slowly and without a note of malice she explained what she was about.

'Huh!' Margaret replied as if that said everything.

'Would you like to explain that, Margaret? It is a little inarticulate as it stands. So unlike you, my dear.'

Philippa could hardly believe her own ears. Yes – she had said it. The worm had turned! She felt quite calm. With superb self-control she watched her comment strike home.

Margaret was stunned. She blinked. She flushed. One of the servants sniggered ... or was it a stifled sneeze? Margaret flashed a terrifying glance in the direction of the sound. It died a suffocating, strangled death. Philippa brushed back a wisp of stray hair and repeated the question. Now her tone was flat; no civility in it at all.

'There was nothing wrong with those rushes, nothing whatsoever! Only a weak-willed servant girl would have found offence in them. This house cannot afford the tastes of such as that; nor can such extravagances be ...'

Margaret's words dried up. Philippa had quite ignored her and was pointing out a patch to a gawping servant.

'Dog's vomit! There, that's right. Remove it and the filth around it. Emma, put some new ones down where the filth was. Just there.' Emma was frozen. She could not comprehend what was going on. 'Emma, my dear, put the clean rushes down – there.' Philippa's voice was sweet as smooth honey.

Margaret was bright red. Each freckle stood out as a dark island in a pale pink sunset sea. A pulse twitched in her cheek. She looked a candidate for apoplexy.

'I'm sorry, Margaret, what were you saying?' Philippa worked hard to keep the honey flowing. 'I must have misheard you. I thought you had said how the state of the floor was exactly as you liked it and should not be altered.' Philippa watched the servant clean up the reeking floor covering, then turned back to the now scarlet Margaret. 'What was it you said? Did I hear you aright?'

'How dare you, how dare you, how *dare* you?' Margaret's voice rose in pitch and fury. She was almost shrieking as she reached the last 'how dare you'.

The servants stopped working. Agnes Bakwell's head appeared round the side of the screen at the far end of the hall. Thomas and John, who had just descended to the dais, stopped in horror.

'How dare you speak to me in such a way? In front of . . . in front of these!' She flung her arms in the direction of the servants.

Then Philippa produced her winning hand. Even afterwards she could not truly believe that she had done it. She did the most destructive thing she could do. She did not shout. She did not scream. Neither did she retreat in her usual fluster. Instead she leant close to Margaret's flaming face and summoned up her sweetest tones.

'Margaret, dear sister . . . you must not exert yourself so. I fear that if you continue to do so you will have a stroke.'

For a moment she thought Margaret was going to hit her. Her hand swept back. The servants gasped. Then she turned and swept across the hall. For a brief moment she stood in front of Thomas and John.

'I will not stand it. I will not stand it. I will not take it from . . . that woman.' She spat out the last word, then almost ran up on to the dais and vanished up the wooden stairs.

There was silence in the hall. Agnes Bakwell's eyes were almost popping out. Thomas and John stood stunned.

Emma looked from the dais to her mistress, back to the dais and then back to her mistress.

'Mistress Philippa,' she whispered breathlessly, 'you were wonderful!'

'Thank you Emma,' Philippa replied. 'I was, wasn't I?'

John and Thomas had been astounded by the outburst in the hall. They had never seen Margaret so combustible before. Her explosion in front of the servants was as improper as it was unexpected.

John was in the unwinnable position of loving both participants in this female rivalry. Taking his wife to one side he attempted to untangle the motives behind the explosion.

'You should not be so surprised, John,' Philippa commented. 'She has hated me ever since I arrived in this house.'

'No, my dear, you must not think that.'

'Think? Think? I do not think it, John. I know it! Ask any servant! Ask how many times my instructions have been countermanded. Ask how many times my authority is undermined.'

'But why, Philippa. Why is this so?'

'Because she is jealous beyond words of another woman in the house. She cannot control her jealousy, nor can she control her temper. You saw that today.'

John could not deny it. 'Can you not meet her halfway? Is it not possible to share the duties?'

'Share? Who is wife to the heir of Thomas Mentmore? Besides which, I have made every effort to "share". I have retreated before her advances, but does she rest easy with her gains and my losses? She does not! As I give way she seizes more. Only complete control will satisfy your sister. Ask her about "sharing", John. If you were truly master in this house you would not ask me how things are. You would know!'

'Enough!' John snapped.

'At least I wait until we are alone. Your sister, you will recall, entertains all comers!'

John was speechless. Philippa was transformed. Her meekness appeared to have dissolved and a new strength seemed to be flowing up from unknown depths.

'I shall speak with her,' he concluded.

'Aye, John, speak with her. Tell her who is wife to the heir of the House of Mentmore and remind her that she still holds the keys – my keys!'

Philippa was hurt and angry that John had not taken her side without reservation. Whilst she had acquitted herself well in the hall, she felt more isolated than ever in the household. Taking herself up to her chamber she sat quietly for a while. Then she cried and cried.

John, meanwhile, was experiencing anew the fury of his sister.

'She meddles in all things. She has no understanding of the

house!' Margaret, standing in the solar, was haloed by the sunlight. 'She orders swan and rabbit regardless of the cost.'

'But Margaret, this is for a special meal. She was told by father to spare no costs.'

'Spare no costs? When was I ever given such authority? I who have slaved to hold this house together for years. Now I am cast aside and she can take my place, can she? She can order forks, can she? Forks! Ha! Such extravagance! Besides, she has no grasp of dishes. She would have served them fresh fruit and salads. Even a child knows that such poisons a guest.'

'Look, Margaret, you must find ways of sharing the – '

'Share? I have made every effort to share. From the beginning I showed her only sisterly kindness. It is she who has poked her nose into every corner.'

'Margaret, she is my wife!'

'Oh, I should have known you would take her part in this and refuse to see my side. Leave me, John. I am tired and this goes nowhere.'

In confusion, John retreated. He began to feel he had failed with both women. The negotiations with the weavers were as nothing compared to this.

That evening Thomas attempted to put his foot down and pleased no one. The two women sat before him as he paced around the parlour.

'I will not, cannot, have such discord in the house. It grieves my heart to see sisters – for such you are – divided against each other. Nor shall I have your ill feelings aired before the household. I should think the whole of London knows of it now.' He stared at Margaret, who faced him squarely with defiant eyes. Wisely, though, she held her peace.

Thomas continued: 'We must learn to work together, for unity is our strength. Without it we shall fall. Of this matter of the running of the household ...' He paused. This was going to be tricky. 'You, Margaret, may hold the keys that you have held for so long. The household duties are large and a sharing of the burden will be beneficial to Philippa.' Margaret smiled faintly; Philippa's eyes narrowed. 'But major decisions in the household shall rest with Philippa Mentmore.' He emphasised the surname. 'For she is wife to my heir.' Margaret's smile faded away; Philippa nodded slightly.

Both women fixed their gaze on Thomas; he had given to both and denied both. His juggling act had therefore succeeded in satisfying neither of them. Thomas was clearly aware of this. When the women had retired he turned to his son.

'This business of Giles and the cloth trade. You did say you planned to spend time away from the city?'

'Yes, father, given your permission, of course. I would go alone initially but once the contacts were established I had thought to take Philippa on some trips to the country.' He let the idea hang there.

Thomas mused for a moment. 'I have thought of what you have said, John. I am prepared to go this far: make your enquiries; visit Giles's manor and explore the possibilities of expansion. "Explore", I say. Do not commit us yet. I shall have final say on this matter. One day the household will be yours but until that day . . .'

'I understand. I am to explore but not irrevocably to commit.' John's quiet acceptance of Thomas's authority hid a swell of triumph. At last he could move forward.

'That is so, my son.'

'Thank you, father. You will not regret this, I can assure you.'

'We shall see,' Thomas said. 'But it will be wise to give Philippa and Margaret some time apart.'

'Once I have made my initial enquiries that should be possible. Yes, it will be possible.'

So at least someone was happy. John went to bed jubilant. It was a jubilation which he was wise enough to withhold from his wife. He had seen, as Thomas had, that neither Philippa nor Margaret was elated at Thomas's imitation of Solomon. Later he would tell her of the future. Beside him – apparently fast asleep – Philippa also lay awake. She too was thinking of the future. Her pillow was damp.

The next morning dawned clear and the day, though busy, went well. Margaret and Philippa somehow managed to avoid each other. For the time being the strategy worked. How long it could be kept up was hard to tell. For much of the late afternoon Margaret contrived to be away from the hall. At any other time such an absence, on the brink of a major social event, would have been unthinkable. This time, however, it was put down to a belated sense of diplomacy. Her absence gave Philippa time and

freedom to finalise preparations.

Margaret, though, was less concerned with diplomacy than with Robert Newton.

'Your brother watches me strangely,' Newton remarked.

'Do you think he suspects the truth concerning our love?' Margaret asked.

'I do not know. Perhaps, perhaps. I come to your house rarely now but I feel he watches me carefully.' Robert shook his head. 'I wish I could explain to him . . .'

'No!' Margaret interrupted. 'He would not understand and you would destroy everything. Do not be fooled, my love. There is peace between you now but an extorted peace. The Mentmores did not come willingly to it.'

'Nor generously!' Robert retorted. 'Six pence we were promised, five pence we have received.'

'I know, my love, but do not let us quarrel. All I seek to show you is that peace with the Mentmores does not equal love. John and my father must never learn of us or they will destroy us.'

'Never? Never?' Robert's face was marked with sorrow.

'My father is ambitious, Rob. He will not see me married to a minor guildsman.'

'Ha, a fat goldsmith perhaps? Or another mercer or draper?'

'My father will not force me, Rob, In that, at least, I am both blessed and rare! But he will not countenance a marriage 'down' either. He has dreams. John has dreams. If he has his way he will take the family beyond London . . .' She stopped, realising the secret she was sharing. She knew nothing of Thomas's final agreement but had been privy to the discussions following the coronation.

Robert's eyes grew shrewd. 'And how would he do that, Maggie?'

Margaret flushed. 'I know not.' She whispered her lie fearful that God, in the silent church, would hear.

Robert was staring at her oddly. 'Come with me, Margaret,' he said at last. 'Come with me and marry me. I need no dowry to love you.'

Margaret's face must have shown the depths of her shock.

'You cannot pretend you have not thought of it,' Robert continued swiftly. 'You yourself have said Thomas will never agree to our marriage. The word "never" was your word. Come away with me, my heart, marry me.' His voice was almost pleading.

Margaret had thought of such an option. Relentless logic had forced her to it on many a sleepless night. It had forced her to it, but she had not embraced it. Such an irrevocable severance of her family ties appalled her. She loved this man, but this much? She shook her head in despair.

'I cannot, Rob. No, I cannot.' Tears misted her ice-blue eyes. 'No, I cannot. I must not.'

'Oh, my heart, my dear love.' He reached out to hold her.

'No, Rob. No.' She struggled free. 'It cannot be. It serves no good to torture ourselves so. It cannot be and we cannot be. I shall . . .' Her voice trembled then broke. 'I shall see you no more.'

She turned and ran from him. Her feet echoed in the nave. At the door she wiped away her blinding tears with one long, loose sleeve, then she was out into the street, By the time Robert reached the door she had vanished.

Thomas's party was a great success. Each guest was carefully seated so as not to be offended by his neighbour. Each guildsman and his wife shared plate and cup and ate and drank to their heart's content. Philippa had laid out the tables perfectly. Cutlery and cloths were clean, the silver salt cellars were aglow and the heaps of spices, in a jewelled model ship, were brought in amidst much ceremony.

Thomas and John were acutely aware of the silent reservation of Margaret, but such emotional complexities were thankfully lost on the eager guests. They tucked into mustard brawn, roast heron and bittern, sweet cakes and jelly with enthusiasm. Wine flowed. The household consumed gallons of beer. John Philipot seemed more than pleased with the feast held in his honour. Sat next to Thomas, he ate and drank with a will. From the gallery musicians played non-stop.

When the table was clear the servants brought roasted pears and apples to ease the extended stomachs. They also brought the mazer bowl to Thomas. Handling the polished maplewood cup, he rose to propose a toast to the guest of honour. The rush and candle light reflected on his balding head and jewelled fingers. He was quietly exultant. Only that afternoon, Thomas of Woodstock's steward had brought a tapestry commission to him. Now, with the feast a success, he rose to crown the triumph of a glorious day.

'My friends,' he said to the hushed gathering, 'I give you the toast, to John Philipot who has protected our noble trade and city.' The gathering thundered its approval. Thomas waited for silence. 'And I toast the great assembly of guild masters here present who represent the power and the majesty of this great city.'

With much pushing back of benches all present echoed his toast. Thomas passed the mazer cup from hand to hand around the table raised up on the dais.

The merriment went on until very late and so it was a much disgruntled Thomas who was awoken from his bed early the next morning. Since his room opened off John and Philippa's chamber (as did Margaret's room) they too were awoken and it was a sleepy and bad-tempered pair of mercers who descended to the hall. Had the visitors not been important they would have been left to stand there.

Lionel de Roos, tapestry maker to King Edward III, deceased, and to King Richard II was waiting in the hall. He was not alone. Around him stood a small group of richly dressed men – his confederates.

Lionel was sallow cheeked with bad teeth. His lip raised a half sneer as the two male Mentmores appeared. 'Did we drag you from your beds?' he enquired maliciously. 'It is well after prime.'

'Aye, aye,' Thomas muttered. 'Will you come to the solar, gentlemen? We can talk business there.'

'We've not come to talk business, Thomas Mentmore.' De Roos's voice was high-pitched and aggressive.

'Oh?' Thomas said. He had caught the tone in his visitor's voice. 'Then what, pray, brings you to my house?'

'You have supplied tapestries to the Duke of Lancaster.' De Roos's words were challenging.

'What is that to you, Lionel de Roos?' Thomas said. John hissed an intake of breath. He did not like de Roos.

'And he promises more? A great commission?'

'I asked, what is such to you?' Thomas was angry.

'And now his brother Woodstock, the king's other uncle, approaches you. Is this not so?' Lionel's eyes glittered with undisguised menace.

Thomas stared at de Roos, then answered him coldly. 'Thomas of Woodstock, Duke of Buckingham – whom you term "Woodstock" – has approached me, yes! He is the liege lord of Giles de Brewoster, my brother-in-law and Lord of Woodlands and Knolton and Lord of Upton. He has approached me with a commission. What is it to you?'

'We are chartered tapestry makers to the king.'

'John Duke of Lancaster and Thomas Duke of Buckingham are not kings, de Roos. I ask once more: what is any of this to you?'

'Gaunt would make himself king,' one of de Roos's company sneered.

'Be quiet, man!' de Roos snapped.

'Do I hear treason?' Thomas replied mildly. De Roos ignored this question.

The man who had slandered Gaunt would not be so easily put down. 'We know your game, Thomas Mentmore. You seek to steal our work. You connive to take bread from out of our mouths.'

'Be silent, or answer with a sword,' John spat out.

Thomas put a hand on his son's shoulder. 'Be very careful, de Roos, and your lackey too. My commissions from Lancaster and Buckingham do not contravene your legal monopoly with the King. I act within my rights.'

'No man should work two mysteries,' de Roos whined. 'It is illegal to do so, Mentmore. You are a mercer – keep to that. Be a middle man and grow rich, but do not produce. Do not take on another mystery. Keep off the mystery we hold dear.'

'If my father breaks the law, take your complaint before your alderman; take it to the Common Council; let a sergeant-at-law decide in the courts of this city!' John was furious.

'Get out of my hall, de Roos,' Thomas ordered. He clicked his fingers. Liveried retainers appeared, full of menace.

'Be warned, Thomas Mentmore, be warned. We shall not stand idly by. We see everything you do. We see your clerks scurrying about the city. We saw Adam Yonge poking and prying. We see your son – and you – making plans to rob honest men.'

'What do you know of Adam?' John roared, and lunged at de

Roos. The pale tapestry maker was light on his feet. He danced away. 'What do you know of Adam Yonge, you rogue?'

'Enough, John.' Thomas caught at the sleeve of his shirt. 'Get them out of here,' he called to his servants.

Roughly and without ceremony the visitors were propelled out of the door. They shouted and cursed as they were manhandled.

Both Thomas and John were shocked at the unexpected intrusion and threat. John particularly was stunned by de Roos's acid reference to Adam, the murdered clerk. All that day he could not shake off the words. He slept badly that night, was up early and, over a mug of wine, tried to piece together their significance. That day, too, he worked without concentration. Philippa noticed it – who would not? – but she could not penetrate to his concerns.

Two nights after the triumphant feast, John awoke from a nightmare. Once more he had seen Yonge's butchered body only this time it was on fire. Cruel snakes of flame writhed over the corpse.

Soaked in sweat, he tossed uneasily. The dream was past. Yet still he could smell smoke. It was close. The scent of burning wood was clear in the room. Suddenly he leapt from bed.

'Fire, fire!' he howled, and knew it was no dream.

Chapter Seven

The night of the fire haunted John's thinking. The smoke and screams, the wild panic and the rushing feet provided fodder for innumerable nightmares.

Fire was the terror of the age. As the Mentmores and their streaming-eyed servants had fought the blaze, they had done so in the company of neighbours fearful for their own timber-framed tenements and sheds.

The seat of the fire had been the tapestry workshop. Separated from the main hall by an alley linking the street to courtyard, the wood-beamed shed had burnt with ferocious force. All within it had been reduced to ashes. Only the frantic efforts of the local populace – and the dividing alley – had saved the house. As it was, the wall had been burnt in many places and the jetty overhanging the street had its whitewash blackened by the soot and wood ash.

The vagaries of the wind had also helped. A northerly breeze had lifted the flames and blown the sparks southward. It had cost the Mentmores' neighbour – a draper – his house and shop, but spared the Mentmores' hall. Nevertheless, this narrow escape had not come cheap for Thomas and his family. The weaving shed represented a considerable capital investment. The Mentmores would take time to recover from such a blow.

Standing in the cold ashes, John's face was creased with puzzlement. The ferocity of the fire pointed to arson but the act had consumed the evidence – if ever any had been left. It hardly seemed coincidental that the disaster followed so hard on the heels of de Roos's threatening visit. However, as with Adam Yonge's killing, that was all John had to go on: coincidences and grave suspicions.

Thomas, of course, had furiously denounced the tapestry

makers before the Common Council. His friends had sided with him, his rivals had requested proof. There was no proof. No one had seen or heard a thing. And why should they have? Honest citizens had been sound asleep in their beds. The curfew had been in force. The city had slept. As with the killing of the clerk, the trail was cold. Days turned to weeks and weeks to months and nothing was resolved.

The visit of de Roos and the loss of the tapestry shed only added to John's list of rivals and enemies. He had not seen Robert Newton for weeks. The man had rarely been to the house before the fire; now he seemed to have vanished altogether. Added to which was de Roos's casual reference to Adam Yonge. What had he meant by it? John wondered. Was it a threat? 'See what we have done to your busy clerk, now see what we will do to you if you do not leave off this work!' The fire would support such a conclusion. Or was it a remark without consequence? 'Just as Yonge represented your expansion, now you, John Mentmore, are seen scurrying about the city. Leave us alone!' Little did they know that John's scurrying about the city had nothing to do with tapestry work.

Yet Dick Appulby had clearly said that Adam Yonge had been a regular visitor to Robert Newton. Yonge had never revealed such regular contacts to John. Appulby had also suggested that there was bad blood between them. Against this stood the fact that Newton had accepted the Mentmores' offers and seemed to be reasonable. Or was he playing some deep game? And where was he now?

John was called out of his private, muddled thoughts.

'Your father has a guest and seeks your company in the solar. He will take supper there tonight and wants you alone to join him.'

John nodded absent-mindedly. 'Thank you, my dear.'

Philippa watched him go. She had changed since the public fight with Margaret. No longer submissive and yet not allowed to take charge of the whole household, she was not satisfied but was no longer cowed. No more did Margaret cross her with impunity. Whilst Philippa deeply resented her sister-in-law's possession of those symbolic keys, she made the most of Thomas's decision to make her the final arbiter of the household. Whether John supported her or not she would resist Margaret.

John had noticed the change in his wife. He was not so lost in his thoughts as to be blind to such a transformation. He felt a distance between them and did not know what to do about it. Oddly, in his opinion, he felt the same with Margaret. She too was cold and aloof. Whilst Edmund had always been the favourite brother, it was hard to explain this sudden reserve with regard to himself. He was sure he had dealt with both women even-handedly. What then could have led to such a chill?

This was on his mind as he entered the solar. For a moment he thought of another occasion, long before, when Hugh le Breton had risen to greet him. Those days seemed far distant.

The visitor was John Kirkby. A wealthy merchant, he was one of the leading anti-Lancastrians in the city.

'Welcome, John. Kirkby, you know my son?' Thomas enthused.

'Aye, I know John. It's good to see you again,' Kirkby said.

He was a big-boned but active man. His movements belied the heavy appearance of his body. His cheeks sagged into dark jowels but his eyes were quick and alert. He wore a fine jewelled sword. A rich purple cloak was carelessly tossed over the bench.

'Welcome, sir,' John said cautiously. He knew exactly why Kirkby was here — money! The firing of the weaving shed had left Thomas in need of some quickly available cash.

Gaunt's return from France had brought the promised tapestry commission and Woodstock had also made his much publicised approach. The orders were there; the means to fulfil them were not. Only the week before Thomas had entertained Richard Lyons in a similar, private fashion. The meeting had secured a hefty loan from the tremendously wealthy Lyons. In that case, of course, the Lancastrian sympathies of the guest had helped to oil the cogs somewhat. The same could not be said of Kirkby. Perhaps this was a symbol of the success of Thomas's juggling act. Or perhaps Kirkby had his own price to name!

A servant brought in silver goblets and wine of Auxerre — expensive stuff, what with the war.

'To our mutual benefit,' Thomas suggested. The three men drank deeply. 'We shall eat here and discuss a little business arrangement which is of benefit to us all.'

It was unusual for Thomas to take supper apart from the family and household. Even family meals alone in the parlour were unusual. Whilst dinner was the main meal of the day, this last meal, too, was most regularly taken in the hall. Thomas did not break with tradition without reasons.

The September daylight had faded away. An attendant lit up beeswax candles and set them on the table. No mutton fat candles for John Kirkby, John reflected. Father means to impress.

Since it was the eve of the feast of St Matthew fish was served, but Thomas had clearly given instructions to spare no cost. Now John realised why Philippa and Emma had hurried off to Billingsgate market that morning. The products of their planning were now carried in on wooden boards: fish baked in bread, broiled on coals, stewed, cooked in spices. And with them came the usual array of jellies, stewed fruit tarts and custards.

As they ate, they talked over business.

'How have you coped with the results of the fire?' Kirkby enquired.

'Oh very well,' Thomas replied. 'It is only a sideline, a mere diversification. It has been an inconvenience but the main work is quite untouched.'

'A mere diversification but a lucrative one, I hear. So successful that the King's tapestry makers have petitioned the Common Council to fine you for breach of a mystery.'

'Ah, yes.' Thomas nodded. 'But so far they have not succeeded.'

'Quite so,' Kirkby said and added, 'But my point was not a legal one. I meant instead that it is a money-making concern, one which would quickly repay a loan.'

Thomas eyed his guest carefully before responding. 'Yes, it is a worthy investment and when present projects are completed should – will – turn in a handsome profit.'

'How large a loan would assist the completion of these present projects?'

John munched on a baked pear and watched his father and Kirkby fence.

'To rebuild the sheds and re-equip them would cost perhaps a thousand pounds,' Thomas replied as if he were reading out a shopping list.

John winced inwardly at the cost. Kirkby seemed unmoved. He was obviously used to such figures.

'What kind of loan would you have in mind, Thomas?' he enquired politely.

'I have secured loans up to eight hundred pounds. I now require a loan of two hundred.'

'Over what period of time?'

'Two years.'

'With your regular textile stock as security against the loan?'

'Of course. As I said the sheds are full of fine merchandise and the company is healthy.'

Kirkby picked at his fish. He evidently had one more stipulation and was considering it. At last he spoke. 'I will make you the loan, Thomas. But I will only require you to pay back a hundred pounds of it.'

Both Thomas and John drew in breath.

'I do not follow,' Thomas said.

'I will only require that amount to be repaid, if you will assist me with a little . . . a little project; a mere diversification of my own . . .'

The silence within the room was intense. The sound of the household noises from the hall came as from another world. Within the solar the three men sat in an awkward stillness. John caught his father's glance. He twitched an eyebrow. Thomas's eyes narrowed slightly.

'And what is your project? Your diversification?'

Kirkby shifted his heavy body on the bench. The wood creaked. He smiled a thin smile. It was a knife slash in his heavy face.

'I need to take two men to Westminster. By night. They are – how shall I put it? – desirous that they travel unobserved.' He smiled again.

'May I ask the names of these men?' Thomas asked in a voice that was barely above a whisper. 'And from where will they begin their journey?'

'Their names I would withhold – for now. They will begin their journey from outside the tavern in Tower Street.'

'But that is only half an hour's ride from Westminster,' Thomas protested. 'What need is there of our assistance to convey them there? Besides, any man could direct them hither!'

Kirkby was no longer smiling. 'Mayhap they do not wish to ask the way. Mayhap they need to go via back streets and early in the morning. Mayhap they would hope to move after the curfew and yet evade the city watch. Mayhap they need the company of one who can be trusted absolutely, one who has wit and discretion.'

'Who are these men?' Thomas insisted.

Kirkby did not reply. John chewed at his lip with vigorous concentration. 'Who else but men leaving the Tower without their host's permission and seeking sanctuary? Am I right, John Kirkby?'

'By God, man, your son is a plain speaker and does not dally with niceties!' Kirkby was not angry. Rather he seemed faintly amused by John's directness.

'Who are they?' Thomas repeated.

'Their names will lie doggo for now, Thomas. Truly that is for the best. Suffice it to say they have run aground on Gaunt and now he has made them his guests against their will. However they are not without friends. They are known to me and have made contact with me via the good offices of a guard – '

'Who has been bribed handsomely, no doubt?'

Kirkby shrugged off John's question. 'They have made contact with me. They desire it that I should convey them safely to sanctuary, but I am not a young man. I require the assistance of another, a young, brave man whom I can trust. Their leaving of the Tower is no concern to such a man. I simply require their swift conveyance along the river by night.'

Thomas was considering the potential consequences of such a venture. John of Gaunt would hardly smile upon those who were party to such an escapade. His fury would be terrible. More than that, Thomas was acutely aware of his reliance on Gaunt.

Kirkby seemed to be studying Thomas's private agony. It seemed obvious to John that the perceptive guildsman had the full measure of the Mentmore dilemma.

'Some say you lean towards the duke, Thomas. Surely this is not so?' Again the sardonic mask.

Thomas reacted as if stung. 'Who says so? I am my own man! By St John, I feted Philipot as a hero. I am not the lapdog of the Duke of Lancaster. All know the magnates around the duke condemned Philipot's brave efforts on our behalf. Yet I was not abashed. I feted him and you were there. I gave every support to his becoming mayor this year. Who says I am of Gaunt's party?"

John, too, was conscious of a veiled threat behind Kirkby's suggestion. He tapped the trestle table. 'The house of Mentmore stands four square for the good of this city, its charter rights and freedoms. The Mentmores are not bought or sold. When men speak of Philipot and Walworth they also speak of Mentmore. We defend the city and are not puppets of the duke.'

Kirkby showed no emotion. 'Yet you do support John of Northampton, do you not? Men wonder at that.'

John sucked in a sharp breath. Yes, men did wonder at that! Philipot and Walworth were not only critics of Lancaster, they were also great guild masters. They were allied against Northampton's attempts to make the city's government more accountable to the guild members – especially the lower craftsmen guilds. If they had their way the city would once again be ruled, in effect, by the oligarchy of mayor and aldermen. They would reduce Northampton's Common Council to a talking shop.

Thomas Mentmore's promise to the weavers to support Northampton had caused a stir of alarm amongst the masters of the richest trade guilds. It had seemed to be a curious kind of defection; a betrayal of the exclusive group to which the Mentmores belonged.

Thomas was not happy at the turn the conversation had taken. He picked at a flat cake of bread stuffed with spiced fish. In the end, however, it was John who completed the defence of his family.

'We accept the duke's commissions. What trade master at the head of a mystery would not do so? We support Northampton against the fishmongers at the behest of the crafts guilds who supply us, and because the fishmongers have no right to use their monopoly against the whole city. Do you relish higher prices?' He paused to let this sink in, then continued: 'That John of Northampton is said to be of the duke's party is of no interest to us. We chart a free course – for the Mentmores and for the city!'

'Then you would be free to act against the duke?' Kirkby's question hung heavy in the air.

Thomas stirred. 'We are free. Yes, of course. We are free.'

'Splendid,' Kirkby retorted. 'Then our venture would be of mutual benefit. No?'

Thomas nodded, stony faced.

'I think my brother Edmund would be better suited to your

venture,' John said.

'But Edmund is not here and I must move soon and quickly.'

'That is quite true,' Thomas agreed. 'Edmund is not here. He has fought this year with the duke in France. He has been there throughout the summer.'

'He fought?' Kirkby was ironic in his surprise. 'Did not the duke sit out the siege at Brest with Katherine Swinford? Did not his army find free shelter with the towns of Brittany until they could afford no more . . . hospitality?'

'My son fought off Bayonne,' Thomas remarked coldly. 'His young squire, a tenant of my brother-in-law, de Brewoster, fell badly wounded in that heroic victory. Long did Edmund spend with the boy in France. Now both are at the Dorset manor of the boy's father. The boy mends slowly. Edmund attends to the manors of de Brewoster, for he is de Brewoster's heir.'

'So Edmund is not here.' Kirkby's simple assertion seemed to deflate Thomas's proud account. John decided that he did not care for this bull of a man despite his much-needed loan.

'No, he is not here,' Thomas concluded. 'John alone of my sons is with me. William is at Oxford.'

Kirkby laughed. 'I did not presume to send a clerk, Thomas! This venture calls for swords not quills. I need a man who will act the hero not the lawyer!' His dismissive reference to William brought colour to John's cheeks.

'I am my father's heir,' John declared. 'If my father accepts a part in this . . . in this enterprise, then I shall be prepared to uphold the Mentmore side of the agreement.'

Kirkby looked appraisingly at John. 'Men speak well of you. They say you are clever and cool. Both will be needed to carry off this task. You will do it then? If your father agrees?'

'I will.'

'And what do you say, Thomas? The final decision is yours. If you can assist me I shall be pleased to help your business, as we have outlined. I shall advance two hundred pounds but be owed but a hundred.'

The mention of the money brought the conversation full circle. It only emphasised the fact that Kirkby must be making a great deal of money out of the escape.

'I agree,' Thomas said. 'The Mentmores agree to your terms.'

John was less than happy with the arrangement. The risks

seemed fearful. The family could lose all in this gamble. And yet, as with any gamble, the stakes were worth playing for. Kirkby's offer was a substantial one. It was no secret that the fire had hit the Mentmores hard. It could be carried by the family but it would slow down Thomas's response to the recent lucrative commissions. He and his son knew all too well that such opportunities would not repeat themselves. Both Gaunt and Woodstock had opened windows of opportunity for the family. Whoever had set up the fire had sought to shut the windows – and firmly.

Thomas was no less concerned than his son. He knew how terrible Gaunt's wrath would be in the face of Kirkby's planned humiliation. It was a bitter irony that he was being tempted to flaunt Gaunt's authority in order to benefit from his patronage. The dangers inherent in such a game of chance were hard to exaggerate. He and John talked them over as September 1378 drew to its close. Neither could deny the risk. Neither could deny the potential monetary gain.

These thoughts were whirling through John's head as he stood in the stone-built store on a pleasant late September morning. The swallows were swooping and diving in playful pursuit of the last of the summer flies. A kestrel flew low over the yard in search of absent-minded sparrows. It was a September day when autumn seemed far off and winter a hollow threat. The sky was a canvas of pale starling's-egg blue.

John Mentmore did not think on these pleasantries. His mind was off on a less sunny journey. As he watched the arrival of a batch of cloth he had to concentrate on the exercise of his mystery with real effort. Ten ells of velvet lay stacked on the bench beside him. He ran his fingers over the dense, smooth, piled surface of the exotic cloth. Its colour was deepest wine. Even in the shadows it was luxurious.

'A fine cloth, sir.' The journeyman ran his hand over the material too. 'A fine cloth and no mistake about it.' His fingernails were buffed smooth by the constant handling of textiles.

'Aye,' John agreed, 'and a pretty penny it shall be worth.'

Laughing, the journeyman ordered two of the workers to stack the bundle on a shelf out of harm's way.

'And where will you have the damask stored, sir?'

'Beside it,' John decided with less than full concentration. The bale of rose-coloured, wave-patterned silk was duly transported.

'And the wool cloth?'

John was beginning to feel irritated. The journeyman was quite capable of making such decisions on his own. He had been in the household for over ten years and knew the mystery backwards. Only lack of funds prevented him from buying into the mercer guild as a master himself. Nevertheless, John's presence was clearly hamstringing the man this morning. His constant questions were spoiling John's line of reasoning.

'Wherever you will, Tom. You decide. You know as well as I.'

Tom looked doubtful but could scarcely deny such a compliment, even if delivered with a peevish intake of breath. He duly made his choice.

'It'll cause trouble, you know,' he intimated in subdued tones.

'By St John, man, it can matter not at all. You've stored it safe and sound and it will come to no harm where it is now put.'

'No sir, not where it is put; rather what it is that we put there.'

John frowned at the incomprehensible nature of this information. 'What are you talking of, Tom? I cannot see danger in bales of cloth.'

Tom was stung. 'But what is it?' He seemed amazed that no one could share his concern.

Shaking his head, John examined one of the bales. 'Lincoln Scarlet.'

'And around it? All around it?' Tom was agitated. Really, John thought, for a man in his twenties he fusses like an old woman.

'Twenty ells of Stamford cloth; no, thirty by the look of it. More scarlets. A bale of Beverley Blues and – '

'Good cloth but woollen cloth not fine cloth. The drapers don't like it. They don't like it and they are talking again. Talking about infringement of mystery.'

John raised his eyes in exasperation. None of this was new. Not for the first time were drapers carping about mercers stocking less high quality cloth. It was an old story. According to tradition and regulation the mercers dealt in fine cloth and the drapers in sewing materials and less high quality fabric. Neither could sell buttons or ribbons. That was the prerogative of the guild of haberdashers. The moot point was where to draw the line. Thomas had always drawn it with an eye to inclusiveness.

To the drapers this smacked of intrusion. The Mentmores were beginning to get a name for this.

'It's old news, Tom. They complain but cannot enforce their jealousies. There's no coarse cloth here. All the woollen cloth is fine spun and within our mystery. They push to see how far they can go.'

'Mayhap 'tis – '

'Fret not, Tom, or you'll die ere you're thirty. It's not the first time we've faced this.' John was finding a source of irritation in the trade restrictions. He knew where it could lead. The blackened spars of the tapestry shed were at his back. They served to remind him where a charge of 'infringement of mystery' might take him.

Tom was not convinced but was unable to press his point. At that moment Philippa entered the storehouse. She was dressed in a saffron cotte with full flowing skirt and looked as if she did not have a care in the world. Her face shone and she was in high spirits. Much of this was lost on John who was not in the mood for talk. Philippa had been rather frosty of late and despite her genial expression John was cautious with his wife. That sense of caution fed his irritability. It was a worrying combination of emotions. The matter of Kirkby and the journeyman's alarm did not mellow John's mood.

'Good morning,' she beamed and John grunted. 'Can I see the new stock?' She stepped lightly amidst the bales and surveyed the carefully tied and piled bales of merchandise. She seemed taken by the damask. She caressed the rippled cloth. 'Can I have some, John?'

'No,' John replied with annoyance. 'We have scarcely tallied the stock or inventoried the new bales.' He was right, but even as he spoke apprentices were cutting notches in different coloured tally sticks. Each notch a bale; each tally stick colour a different grade of cloth.

Philippa pouted. 'Ah, John, you are in a bad mood.' An apprentice smiled and John blushed. This really was too much.

'I meant it, my dear.' His civility was rather forced. 'You may pick from the new stock when it is counted in and measured.'

Since the explosion with Margaret, John had been nervous in the presence of his wife. Nothing in his upbringing had prepared him for a feeling of inadequacy in the presence of a woman – let alone a wife. He had often privately scorned the parish priest's insistence on the wilful nature and awful power of the daughters of Eve. 'Vain and weak in flesh,' he had often pontificated, 'but it was Eve who tempted our father Adam to sin. Never ignore the temptation housed in such frail vessels.' John was reluctantly converting to that celibate's theoretical view of Eve's offspring. The preaching reassured him but did not truly comfort him. Nowadays he was quick to sense slights to his authority and to put his foot down. Something of his mood must have transmitted itself to Philippa. Her sunny features clouded. She flushed and pushed out past him. He followed her. He was alarmed by her displays of emotion. This was not the girl he had married. Something had changed.

'He should take a stick to that one,' an apprentice commented with a smirk. 'Or if he'll not, I'll gladly do it.'

'Shut your mouth,' Tom snapped. 'If John Mentmore hears you, he'll take a stick to you.' Tom sighed. Perhaps the apprentice was right.

Outside in the yard, John caught his wife's arm and firmly turned her round to face him.

'Enough, woman. You shall submit to your husband.' He laid stress on the word 'submit'.

Philippa was hurt. John's resistance had come as a total surprise and for her the sunny day was ruined. Tears were welling up in her eyes. The sight of them brought a deep distress to John. Despite her hurt she was also angry. The spark, never far from her these days, was also in those brown eyes.

'You have no need to treat me like a churl, my husband. I only asked. You said that I might ask.' She was feeling sick. She had but picked at her food for some days. John had not noticed. More important than even the dull nausea, she was aware that her period was long overdue. She had felt elated as she went to tell John her conclusion. Now she felt brittle and fragile. 'I only wanted to dress for you and to tell you . . .'

'But you know I must check in cloth and I am not to be disturbed until all is settled.' John's anger had ebbed away.

'And now it is spoilt.' She was pale and her eyes were wide. 'It is spoilt and to think I had rejoiced to tell you of it!'

'Tell me? Tell me of what?' John said, mystified.

'I'm to have your baby,' she blurted out through her tears.

Then, her face crumpled in distress, she ran into the house.

John would have gone after her. Despite his need for dominance he was desperate to follow her. Then his father was calling to him. Thomas stood at the entry to the hall. Philippa had dashed passed him. Beside the Mentmore patriarch stood Kirkby, a faintly amused smile playing over his heavy lips. The die is cast, John thought miserably. There is no turning back. No turning back for any of us . . .

John had no time to comfort his wife. Kirkby's arrival signalled that the hour was almost at hand for John's adventure. The news brought little joy to John and Thomas, too, was far from at ease.

Kirkby seemed to have considered his plans carefully. He had also crossed with silver the palms of some of the city watch. His money promised that no one should be over-vigilant in checking for curfew breakers about East Chepe. He seemed confident and calm. His presence annoyed John as much as Tom's clucking concern. Indeed, it was far worse. John had an uncomfortable feeling that Kirkby was laughing at him. His hooded eyes were the last ones John would have chosen to witness the tearful retreat of Philippa. John doubted whether Kirkby brooked such displays in his house.

Kirkby and John left the hall separately for neither was keen to be seen with the other. John went to hear vespers sung at St Magnus Martyr and prayed for God's blessing on the whole venture. Somehow, though, he could not relax. Whilst the priest led the singing of the Daily Office his mind was darting in and out of alleys and going over his chosen route again and again.

He drifted through the five psalms but was caught by the recitation of the Magnificat: 'He has performed mighty deeds with his arm; he has scattered those who are proud in their inmost thoughts.' John hoped that this was a sign of God's blessing. There was no prouder man than Gaunt. But still the mercer was troubled. Was it a Christian duty to seek a man's patronage and then to betray him? Indeed, if he was so sure of Gaunt's pride, was that not a sign of his own lack of humility? He shuffled about and disturbed those standing near him. The church was half full. Candles cast shadows about the chancel. Somehow he doubted whether Edmund ever entertained such thoughts. This was a job for Edmund. He was experienced in these matters. Indeed he truly relished danger. Why was he not here? Why was he still in Dorset?

The priest recited the closing prayer and the congregation joined in the familiar words of the Our Father. John prayed 'deliver us from evil' with unusual fervour. Those about him glanced at the fervent piety of the cloaked young man. He seemed not to notice them.

It was dark before he left the church and slipped away towards the Customs House. Down below the wild drop of London Bridge, the pent-up Thames once more sunk into a strange lethargy.

John watched the moonlight on the torpid waters. It was getting cold. The night was cloudless. There was a frosty feel to the air. He pulled his cloak about his shoulders and drew up the hood. He was the image of melancholy, gazing out over the dark river.

Soon the last inn had closed its doors. In the darkness only the protruding 'inn stake', with its bundle of leaves, betrayed the presence of a tavern. The last drunken voices died away, the gates were shut, the city slept. John gazed out over the river.

He stood there for what felt to be an age. Then, keeping to the shadows, he followed the river bank eastward towards the Tower. The black bulk of that mighty edifice stood out against the sky like some sinister mountain.

Kirkby was waiting. He was restless. The sight of his nervousness reassured John. Two men were with him. They too seemed ill at ease. Both were cloaked. Nearby stood one of Kirkby's retainers. He was heavily built and carried a wicked looking dagger which he made no attempt to conceal.

'I'll come as far as St Benet, Thames Street,' Kirkby hissed. 'Then you must get them into sanctuary at Westminster without delay.' He tugged at John's cloak. 'They are Shakell and Hawley.'

'Holy Mother of our Lord!' John blanched at the two names. His shock prompted Kirkby to grin. John was furious. 'By Our Lady, Kirkby, have you gone mad? What incubus possesses you? Gaunt will slaughter us for this – '

'Hst, man, and play the valiant,' Kirkby taunted. 'You'll not deny that this is worth a hundred pounds.'

The two silent strangers were restless. John's fear was infectious. They muttered to Kirkby to 'get on, get on'. They spoke in French, still the language of aristocracy though giving way to English with the drawn-out war with France. Kirkby answered them, also in French. Kirkby smirked. John's distress seemed to have restored his confidence.

Ignoring John's carefully researched route, Kirkby led the way through the darkened streets. In the alleyways were no sounds but their own hurried footsteps. It felt like a dream. Kirkby's faithful hound padded at the rear. Past the Steel Yard they hurried. The Hanser guards watched them go. It was no business of theirs. At St Michael Paternoster Royal the city watch appeared. Kirkby made a sign and his party became invisible. The watch passed by. Such was the power of Kirkby's silver pennies!

The Thames lapped close to the road at Queen Hythe and Kirkby leant out into the darkness. Around him the jettied buildings and plank warehouses were in total darkness. Down in the shadows a rowing boat bobbed on the full tide. One of Kirkby's henchmen was at the oars. Even in the shadows his coarse face exuded violence. John shuddered.

Kirkby and his henchman hurried their three companions down the slippery jetty steps. They clambered awkwardly into the heaving boat. It was amazing how the boat moved, even on the controlled current. John hated water and felt sick with fear.

Kirkby moved away into the darkness. The boat pulled out. Oars struck and splashed the moonlit waters.

Back on the wharf a startled cry split the darkness. Oaths and shouts poured from a mass of shifting shadows. There seemed to be some kind of scuffle going on in the street. From the water it was not possible to make out the protagonists in the strange eruption of noise.

'Row, for God's sake!' John exclaimed.

'Yes, row or we're dead men.' It was one of the muffled strangers. His eyes were full of fear. 'Row . . . row . . .' His panic-stricken French beat on the air like bird's wings.

In a flurry of splashes the boat pulled out from Queen Hythe. Back on shore the noise was punctuated with screams and the sound of clashing steel. The burly boatman took the vessel upstream. The tide was hindering them. On their right Baynard

Castle loomed, a dark shoulder of stone.

John felt utterly wretched. He knew what he had taken on. Kirkby had not thrown away his hundred pounds. Slumped in the heaving boat were the two squires, Shakell and Hawley. These two young warriors had been the talk of the city. They had refused to hand over a Spanish hostage to Gaunt and had stubbornly defended their right to hold him as a trophy of battle and ransom him themselves. Gaunt, who intended to use the hostage to further his claim on the Castilian throne, had reacted with fury. Seizing the squires he had incarcerated them in the Tower. John knew how wicked the duke's anger would be when he discovered his prize birds had flown the nest.

More than ever John longed to be rid of the burden of the two death warrants, but the boat made slow progress. It was agonisingly tedious. Water pushed hard against the planking. The rower swore. The gardens of the bishops' houses along the Strand drifted by one after the other: Exeter's, Bath's, Worcester's and Llandaff's. It took an age to pass them. Then came the Savoy itself. Unconsciously John held his breath as its towers and walls came into view. He could almost feel the white-hot ire of Lancaster emanating from the great complex. Yet there was no alarm. All seemed tranquil and lost in sleep.

More gardens appeared and vanished. Then it was the Hospital of St Mary of Rouncevalles. Westminster was close now; very close. The night was passing. The occupants of the rowing boat were silent, except for the cursing boatman. He alone produced a torrid conversation of oaths as he pulled on the oars.

Beyond the hospital and before the town house of the Archbishop of York, a jetty jutted into the river. They made for it and pulled alongside the stairway. John and his dangerous cargo tumbled out of the boat and up the steps. All were wet, tense and frightened. They began running. The dark towers of Westminster were clearly visible. All subterfuge evaporated. A kind of nervous energy propelled them forward. Harder and harder they ran. Their boots pounded. The blood throbbed in their temples. Ahead was the iron ring of the great door. Within lay sanctuary. Hoods flew back. Stitches caught at their sides but there was no respite.

In the Palace of the Savoy torches were blazing. Horsemen

milled about the colonnaded courtyard, snorting and stamping their feet. Armed retainers ran to and fro in confusion.

Gaunt had been disturbed from sleep by his commander of the Tower and had listened to the tale of escape with mounting fury. Hugh le Breton appeared. Gaunt conferred with him in gabbled French.

At last, the duke turned to his liveried retainers. 'Yes, yes. They have escaped, but not for long. I want them back and I want them now. Like mice they will have scurried to sanctuary. But by Our Lady I want them seized and taken. Yes – taken. Even if it's from before the altar itself. I shall not be mocked!' His guard commander bowed and hurried out.

The precincts of the Abbey of Westminster were in darkness. The complex of buildings on the Island of Thorney seemed a pool of tranquillity in a night beset with danger and alarms.

The three conspirators entered the precincts by way of the Dean's Yard. To John it seemed an eternity since the cobbles had echoed to the joyful cries of the king's coronation. It disturbed him to think how his present visit was more akin to the dark funeral column which had carried Edward III to this very spot. Now it was night which draped the stones in its own black crepe. Death felt very present. John could almost feel it in the deep shadows and the dark corners.

Despite the early hour – it was not yet dawn – hooded brothers were already going to lauds in the church. In silent groups they threaded their way from their dormitories. This sign of life gave John hope. The very presence of men engaged in worship seemed an antidote to the poison of the silent, mocking darkness of his private fears.

As John, Hawley and Shakell crossed the court, no word was exchanged. The two squires kept their own company. It was John who was the outsider, the intruder. The risking of his own life had not bought their trust. Their confidence was less easily purchased than that of the city watch.

They were challenged by a leather-jerkined porter, whom they ignored. Sanctuary was too close now. It was not to be jeopardised by delay. Explanations could wait. Cowelled heads turned in surprise, heads craned to take in the nocturnal visitors. The porter, puffing and wheezing, was running over the cobbles.

John felt the cold ring of the door knocker. The rough oak beneath exuded strength and certainty. He pushed at the door. Inside candles were burning. The beeswax was fragrant.

'I am Prior Richard. What mean you to come at this hour to this place?'

The voice was stentorian and brimming with authority. A gaggle of monks drew back. They too recognised both voice and authority. The muttered speculations concerning the identity of the intruders ceased.

John pulled his hood askew across his face. Bales of Mentmore crepe had been officiously checked over by this very monk. Would he recognise the man who had ridden down with it so jauntily with his new wife? John's apprehension rose like moths in flight. He almost choked on his fear. Swallowing hard, he half turned.

'Now, man, now!' Prior Richard was not used to delay. 'Answer! Pull down your hood. Pull it down and identify yourself.'

'These men seek Nicholas Litlyngton,' John said. 'And God strike down any who stand between them and life.' His voice was thick and gruff. His attempt to disguise it almost smothered his words.

His use of the abbot's Christian name and his call for divine judgement shocked and stilled his listeners. There was an audible intake of breath around him.

The prior made as if to speak. At that moment the agitated squires exchanged some muttered words then elbowed the prior aside and pushed into the church. Dignity affronted, the cleric hooted with annoyance. He sprang forward to follow the two men and some of the monks made as if to seize John. They did not have time. Mounted men clattered into the yard and the porter turned to confront them. They rode him down.

Chapter Eight

The room was cold, in spite of the brazier. Windows, glazed with oiled linen, were tightly shuttered against the night. Despite these elementary precautions the draughts wormed their way between the planking of the wall. The tallow candles were crowned with softly fluttering flames. Beyond their dancing light the winter shadows hung like threatening cobwebs from the beams of dark, smoke-grimed oak. Outside a rising wind blew gusts of wet snow against the hall.

It was Holy Innocents' Day, 28 December 1378. A wet, chill November had succumbed to the hoar breath of December. Days of cold had preceded Christmas with aching monotony. Ice had frozen thick on ponds and fish stews, water jugs and chamber pots. Each morning, dark and illuminated only by the stars, had been lace-frosted with cold. In hall and hut the log fires could not keep pace with the falling temperature. Out in the fields even the ploughing had fallen foul of the severity of the frost. Cursing villeins and freemen alike turned their chapped thoughts to hauling in more timber for the fires and clearing dead wood from the manorial orchard. Those fortunate enough to have cattle surviving the autumn slaughter took crumbs of comfort from the animal heat conserved in stinking stalls. Here and there a swineherd still drove his squealing pigs out to the edges of Wychwood forest in search of fern roots. Soon even this became impossible, with iron-hard ground.

Even the Christmas festivities were muted. The cold seemed to have slowed down men's hopes as well as their bodies. The capering Jack in the Green – the fool of celebrations in hall and village – called to mind the desperate desire for the return of spring and all things green. Holly and ivy, hung in wreaths, pointed to an unspoken hope that life and fertility would once again make the earth fecund and banish death.

Then, on St John's day, the temperature had risen. Villagers and woodsmen sniffed the air and nodded. Snow was coming.

Giles de Brewoster pulled a cloak more tightly around his muscular frame. He was not a big man. The giant folds of the Lincoln Scarlet cloak closed about him like some great and flabby hand. A gnawing ache of arthritis ate away at the base of his spine. The pain had increased of late and it made his temper brittle.

Across the room Edmund threw another log into the brazier. The solar was full of smoke but no one seemed to notice or mind. Like his uncle he was closely wrapped. Even the coming of the snow had not brought sufficient comfort for a cold world. Edmund, like Giles, was sprawled on a patched floor cushion beside a stiff backed, roughly carved chair.

In front of the chair John Mentmore was pacing up and down. Unlike his brother and uncle he was not cloaked. That particular piece of clothing had been carelessly flung on to a pewter-laden trunk. Other things than the cold were clearly occupying his mind. The usual cheek chewing signalled that it was not a source of contentment.

'Go on.' The voice was that of Giles. It was tinged with the world-weariness of one who has witnessed a multitude of madcap ventures and will not be shocked by the retelling of another.

John frowned, as if recalling a long-buried secret. He shook his head.

'I take it you've not forgotten the finale, brother,' said Edmund teasingly. He was enjoying the tale and ignored the scowl which his joke produced.

'It's not a laughing matter, Edmund.' Giles was animated now. 'God's blood but it's not! By Our Lady, I cannot believe Thomas let himself be talked into such a crazed scheme. That whoreson Kirkby should be pilloried for ever dreaming of such madness.'

'It was not only Thomas!' John had no great love for Kirkby but Giles's rebuke stung. Anyway, he felt Kirkby was well on his way to paying heavily for his part in the escapade. And paying in a coin not of his own choosing!

'Quite.' Edmund laughed. 'It was not only Thomas, nor that fool Kirkby. Tell us how *your* part in it ended, John.'

'I told you how Gaunt's men surprised us at the Abbey?' Giles and Edmund nodded. 'Well, their arrival caused an uproar. Shakell and Hawley were in the church. In the Dean's Court it was chaos. The soldiers were shouting. The horses were slipping on the cobbles. The monks were running about like headless chickens.

'It was that which saved me. The chaos, I mean. The monks lost interest in me and I ran for it. The prior, too, forgot me and vanished into the church. That much he and the squires held in common. They thought they'd find sanctuary before the altar. But they were wrong . . .'

'What do you mean?' Giles knew the laws on sanctuary, but he guessed what was coming next.

'Oh, Gaunt has no fear of God or His church. His soldiers burst right in. They went in like a stoat after a coney. By St John, two actually rode in. I saw the sparks from their hooves on the stone.'

'The whoresons never rode into the church? God's blood, John, but not even Gaunt would be such a fool.'

Giles cast a disapproving glance at his nephew and heir but forbore to check his attack on the king's uncle and the brother of Giles's liege lord.

'Gaunt is no fool, Edmund. He simply plays to a different set of rules to other mortal men.'

'Not a fool? You should have seen him at St Malo, John. Had he put more effort into penetrating the town and less into penetrating Swinford we'd have had a victory.'

'Enough, Edmund,' Giles broke in. 'Go on, John. Tell us the worst.'

'Well, it's the worst you'll hear too. They rode down the monks and seized Shakell and Hawley before the high altar itself. They killed Hawley in the struggle and dragged the other down the nave. By now, you understand, Litlyngton had stopped the mass.' His gallows humour failed to raise a smile.

Edmund was amazed. 'Let me get this right,' he said. 'These bastards rode into the church. They killed a man in sanctuary and dragged the other back to Gaunt? All for a Castilian hostage? By Our Lady, has he no fear for his soul?'

Edmund was rarely so serious. He scratched at his bobbed yellow hair in disbelief.

'That sums it up, Edmund,' John replied wearily. He stopped pacing and sat down on the chest. The pewter jangled. 'But there's more. The Bishop of London excommunicated the men who violated sanctuary. Gaunt retorted by saying that he would seize the bishop.'

'And did he?' Giles was pale.

'No. At that, at least, he baulked. And a wise move too. The city was up in arms. At West Chepe they threw filth from the common sewer on to the pillar carrying his arms displayed. Gaunt's men have taken to wearing no livery again. Even the Duke of Lancaster cannot find pleasure in such hatred. He did not grab the bishop but, by God, it was a close thing.'

'And what of Kirkby?'

'That's the irony, Edmund. He was nowhere near any of this and yet he's in trouble up to his neck. He was surprised on Thames Street by a party going back to Baynard Castle. Genoese they were, carrying a royal seal to be about business and be out after curfew.' John paused. 'It's strange, you know. It makes me feel that it was fated. Kirkby was such a gambler. He could start a game and make it his. God knows he would take more risks than father or me, and yet he'd stopped seeing them as risks. He knew the game so well he thought he was familiar with every twist. He was so sure it was almost as if he played with loaded dice.

'But that's just it, isn't it? No matter how you throw the dice, no matter how many times you do it and anticipate it correctly, it never eliminates chance. Does it?'

He stared at Edmund, who seemed a little bemused at John's ponderings. And then a troubling thought crossed John's mind. Within an ordered universe was there room for a concept like chance? Rather, was Kirkby's downfall a product of the hand of God? John too had been closely bound up with Kirkby's stratagems. Could the hand of divine providence be working against him also?

Giles leaned forward. 'What happened to Kirkby?'

'He'd been in a dispute with one of these Genoese before. Word had it they were here on Gaunt's behalf. They aimed to persuade the king to ship more of his wardrobe's goods out of Southampton. The Genoese galleys have been encouraged there, and the men of Southampton obviously like the idea. It appeals to Gaunt for a simple reason: it would hurt the Londoners. And Gaunt hates them. Well, you can guess how such a scheme was received amongst the trading guilds.'

'Like a leper in a brothel?' Edmund suggested helpfully.

'Quite – not that we have lepers any more. A new ordinance . . .' John grinned at his own habit of getting off the point at times. 'Anyway, Kirkby got into a terrible argument with these men. Murder was almost done. But that had to wait . . . As luck – or providence – would have it, these passing Genoese recognised Kirkby, even in the dark. They outnumbered him, of course. He only had one servant with him. I'm sure that he'd have let it go this time but they were out for trouble. Accounts are confused. Some say the Genoese pulled knives, others that Kirkby stuck one of them. How anyone knows is beyond me, but you know how it is. Who needs evidence in London? The long and the short of it is that a Genoese was killed and so was Kirkby's servant. Kirkby himself made off. He's vanished. Probably left London.'

There was silence in the room. The shocking turn of events had gripped the imaginations of the listeners. Like John they were amazed at such a bitter – and bloody – coincidence. Out in the hall the rough games of Giles's household could plainly be heard. It was a drab night and the retainers craved diversion.

'So Kirkby is sought for murder.' Edmund's voice was low.

'No. For treason.'

'Treason? What makes it treason?'

John smiled a thin smile. 'They carried a royal seal, did they not? They were aliens travelling under royal protection. Richard had given them ambassadorial status. That was Gaunt's doing.'

'So, if Kirkby is taken?'

'He'll be hanged, drawn and mutilated.'

'Sweet Mary, what a bitter potion to swallow! And all on the night when Gaunt had ridden roughshod over his carefully laid plans.'

'And mine, Edmund. I too had made plans.' John's voice trailed off.

'Aye, John, and over yours too, by God.' Edmund's voice was surprisingly soft. There was real concern written in his eyes.

'So you can see why I left London. Father had meant to go with the city delegation to the autumn parliament in Gloucester.

Both sides in the victualling dispute had planned to send men to petition the king.'

'What dispute, John?' Giles asked.

'The fishmongers are fighting to hold on to their monopoly. The fight is not new. Father first made his play just before my wedding. Now, though, he's more determined. Opposing Horne and the fishmongers is popular with the lesser guilds. It wins friends cheaply. After all, what can Horne do about it? It was my idea to declare openly for John of Northampton. It wasn't new but it has raised the profile of our position. The yeoman guilds like that. It's all a game really.'

'Kirkby played games, didn't he?' Giles added sombrely.

John shrugged. 'Anyway, I left the city with the delegation. There was nothing strange about that. What with the fire and the tapestry makers breathing murder, it was no surprise that father remained. And the rest you know. Father wrote to me in Gloucester. Told me Gaunt was still baying for blood, told me Kirkby had fled. It seemed best to stay away for a while. Keep quiet; keep low. To any who asks, father tells them I'm making contacts in the Cotswolds and Christmassing at Giles's manor. All very innocent, don't you think?'

Edmund laughed. 'Big brother, you really do get into some scrapes, don't you? I thought I was supposed to be the hell raiser! With William coming here for Twelfth Night, it will be a real family reunion.'

Later, as the household retired, John had time to ponder anew on the tale of woe with which he had regaled his brother and uncle. He was not happy with the twists of fate. Whilst he had escaped without injury, the sheer risk appalled him. He knew that he had sailed very close to the wind.

Giles, Edmund and John shared a common sleeping room. Bedded down on mattresses of flock, it made the separate chambers in Thomas Mentmore's house seem the height of luxury. Apart from two chamber pots, the bed pallets were the only furniture. Before they slept they were joined by Stephen de Knolton, Edmund's squire, who slept by the door. Giles's personal servants bedded down in the solar. The rest of the household slept on the soiled rushes of the hall.

John was almost asleep when Edmund rolled towards him. 'What happened at Gloucester?'

John yawned. 'What?'

'At Gloucester. Did you win or did the fishmongers?'

John muttered an oath. Why on earth did Edmund want to know such trivia at this time of night? It was almost nine o'clock.

'We did. They've lost their monopoly in selling fish.'

Edmund grunted and the two brothers settled back to sleep. Soon the chamber echoed to the rise and fall of Giles's snores. Outside the wind shrieked about the hall.

In the morning a white dawn revealed a snow-crusted creation and it snowed steadily throughout the day. The servants and their masters were confined to the hall. It was a cramped existence, without private moments. Yet everything in their upbringing had pointed them this way. They were not private people, because they could not be so. At all points – sleeping, thinking, praying, eating, love making – their lives touched upon those of others. In hall or solar there was no privacy. In hut and farmstead it was an unknown phenomenon. There, animals and men jostled for room and thanked God for the moments of warmth on a winter night.

By the Feast of the Circumcision of Our Lord, four days later, the snow had stopped. A steady frost held it. The world was newborn in virgin splendour. John paused in the yard and surveyed Giles's manor. It was an impressive establishment. Surrounded by an earth wall and palisade was an assortment of buildings: dovecot, barns, hen houses, stables, bakehouse. In the centre lay the hall itself. An impressive stone building, it was largely the work of Giles's grandfather, Edward de Upton. Its ground floor was a stone storehouse. On the first floor was a wooden-built hall and chambers. This was thatched. Wooden steps led up to the living quarters.

Edward de Upton had lived in dangerous times. As a young squire of eighteen in 1264 he had fought with Henry III at Lewes and barely escaped the battle with his life. His experiences had coloured his outlook. When he had rebuilt his manor he had done so with defence in mind.

Outside the palisade a great ditch bounded a quarter of the perimeter. It had never been completed. Work had halted with the death of Simon de Montfort at Evesham in 1265. An end to civil war had caused the abandonment of such efforts. Now it was backfilled in places and rank with nettles thriving on human sewage.

Beyond the palisade lay the orchard and a mill. About that were the jumbled cottages and byres of the village of Upton itself. Giles held many manors, including Knolton and Woodlands, but Upton was his 'caput', his 'head manor'. Here he had his greatest concentration of demesne land and his place of personal residence.

John breathed in the cold air and felt it burn in his lungs. It was on Giles's manors that he intended to hang his new Mentmore empire. They would provide the bases for his expansion. Even as he stood – and stamped his feet in the frost-crisp snow – he could hear the soft bleating of the breeding ewes, happily cooped up in the byres with precious meadow hay. On Giles's manors and on those sheep he was pinning his hopes.

Strangely enough he was not thinking of cloth this morning. Rather he was thinking of Philippa. He had scarcely spoken to her since the argument outside the cloth shed. The disaster at Westminster had propelled him from the city in some haste.

Now he thought of her. A serving girl was carrying eggs across the yard. She was young: perhaps sixteen years old. Her cheeks were rosy, if grimy. She walked with exaggerated care because of the snow. Her hair, though greasy, was white-gold fair. She caught John's eye but did not blush. There was a knowingness in her smile. John swallowed. He felt his need, hard and undeniable. He had not slept with his wife for over three months. The muscles knotted in his neck.

He wondered if Edmund had had her. His brother was renowned for his amorous adventures. His fame was due to chivalric courting of wealthy ladies. John knew, though, that his brother was sure to have taken a tumble with the serving girls in Upton. There was at least one bastard son in the village beyond the palisade.

Whilst in Gloucester John had not visited the whores in the city stews. He was not sure why. No one else had shown such restraint. Before his marriage he had bedded more than one whore in Southwark. What was different now?

Marriage was simply a convenience. A matter of policy for guildsman, as for nobleman. Virginity and marital faithfulness were the prerequisites of bride and wife, not of groom and husband. John was quite at a loss to explain his abstinence. More than one night in Gloucester he had lain awake burning, and yet he had not satisfied his natural desire.

Now this sixteen-year-old was before him. She lowered her eyes meekly. Then she raised them.

'Would ee loik to choose thee oiwn egge, marster?' she drawled. 'Oive enough layers amarngst the hens, zur. Would ee care to choose thee own?'

She did not wait for a reply. Instead she retraced her steps to the barn. John followed her.

Inside the barn it was twilight. The girl was in one corner. She stooped to pile up hay then lay on it. She raised herself on her elbows and smiled at John. With one hand she pulled up her coarse, undyed woollen robe.

John moved towards her and crouched beside her. He caressed her naked thigh and pushed his fingers against the rough wool. She wore nothing beneath her robe. He caressed the silk-smooth skin on the inside of her thighs. Urgently he fumbled and groped between her legs. She giggled. Then she moaned with pleasure as his fingers got to work. Few men took time with a woman. For her this was a new sensation. She was used to rough partings of her legs, penetration and a hard, desperate male ride to climax. This was new. She liked it.

John had confidence now. Philippa had never shown such eagerness. This girl wanted it as much as he did.

She reached for him and pulled him down. Their mouths met in throbbing, tongue-probing passion.

He was on top of her. Her legs were open. He thrust between them. With experienced hands she grappled with his chausses. She could feel his masculine force hard against her. She wanted it.

Then something absurd happened. She pulled open her gown and revealed her breasts, nipples erect. She guided John's searching tongue to them. John gazed at her nakedness. By some strange chance her breasts were clean. Virgin white. They looked like Philippa's breasts.

Suddenly he saw Philippa on their wedding night. He saw Philippa crying outside the cloth shed. He saw Kirkby's sardonic smile at his wife's distress. Swearing obscenely, John pulled himself away from the girl. He staggered to his feet. His passion and confusion blinded him. He reeled towards the door.

Back on the hay the panting servant sat up. Her hair fell in golden folds over her breasts. She wore a look not only of intense disappointment but also of utter astonishment.

The next few days were an agony for John. The close confinement of the hall in winter meant it was impossible to avoid the Saxon-headed servant girl. She looked at him with the knowing eyes of an old whore. Now, however, those old eyes in the child's nubile body did not arouse John's desire. Rather he read contempt in the glances she gave him. He was also acutely aware of the other household servants. How many of them had she regaled with the tale of the incapable young master? His pride stung to think of such crude joking in the hall when Giles and his family retired. Despite his humiliation there was no escape. The daily round of dinner, seasonal mummery, conversation and light supper rolled on towards Twelfth Night. Outside, the snow held firm.

Three days before the Feast of Epiphany, the January weather changed. The first herald was a breeze rising from the southwest. It was a damp wind bringing warmer air and rain. The coming of the rain transformed the frozen stillness into a melting morass of mud and slush. Below the manor house the sluggish waters of the Knee Brook – a tributary of the river Stour – were fed on the meltwater. Soon the mill was flooded. The village across the stream, on lower land, was reduced to a dark lake. The cruck-built village houses, with their walls of wattle and daub, stood like islands in a dirty sea. What had once been a cold white misery was utterly transformed into a wet dark one. Cattle and pigs stood hock deep in their byres. Villagers cursed and splashed their way through the chaos.

On Epiphany Eve William arrived. He was in an ill humour when Giles, Edmund and John went to meet him. The road from Oxford was a river of mud and William and his mount were painted with the oozing clay. With one filthy hand he sought to disentangle his grimy beard.

'Mother of God!' he exclaimed bitterly. 'The road has been a nightmare. From Woodstock to Chipping Norton it was bad enough but nigh on Moreton it was hell itself!' He ran his fingers through his mouse-coloured hair. 'What say the folk hereabouts of Moreton, uncle?'

Giles laughed. His scarred face was creased. 'Why Will, 'tis commonly called Moreton-in-the-Marsh.'

'By God,' William spluttered, ''tis not misnamed. Moreton-in-the-lake would be better though. Aye, much better. And to cap it all, I'd turned north on to the Fosse Way when my horse stumbled; pitched me into it.'

It was rare for William to swear. He did not go in for the popular oaths and curses of his generation. His excitement generally had a more boyish, perhaps bookish charm. John watched his brother with real surprise. Edmund was grinning broadly. Household servants, ankle deep in mud, stopped to gawp at the strange apparition, oozing filth until Giles ended his cleric nephew's misery. Gingerly taking him by the arm he led him away to the hall to change and wash.

A clean cloth was laid over the soiled rushes in the solar. On it William stood, as naked as on his entry into the world. Two servant girls were lathering him and splashing him with tepid water from iron-bound wooden buckets. Had Giles had a wife, she would have done William this honour. The soft soap – wood ash, mutton-fat and caustic soda – lifted the worst of the grime and soon William was shining before the brazier. About his neck and back red flea bites stood out against his pale body. He was so slight he could almost have been in his teens. He scarcely looked twenty, let alone twenty-four.

'Now, Will. What's new in Oxford?' Edmund was keen to hear. Months spent in Dorset and on Giles's head manor had starved him of diversions. Only the ready availability of village girls had served to satisfy some of his restless desires.

'There's plague, for a start.' Will pulled a sour face.

'Again? Surely the pestilence burnt itself out last summer in the city.' John shuddered to think of the deadly corruption of the air hanging over the city as a foetid, noxious miasma.

Will shrugged. 'A learned doctor of medicine at Queen's College is of the belief that this new corruption of the air is from a marrying of the movements of the stars with the strange vagaries of the weather these past months. Such changes and turbulences of the air have made the elements noxious once more.'

Giles crossed himself. 'It was so in your grandfather's time. Just so. Then they say that tempests rained down all manner of venomous beasts hard by Greater India and Cathay. This curse was followed by the falling of sheets of fire which burnt up men and animals and crops.' The grizzled old knight shuddered at the thought of the divine fury behind such horrors. 'By these tempests whole provinces were infected with poisonous vapours and winds from the sea blew the vapour across the world. I was but twenty-eight when its poison reached this realm. Your grandfather, Henry Mentmore, later died from it and Elizabeth his wife. So did your father's elder brother. He was but one year older than myself.'

Silence settled on the room. Despite the virulence of the pestilence, men and women had come to terms with the cataclysm of 1348 and 1349. The survivors had learned to live with it, had, by some communal effort of will, accepted it and ceased to dwell on it. It was now rare to hear conversation centred on it. And yet, beneath the calm of coming to terms with this horrendous reality, a gnawing curiosity could not be denied.

'I heard it was a war 'twixt sea and sun did cause it,' Edmund ventured. 'The waters of the ocean being drawn up as vapours did slay fish beyond count. Such vapours could not fall as healthy rain but drifted off as a killing mist.'

Will snorted. 'I've seen plenty of fish killed and burnt at Billingsgate. God rot the fishmongers but I've never known them, or it, to kill an entire city.'

'Or to return. To return again and again.' John's haunted comment halted Edmund's angry response to Will's rebuff. 'Was it not the pestilence which killed our mother in the year of grace thirteen sixty-one? Did it not also slay Philippa's mother that same year? That year, they say, it killed mostly children – '

'That is true,' Giles interrupted. 'So true that some call that time the plague of children.'

John was talking softly. He seemed not to have heard, or registered, Giles's information. 'So why does it return? Should not such a vapour disperse? Should not fresh winds scatter it and weaken it?'

'Mayhap so, John.' Will was looking at his businessman brother with a new respect. He had rarely heard John so philosophical.

'Mayhap that is why it comes and goes. It is not as strong as it was. The poison lessens, grows dilute.'

John nodded. 'Could it not, though, reside in a man's breath? Be passed, breath to breath, from the dying to the living? I've heard it said that as a man dies his last glance may pass the poison to a neighbour.'

John shuddered. The room was cold. William pulled his cloak over his nakedness. The serving girls left, splashing dirty suds on to the sour rushes.

'Some say it can be seen – a plague maiden. She waves a yellow rag through open windows and poisons those inside. Mayhap if a man should cut that arm off – could sever it – he might save his fellows . . .'

'And kill himself!' Edmund had grown tired of this morbid intellectual search for answers. 'I'm going for more wine!'

John laughed. The spell was broken. Edmund was right, of course. What did it matter anyway? Providence would not be mocked. What good could come from such idle speculation? Life belonged to the living. Mankind had stared into the face of death but found it more bearable to turn to more basic things – to life!

And Twelfth Night was for the living. A wild exuberant celebration, it ended the season of Christmas with anarchic splendour. The Twelfth Night dinner was a raucous affair. Outside the mid-morning was dominated by a thin drizzle, inside the Lords of Misrule held sway.

Giles's household cook and mainstay was a redoubtable north country woman whom all called, reverently, Mistress Holland. Fiery she could be, but she knew her job and ran the household with a firm and practised hand. Woe betide the starry-eyed maidservant who mooned lovestruck about Mistress Holland's kitchen. Those blue eyes would flash and reduce the girl to tremulous confusion.

Despite this, despite the almost universal caution in crossing her, Giles held her in deep respect. He knew her for what she was, a proud and professional servant who loved her duties and who performed her work with skill and efficiency. Between the two of them was a curious bond of affection. John had come to realise that only the inefficient and the wavering need fear Mistress Holland. Beneath a defensive exterior lay a sensitive heart. To the resolute and hardworking she was equal – and more than that: friend. John marvelled at the frankness in the conversations between Giles and this servant. Mistress Holland served but was never servile!

Giles's plank-walled thatched hall did not have a dais. The

head table was on the same level as the side trestles, and to this head table Mistress Holland brought two great plum puddings. The dark masses steamed and the hall cheered. Carefully skirting the blazing central fire, she laid the wooden platter before Giles. She wiped her hands on her kilted, homespun brown robe and looked Giles full in the face. Her blue eyes sparkled. The hall fell silent. Two dogs snarled over a bone in the rushes. No one spoke.

Giles's chaplain, Godfrey de Avalon, rose to his feet. A long-faced Franciscan, he had little taste for what was to follow and his lack of enthusiasm was evident. Deepset black eyes were flat, like dark, dead, moorland peat-pools. His discomfort was obvious. Someone far down the trestle tables giggled. That it was a woman did nothing to minimise its impact on this celibate mendicant. He flushed to his tonsure. With a rapidity of speech, indicative of disdain, he blessed the puddings. Everyone roared and cheered.

Then Mistress Holland began the ceremony: starting at the top table, one pudding was carved up for men; the other was divided between the women.

John was sitting between Edith, wife of Giles's bailiff Wyloc, and Ellen his daughter. The women began to search through their pudding, possessed by an insatiable curiosity.

Ellen turned to John in disappointment. 'It's not in mine.' She was only ten and was genuinely distressed.

''Twas not in mine either,' John consoled her. 'Next year, perhaps.' The girl nodded stoically.

From down the hall came cries of triumph. One of the herdsmen had found a dried bean in his pudding. Soon a shriller cry heralded the discovery of a dried pea.

The hall dissolved into chaos. Whooping wildly, 'King Bean' and 'Queen Marrowfat' were carried shoulder high up the hall. It gave John no pleasure to learn the identity of the king's consort. The golden-haired servant girl was coming in triumph to the top table.

Giles graciously gave up his seat. His chaplain gave up his, with less approval. Soon the two monarchs – the Lord and Lady of Misrule – were installed. Their 'courtiers' paid them mock homage. Bowing and curtseying, the servants and the Lord of the Manor himself brought wine and meat to the rulers of the day.

The Lady of Misrule seemed to gain an inordinate amount of pleasure in ordering John Mentmore to wash her feet. He was both humiliated and outraged but was powerless to oppose tradition. An earthenware basin and jug were produced, and a pair of chausses were tossed to him as a towel. What now was the owner wearing? John did not have time to speculate as he attended to his humble task.

With red-faced haste he washed the shapely if grimy feet. To popular applause, the queen ruffled his hair. Ribald comments turned the air blue. With provocative calm she brazenly lifted her skirt over her knees and looked at John with the eyes of one finally vindicated. John thought of his wife and wished himself home.

He was saved from his predicament by an altercation between Will and Giles's chaplain. The two of them had fled the chaos of the top table and, along with Giles and Edmund, were now occupying a wide, shuttered window seat. The argument was taking place in anglicised French. That much at least had been conceded to propriety.

As John approached the group he deduced that the disagreement seemed to be centring on William's opinion of friars. He caught a rather heated retort from William.

'Is it, then, small wonder that the country people call the cuckoo pint the "Friar's Billycock"? Such is the moral grandeur of the mendicant orders.' Godfrey flushed with fury but could not halt William's criticism.

'Perhaps alone of the orders of monks, the Carthusians still stand by the love of poverty. All else have sold out to the pleasures of the flesh and the love of worldly praise.'

'By God, sir, you do walk with little fear for your soul. You speak of those dedicated to the highest calling – the religious life. How dare you heap calumny and old wives' tittle-tattle on the celibate sons of God? Our Holy Father himself honours the friars as poor brothers of our Lord.'

William laughed. It was a hard and contemptuous sound. 'Poor brothers of our Lord? A friar could wheedle out the widow's last mite! Our Lord tells of a man who found a pearl of great price. Desiring it, he sold all he had, returned and bought it. I tell you, had a friar been present the pearl would have been gone ere our honest man returned to buy it.'

'By Our Lady, sir, mind your impious tongue...'

'And speaking of the Holy Father: which had you in mind?'

Godfrey blanched. He opened his mouth, then snapped it shut. William's jibe had struck home. Only the previous September, western Christendom had been shocked by a schism in the very core of Mother Church. The death of Pope Gregory XI had led to an escalating crisis. A murderous Italian mob had insisted on the election of the Italian Archbishop of Bari to the Holy See as Urban VI. In reaction to this new pope's moral failures, all but three cardinals had retired to Anagni. Here they had elected a Frenchman – Robert of Geneva – as a rival pope, Clement VII. By Christmas western Christendom had two popes: Urban in Rome and Clement in Avignon.

Edmund, ever the fisher in troubled waters, added, 'And now I hear that the Frenchman has gained the support of France, Scotland and Castile; whilst England, Flanders and most of Italy adhere to Urban. Decisions accompanied by much prayer and fasting, I am sure.'

'Edmund!' Giles growled in defence of his bristling chaplain. But it was too late to stop William, who scented blood.

'Perhaps, Father Godfrey, you could tell me: is it true that Bartholomew did assault the Bishop of Limoges? I hear also that he shouted down the Cardinal of Milan whilst in the middle of a service. Can this be true?'

Godfrey took immediate offence at William's reference to Urban's pre-election name. He snapped: 'You jest at Holy Church as if you were no better than a Jew or a Saracen. Is this what Wyclif teaches you in Oxford? To mock God's church?'

At that moment a staggering group of dancers spilled against them. John dodged the wildly moving crowd. When the revellers returned to the centre of the hall, William was ready with his answer.

'John Wyclif holds that morality is the mark of God's election. True lordship can only be exercised by righteous men; by those who are not merely "hearers of the word" but "doers of the word". Should priest, cardinal or pope fall down on such a sacred trust, he should be deposed by the civil power. That is what Wyclif teaches.'

This was radical. Godfrey sneered. Giles, whose doctrinal

conservatism was rooted in the opinions of his chaplain, looked astonished at William's claims. Surely this laid an axe to the very root of the tree of faith?

William was quite unrepentant. 'It is holiness that Wyclif preaches.'

'And is it also true your Wyclif claims a common priesthood for fathers of the church *and* for ignorant cow-herds? Does he not also justify the withholding of this realm's holy offering to the See of St Peter? Are these things not true?'

'Aye they are true . . .'

'And so Gaunt uses him to beat the church, to attack those bishops who would oppose his tyranny. A worldly prince defends your worldly clerk!'

This time Giles frowned at his chaplain. It would not do. Godfrey's line of attack opened up the complex undercurrents of loyalty which swept through de Brewoster and the Mentmores. On one hand William was the partisan of Gaunt because he was the protector of Wyclif. On the other hand Giles was fiercely loyal to Woodstock and Gaunt, but drank distrust of Wyclif's 'heresies' at the fountain of Godfrey de Avalon.

Between the two extremes lay John and Edmund. Edmund possessed a professional contempt for Gaunt and lack of interest in Wyclif's theology. All that mattered to Edmund was that Wyclif criticised the more worldly and hypocritical aspects of ecclesiastical life. John had a pragmatic attitude to Gaunt but also feared him. Alone in the group, he was fascinated by the possibilities being outlined by Will. As a true son of the church he was shocked by, but also attracted to, Wyclif's reasoning. And yet he had his own peculiar doubts about his words.

Like the rest of his generation John was profoundly moulded by the faith of the church. Its fasts and feasts were the barometers of his life. Its pageantry and beliefs were the sole touchstones in a wild world. He could not conceive of existence apart from the reality of the Christian gospel. Yet he shared with so many of his fellows a cynical distrust of the earthly vessel which sought to hold and monopolise those sacred truths: the church and its priests and monks.

He was held in a terrible tension between a God he would never, could never, deny, and a church which claimed exclusive rights of access to God through its priesthood which was so often corrupt and morally bankrupt. In this awful tension he could spill from faith into anti-clericalism and back again. It was a painful and a frightening place to be. For the church he might so freely criticise claimed power to be able to shut him off eternally from the God he could not live without.

Godfrey de Avalon was confident now. 'Your Wyclif would also let churls and housemaids read the scriptures, if they could. Is that not so? Truly the man would turn the world upside down and give the kingdom to the base and ignorant.'

Giles could not read Latin and so Godfrey's Vulgate translation of the Bible was closed to him. Whilst a few literate laymen owned the Anglo-Norman translation, Giles was not one. Besides which, he was not a very literate man.

'God's blood, Will,' Giles said, 'your Wyclif plays with fire. The countryside is unsteady as it is: sturdy beggars walk the roads, hedge priests preach rebellion and heresy, villeins refuse boon work on the demesne land – and your Wyclif would let such be arbiters of God's word?'

John felt Giles was less concerned with theology than its consequences. He too felt a twinge of alarm.

''Tis worse still, my lord,' Godfrey said icily. 'Wyclif would even sanction the despoiling of God's house. Would he not, William Mentmore?'

William bit his lip. The bagpipes wailed. The dancers' feet thudded on the planks.

'Well?' Godfrey said.

William swallowed. ''Tis true that Wyclif appeared before the Gloucester parliament. He argued that Hawley and Shakell had no rights to sanctuary; that Gaunt committed no sin.'

'Yes, I heard him.' John's voice was low and brittle. He had almost choked as he recalled Wyclif playing Gaunt's part at Gloucester. He simply could not decide what he felt about that stiff-necked Yorkshire cleric. How could he ever excuse what he had said at Gloucester?

Will caught the look in John's eye and felt his throat go dry. Godfrey also saw it. He beamed to discover an unexpected ally.

'But surely, John, you can see Wyclif's point? In the case of Shakell and Hawley . . .'

'All I can see is that a man is now dead.' Despite the weather John felt hot. His eyes burnt with emotion, confusion and wood-smoke. The party at the window seat watched him go.

At the door of the hall, John turned. In one corner, away from the chaotic reels and carols, a group of grubby children was playing. He instantly recognised the game: hoodman blind. With a reversed hood covering his face a little boy was groping about. His companions squealed with glee as he caught one and tried to guess his squirming prisoner's identity.

John bit at his cheek. How like me, he thought. Adam Yonge; John of Gaunt; the weavers; Shakell and Hawley; Wyclif . . . I am but groping in the dark. I know not where I am going, nor whom I have found. I am the hoodman blind. And there was one more name that he added to that list of enigmas; that list of confusion and of doubt. He wondered what Philippa was doing now.

Outside, the late afternoon was darkening under a lead heavy sky. The cold drizzle fell like the tears of the lost.

PART THREE

A Game of Fox and Goose
1379-80

Chapter Nine

John remained at Giles de Brewoster's manor of Upton until the end of April 1379. By this time he had been there for five months and away from London for over six.

William stayed at the manor until February. His fear of the pestilence raging in Oxford was greater than his discomfort in the acerbic presence of Giles's Franciscan chaplain. At last the pedlars brought news that the disease was waning and on 28 February William rode back to the city and his studies.

The mild weather of Epiphany held. Soon the woods and common lands were carpeted with early snowdrops and the pastel shades of primrose flowers. Wild daffodils fluttered in the slight breeze like fragments of earthbound sunshine.

John did not let his forced exile turn into idleness. In the company of Edmund and Stephen de Knolton he visited Giles's outlying manors and sheep granges. As the weather grew drier, the three of them went hunting in the lime and oak woodlands of Wychwood forest to the south-east of Upton. Here they picked up news of the wider world from monks from Winchcombe, overseeing the Abbey assarts in the ancient woodland.

What John saw of Giles's manors and those of his neighbours convinced him of the rightness of his business plans. Throughout the rolling hills of the dip slope of the eastern Cotswolds, thousands of sheep were grazing. In the sheltered valleys the wood-framed fulling mills had sprung up to capitalise on the abundance of wool.

The lack of organisation amongst the textile workers encouraged John. Toiling on their upright looms, their wives and daughters spinning on the distaff, they were ripe for large-scale organisation. Already the local towns of Stroud and Cirencester were feeling the impact of this cheap, guild-free, cloth manufacturing. But John Mentmore had a greater vision. He saw Gloucester and Bristol, London and beyond. No, his exile was not a time of idleness.

On St George's day John visited the fair at Chipping Campden. He and Edmund returned to Upton late in the afternoon and were greeted by Stephen de Knolton. At first John had not warmed to the silent gangling youth with the languid chestnut eyes and straw thatch of hair. That had changed. He could not help but notice how devoted Stephen was to Edmund. All squires were required to be dutiful: waiting at table, learning etiquette, learning the art of knight and of lord. Nevertheless, Stephen seemed tireless in the service of his more ebullient master. Edmund, too, seemed very fond of his squire. The more John observed Stephen, the more he concluded that he was a conscientious and reliable young man. His affection for the boy grew.

In the solar, Giles was in rigorous conversation with a new arrival.

'Yes, my lord,' the man was saying, 'that is the latest I've heard. It was the talk of all the villages between London and Oxford.'

Giles paced up and down. His weatherbeaten face – scarred like old leather – was furrowed with a frown. 'You are saying that the villeins at Harmsworth refused to do service for their lord . . .'

'And opened the river sluices, my lord, to flood the meadow.'

'Soul of Mary! And you say that the jury acquitted these whoresons after this?'

'Aye, my lord. That was the talk in Wycombe where I watered my horse. They also say that the Chilterns are thick with runaway villeins and the roads are scarcely safe for – '

He broke off as John and Edmund entered the solar. John saw that his cheeks were a fine map of broken veins – a badge of years of hard riding. Giles turned. His concern vanished in a grin of welcome.

'We've news from Thomas, John.' He handed over a letter. The sealing wax, a blob of scarlet, was unbroken. John recognised the florid 'M' of the guild house of Mentmore, and the face of one of his father's riders.

John tore open the sealed message. Sitting on the box, with the pewter, he scanned the vellum sheet. As he did so, his face broke into a broad smile.

'Good news?' Giles suggested, with some certainty.

'Aye,' John replied. 'It seems my father's business here is completed now. He would have me return to London. He says that from his reading of opportunities in the city there's no reason why I should not return immediately. He has sent the courier to escort me home, since he fears the roads are not safe.'

'There is another thing,' Giles said slyly. He produced another letter. 'It seems to be to you, from yourself!'

John could not conceal his surprise. As he took it from his uncle he saw his own seal. Then he understood. He had left it in London in the possession of his wife. Nervously he broke open his own seal. Could the others read his lack of confidence? Then he was grinning.

Two days later John was on his way home. He was in a good mood. The spring sunshine was warm. Thrushes were singing in the woods.

His escort was taciturn and not inclined to talk. Still, John was not hampered by the lack of stimulating company. After six months in exile he was going home at last. No less important, he had a letter tucked inside his linen shirt. A letter from his wife.

Philippa paused for breath. She was now entering the eighth month of her pregnancy. At the start there had been nausea and loss of appetite; then there had been the easy middle period when the baby was light and the sickness gone; now she simply felt heavy and tired. She remembered travellers' tales of vast fish beached on the shore after a storm. When she lay down, she felt like such a fabulous creature.

At times she felt faint, and then she was especially grateful for the presence of Emma. The awkward but well-meaning girl had changed into a young woman with poise and perception. It was as if she had suddenly grown up. It was as if both she and her mistress had done so together. There was a peculiarly strong bond between them. It had been forged in conflict and isolation. Both mistress and servant had been uprooted together and then replanted in a strange place. Emma was Philippa's Stephen de Knolton.

As Philippa sat on the edge of her bed she pondered on the

months which had passed since she had last seen John. They had not been easy. Margaret had never fully recovered from the rebuff before the feast for John Philipot and now there was an icy gulf between the two women. There was no conflict. Emotion seemed to have been frozen and destroyed.

John's flight from London had not been easy either. It had surprised her how much she had missed her husband. After the argument outside the cloth store she had feared she had gone too far. For a while she had truly felt she might be beaten for her impertinence.

Then that concern had been swept away in some night-time adventure which John could not, or would not, speak of. Within days he had left. Philippa was no fool. The city was full of gossip about a murdered Genoese and the disappearance of Kirkby. It was also abrim with outrage at Gaunt's breach of sanctuary at Westminster. Whilst John refused to divulge any details, it was obvious to his wife that he was caught up in these terrible events in some way.

It was fear for him that had first signalled her feelings for him. Night after night she had lain awake dreading news of disaster. Then arose a real feeling of longing. It had come as some surprise to her to discover just how much she missed her husband. She doubted if he missed her.

Her chamber was cramped. As well as her marital bed it contained Emma's sleeping pallet and a chest of black poplar. On the chest lay a book. She smiled as she reached out and touched this extravagance. It was the *Book of the Knight of La Tour*, a gentle French guide to chivalry and female manners. It had cost her a pretty penny and she blushed to think of it. There were only two other books in the entire household. One was owned by Margaret. The other was Thomas's, an English copy of *The Travels of Sir John Mandeville*. Oft times, when the family took light supper in the solar, Thomas would summon his literate clerk to read to them. It opened vistas on to worlds both new and strange.

'Will the clerk read to us again tonight, my lady? I do like to hear of love and courtesy and of the manners of knights and ladies.' Emma was busy turning up plaits on either side of Philippa's face.

'Mayhap, unless my husband arrives home.' Philippa felt a

smile suffusing her face.

'Oh, I do hope so, Madam.'

Neither Philippa nor Emma could read. Whenever Philippa wrote, as in her letter to John, she dictated to one of Thomas's clerks. There were no secrets in her life! Even her tokens of love to John were carefully written in a man's hand. Lately she had summoned the clerk to read to her and Emma in the afternoon, or as they sewed in the solar. It had become a particular pleasure.

Their conversation was interrupted by Margaret. Both she and Thomas had tiny chambers opening off John and Philippa's room. She crossed the room to her chamber without a word. Returning with her outdoor pelisse, she would have recrossed the room in silence.

'That is a pretty colour pelisse, Margaret. Is it new?' Philippa made an effort to be civil.

Margaret reddened. 'No, sister, it is not.' She cast a withering glance at her 'extravagance' now open on the bed. Within the wide sweep of a capital 'C' a Wyvern cavorted with a phoenix. 'I make do with what I have. Since the fire I have not taken money from my father.'

She stalked out of the room like a cold winter wind. Philippa shuddered. Safely out of sight, behind her mistress, Emma poked her tongue at Margaret's retreating back.

'Returning to your question, Emma. Yes, the book will be read tonight. We shall hear of the proper manners to be expected *between* ladies!'

Emma giggled. She took the message plainly. 'Oh yes, mistress, it would be so lovely. I hope mistress Margaret will enjoy it too.'

However, Margaret, Philippa and Emma were not to be delighted that night by a reading from the *Book of the Knight of La Tour*. Hardly was mid-morning dinner cleared than John Mentmore arrived home.

It was a joyful reunion. Even Margaret thawed at the sight of her brother and Thomas embraced his son with hearty enthusiasm. He had missed his right-hand man.

Emma, who observed all with detachment, was particularly gratified by the reunion of her master and mistress. John kissed his wife's palms as a lover would and the servants giggled.

Philippa flushed, but it was joy not embarrassment which coloured her cheeks.

In the solar, John took a most unmasculine interest in his wife's pregnancy. He felt for the kicks and put his ear to the sweeping curve of her stomach. Emma was delighted. Margaret soon tired of this and left to attend to more gratifying duties, away from Philippa. Thomas beamed.

When at last they were in bed that evening, Philippa gently laid her arm across John's chest. She had listened with unfeigned enthusiasm to his tales of life on Giles's estate and now they were as alone as they would ever be. On her pallet by the door Emma was sleeping.

'Truly John, I did miss you,' Philippa whispered.

John half turned and kissed her on the velvet tip of her nose. 'And I you, my heart. I counted the days until my return. I rode my horse to a lather to get back.' He was thinking of the whores at Gloucester and the girl at Upton. Yes, they had promised passion. But this they had lacked – this clean wholesomeness. This sense of peace.

'John, I fear I bought a book . . .'

He laughed. 'I know! And Margaret is not best pleased.'

'Dear heart, I only bought it to learn to be a better wife. I – '

He silenced her with a kiss. 'Philippa, hush. I would not care if you had bought two books. I do not mind. We shall hear it read together.'

It was pitch dark. John could not see her tears, but he could feel them on his shoulder. 'I did miss you, husband.'

'And I missed you.' He kissed her again, firmly but tenderly.

May 1379 was the happiest month of Philippa and John's marriage. Together they took part in the 'Maying' pilgrimage to the heaths and commons beyond the city walls. Laughing and joking they gathered armfuls of the sweet, white hawthorn blossom. Willing servants carried it home to decorate hall and solar. Great boughs of green-leafed splendour were hung up outside the house. Philippa, too late in her pregnancy to clamber and climb, directed operations.

On West Chepe the fair-going crowds hemmed in the looping and weaving maypole dancers. The city seemed caught up in a wild affirmation of spring and of life. All winter its citizens, in common with townsfolk and villagers across the land, had suffered wet and cold and frost, had eaten first salted and then rancid meat; had watched for signs of returning life. Now their celebration of spring was a release known only to those who have sat through winter nights, and feared that green things would never rise again, through cold, dead earth.

It was a springtime in Philippa and John's relationship. The parting had made two hearts grow fonder. Two strangers had been forced to assess what they knew and liked about each other. Both had become stronger from the re-evaluation.

It was not lost on Philippa that John had so easily dismissed Margaret's condemnation of his wife. The red-haired Mentmore sister's last grip on her brother had been broken. Next, thought Philippa, I'll again broach the subject of the keys.

In late May a tournament was to be held at Smithfield, where open land lay beyond the city walls. Edmund and Giles were attending and mixing business with pleasure. Every lady of fashion was preparing for the event. Mercers, drapers and haberdashers waxed fat on the preparations. The Mentmore household was seized by excited activity.

Philippa was busily engaged in the duties of wife to the heir of the house of Mentmore. Each day brought a host of tasks to be attended to: wine needed to be bought and stored; bread of all types required checking and its age recorded for its various uses; soap needed to be made; rushes needed replacing; meat needed salting down for the winter.

During the winter she had seen these tasks as an unavoidable part of life, a chore without escape. Now she felt transformed. John's return had lightened her spirits. Even the tiredness of late pregnancy seemed eased by her new-found happiness.

Occasionally she accompanied John down to the wharves to check in galleys and cogs carrying expensive satins and silks and velvets. John was very protective of her. He worried if she tired and insisted that she sleep after mid-morning dinner. It was an indulgence which did little to endear her to her sister-in-law. Wisely, though, Margaret held her tongue. She seemed to have noted the change in John's attitude. She clearly did not feel sure of herself in his presence any more. She had guessed – correctly – that he would not brook criticism of his pregnant wife.

As the date of the tournament approached, so did the expected date of Philippa's delivery. John was not sure that she should go out amongst the jostling crowds of Smithfield. Philippa was quite undeterred.

'I feel fine, John. A first baby is often late. I do not think I shall be forced to give birth in Edmund's armouring tent. Truly I do not!'

She smiled at his concern. If the baby made her more important in his eyes, then so be it. She would enjoy it while it lasted. Seeing that his resolve was wavering, she added quickly: 'Besides, I have had Emma sew me up a pelisse to fit my new size. I took the Beverley Blue wool, my love. Poor Emma's worked so hard to finish it in time.'

John grinned ruefully. 'It would be a pity to waste such a good woollen cloth. But, my love, you should be in Sitrine silk or Alexandrine velvet. The Beverley Blue is fine, but – '

'Hush, husband!' She put one finger up to his lips. 'I would prefer to wear such when I am ... am a more fashionable size again. Till then the blue finespun will be perfect.'

'Very well,' he conceded, 'but as soon as the child is born you must away to the warehouse and pick out some rolls of silk. I'll not have my wife in anything but the best cloth, if I can help it.'

His generosity stirred her. It was in stark contrast to the bitter scene in September.

'Thank you, my love, I shall not deny you your rights!' She smiled and fluttered her lashes provocatively.

John snorted. 'You have no shame, woman.' But his eyes were shining and his mock horror only made her laugh.

Margaret, who was working at her sewing frame, looked up. She had been sewing throughout the conversation and took no pleasure in the sugared pleasantries. A sour smile lingered on her lips and her eyes were smouldering with jealousy and resentment.

'What will you wear, Margaret?' John's question was innocent enough but his sister bridled.

'We cannot all be away from the house, brother. Someone must stay to mind the running of it.'

This was nonsense, of course. Agnes Bakwell was more than capable of holding the fort. Like Giles's Mistress Holland she was an able and independent woman. Margaret's answer made no sense and John told her so.

Margaret rose stiffly from her bench. Without a further word she left the room and went down into the hall. John could have stopped her. As heir to the household he could have ordered her to stay and to be civil. Instead he chose to watch her go. As the red-headed firebrand left the solar, John Mentmore at last began to realise what his wife had been through since February 1377. It was a painful thought.

'She will come, for Edmund will be mortally offended if she does not. If Maggie will not do it for you and I, she'll do it for Edmund.'

But Philippa was not so sure. She had had more time than her husband to acclimatise herself to Margaret's moods. She scented a storm coming, even if she could not tell why.

Edmund and Giles arrived two days before the tournament with a gaggle of servants under the general command of Stephen de Knolton. Whilst Edmund and Giles were to be accommodated within Thomas's chamber, Stephen oversaw the establishment of the servants' camp amongst the sprouting tents and banners around Smithfield. Then he returned to the Mentmore hall to wait upon Giles and Edmund. He brought two pages with him to assist.

Edmund and Margaret quarrelled bitterly over dinner, much to Thomas's chagrin. At last she agreed to come to the ground at noon to observe the mêlée. He had to be satisfied with that.

'She should be soundly thrashed,' Giles remarked to Edmund, as they made ready for bed.

''Tis too late now, I fear,' Edmund retorted. 'Father has indulged her for too long. He raised her to be a high-spirited filly and no mistake.'

'And what good will come of it, I ask you? What horse is of use until it is broken? What woman will gain a husband if her will is as unbroken as a wild stallion? 'Tis not good, Edmund. Your father should have beaten her more often. She'd have loved him for it in the end. Mark my words, lad. Never forget that a daughter and a wife improve through discipline. A use of the switch now and again is little enough to endure but produces a harvest of good things. Never forget it!'

At that moment Thomas entered the chamber and the talk ended. As Edmund settled down on his mattress on the pallet he could not help but think of Anne Glanville. There was something of Margaret in that filly. Edmund pondered on the jet-haired, alabaster skinned beauty and reflected on the unlikely circumstances which would reduce a man to beating her. No, she and Margaret were horses from the same stable. Edmund was not one who desired a sedate ride. When it came to Anne Glanville he was prepared to take a few risks.

The day of the tournament was hot soon after dawn. A breathless morning was ushered in with golden sunshine and that slight haze which portends shimmering heat by noon.

Giles and Edmund were up before dawn. Along with Stephen de Knolton they had business to attend to at Smithfield. The rest of the family rose at first light and breakfasted lightly as was the norm. Margaret was silent and only picked at her sop of wheatbread in wine. Immediately after breakfast Thomas, John and Philippa processed with their servants to Smithfield. As the day was fine they walked. Retainers led horses behind them: palfreys for the men and a white jennet for Philippa.

Smithfield was a wild confusion of tents and banners. For a week past royal carpenters had been hard at work. Barriers had appeared to separate crowd from combatants, great stands shaded with multicoloured awnings had been erected for the nobility and the guild masters. The environs of the tournament had taken on the appearance of a fair. Wrestlers and jugglers vied with each other for public attention. Fire eaters, blacked to look like Moors and Saracens, astonished wide-eyed children. Even a dancing bear stamped and ambled in a rough rhythm to a shrill pipe.

The whole city seemed to be there. Beggars begged, hawkers sold sweetmeats, prostitutes plied their trade and still more people arrived. Around the knights and their ladies, in their tented shade, armed retainers stood guard. Gaunt was here. A great pavilion was decorated with his arms: the leopards of England surmounted by an ermine trim like a sideways 'E'. Soldiers patrolled the immediate area around the tent and kept the gawping crowd at some distance.

From the royal arms, fluttering above the principal stand, it was evident that Richard, King of England, was already present.

Liveried retainers in blue and gold forced their way through the crowd. Behind them rode Mayor Walworth and a host of fishmongers as well as the aldermen of the city wards. Walworth saluted Thomas with a civil raising of the hand. Philippa blushed as she met the open gaze of Ralph Horne, the handsome son of the alderman of Billingsgate. He studied her nonchalantly, then passed on. She felt as if she had been weighed and evaluated like a shipload of cod. Damn him, she thought furiously. How dare he stare at me like that? But then she thought of the humiliation which had undoubtedly accompanied Roger Starre's rejection of Horne's suit in favour of the Mentmores'. Perhaps he had good reason to show proud disdain. Still, he was a handsome young man.

'Did you see the look Horne gave you?'

Philippa turned scarlet at John's question. Had her husband really seen it? Had he understood its significance? She turned in a real flutter. 'I do not know. What look?'

'Aye, but it's hardly a surprise.'

Thomas had begun to answer his son's question. He stopped and Philippa put her hand to her mouth. Suddenly she realised John had been addressing his father, not her. John cast her a questioning glance. Thomas shook his head and continued.

'Aye, I saw the look, John. But 'tis no surprise after the work accomplished at Gloucester. You'd hardly have expected us to have won the affection of the fishmongers, would you?'

John grinned. 'Hardly,' he said. 'But I think we can weather their criticism.'

They made their way to one of the stands. Draped in crimson crepe, it had been erected at the expense of the mercers. From its vantage point John could just make out the pennant flying from Edmund and Giles's tent. They were well placed, at the south-west corner of the tourney ground.

Out of sight, behind the tent, Stephen de Knolton was steadying a great chestnut destrier. The warhorse was trampling the ground and Stephen was doing his best to avoid the raking teeth of the savage beast. Settling the animal at last, Stephen left it with a couple of nervous grooms and retired to the confines of the tent. Here Edmund was waiting his arrival with some impatience.

'Come on, Stephen lad. We don't want to keep the victim waiting.'

'Go easy on them, sir,' Stephen said, 'or there'll be no one left for the late arrivals.'

Hurriedly he helped Edmund to don his armour. Edmund was already wearing the quilted tunic, or gambeson. It was a new one and he felt the supple patches of linen beneath the leather. He nodded with approval as Stephen swiftly fitted the metal breastplate and helped him to pull on the tight fitting jupon, or surcoat. Stephen had come a long way since the desperate fumble aboard the *Gabriel* off Bayonne.

This time, though, Edmund did not pull on his visored bascinet. For the tournament the great helm – an eye-slitted pot of metal – was still the favourite protection.

'Well, how do I look?'

Stephen de Knolton smiled with obvious pride. 'Magnificent, my lord. Shall I?' He reached for the helm.

'Aye, lad. I'll not put that on until I have to.' He winked at his squire.

The tournament had a strict programme of events. In the morning were the individual jousts on horseback. Armed with shield and a blunted lance, the knights, on their destriers, would fight in single combat. It was a wildly dangerous sport. The church had often condemned it but had never succeeded in banning it. Later came a series of single combats on foot, fought in the arena at the same time. In the afternoon a mêlée had been planned. This was the old-style tournament and looked like a slightly organised brawl. Dozens of knights were grouped into two rival armies who then fought each other to a bloody standstill.

From their places in the stands the Mentmores watched with rising excitement as the trumpeters announced the arrival of Edmund and his opponent in the lists.

Edmund pulled hard on his reins. The destrier brought its head up with a furious snort. Edmund knew never to underestimate the power of such a beast. The destrier was not built for speed but for brutal courage and immense strength. He could feel its enormous power quivering beneath him.

His opponent, Reginald de Hamelak, a Yorkshire knight, cantered towards him. Together the herald led them before the king's stand. Dipping their lances they saluted the young monarch. Away, at either end of the long tourney ground, stood the opposing squires and retainers clutching the helms and spare lances.

The salutation over, the two knights rode their lumbering destriers away in opposite directions. Halfway along the lists Edmund reined in his beast. Turning it in a snorting half circle he faced Anne Glanville.

This was no coincidence. He had scouted out the terrain, using Stephen as his eyes and ears. Leaning forward he pointed the heavy lance at her breast.

'Your favour, lady? Pray let me wear your favour humbly.'

It was a request of exquisite courtesy. The crowd clapped. Heads craned to see Glanville's response. Her father and brother eyed Edmund warily. Around her, her guild relations looked sourly at the mercer's son.

Anne Glanville was wearing a flowing surcoat of green Alexandrine silk. Looser and lower-necked than the older style bliaut, it was drawn in upon her body by a low-slung hip belt. Her shiny black hair was held up with a net of gold. Around her the older women looked severe in their coiffes and wimples. Amongst such, Anne stood out like a queen.

Slowly, with great care, she raised long, cool fingers. Between them she held a fine veil, as shimmering as morning mist. With confident movements she tied it about the tip of Edmund's lance, which was aimed at her heart. Ignoring the scowls of her London relatives, Edmund Mentmore raised then dipped the lance in salute.

Back at the end of the ground, Stephen was holding the helm. It was topped by a stiff wooden swan's head, painted white. He lifted the helmet to his knight, then the tournament shield with a notch cut to rest the lance on.

A trumpet brayed out across the field. Edmund tensed. He swung up his lance and drew his shield across his chest.

The trumpet brayed again. With gathering speed the two destriers rumbled towards each other. The crowd roared. Money changed hands. Children gawped. Anne Glanville could see her veil fluttering on Edmund's lance.

Almost immediately in front of the king the two knights met in an explosion of violence. At the last minute de Hamelak lunged to the right. Edmund's lance sliced inches above his bull's head helm. De Hamelak's lance hammered into Edmund's shield with a splintering crash.

Edmund felt his face slam into the front of his helm. He tasted blood. The shock coursed through his body like lightning. His feet thrust down on his stirrups. His entire body jerked backwards. Then they had passed.

Cursing foully and spitting blood, Edmund turned and forced his horse forward. Again they faced each other. Once more they began that steady, irresistible charge. This time Edmund had learned. The moment before impact he flung himself forward on to his horse's cloth-draped neck. De Hamelak's lance thrust smashed the swan's head to shreds.

Edmund heaved on his reins with unbelievable savagery. His destrier pulled up in a wide-nostriled, rolling-eyed fury. Clods of earth flew as it slid to a terrible halt. Edmund swung in the saddle. His lance described a wild arc. De Hamelak began to pull away. Not quickly enough. Edmund's lance tip slammed against the side of his helmet. De Hamelak was flung forward and off by the force. He hit the turf with a metallic thud and lay still.

The crowd was delirious in its acclaim. De Hamelak's squires pelted down the list to their fallen hero. Edmund saluted the king, then Anne Glanville. This time her father and brother were smiling. They basked in the reflected glory of Edmund's victory.

Whilst Edmund rode away, the next contestants lumbered forth. Soon the arena was again ringing to the sound of wood on metal. Edmund fought once more that day. This time the battle was longer and more drawn out. With both lances shattered, the conflict continued on foot with sword against sword. His opponent matched his own skill and the brutal slogging match soon took its toll of both knights. In the end it was Edmund's experience and greater fitness which told in his favour. As his opponent tired, Edmund at last began to suspect that victory was in his grasp. There had been times when he had begun to doubt whether he would win. An opportunity presented itself as his opponent slipped on the smoothed grass. As he stumbled, Edmund gave him a stunning blow on the arm and then on the helmet.

With the battle over, Edmund sunk to his knees. He was bathed in sweat and his breath was coming hard and fast. The crowd roared its approval but Edmund Mentmore decided he had had enough glory for one day. Acknowledging the cheers of the onlookers, and assisted by his squire, he retired to his tent to take wine and be stripped of his armour.

The sight of Edmund in triumph had made the day for the watching Mentmore clan. When Edmund was clothed in chausses, shirt and long-sleeved embroidered tunic, he joined his family in the stands. As usual he was the centre of attention. His long, pointed shoes were the height of fashion as was his bobbed hair. Ladies smiled demurely but kept their eyes firmly fixed on the victor of two fierce encounters.

John did not resent his brother's pre-eminence. He had enough to keep him occupied. Giles de Brewoster had ridden up to London in the company of a number of Cotswold knights. Like himself they held extensive manors in Gloucestershire, Oxfordshire and southern Warwickshire. As with de Brewoster, many had turned arable over to sheep to reduce costs, or had cottage textile industries flourishing amongst the more prosperous yeoman farmers. John made the most of his opportunity by talking at length with Giles's neighbours. Before he had finished he had established a number whom he would visit in the late summer and autumn. He was determined to capitalise on the interest which his enquiries produced.

One person notable for her absence, however, was Margaret. Despite her assurances she did not come to the mêlée. Edmund did not hide his peevishness and Thomas was visibly angry. Giles was prudent enough not to make any comment. His glance at Edmund said it all.

Back home, Margaret had busied herself with mundane tasks during the morning. She was so obviously in a bad temper that the servants kept their heads down. Shortly before noon a visitor came to the hall.

'Sweet Mary!' Margaret exclaimed as she greeted the dark-eyed weaver. 'What madness brings you here, Rob?'

Conscious of the stares of the servants, she led him towards the dais. He was nervous.

'By God, Margaret, I cannot abide being without you. Leave London with me!'

Margaret gave a low laugh. 'Are you insane, Rob Newton, to come here in daytime and before the household?'

'When else could I come?' His eyes were brimming. 'And besides, who will suspect ill of so brazen a visit?' Margaret did not seem convinced, so he added: 'And you are mistress here.

What care you what scullery maids think or say?'

Long afterwards, in dark days, she would recall that chance use of words. It was that simple question which propelled her into what was to follow. For she was not mistress any more.

When the tournament was over, the Mentmores rode back to Roger Starre's hall by Newgate. There they took a light supper, along with Giles de Brewoster. It was therefore getting dark when they rode back to their own home. The curfew was soon to be enforced and city gates were being shut. It was a golden evening. Sunset spilled across the sky in a profusion of suffused pinks and red-tinged grey.

John was very thoughtful. Before they had left Smithfield, Anne Glanville had come to thank Edmund for so gallantly wearing her favour. Her father and brother stood at a discreet distance. Before she left she turned to John and said: 'Be careful, John Mentmore. Some men say you fly too high.'

It was said with real concern, which pierced John's defences. It had been totally unlooked for and he was astonished. He longed to stop her and ask for an explanation and even Edmund looked disconcerted by this surprising comment. However, there had been no time for further discussion. Her father – plainly displeased at the length of the conversation – had whisked her away.

John steered his way out around a group of beggars beside the narrow lane. The street was almost deserted and he was mildly annoyed at their occupation of much of the road to one side of the central gutter. His mind was on other things. Only at the last moment did he recognise the vagrants as lepers. They had emerged out of a nearby alley and he could see the dirty rags tied across their faces. He grimaced in horrified disgust and pulled on his horse's reins.

They moved towards him, begging bowls in one hand and bells or clappers in the other. They cried out pitifully. John turned his horse away, loath to see the rotting cankered faces. Had he been less preoccupied he would have recalled a new ordinance banning lepers from the city. Only at the last minute did it occur to him. There should be no lepers in London.

The knife slashed his reins. His horse reared in panic and collided with Philippa's jennet. The jennet stumbled and pitched Philippa forward.

The rearing horse saved John's life. As it rose up, in pawing panic, more knife thrusts missed their mark. One jabbed into the horse's leg. His high, wild neigh echoed along the street.

Edmund and Stephen urged their mounts forward. At front, Giles and Thomas savagely dragged their horses about. John's hat and purse flew across the lane. Silver pennies scattered in the mud and filth. One beggar snatched the prize from the sewage-filled gutter.

As Philippa fell she collided with one of the lepers. Arms flailing she raked her fingernails across his face. Bandages were stripped away. For an awful moment she gazed up into a brutal, brawny face. The 'leper' knelt beside her. His cheek bore the parallel furrows cut by her nails.

Then the 'lepers' were gone. They fled back down their alley and the horses could not follow. Edmund and Stephen dismounted and gave chase on foot, to no avail.

Badly winded and bruised, John crawled over to his weeping wife. He cradled her in his arms and with one hand wiped filth from her grazed face and pelisse.

'My God, are you all right? Oh, my darling, my darling . . .'

She collapsed shivering into his desperate embrace.

The attack in the alley came too hard on the heels of Anne's cryptic warning to be a coincidence. But she was gone. She had returned to her father's manor in Wiltshire.

John was intensely worried about his wife. Her resilience amazed him. Given the stage of her pregnancy it was a miracle her labour did not begin on the spot, but it was over a week before her contractions had reached sufficient force and regularity to require midwives.

Impotent with rage, John paced the hall vowing vengeance on the swine who had endangered his wife and child. He was quite oblivious to his own injuries. Assiduously kept away from the female preserve of the birthing chamber, he could only vent his anger on the servants. They kept out of his way whenever possible.

Edmund tried to entice him to the solar but his restless energy could not be so easily channelled. Neither, though, could he seriously concentrate on any one task. While Philippa writhed on the birthing stool her husband suffered his own form of slow torment.

Philippa gave birth to a girl early in the morning of 9 June.

It was two days before the feast of St Barnabas. John recalled that the name meant 'Son of Encouragement'. Without a shadow of doubt the name was appropriate. After the trauma in the alley the safe delivery of a healthy daughter was encouragement enough for any man, even if it was not a boy.

Despite her fears, the birth, for Philippa, was without complications. She and John resolved to name the child Anne, after John's mother. As John cradled the pink scrap of sleeping humanity in his arms he felt an intense satisfaction which quite surprised him.

'It becomes you, John!' Philippa smiled at the nervous way her husband held the baby. It was as if he thought he might break her.

The family had employed a wet nurse and when John had had his fill of fatherhood he handed the baby over to her. Contentedly fed, baby Anne sucked one tiny thumb earnestly.

'See? She even has tiny fingernails.'

Philippa laughed. 'Of course she does! She came complete, John Mentmore. Never fear.'

Still John gazed on those tiny hands. It was amazing. He frowned. 'You know I must go to Giles's manor soon?' There was a lack of resolution in his voice, but Philippa knew better than to capitalise on it. She had no wish to jeopardise her newfound intimacy with her husband.

'I do,' she replied.

'If I could do other, I would. God knows I would not wish to leave you at this time.'

She winced at the words 'at this time'. The attack in the alley hung like a cloud over the whole household. They felt as if they were under siege. It was a claustrophobic experience. It stifled.

'I know, John. I do know.'

He scratched at his beard. 'I have spoken to Edmund. He has agreed to stay here for a while. Father can make use of his talents and Giles has acquired a manor in Essex. He is content for Edmund to familiarise himself with the place, from here. Edmund will keep an eye on you. Do not fear.'

Philippa did fear. She had seen how the muffled attackers had aimed their knives at John. She feared for her husband.

'Besides which,' John continued, 'Edmund has a passing interest in Anne Glanville. And, now, so do I!'

Philippa smiled bravely. She did not feel very brave.

John left at the beginning of August and returned to Upton. He promised Philippa that he would write as soon as he was able. He promised to employ a courier to carry his letters for him. It was not much to cling to, but for Philippa it had to be enough.

A week after John's departure, Philippa and Emma went shopping on Chepeside. Thomas had always insisted that a male retainer accompanied female family members, a rule often flouted by Margaret who traded on her father's indulgence. This morning the men were busy unloading a cargo of cloth and Philippa would wait no longer. She stole out of the hall accompanied only by her maid. Thomas was not about. He was engaged in a fierce debate with a neighbour over the proximity to his land of a new earth closet.

Philippa and Emma browsed along Hosier Lane and up on to West Chepe. Thomas was preparing a midday dinner for the mercers' guild and Philippa had a week to take stock of the available produce. The two women made their way up to the butchers' quarter around St Nicholas Shambles. It was near the church of Holy Sepulchre, on Newgate Street. For Philippa it was very much home territory.

Off from the main meat market an unfortunate was locked into a pillory. Guild officials were busy burning meat below his nose. The smell was stomach-turning.

'Putrid meat,' Philippa said to Emma. 'That will teach him to sell it.'

Emma wrinkled her nose. 'It stinks like death, madam.'

'You should see the cleaning ground at Knightsbridge if you think this is bad. And when my mother was alive they even used to clean the carcases and dispose of the entrails just beyond the city walls.'

'Ugh, madam. Never so close to the city!'

'Yes, Emma. At Seacoal Lane, down by the Fleet.'

Emma pulled a face. 'The whole Fleet is a sewer, madam.'

'It is that, but the butchers did not make it any the less so with their actions. My father says that the prior of St John of Jerusalem himself ordered the site moved.'

Philippa, of course, had never seen either site, but had heard of them from clerks and from her father. Now she talked of them with a disgust which carried real conviction.

When the business was completed at the Shambles and a date agreed for the collection of the carcases by Agnes Bakwell and the servants, Philippa and Emma progressed back along the north edge of Chepeside.

At The Poultry, Philippa froze. A face had appeared and then disappeared in the crowd. She knew that face. She recognised the scratch marks. And who else wore a hood up in August?

'Quickly, Emma, back to the hall and get master Edmund.'

'But my lady, I cannot leave you. What if . . .?'

'Hst, girl. I'll not hurt standing here. I can buy a new purse for my husband. Now run – quickly.'

Emma was not convinced. She opened her mouth. Then she thought better of it. She turned and pelted away, cotte flying, legs flashing white.

Philippa was wrong. She could not simply stand and wait for the armed arrival of Edmund. The man was drifting away. She followed. West of Walbrook he turned north into the ironmongers' quarter. Philippa followed at a distance. The streets narrowed. Jetties projected overhead. The man was now in a hurry. He turned right towards the tailors' and the weavers' quarter off Threadneedle Street.

Philippa began to feel qualms. Then she thought of John. No, she would not let him down. She would see to which weaver's shed this man went.

The alleys were dirty. The gutters which ran down the sides of wider streets ran down the centre of this one. There had been no rain for days and the gutter was full of nauseating litter and effluent. Philippa sidestepped to avoid animal dung. Here and there a householder had piped his latrine into the common drain. Quite illegal, it only added to the monstrous state of the street.

Philippa was wearing the pelisse of Alexandrine velvet which John had promised her. Her hem was soon dark with splashes. Really, she thought, this is utter madness.

She had lost sight of the man in the tangle of tenement buildings. She began to panic and broke into a run. A group of scruffy youths, in patched doublets and hose, watched her with interest.

They lolled on either side of the alley. Philippa's mouth went dry. A hand caught at her. She struggled. More rough hands groped at her. She saw faces with black teeth and fingernails grimy and broken.

She struck out. They laughed. A violent hand tore her pelisse. Held against a wall the hand ripped her tight-fitting bodice. Eager fingers grasped her breasts. She felt a hand stifle her screams. More hands tore at her cotte and groped up her legs.

Then Edmund was amongst them, spitting and snarling like a wild cat.

Chapter Ten

Adam Attechurche was not a well man. Nobody else seemed to pay his illness much mind, but he was well aware of it. Try as he might he could no longer shake off his debilitating melancholy. The dark days of winter only added to his sense of loneliness and utter isolation.

He stood at the door of the church and watched the grey curtain of November rain. It seemed to have rained since Michaelmas. He remembered the dismal autumn when his wife died. It was as fresh as yesterday and yet separated from now by an uncrossable void. His mind drifted back to the wet churchyard, smelling of earth and sodden vegetation. It must have been ten years ago, he thought. It was the year after the cattle murrain wreaked havoc on the herds. The autumn before the reeve's young daughter drowned in the mill leat. The memory seemed to gather other dark incidents to itself. It lay in his mind like a deep, dark pool of sorrow. Yes, it must be ten years ago.

Adam no longer found it easy to construe the exact dates of passing events; rather he was aware of their ebb and flow in wide currents. He had slept badly since her death. For a moment he dared to think on her name: Cecilia. It was a very lovely name. An exotic name. God alone knew where her parents had heard it. He brushed a tear from his cheek. There – his mind was wandering once more. That happened frequently these days. Very frequently.

He had found that mandrake and henbane in a little watered wine helped him to sleep. Sometimes he added thornapple, when he could get it. Now he took it almost every night. His remaining stocks he hoarded with the fanatic urgency of a miser. Sometimes he drank in the day too. It helped him to relax. It helped him to forget.

The rain was quickening now. No longer drizzle, it turned into a full downpour. Adam retired into the church. It was early afternoon and the place was dark. One mutton-fat candle burned smokily by a side altar. On the walls the luridly painted images of death and judgement seemed to move in the quickening shadows.

Adam had been the resident curate at Todenham for almost twenty years. The actual rector was an absentee. Away at Oxford, lecturing in Canon Law, he had employed Adam as his replacement vicar. The living was not a rich one. The rector kept the great tithe on crops, sheep and cattle. Adam survived on the produce of the glebe farm and the lesser tithe on pigs, geese, poultry, fish and garden produce. In a good year his income might exceed five pounds. It was little more than his father had made, toiling on his twenty acres of ploughland.

Lately the tithe had fallen. The pestilence had carried off too many of the farming families. The lord had turned some of their holdings over to sheep walks, and Adam now took nothing from that land.

Thought of the pestilence brought back memories of Cecilia. He would never forget her death. The lords of Mother Church might not recognise her as a true wife, might scornfully call her a concubine, 'a carnal indulgence'. Yet she had been all Adam had had. Bitterly he recalled the scathing words of his lord's chaplain. They bit deep into his soul. 'A carnal indulgence.' Adam leant against the font. God damn Godfrey de Avalon, Adam cursed with silent venom. God damn him to his own pit in hell.

Adam gazed up at the wall. Figures of the doomed were plunging headlong from grace into fire. He picked on one writhing figure. With all his heart he wished it was Giles de Brewoster's chaplain. Which was strange; for Adam Attechurche was a kindly man.

There was a movement at the church door. Adam did not notice. Below the chancel step he had secreted a flagon of blackberry wine. He was secretive about that particular beverage. The previous year he had picked the berries late in the season. It had been after 11 October, Old Michaelmas Day. Adam knew, as well as anyone, that blackberries picked beyond that date were cursed. Any who ate them would sicken and die. And yet it had not deterred him. He had grown careless even of such vital matters. That troubled him. But he drank the blackberry wine nevertheless!

At last Adam could not fail to notice that he was no longer alone. Disappointed, he turned to face the intruder. He recognised the face. Like everyone in the village he was suspicious of strangers. This man was not of the community. He came from another world. Some whispered that he hailed from London. Adam shivered to think of that sinkhole of sin and moral depravity.

It took a while for John Mentmore's eyes to grow accustomed to the gloom. When he did so, he became aware of the grey-haired man watching him. Even in the shadows he could read hostility and wariness in those hooded eyes.

John had met a fair amount of hostility since he had returned to Upton in the summer. He had soon been identified with a manorial lord who was turning arable land over to sheep walks and who refused to relax his traditional demands on the villein holdings. There was bad feeling in the air.

'Can I help you, my lord?' Adam's voice was low and reticent.

John forced a smile. ''Tis the rain. I seek sanctuary from the storm outside for a while.'

''Tis but a short ride to Upton, my lord. Mayhap you would find fire and fresh clothes there.'

Adam's suggestion had the merest hint that his guest was not welcome. John shrugged and threw off his sodden cloak. Dark droplets splattered the flag floor with a sudden shower.

'You are Adam Attechurche?' John did not pause for reply. 'My uncle speaks well of you. Says you are a goodly man of God.'

A wintry smile played on Adam's face. Godfrey would choke to hear him so called. 'My lord does me too great a service.'

Adam had retreated from the font and was halfway to the screen, before the chancel. John strode towards him.

''Tis dark early.'

'Aye,' Adam said guardedly but the remark seemed innocent enough.

'I'm surprised you can see well enough to read the service. These dark winter days, 'tis surely – '

'No, sir! I can read the Latin well enough. No one in the village finds fault with my matins or mass.'

He had stiffened at John's remark. Adam was conscious of his rudimentary Latin. His father had scraped together precious pennies to purchase his son a shallow knowledge of the venerable tongue. Adam knew how scholars despised simple parish priests. He had often read the disdain on the high-cheeked face of Giles de Brewoster's mendicant confessor. In his heart he resented that man's intrusion into his life; his community. Now this stranger had sought to humiliate him in his own church. Adam's lip trembled. He was shocked at how deeply the casual criticism had hurt him. Once more he felt tears well up.

John was taken aback at the old man's distress. He had meant no hurt.

'You misread my words, I assure you. By Our Lady Mary I meant no slur on you as priest of this place. I meant only that the light is bad and you have only one candle. And that a poor one . . .' His voice trailed off, fearful of creating more offence.

Adam saw the honesty in the young man's face. Seeking to make amends, he gestured down the church.

'I have a little blackberry wine . . .'

'It would be a godsend on such a day as this!' John said with a relieved smile. He had witnessed enough hostility without unwittingly creating more.

Adam poured the fragrant liquid into a green glazed bowl. He handed the palm cup to John, who took it eagerly.

Adam recalled how Our Lord had promised that the elect might drink poison and not be harmed, and looked curiously as the Londoner downed the cursed wine. Would some awful fate befall him? Here, before the rood screen itself?

'Thank you.' John returned the bowl.

Adam raised his eyebrows. Surely a Londoner could not be of the elect? Yet the young man seemed sound enough and no terrible end came on him. Adam shrugged. Pouring himself a drink, he was rather relieved. He had begun to feel a liking for this young stranger.

'You're one of the few villagers who shows me any welcome.' As soon as he had said it, John bit on his lip. When would he learn to bridle his tongue?

Adam sat down on one cold step. 'What welcome do you need from us? You are kin to our lord of Upton.'

John laughed. In the empty church it echoed. The man was right, of course. What did it matter how he was welcomed? His plans were working out well. There seemed to be no obstacle to his seizing the initiative in the local cloth trade. Mentmore money had bought him friends where it mattered. Giles's neighbours were only too keen to find wider markets for their wool. The rural weavers, unprotected by guilds and unfettered by regulations, welcomed his money and his promise of markets further afield than Moreton and Chipping Campden. Already he could envisage convoys of pack animals en route to Stroud and the great fairs of Gloucester and Bristol.

Yet he was increasingly aware of an undercurrent of resentment. It concerned him because it was so strong. It was like that powerful undertow which could suck a swimmer to choking destruction. It was like that sudden hand of fate which had swept aside Kirkby's schemes and turned his game into chaos.

John shivered. The cold was more than just the autumnal rain. He felt menaced and isolated and he wished that Edmund were here. More than that, he wished he was home with Philippa and their baby daughter.

Adam poured out more wine and offered the bowl to John, who took it gladly.

'The villages are restless.' Adam watched the effect of this statement on his visitor. 'The villeins refuse boon work and would have it exchanged for cash payments.'

'And yet on other manors they are eager to take up villein holdings. Willingly seek land with obligations.'

Adam sighed. How much this man had to learn about the countryside!

'Yes, they'll do so for it's an ill wind that blows no good. Even if that is the only way to increase their holding they'll do it. A man will dice with death himself to gain more land. But now they grow greedy and, left to themselves, would do no villein work at all. They would be free of all dues to their lord.'

'And to church, too,' John interjected.

Adam fell silent. As the son of a peasant he sympathised with those who would shake off their servile bonds and become free tenants, holding land for a money rent only. More than this, he feared Giles's obsession with turning over depopulated holdings to sheep. He could almost see his tithe decline before his eyes.

Yet he too depended on the obligations of his parishioners. He was caught between two worlds.

'Aye, and to church too,' he conceded.

'You'll not deny the wickedness of those who despise the authority of their temporal lord, the outlaws who destroy hay and open sluices by night and who deny church her rightful dues. You cannot tell me that the villagers give up their tithe with a joyful heart.' Adam looked old and sad. John continued: 'For they would as eagerly deny their obligations to you as their lord. What household would give up its second best beast to you on the death of the tenant if it could avoid it? They must resent the payment of the church heriot as much as the tithe.'

Adam nodded slowly. He knew how desperately he had to press his parishioners for the lesser tithes. He also knew how they resented him every egg, every cup of honey, every handful of flax. Each year he sought to harvest more from the fifty acres which made up his glebe land in the strips of the open fields.

'And from your pittance you must devote two thirds to the upkeep of the chancel and to the relief of the poor. By St John, man, you must feel every pinch of those actions which deny you your rights.'

'I'll not deny it,' Adam said flatly. More than John Mentmore, he felt the unrest and rebellion about him. The very system of feudal obligation was creaking and groaning under the titanic strain of popular resentment. He was finely meshed into it. It was his life. He had nowhere else to turn. Its sinews bound him. All that threatened it threatened him.

He rose to his feet. 'It's stopped raining.' He sniffed the damp, musty air as if it was that sense which had conveyed the message to him. 'You will find your ride back to Upton easier now.' He moved away into the chancel. His drifting, absent-minded gait reduced any offence which might have been given by his virtual dismissal of his guest.

'Thank you for the wine,' John said softly. There was an intense loneliness about this man which stirred him.

Adam seemed not to hear. 'Mind the torrent at Ditchford. It rises with the rain. I've known a child drown there, a long time ago . . .'

The deeper darkness of the chancel swallowed him. John caught up his damp cloak. Puzzled at the old priest's behaviour, he made his way down the nave. Soon he was outside in the fresher air.

The churchyard was rank with grass and weeds. White deadnettle and hawkbit brushed against his boots. His horse was waiting. Around it the grass had been mown clean. John mounted and turned the horse's head towards the narrow, muddy lane which led to Upton.

Back in the chancel, Adam Attechurche stood in silence. In his head a wild hunt of thoughts flashed in wild pursuit of answers: sheep grazing on old arable plots; a sluice gate open on a field of the lord's hay; reluctant villagers counting out a tithe of cracked duck eggs. He felt confused and sad. With slow, deliberate, effort he poured himself another bowl of the blackberry wine. With trembling hands he brought the bowl to his cracked lips.

December, too, was wet this year. The roads were reduced to rivers of mud once more. Cattle had been slaughtered and the villagers celebrated the killing with a horn fair. Far into the night, the men and boys of Upton and of Todenham sounded their horns; bonfires lit the night. On 21 December, St Thomas's day, the women and girls of the villages went on traditional rounds, begging money and sweetmeats from their richer neighbours.

John watched these shameless beggars as they came, giggling, to the hall. Each carried a holly wreath to reward a generous giver and soon Giles's hall was decked with the seasonal gifts. Godfrey was disapproving of this custom but Giles saw no harm in it. Indeed, John felt that a flood of benevolence might be a shrewd move in the midst of an unsettled winter.

The next morning Giles and John were disturbed at breakfast by an agitated groom. He led them out to the main gate of the manor stockade. The morning light was thin and grey. A holly wreath was nailed to an upright of the gate. It was dark with a sticky substance. A trail of the same liquid ran down the upright and gathered in a muddy pool. John reached out and touched the wreath.

"'Tis blood,' Giles commented crisply. 'Bull's blood, I'd wager.' John pulled back his hand and gasped.

'By all that's holy, my lord, 'tis a curse. A fiendish curse.' The groom wrung his hands in very real horror. He knew well the efficacy of such witchcraft.

'John!' Giles's eyes were hard and cold. He held his nephew's glance. ''Tis nothing. 'Tis the foolishness of old women. Go fetch pliers and have it down,' he said to the groom. 'Go, man. Look lively.'

'Uncle, what does this evil act mean? Can you truly think . . . ?'

'For God's sake, John, hide your thoughts! The servants must not see you so concerned. To them you must appear beyond such things. Make out 'tis but a simple foolishness. It has happened before – '

'Before – ?' John interrupted. 'You mean this is not the first time?'

Giles smiled grimly. 'Not the first and by no means the last.'

On that score, Giles was proved right. The bloody holly wreath was the start of a campaign of intimidation. On Christmas Eve the head of a ewe was tossed into the yard. On Twelfth Night some darker 'Lords of Misrule' burnt down the croft of one of Giles's shepherds, away by the sheep walks of Charingworth beyond Stretton-on-the-Fosse. It was a bleak Christmas.

In January the third poll tax in as many years put a torch to the kindling of an unhappy countryside. It was only a matter of weeks before the flames licked at Upton.

Giles and John discussed the matter at dinner. It was a blustery Shrove Tuesday. Neither was encouraged by the news. Rumours of mass tax evasions and of mindless attacks on landlords were also filtering through to Upton.

'It's a flat rate this time – one shilling a head. At least that cuts less harshly into us,' John mused.

Giles nodded in agreement. 'That much at least is better than the last one. I paid fully a pound, as did your father. They say the Duke himself paid ten marks.' He pulled at his sweet pancake with little relish.

'But did it raise the money required?' John's question was rhetorical. He knew that of the fifty thousand pounds to be raised only twenty thousand had ever seen the coffers of the young king. 'So now we pay again! And the countryside is already seething with resentment at high taxes. I fear we may see more than bloody holly wreaths this spring.'

Mistress Holland, all bustle and bonhomie, brought up fresh platters of pancake confections. She frowned to see how bad news had diminished appetites.

That very afternoon brought news of damage to sheep pens out at Great Wolford. A distraught shepherd brought the news. Great Wolford lay beyond Todenham. The poor man had been running. His breath came in short hard gasps.

'Men, sir ... armed men, sir ... villeins, sir ... black-hearted scum,' he panted. 'We could do nothing, my lord. They came with staves and cudgels. They have broken down the hurdles and killed some of the sheep. We could not stop them, my lord. Indeed, we did try.'

He rubbed one grimy hand over a raw wound on his forehead and winced as his fingers touched the ragged graze.

Giles's red-bearded bailiff, Wyloc, appeared at the evening hall. 'My lord, I have only now heard of this outrage. I was out inspecting the runs at Stretton and have just returned. What would you have me do?'

In one corner of the room his little daughter, Ellen, watched her father with concern. Even at eleven years, she could sense the danger menacing them. Her mother, too, looked pale.

Giles was aware that all eyes were on him. Conscious of their stares he slowly scratched at his tight-knit curls. He was determined to look unflustered.

''Twill be too late to apprehend these rogues tonight. Ride over to Wolford tomorrow and take names enough to see hung.'

With a nonchalance born of years on the battlefield, he signalled for his nephew to join him in the panelled solar. Once isolated, he vented his true feelings.

'God's blood, but I'll see ears cut off and noses gouged out for this.' His arthritis was drilling at his spine and he was in a foul mood. 'Damn them! I shall see they hang for this day's work. And I shall show Compworth and his nest of vipers that I shall not be intimidated.'

John frowned; his blue-grey eyes revealed puzzlement. 'Compworth? Surely Wyloc said it was disgruntled villeins. No doubt they hate the use of sheep on holdings they covert or desire – '

'Have you ever seen a bough fall from a tree, John?' Giles's abrupt question halted his nephew in mid-flow. 'Have you seen it crash down in a storm?'

John could not see what Giles was getting at. It was not like the old knight to talk in riddles.

Giles was calmer now. 'Though the tree be rotten is it from its will that the bough breaks and falls?'

'No. Mayhap the force of the gale plucks it off.'

'Quite! You speak of what is rotten in the tree. You speak of villein dogs who dare to dictate my use of land, or demand to be excused from labour on the demesne. You speak of what is rotten in the tree. But, by God's blood, I speak of the gale blowing through the wood.'

'You mean you think a hand guides these actions?'

'Yes, and I know the name behind the hand.'

'The one you call Compworth?'

Giles nodded. Suddenly tired, he sat down on the trunk. The pewter jangled. 'It's a long story, John, but you should know of it. It will perhaps explain more than you could guess. It began when my elder brother held this manor and the other lands this side of Wychwood. I was away in France, with the old king.' He paused for a moment. To John it seemed that nostalgia glinted in his eyes. Then the warhorse shrugged. 'Out towards Great Wolford the village is divided between two manors. We hold the one – where those sheep runs are – and the Compworths hold the other. Their caput is across the Nethercote Brook, at Little Wolford.'

Giles's caput at Upton, and its village, was to the east of the great Fosse Way running north-eastward towards Warwick. The manor of Stretton lay up against the highway itself. To the south-east, across the Knee Brook, was Todenham. Further to the south-east – perhaps one mile – was Great Wolford with its newly wrecked sheep grange.

'These Compworths. They have not figured in the list of your neighbours you gave to me. They are not your friends?'

Giles's laugh was a bitter one. 'When I was away in France they led my dear brother a merry jig. He was a good man, John, but too tender in his actions. The Compworths took his measure and would have taken him, if they could. They rustled his cattle. They stirred up his villeins to revolt. They abused his plough teams and fired his ricks.'

'But why, uncle? What did they hope for?'

'What do brigands always hope for? Easy plunder! They would have had him buy them off! Oh, do not look so surprised, John. This countryside is no Eden. God's blood, I've known the king's own judges taken by the likes of the Compworths and held to ransom. And what jury will find them guilty if they have put silver into some hands and knives into others?'

'You never mentioned this before.'

'There was no need, John. I returned from the war. My brother died. I inherited these manors. I am not as my brother. I am less . . . less tender with the likes of the Compworths.'

John understood all right. 'So they learnt to leave you alone?'

'That they did. I repaid bloody nose for bloody nose and cracked head for cracked head. They learnt to pick off weaklings elsewhere. They have given much grief to the monks of Winchcombe in Wychwood. But me they have left alone.'

'Until now,' John said.

'Until now. Yes. Something has stirred them. They have scented an opportunity. 'Tis this matter of the sheep, John. They have smelled out trouble. They are wolves. Mark you, when Wyloc returns tomorrow he will have news of the Compworths. They have long wished to hold all of Great Wolford; they'd not share its rents with another if they could help it. When Wyloc returns he'll have names, and they'll be from the Compworths' manor as well as from the dregs of my own.'

With that, John had to be content. He would have ridden out with Wyloc himself, but Giles forbade it. He had alternative plans. John would ride the three miles to Charingworth Grange to supervise the reconstruction of the shepherd's hut there. After that he would ride over to Giles's neighbour at the manor of Ebrington. Giles was keen to know if he was being singled out for special attention.

Due to this, Wyloc rode out alone in the morning. It was Ash Wednesday and he had begun the Lenten fast. Already he was feeling hungry. As he rode he had visions of piping vegetable gruel, rye bread, meat and cheese. He had been Giles de Brewoster's bailiff for some twelve years of his thirty-five. With his fifty-two shillings a year, stabling and a peck of oats per day for his horse, and free repairs for his house, he was a substantial figure in the village community. Giles was a firm master but not a hard one. Despite the vagaries of the harvests, it was a rare year that

Wyloc had to make good the deficiencies from the set profit plan for the manors.

He had lived at Upton all his life and his family before him had done likewise. Comfortably off freemen, they had habitually named their eldest sons Wyloc. In so doing they had confirmed a Saxon lineage stretching back beyond the reign of William the Bastard. Within the close-knit community, they occupied a position of some honour. The bailiff ensured that villeins performed their labour service on the lord's lands and his family basked in the light of this power. They took their status from his authority. Below lay the lesser ranks of reeve and beadle, cart-, hay- and woodward. Life was reasonably good for Wyloc the bailiff and his family.

At Great Wolford he inspected the damaged sheep pens and quizzed the villeins and tenants summoned from the sowing of beans in the great south field. They were subdued. He could not tell if it was resentment or fear which bound their tongues. He berated the reeve for not going to the help of the shepherds. A coarse-featured man, he glowered and sulked.

'Saw nothing. Didn't see anything. No one did.'

Wyloc growled in fury. It was the reeve's duty to assist the bailiff. The fact that the reeve was elected by his fellow villeins should not have affected his loyalty. He would have struck the man, but he saw that the mere mention of the shepherds had caused a stir amongst the watchers. Clearly they had no love for the lord's sheep in their newly erected closes. The mood was subtly changing from subdued to angry. Suddenly Wyloc was painfully aware that he was alone.

With a dismissive wave of contempt, he remounted his horse. 'The lord of the manor will hear of your sudden afflictions of blindness, deafness and dumbness.'

There were muttered comments but they did seem genuinely worried at the content of his threat. Spurring his horse, the bailiff rode back along the greenway track between the ploughed strips of land. As he neared Todenham he could see a large crowd gathered before the church. He did not recognise half of them. That should have given him pause for thought. Instead it made him curious; curious and a little angry. Who were these loafers?

A Jack of Lent was being carried through the muddy streets between the cobwalled cottages and the wicker pens of livestock.

A grotesque scarecrow of a figure, the representation of Judas was being pelted with filth. Wyloc guided his horse past the squabbling pigs. Ducks and geese scattered before the splashing hooves. He came up to the Jack of Lent. The man carrying it was known to him. It was the Todenham reeve.

Some of the strangers jostled his horse. A clod of mud struck him on the face. He was stunned and almost fell from the saddle. Turning in fury he faced a jeering anonymous crowd of peasants in patched tunics and chausses. Some had their chaperons drawn up over their heads. Half hid beneath their hoods, the faces of malicious strangers leered at him.

A stone hit his horse. It shied in fear. The Jack of Lent swung against him. Its grotesque face grimaced at him. More stones were thrown. The horse whinnied and turned about, stamping its hooves.

'Back, you dogs. Back! I am the bailiff of Giles de Brewoster.'

A sharp stone struck his forehead. He plunged backward from the saddle. The hooded men surged forward. The Jack of Lent jigged about like a hideous standard. Sticks and cudgels rained upon the desperately writhing man.

'God's blood, have mercy, have mercy! Jesus help me . . .'

Oak staffs smashed on his raised arms. Blood coursed down his face.

From the door of the church Adam Attechurche watched in fascinated horror. His stomach turned. Vomit, acrid, was in his throat. He wanted desperately to intervene. He longed to stop those pitiless kicks and blows. He longed to stop the murder being committed before his very eyes, but he did not do so. Adam Attechurche was not a brave man.

Soon the butchery was over. The hooded men fled back across the fields towards the Compworth manor. Behind them the villagers - few of whom had taken part – drifted away. It was as if some terrible spell had been broken. Whispering, in hushed tones, they turned towards their cottages. Ploughs would lie idle this day. There was an awful hush over the village.

Behind them they left the battered and lifeless body of the bailiff. His horse, terrified, had bolted.

Adam Attechurche slowly moved towards the fallen man. Bailiff and Jack of Lent lay huddled together in an obscene union of mud and blood. Adam knelt down and turned the man's head.

The face was swollen with angry bruises. The eyes were staring. With thin fingers Adam closed the lids and folded the arms. Then, in a steady rhythm, he began to recite the office for the dead. The familiar Latin phrases tumbled from his lips, only this time he prayed with a new fervour. He felt that something of himself lay broken in the mud. He prayed for the bailiff and for Cecilia; for the reeve's daughter drowned in the mill leat; for all the sad victims whom he had buried in God's acre. And lastly he prayed for himself – for his own cowardice. Beneath his prayer, the body of Giles's bailiff grew cold.

When John returned to Upton from Ebrington he brought news that, whilst the manor was experiencing its own share of unrest, it had experienced nothing like the pattern of violence currently being played out at Upton. John's ride home had not been a happy one. It was difficult to deny Giles's belief that he was the target of more than the usual rural unrest.

At the edges of the ploughed open fields the dividing sikes and grass tracks were alive with shepherd's purse and the first star-like flowers of chickweed. John saw none of it. His mind was far away in London with his wife and baby daughter. He had begun to wish that his schemes had never brought him to these troubled regions of the eastern Cotswolds.

As he spurred his horse forward, the villeins ploughing the curving selions scarcely glanced up. The plodding oxen tugged the plough under the hazel switch. The foreign rider rode by on the furthest edges of their world.

Back at Upton, the compound was in a state of alarm. Giles's horse was saddled and ready and those of the other household retainers stood nearby. John soon saw the cause of this alarm: the bailiff's big, black mare was lathered in sweat and her quarters were cut.

'What in God's name has happened?' he cried to his stone-faced uncle.

'What, indeed? This is how Wyloc's horse has returned; without him!' Giles was wearing a cloak over a broadsword. John noticed that the retainers were likewise armed. Three carried longbows – relics of the French wars.

'You've had no word from him?'

Giles swung his stocky frame up into the saddle. 'His mount is the only message we have received. No more.' Then, as he wheeled his horse about: 'What news from my neighbours?'

John rode alongside him. 'There's unrest about Ebrington. Disruption of work on the demesne by disaffected villeins but nothing like here.'

Giles's face was pulled taut as he sneered savagely, 'No, by God! The Compworths take a manor at a time!' He dug his heels into his horse's flanks. The dappled palfrey sprang forward. Watching servants scattered. Giles and his men rode out under a low grey Lenten sky.

The riders – some twelve in all – crossed the Ditchford of the Knee Brook in a confusion of spray and hooves. Ahead lay the spire of Todenham church. Todenham village was strangely deserted. A foraging sow ran before them, piglets squealing in the muddy main street. The timbered huts and hovels were shuttered and silent. Apprehensive of the coming storm, the people of the village had taken shelter.

Giles would have taken the greenway across the open field to Great Wolford, but the deserted state of Todenham aroused his suspicions. His answers, or at least some of them, would be found here. The church door was open. Giles reined in his horse and leaped down from the saddle. His landing jarred his back but he was beyond such concerns. Hurried steps took him into the silent house of God.

Adam Attechurche was kneeling in the bare expanse of the nave. He looked up at the sound of boots on the flags. Fear was etched on his tired, old face. Giles took one look at the muddy body of the bailiff.

'Who?' His voice was abrim with fury. 'Jesus God, who?'

Adam was trembling as he rose. Blackberry wine stained his faded coat. 'Lordless men, sir. 'Twas not of this village. 'Twas lordless men, sir. Robbers and wolf's-head men.' He tried not to think of the villagers who had joined in the assault. There had been very few. Least of all did he ponder on those who had simply stood and watched; those who, with Pilate, had washed their hands.

Giles had seen the Jack of Lent in the churchyard. He rounded on Adam and his words flew like goose-feathered shafts. 'And no one saw? No one heard? No one helped him?'

His awful questions hung in the air. They had the heart-piercing sharpness of the judgements of God. Adam blanched. 'I ... we ... we could not. They were too many. If only ...'

'God's blood, man, but there will be a payment made for this day's bloody work.'

If Giles had ever toyed with the conversion of his villeins' labour service on the manor's demesne land to cash payments, that moment in Todenham church destroyed it for ever. Let them all rot, he thought viciously. Let them all rot and labour to the twentieth generation from now.

Outside the church, John and the others steadied their restless mounts. Giles reappeared like an avenging angel.

'The bailiff is ...' John's words trickled away like water in sand.

'Wyloc is dead. We ride to Wolford.'

Did Giles mean to Great Wolford for information or to Little Wolford for vengeance? None of his attendants dared ask.

Giles drove his horse hard and John strove to keep up with the breakneck pace. Ahead lay Great Wolford. North of it spread the dark mass of High Furze. Here and there twists of grey smoke betrayed the location of assarts on the edge of the woodland. Giles pulled up his horse. John almost ran up his back. Mud flew from flailing hooves.

'There!' Giles pointed away to the east.

John followed the accusing finger's direction. Between Great and Little Wolford, men and sheep were moving away towards a crossing of the Nethercote Brook. The stream marked the boundary between Giles's manor and that of the Compworths.

'Those men! My sheep!' Giles's rage twisted his words. His message was clear. He was witnessing the rustlers at work. In broad daylight.

With fierce cries, the de Brewoster riders bore down on the thieves. Across the bean and madder fields they poured in a ragged line.

Seeing the impending vengeance the rustlers gave up their task. They ran headlong towards the shallow brook. Here and there, one bolder than the rest stopped to resist. Giles brought his sword down on the head of one of the fleeing criminals. John slashed at another with his dagger. The mounted archers loosed off a small volley. Two of the fugitives plunged into the brook, arrows in their backs.

Giles's pursuit stopped at the edge of the brook. One of his men, who had crossed it, thought better of it and retired. Around them sheep bleated in panic. On the rising ground beyond the brook lay the fortified Compworth manor. Between it and the brook men were gathering.

'Sweet Mary, my lord, look at them!' It was the man who had inadvisedly crossed the Nethercote. His nervous horse wheeled. 'The whoresons have an army!'

The man scarcely exaggerated. A formidable force, perhaps fifty strong, held the high ground. Although some three hundred yards away, it was plain to see that they were well armed. Maces and wickedly pointed bills and pole-axes were all too evident.

''Tis no mere posse, this,' John muttered and cast an apprehensive glance at his uncle. Giles was watching the show of strength with narrowed eyes.

It was abundantly clear that the Compworths had done more than just call up the men of their tithing in a 'posse comitatus'. This array of might could only be interpreted in one way: the Compworths had bought the loyalty of ex-soldiers and lordless men. John paled at the thought.

'We cannot face this. Not yet.' Giles's words betrayed no hint of emotion. 'Quietly now. Turn the horses about and back to Upton. Quietly now. 'Tis a withdrawal, by God, not a rout.'

With calmness beyond belief, Giles turned his mount around. John and the others did likewise. Behind them the Compworth army jeered and cat-called.

The ride back to Upton was miserable and silent. At Todenham, Giles left his archers to retrieve the body of the bailiff. John would never forget the look on young Ellen's face as her father's battered body was brought in. It seemed an age since the two of them had searched for bean and pea on Twelfth Night a year before.

Giles did not waste time. He immediately made plans to defend the manor. The gates were shut and barred a good three hours before dark. All male retainers were armed. A watch was set up about the stockade.

In the hours of darkness Giles laid out his plans to his nephew. Far from being dismayed, the elderly knight was bitterly determined.

In the early hours, Giles and John were aroused by Godfrey de

Avalon. Standing at the stockade they watched a glow rising in the night sky.

'They're burning one of the sheep granges.' Giles did not seem particularly shocked.

'But the sheep,' John protested. 'What of your sheep?'

Giles pulled a wry face. 'I had the flock moved away toward Charingworth ere it grew dark. I had expected this.'

John's mouth was dry as he watched the distant flames. He bit at his cheek in anxiety. With all his heart he wished he was back at his father's house.

In the morning a constable appeared at the hall. He was in the company of one of Giles's archers and had the look of one who would have avoided this duty if he could. He was a weather-beaten, old greybeard and very, very scared.

Since the Statute of Westminster in 1285 all free men aged between fifteen and sixty years had received the right to bear arms. More than that, they shared the duty of appearing in the Hundred Militia – the 'posse comitatus' – as an instrument of local defence. Their organiser was the constable; his superior was the shire sheriff himself.

Briskly Giles informed the man of the outrages perpetrated against his manor. Living at Moreton the constable could hardly have been unaware of the civil war growing on his doorstep, yet he bore the look of one who could not see how the issue involved him.

'What would you have me do?' he asked lamely.

'You are constable of the Hundred court?' Giles asked. The man nodded.

'Then call out the Hundred posse, man! There is murder and arson stalking the land and you would ask what you should do?'

The constable shifted his feet and twisted his hood in white-knuckled hands. He was adept at pursuing the odd horse thief. Indeed, he had once led the posse against robbers operating from Wychwood itself. Here, though, he was way out of his depth. It had been five years since he had led the Hundred in concerted action of the kind envisaged by de Brewoster, and then he had done so under the command of the sheriff. More than this, it had been a generation since the King's Commissioners of Array had summoned the shire levy to any great task. A professional army had changed all that. Now the constable was being asked to lead the posse in a civil war.

'I . . . they will not . . . cannot.' His eyes swept the floor. He would not look up. 'They are afraid. They cannot go against the Compworths.'

Giles cursed bitterly. 'By Our Lady, you are telling me that you will not act? Is that it?'

The miserable man shuffled his feet.

'Get out,' Giles hissed. 'Get out, you worm!'

When the constable was gone, Giles exploded into a chain of curses. Godfrey de Avalon looked pained.

'By St George, do you like it? The man is afraid to call up the Hundred. By St Christopher, I'll wager the Compworths have had no such trouble putting their hands on armed men! By God!'

Giles was correct. The arming of the population since 1285 and the archery practice encouraged by the late King had created a large number of the populace trained to act as a rudimentary military unit. It could make for serious trouble if that experience was manipulated by lawless hands.

'Indeed you are right, my lord.' Godfrey's black eyes glittered. 'One has only to think of the Cheshire rising in the fifties. 'Twas crushed, by God's grace, but it took the Black Prince himself to do it. And the dogs who sacked Oxford University two years later. Who can deny that they acted as an organised force with malice aforethought? It is no different here, as you so rightly say. These dogs would once more rise up against their God-given masters and prove themselves to be brute beasts.'

John shivered at the thought of clandestine armies and secret brotherhoods. It was as if the whole country was shifting beneath his feet. He felt as if he was on quicksand. He recalled the tales of that murderous day in Oxford. A wild day some twenty years ago when peasants from outlying villages had poured into the city to hunt down the students. The hairs rose on the back of his neck as he recalled tales of their black flags and uncouth chants: 'Havak, havoc, strike hard. Give good knock.' There was something dreadfully concerted about such actions. The quicksand was moving again!

'And Wyclif would give authority and power to such dogs,' Giles grimaced.

Godfrey smiled sardonically. 'Those who pull down God's ordered authority can only replace it with their own form of chaos.'

John felt the digs were aimed at him. He was the substitute for William who espoused Wyclif's cause. And yet was Godfrey right? Was it inviting chaos to question the authority of Mother Church; to call for the scriptures to be put in the hands of labourers and maids?

His deliberations were shattered by a hoarse laugh. Giles was clearly not convinced by his chaplain's argument – this time.

'I doubt that the Compworths give a thought to master Wyclif and his heresy. They fish wherever there is troubled water. Having commuted their villein labour service for cash, they are now stirring up trouble wherever another manor has not done so. They use the anger and resentment of the simple and the stupid. See how they have picked out the sheep runs for special attention! They know how they are resented. They know the demand for higher wages by the labourers and how I will not be extorted by ploughboys. They have seen how the greedy and the lazy covet the holdings I have put down to sheep, but they have not bargained for Giles de Brewoster!'

'Can we beat them?' John's voice was edged with doubt.

'We can but it will not be easy. Do you recall the Folvilles and their evil crew?' Godfrey nodded. John did not. 'For sixteen years they terrorised Leicestershire. Sixteen years! And one of them was a priest! They murdered a Baron of the Exchequer and a Justice of the King's Bench. They milked the surrounding manors dry. For sixteen years! Well, the Compworths would do that here. But there is one difference, John. Mayhap you spot it?' John shook his head. 'The Folvilles did not face me, my boy. But the Compworths do. That's the difference. Those whoresons will not intimidate me. By God!'

The grizzle-headed knight could strike courage up in others like a knife on flint. John smiled, reassured.

The next day Giles set out for Chipping Campden to take his complaint before a Justice of the Peace. Since the 1350s these country knights had acted not only as unpaid assistants to the itinerant king's judges but had power to fix wages and, since 1362, try crimes at the quarter sessions. Now Giles put his hopes on dragging the Compworths before the law. With him he took Godfrey de Avalon and a force of armed retainers.

John was to hold the manor at Upton. During the morning, a

force of fifteen men arrived from the nearby manor of Ebrington. It was a welcome neighbourly addition to the manor's defence.

In late afternoon Godfrey returned, escorted by an archer. He wore a look of outrage. John helped the stern friar down.

'Why father, what has happened? Where is my uncle?'

Godfrey's cheekbones showed through his drawn face. 'He has ridden on to Gloucester.'

'Gloucester! Why to Gloucester?' John was astonished and could not conceal his concern.

'Because the king's Justice of the Peace will not act!'

John was appalled. 'Will not act? In God's name why?'

'It seems that the Compworths have made representations to him already. They have laid a charge against your uncle.' John's mouth dropped. He gulped like a trout thrown up on to the bank. 'They claim that his bailiff attacked one of their men in Great Wolford. Furthermore, they accuse your uncle of assault on their shepherds by the Nethercote Brook.'

'This is infamous! By Our Lady, it was their men who murdered the bailiff and their men who were stealing our sheep. Surely the justice dismissed such nonsense?'

Godfrey shook his head.

'Mother of God! He did not believe them?'

'More than that.'

'More? What more could he do? This is beyond belief.'

'He instructed your uncle to appear before the Hundred court and answer the indictment brought by the Compworths.'

'You jest! You must be. This is simply not possible.'

Godfrey was not a jesting man. 'As I stand before you, John Mentmore, so did he speak to your uncle. And should the Hundred court accept the claims of the Compworths . . .'

'Then my uncle will be carried off to Gloucester castle to be tried by a circuit judge of the king at the assize.'

'That is it.' Godfrey's reply was bitter.

'Think you that the justice at Campden is in the pocket of Compworth?'

'I think he is their creature, their puppet to dance as they will.'

John hissed and caught at the horse's bridle. 'And what did my uncle say to this . . . this tissue of lies?'

'Your uncle was not restrained in his response.'

'I'm damn sure he was not.' John laughed suddenly. 'By all

that's holy he must have gone wild.'

'Curiously enough not. He simply promised the justice that he would cut his nose off if he found for a nest of vipers like the Compworths. He was quite calm but not ... not restrained.' Even Godfrey had to smile at the memory. 'And now he has ridden to Gloucester castle to lay his complaint before the sheriff there. If anyone can right this injustice, 'tis him.'

With that, John had to be content. Until Giles returned he could not guess what course of action would follow.

For two days he wandered the hall like a wraith. Although he was numb at the actions of the justice he did not forget to post his guards or to send armed riders out about the estate. Despite his preparation there was no further outrage. It was as if their enemies, too, were watching and waiting.

He was possessed again by that mental and physical tension which had afflicted him the Christmastide after the Gloucester parliament. He missed his wife intensely. It was a chaste existence which left him feeling like a coiled spring. At night he tossed and turned, haunted by the physical desire which threatened to eat him up. He longed for that utter relief which intercourse would bring him; the exhausting, desperate release brought by a coupling.

He became acutely aware of the serving maids and the slightest touch, or glance, could arouse his desire and fan the flames. The flaxen-haired girl, who watched him with mocking eyes, was always so close. There were times when he thought he might wipe that condescending look from her brazen face. He could summon her to his chamber and once there he would rape her. His hard thrusts would turn her mocking glance into pants of desire, like a bitch on heat. She would not look on him as half a man when he forced her writhing legs apart and rutted her to exhaustion. My God, he thought. What am I about? He had sat at table and watched the girl as she moved about the hall. He was conscious of the hot desperation of his own passion. No, by God. I'll not do it. And yet he still could not fully explain why not. It was difficult for him to grasp the true significance of his fevered self-denial: that he loved Philippa.

Giles returned to Upton on the eve of Mothering Sunday and the air in the hall was warm with the smell of simnel cake and spices. He gestured for John, Godfrey and his chief clerk – acting now as bailiff – to join him in the solar.

'The Lord Sheriff of Gloucestershire has given me a warning,' he began. He was tired and angry. He had ridden home through a spring countryside suddenly alive with bluebells and wood edges fragrant with sweet violets, yet this year he had been unmoved by these sure signs of returning life which usually quickened the pulse and brought joy to a population sick of salt meat and dark days.

'Has given you a warning? You?' John was incredulous.

'Yes, me! He has, so he says, received allegations against me from my enemies and has already consulted with others in authority – '

'The justice at Campden,' Godfrey interrupted, forgetting himself.

'The very same. As a result, the sheriff orders that I desist from violence against my . . . peaceable neighbours – his words, not mine – and duly appear before the Hundred court in April. To which I did reply that the late king – God hold his soul in eternal peace – did, in the third year of his reign, remove all sheriffs throughout the realm for wrongful indictments, false returns, wrongful arrests and the packing of juries.'

'And he replied?' John grinned at his uncle's nerve.

'His reply was not suitable to be reported in the hearing of my chaplain,' Giles said. 'I feel, mayhap, he would have seized me there and then, but even a corrupt rogue desires the cloak of legality at times.'

'He would never have dared.' John's grin had faded.

'John, my boy,' Giles said, smiling the smile of one who has seen too much of the work of the world to be so sure as his nephew, 'never underestimate what money can buy. Never underestimate what a sheriff may do! 'Tis barely fourteen years since a sheriff stood accused of torturing a servant till he made false accusations against his master.'

Godfrey coughed. 'I was at York, my lord, in the year after the pestilence slew the children. 'Twas there a jury was so packed by the sheriff that the king's attorney himself did protest. And at the county assize itself.'

'You see, John? Do not underestimate the corruption of a sheriff. Nor what he respects most . . .' Giles dropped his hand to his sword hilt. It was a simple but eloquent gesture. 'And in the meantime,' Giles continued, 'I shall send my new bailiff to instruct lawyers at the Court of Common Pleas to settle this dispute as to my rights in Great Wolford once and for all! And while he is in London he can take my sealed account of what has passed between me and the sheriff to the king's circuit judge for this shire. You may also wish him to take a letter to your wife.'

John nodded eagerly. He had not written since Candlemas in February. He was already planning out what he would say to Philippa.

That night Giles was in a determined mood. After the usual light supper he sat in the solar playing board games with John. For half an hour they played at fox and goose. In the end John was beaten.

'There,' Giles said with the air of one imparting secrets, 'your mind was not on the game. You forgot the formula for winning: the fox must strike at the goose whenever he has the chance. Mayhap the time is right, mayhap it is not. Yet he must not hesitate, John. He must leap to kill when the opportunity arises.' He lifted the solitary fox counter. 'He must jump the goose even if the move carries him into danger.'

He rose from the table, giving his nephew a meaningful glance. It was already nine o'clock and time for bed. Outside an owl hooted. Away in the woods a dog fox was stirring. His bark cut through the night. More distant still, a vixen screamed her reply.

It was traditional on Mothering Sunday for the servants to visit their families in the villages. In these country cottages, where meat was a rarity and fresh white bread a fantasy, efforts were made to make something of this day. A 'toad' of batter and dried fruit might be boiled over the open fire and eaten with cabbages and parsnips from the tiny closes around each dwelling. Here and there a richer woman might sacrifice carrots from her store. It was a day for celebration, despite poverty.

The Saxon-headed girl who had so obsessed John took leave to visit her widowed mother in Great Wolford. It was early in the morning when she set out. If she was to attend church in the village, she would have to walk briskly. In a rough withy basket she carried a precious batch of simnel cakes. Each one was a pastry case filled with fruits, candied peel and spices. These oversize mince tarts had set her back a tidy sum. She carried them with care.

Kilting her skirts she waded over the Ditchford of the Knee Brook. In the nearby village hens were clucking and smoke was rising through holes in rotten thatch. It was a fine, fresh morning. Flocks of redwings and fieldfares swooped low over the waves of turned furrows in the open fields. In the closes between the village and the curving strips the curly heads of kale whispered to each other. Out on the common land scrawny pigs and sheep grazed on the rough turf.

Singing softly some half-remembered ballad of Robin Hood she walked out along the grassy baulk which separated the furlong blocks of strips. To her right the ploughland gave way to a wide strip of meadow. On one side the meadow was bounded by a drainage ditch, or sike. From the shelter of the sike three men were watching her. Had she been at Todenham on Ash Wednesday she would have recognised them as Compworth thugs. As it was she did not even see them.

Adam Attechurche too had risen early. He often woke before dawn, despite his preparations in wine. Mothering Sunday only served to emphasise his isolation. His parents had died of the spotted fever and he had no children. Cecilia had borne two sons but both had preceded their mother into the grave.

Adam had other things on his mind. The Todenham reeve had warned him of a hedge priest sheltering at the Compworth manor. It was not the first time that Adam had come across such an itinerant, unfrocked priest. They always meant trouble. To him they were unregenerate renegades. Even his easy-going nature was affronted by a man who could earn himself a dismissal from his living and the loss of his priestly status. That such a man could then be so bold as to tramp the country peddling the heresy or subversion that had caused his dismissal revealed a depth of naked sin which made Adam shudder.

The bitter taste in Adam's mouth was caused by the popularity of such men amongst the ignorant sheep of a parish flock. Their preaching on the damnation of the rich and the blessedness of the poor was greeted with a warmth which made Adam blush. He knew how easily the more corrupt of such a dangerous breed could be harnessed by the likes of the Compworths. More than this, Adam felt his precarious authority crumbling. For hedge priests did not take tithes.

This early morning he had walked out to the closes of his glebe land where he grew cabbages and the white-headed cauliflower which he loved. He had stopped to watch the fieldfares when he was suddenly aware of the screaming of a woman. Two men were clutching at a struggling girl as a third looked on. Despite her violent movements they were dragging her along a baulk. Laughing and swearing they were heading towards the woodland and wild pasture called High Furze. The woman's cotte was up about her waist. Her slim legs kicked the air. One of the men was virtually carrying her. The other was groping her as they went along. The third was shouting encouragement.

Adam knew the girl by sight. She was a servant of de Brewoster. The two men he recognised also. They were members of Compworth's private army. In the arable fields two hooded Todenham villeins watched the abduction. They made no attempt to intervene. What did it matter to them that three men were intent on raping a girl? She was no relation of theirs. She was from Great Wolford and so a foreigner. More than that, she was of the lord's manor. Let him look to her safety.

Adam felt the blood drain from his cheeks. What could he do? He was not a well man and the church service would soon be starting. The girl was not one of his villagers. Shaking his head, he turned away. He was not brave.

Then her terrified scream came again across the furlongs. Adam froze. He saw the reeve's daughter floundering in the mill leat. He saw Cecilia coughing blood and wide-eyed with agony. He saw sweet innocence despoiled. He saw the destroyer at work in God's field. He saw hell gaping open to devour the souls of men.

Adam Attechurche roared. He roared like a goaded bull. Then he was running across the ploughed land. Mud caked his boots. His black skirt flew. His walking stick was raised like an avenging sword.

'God's blood!' one of the Todenham villeins cried. 'The priest has gone mad.'

For an instant they watched his wild run. Then they too were moving, racing after him.

Adam Attechurche descended on the would-be ravishers like the wrath of God. His stick sent one reeling, blood-soaked. The

Todenham villeins were shouting. Like Gideon at the camp of the Midianites, the terror of the Lord swept the enemy. They turned and fled.

Adam surveyed the scene. 'You – ' He pointed to an awestruck villein. 'Get help from the village. And you, go take word of this outrage to the Lord de Brewoster. Go!'

The two villeins, totally overcome by his authority, ran as bidden.

That day – Mothering Sunday, 1380 – the armed retainers of Giles de Brewoster descended upon Little Wolford with sword and bill. With them was Adam Attechurche, the parish priest of Todenham. They killed or put to flight the lordless men who had sold their swords to the Compworths and shut up the Compworth family in its manor house whilst they fired the outbuildings.

One week later Giles was summoned to appear before the shire court. To ignore such a summons could lead to outlawry. He did not go. Two days later, on the Tuesday of Holy Week, an indignant sheriff came, armed, to Upton with the constable of the Hundred, the Compworths and the posse comitatus.

At Upton he was met by Giles de Brewoster and John Mentmore. Both wore hauberks of mail and carried swords on their hips. With them was the lord of the neighbouring manor of Ebrington. All wore mail. All were in the company of their armed retainers and their sub-tenants.

Also there was Attechurche. Before those present he accused the Compworths of sheltering the killers of Giles's bailiff and the rustlers of his sheep and servants. A wind of change was blowing through Upton. Shepherds and cowherds stepped forward to make similar accusations. The sheriff was pale. He had not counted on a war. Nor had he counted on such stinging evidence.

Then Giles stepped forward, hand on sword hilt. In contemptuous tones he informed those who accused him of the indictment which he had sent to the circuit judge of the king. Then, like a fox facing a goose, he drew his sword.

'And until that day, when I shall accuse my enemies before the assize, let no man violate my manor or any who are mine.' The April sun glinted on the long band of razor-edged steel.

The armed retainers roared. Stamping and snorting, the

sheriff's horse almost reared at the noise. Calming his mount, he nodded. His eyes were bitter but what else could he do?

The point had been made. Giles de Brewoster was not intimidated. The fox had seized the goose.

Chapter Eleven

Ann Mentmore was just over one year old. She had toddled early and by her first birthday was already staggering about the family home. It was remarkable the way her lack of stability was in direct contrast to her speed of movement. Despite tumbles and near disasters her inquisitiveness increased and little fingers were soon exploring everything in sight.

Philippa was pregnant again. She had conceived within two months of John's return from the Cotswolds and now she was experiencing a crippling nausea which defied belief. She scarcely ate, for her appetite had quite collapsed. Despite the common name for this sickness, she found that it was by no means confined to the morning. The constant feeling of dizzy illness knew no such limits.

Dinnertime on this particular day had been a sore trial. Overcome with revulsion of food, she had retired to her chamber and its box bed. The day was hot and Emma attended her. Dipping clean linen strips in a pitcher of water, she applied them to Philippa's perspiration-streaked brow.

'Mistress, this is not right. The sickness should not be so bitter, nor last so long.'

Philippa moaned. 'Mayhap not but it does! 'Twill do no good to lecture it, for it does not listen.'

'Were men to suffer so, there would be a shortfall of infants. My mother did once tell me that a man and his wife should take turns at having children. That way the woman would only bear once.'

Philippa shook her head at her maid's frittering talk. 'How come you by that calculation? Surely the two would double the size of the litter. If dog and bitch whelp there'll soon be no room in the kennel.'

Emma smiled slyly. She had deliberately tried to steer her mistress's mind off her suffering. It seemed to have worked – for a while.

'No, mistress. For they would take it in turns and not miss out a turn. First the man would bear and then the woman. Then it would be the man's turn once more. But men are such feeble creatures they would baulk at such pain a second time. So the litter would end.'

'Oh Emma, you are such a foolish girl. Whoever heard of such a thing?' Then she laughed and Emma was satisfied that her foolishness had not been wasted.

But even Emma's silly chatter could not steer Philippa's mind from the churning pit in her belly. These last few weeks she had begun to dread the yearly occurrences of agonising pregnancy. Ann had been almost easy. This was turning into quite a different story. If her life was to be punctuated with months of such discomfort, it was not a happy prospect.

It alarmed her how rapidly her maternal instincts had dissolved in the fierce heat of this persistent sickness. She had considered buying a jasper stone to hide under her pillow. The crystal's power to prevent pregnancies was legendary. She had purchased some brake root. Taken in wine, it had similar properties. She was aware that such an action was a dreadful sin and consoled herself with the thought that she had not used the brake root, but the awfulness of her intentions disturbed her peace. The priest would be only too keen to remind her: 'In sorrow will you bring forth children.'

Emma wetted her hot forehead. ''Tis not fair that men should cause this but not suffer any of it.'

'Hush, girl. You know how John worries about me. He has scarce left my side since this sickness began. I am blessed to have such a good husband.'

Emma had to agree that John Mentmore had been very dutiful. Most men would have taken no interest in their wife's pain. Nevertheless, she held men responsible for the trouble.

At that moment, the object of Emma's silent accusation was on his way to the tapestry shed. In one hand he held the sticky little fist of his white-haired daughter.

John had grown concerned at Philippa's illness and had

resolved to take Ann away from her mother. The move was proving as demanding as it was revolutionary. The servants stopped to watch. It was not often that a father showed such an interest in his child. The way children sickened and died it could be a waste to invest too much emotion in one so young. The servants shook their heads at his prodigal expenditure of time and feeling on such a scrap. Only Agnes Bakwell smiled indulgently.

The weaving shed had risen from the ashes of the old one. Kirkby and Lyons' loans had helped raise its stout timbers. Despite the hatred of the royal tapestry makers the Mentmores had wasted no time in re-erecting the structure, and while John hid himself away at the Gloucester parliament Thomas had begun work on the new shed. Ignoring the sensibilities of the rival craftsmen he had brought in practised Flemish weavers from Arras. His master craftsman was a Breton who had worked in the great production houses of Paris.

As John entered the shed, he lifted up his daughter to see the hustle and bustle in this hive of activity. Charles de Gouarec stopped his supervision of a group of workers and bid John a cheery good afternoon. The Breton was a good-natured craftsman. His consciousness of his own expertise removed any trace of nervousness in the presence of his master's son. The two men were soon exchanging snatches of conversation in French.

John had not been the prime mover behind the expansion into tapestry work. It had been Thomas's idea and the senior Mentmore tended to keep a close eye on his brainchild, but John was fascinated by the skill and artistry evident in the production of these luxury items.

Before him a superb representation of St Michael killing a dragon was slowly taking shape. The great low-warp loom was stretched out over a trestle table. Beneath the taut thread John could make out the cartoon painted on to a canvas guide. The main lines of the figure were being marked on the vertical warp threads with ink.

De Gouarec and John Mentmore watched the outline begin to be transferred on to the overlying thread.

'What materials are you using for this one?' John enquired.

'The warp is wool, as usual, but for the weft we are using a mixture of wool, silk and silver thread. Between them they will bring out the texture of the piece. 'Twill be a beauty and no mistake. You are watching a masterpiece being formed.'

De Gouarec spoke with real pride. His attitude was infectious. All his workers partook of his high standards and exacting skills. John reached out and brushed the silver threads wound in a spiral on fine silk. It felt as rich as it looked. The angel's crown glowed in the light. Ann reached out a sticky finger too.

'It is beautiful, Charles.'

'Truly it is. But in Byzantium they work solely in silk. That is a sight to see, believe me. The way it catches the light! It is truly a wonder to behold.'

John could believe it. 'How do you follow the pattern so perfectly?' he asked. ''Tis a marvel and no mistake.'

Charles was in his element now. He loved nothing more than a rapt audience. For that he could even begin to forgive the grimy fingers catching hold of a stray warp thread. He signalled the weaver to move and settled himself on the stool beside the loom.

He lifted the small shuttle attached to the cross thread, or weft. Swiftly he wove it under and over the taut warp threads.

'Each passage of the shuttle we call a pick. We use each colour thread only in that area where the picture calls for it. It saves on thread, of course.' Picking up a batten he pushed the weft thread up tight against threads picked earlier. 'When we have finished, the brightly coloured weft threads totally conceal the warp. The warp acts as the bones, but the flesh – that is the weft! Soon the warps are all concealed. You will only see them as tiny ridges in the finished panel.'

John was impressed. 'And the design? It is one of those you brought from Paris?'

Charles de Gouarec chuckled. 'You see this?' He gestured to the cartoon beneath the threads. 'This is based on a design I saw executed for the Duke of Anjou himself by Nicolas Bataille. It filled seven panels in the Bataille workshop in Paris. The cartoon was based on a work by Jean de Bandol. It is of the highest quality and a treasure itself.'

John smiled at the thought of a work by the official painter to the French king being copied in a London workshop. Would Gaunt or Woodstock appreciate the irony of that? Probably not! Come to think of it, the Duke of Anjou would not appreciate the fact that a bastard of his commission was being produced elsewhere. He, though, was the least of John's worries. The Channel and a war separated the Mentmores from the Duke of Anjou.

At the edges of the cartoon template the heraldic devices of Anjou had been replaced by the snarling leopards of England. That gave John a certain grim satisfaction. In a decade which had witnessed precious few English conquests, nothing was to be sniffed at.

Ann was growing bored of tapestries. She was squirming in her father's arms and whining shrilly. John relented and set her down. She tottered off to pester the litter of puppies tumbling and rolling in the straw of the yard. He watched her go with enormous pride. Charles de Gouarec watched her go with relief. He carefully wiped a smudge of plum jam from a handful of golden threads.

John would have lingered amongst the tapestries but he was disturbed by Tom, the Mentmores' senior journeyman.

Sidling up to him he whispered: 'Newton is back in town.'

John's smile vanished and a storm rushed across his previously sunny features. He clenched his fists. 'Is he, by God? Is he indeed?'

When John Mentmore had returned from Giles de Brewoster's estates, he had heard the old news of Philippa's exploits in Threadneedle Street. Whilst he had been touched by his wife's intention not to disrupt his Cotswold adventures, he had wished that she had let him know earlier. More than ever he had been grateful for Edmund's quick wits and savage martial abilities. Few could have dispelled a mob of groping lechers more effectively than that young fury.

With mounting anger he had heard his wife and brother point to the weavers as the source of their discomfort and distress. Once again John had been in the narrow alleyway with the murderous leper. He listened to the tale of the man with the scratched face and the twisting alleys which had led Philippa into danger.

He was moved that his wife had done so much for him. Such loyalty did not go unnoticed. He was also indignant that Edmund's protests to alderman and constable had not turned up the man. He seemed to have vanished into the same hazy limbo as the raspberry-stained killer of Adam Yonge. Without doubt, someone was sheltering these men.

John had few doubts who one such man might be. The words

of Dick Appulby came back to him like a throbbing drumbeat and he could see clearly the pattern behind the attacks upon his family. The trail leading back along Threadneedle Street took his suspicions once more towards one person – Robert Newton.

Yet John had been thwarted of his prey. His immediate search for Newton had turned up the news that he was out of the city. Even that kindled John's suspicions. What was this scheming weaver about? No one seemed willing to tell. Once more John came up against the weavers' wall of silence.

Now Newton had returned, yet he was not lying low. If Tom was correct, the scheming architect of Mentmore troubles was out and about amongst the weaving guilds as bold as brass. As John searched for Edmund, and assembled the burliest of the retainers, he knew that he must strike as Giles had struck against the Compworths.

Edmund was in a bad mood. He had recently returned from Giles's Essex manor and was now busily engaged in contracting for the Duke of Buckingham's planned summer campaign in France. His bad mood, however, did not stem from either of these occupations. He had recently learned that Anne Glanville was to be betrothed to Ralph Horne, the son of the Billingsgate alderman. The woman in question had not been seen in London since her warning to John at the tournament. It was as if she had deliberately kept away from the city. Since Edmund had hoped she might prove to be a pleasant diversion, this had been a disappointment and the latest news came as something of a bitter blow. Edmund had never underestimated the potential problems of a romance between himself and a relative of the fishmongers. Relations between the guilds had been strained for some time and the events of the Gloucester parliament had intensified the enmity. Despite this he had kept his hopes alive, and the news of her betrothal was, to quote his usual phrase, as popular as the proverbial leper in a brothel.

John's plans to invade the weavers' quarters appealed to his more violent instincts. He was spoiling for a fight. Woe betide the man who crossed Edmund Mentmore in this mood. Philippa reacted to John's martial preparations with less enthusiasm. She feared for her husband's safety in such an encounter. She had good cause to fear the violence of the weavers.

John would hear no talk of pacifism. Still less was he inclined to place the matter in the hands of the constable. His experiences at Upton had reduced his faith in the officers of the law. He was determined to face Newton himself. Burning with righteous indignation, he was convinced that Newton's story would crumble before his own carefully gleaned evidence.

It was in this mood that the armed gang made its way to the shed of the weaver in question. Its passage through the streets attracted a following crowd. Any diversion was an attraction to the idle. Both John and Edmund carried swords. The retainers were armed with staves. Tom, the journeyman, led the liveried escort.

As the Mentmores approached the weavers' quarter, word went ahead of them. Looms fell silent. Shuttles were laid down. Faces appeared at doors and at open windows. Robert Newton was in the midst of his own workers. He had clearly been preoccupied with his work and the sudden intrusion startled him. Around the room the upright looms were hung with cloth. In one corner lay bales of finished cloth ready for transportation to the warehouses of the mercers.

The startled weavers left their work as John and Edmund Mentmore burst in. It was not commonplace for a mercer to visit the sheds in person. That the Mentmore brothers came with such a crowd and in such haste signalled trouble. Newton's brown eyes narrowed. John marvelled at the man's duplicity. How could he manage to look the innocent as nemesis approached him?

'Master Newton, you have proved to be a most elusive fellow. Long have we sought to speak with you. Is it your habit to vanish from the city?' John's voice carried a heavy note of accusation. It was as if Rob Newton's unavailability proved complicity in a crime.

Newton's face reddened with anger. 'What have my movements to do with you, John Mentmore?'

There was no hint of deference in him. He jutted out his bushy beard in fury. The scar at his mouth twisted in a sardonic grimace. The other weavers were muttering.

'You do not deny, then, that you have been hiding?'

Newton's surprise could have been genuine. He did not comprehend the question and shook his head in puzzlement. 'What? Who has spoken of hiding? I was not hiding.'

John had made discreet enquiries concerning the weaver's whereabouts. No one seemed to know. Even his own journeymen had found it hard to conceal their total lack of knowledge. This secrecy only added to the weight of guilt surrounding Newton, in John's opinion.

'You'll not deny, I trust, that you have spent much time out of the city and have made a secret of your travels?'

'God's blood, have you been spying on me? My men told me that Mentmore agents were snooping, yet I'd never have cast you as the spy.'

'You knew I sought you and still you avoided me?'

Rob Newton was growing exasperated. He paced the floor of the shed. The eyes of the weavers were on him.

'If you seek me you can find me! It is not for me to come, cap in hand, to you, sir. Besides, I only heard between visits. I had no time to search you out and declare my location. You assume a lot, by God. You assume a lot!'

John sneered: 'And were these visits decided on before or after your men attacked me last summer and assaulted my wife afterwards?'

Newton's jaw dropped. 'What? *What?*'

'By Our Lady, this is a feast of duplicity. So you'll deny it, will you? You'll deny that you have any knowledge of these attacks?'

'No, I'll not deny I know of them. Word travels fast. I heard of them but I know no more than what is carried by common gossip.'

This was not true; Margaret had told him more. He had seen her since the day of the tournament. With any other woman such clandestine meetings would have proved impossible but Thomas Mentmore allowed his daughter a long leash, long enough to take her to Rob Newton.

'And did common gossip tell you that the footpad was a weaver? We know more than you think we do, for my wife recognised one of the scum who so cowardly attacked us. She saw him again. She followed him to your shed.'

The last barbed comment was a lie. Philippa had not known where the man was headed. Newton exploded with spitting fury.

'What? To my shed? 'Tis no business of mine where men wander. You'll not trap me in this accusation, Mentmore. I have done no wrong and you'll not prove otherwise.' Then a look of understanding flashed over his features. 'If 'twas so, why did you not proceed to arrest him? If you truly have such information why did you not act on it? You are lying, Mentmore. Lying through your teeth!'

'You know full well that no court would accept a woman's testimony against that of a guildsman. Besides, I was away. My wife waited until my return. Then I sought you but you were hiding.'

'Ha, John Mentmore,' Newton said mockingly. 'So it is well for you to leave the city but not for me to do so! Besides, even if your story is true – and I'll warrant 'tis a tissue of lies – none of this involves me. You have no charge to bring against me.'

'Not I, perhaps. Not I – But Adam Yonge!' John's voice was raised.

'Adam Yonge? What has he to do with this? Poor Adam has been dead for over three years.'

'Poor Adam.' John imitated Newton's words. 'What care you for Adam Yonge? A man whom you had murdered.'

There was a crystal clear silence in the weaving shed. The charge was out now. No one spoke. Shock was etched on all faces present. Then a weaver moved. A shuttle clattered to the plank floor. The spell was broken. The shed erupted into confusion.

Rob Newton growled and leapt at John. Edmund drew his sword. Mentmore retainers sprang forward. Weavers surged towards them. A weaving journeyman seized Newton and held him back. The hall was on the brink of warfare as the resentments of the past few years came boiling to the surface. Livery guildsmen faced craftsmen; naked hate was etched on their faces. Daggers were drawn.

John shouted, 'His murderous intentions are displayed for all to see. This ... this is the man who knows nothing of violent crime, yet look how he does act. He strikes first. You saw!'

Newton was panting. He pushed aside the journeyman and faced Mentmore. Two feet of blistered air separated them. Both men had clenched fists. Both jutted out jaws in defiance.

'Listen Mentmore,' Newton snarled. 'Listen to me. I am no killer. I am stung by what you say as any innocent man would be stung. By God, I have done you no wrong.' His chest was heaving.

'Will you deny that there was bad blood between you and

Adam Yonge? Will you deny it?'

'On Christ's cross I deny it.'

'Will you deny that he saw you much before he died? That you had words? Will you deny that you saw much of Yonge?'

Robert's face paled. 'I'll not deny that.'

'Hah, hah!' John spat out.

'To see a man is not to kill him. I never did harm to your clerk. I never touched him.'

'Then why did he come to you? With strikes between us, why did he come to you? Surely to accuse you of calumny and so you killed him.'

It seemed a lifetime since Appulby had divulged this information in the tavern by Baynard Castle and it had been festering in John's mind. For all his suspicions, it had never been quite enough as evidence. Then it had been undermined by Newton's willingness to accept compromise and by the realisation that the Mentmores had enemies in more than one quarter. Only since Philippa's trailing of the weaver had Appulby's information been vindicated. Now it was out in the open.

John repeated his question. 'Why did Adam come to you?'

'That is no business of yours, John Mentmore.'

'No business of mine? By God, you have killed my clerk, tried to kill me and my wife and it is no business of mine? By God, you'll tell me! You'll tell us all!'

'I will not.' Newton's mouth was sealed. He would not divulge any more. Even weavers were frowning now.

Edmund stepped forward. For much of this drama he had had doubts about John's tactics, but now he harboured them no longer. The man was hiding something. Edmund was still holding his sword. He gave a menacing grimace.

'You'll do best to speak, weaver. Your life will soon hang upon how you answer these charges. Why did Yonge come to you when there was nought but bitterness between you? He our clerk and you a weaver in dispute with the house of Mentmore? Speak, man!'

Rob had seen the frowns on the faces of his own men. They did not give a damn about Adam Yonge, yet they had expected Newton to destroy the Mentmore accusation. That he had not done.

'I'll not speak. What passed between Yonge and me is of no

business to you. And whoever killed him 'twas not me.'

The last sentence was on a note of pure defiance.

John relaxed. For a few moments even he had begun to have doubts about his tactics, but Newton's refusal to explain his meetings with Yonge condemned him. It was with relief that John now cast a new stone into the pond. Soon its ripples were racing hither and thither.

'Yet you came to our hall, or its environs, the night before Yonge died, did you not? It was the night before the riot. I trust you have not forgotten that.'

Robert Newton looked as if he was going to be sick. He almost swayed.

'Don't deny it, Robert. I have a witness.' John's voice was as cool and smooth as a misericord blade. It was also as sharp. It slipped between the plates of Newton's armour. It wounded.

'I'll not deny it.'

There were intakes of breath throughout the room.

'So,' John continued softly, 'you did see my clerk often, you did go to him the night before he died?'

'I did not go to him,' Newton said.

'Then whom did you see in the neighbourhood of our hall?'

At that point Newton could have exploded John's argument. He could have said that he visited a brothel or a tavern. He could have said anything. He could even have told the truth. Instead, his face crumpled in dismay. He swallowed hard. He would not betray Margaret.

'I will not say. I do not have anything to hide . . . and I will not say.'

The contradiction in that sentence was apparent to all. Edmund reached out to seize Newton, who fended him off.

Suddenly the weavers were galvanised into action. Rightly or wrongly, their master was about to be seized. They surged to his defence. The Mentmores were pushed back. A weaving frame collapsed and cloth and yarn spilled over the floor. A man was stabbed. Despite their anger, the Mentmores could no longer reach Newton. He was separated from them by a choppy sea of fellow craftsmen. More were arriving by the minute.

'We'll get you, Newton!' John yelled. 'You'll not escape the rope!'

Then he and Edmund were forced from the shed by the

rapidly developing riot. The street was crammed with onlookers eager to catch a glimpse of the fighting.

'We'll get you, Newton. By God, you'll feel the burn of a rope.'

Inside the now empty shed, Robert Newton surveyed the wreckage of his life. He reached down and gathered up the scattered cloth. He was quite devastated.

John wasted no time in securing lawyers from the Inns of Court. He was determined to put a noose around Robert Newton's neck. Then, in the midst of this turmoil, William returned home from Oxford.

The mouse-haired scholar was in a bitter mood. The confidence which had so riled Godfrey de Avalon had melted away. The night after his return he sat listlessly with the family in the solar. The women were sewing, the clerk was reading a passage from *The Book of the Knight of La Tour*.

John had passed a busy week since the confrontation with Newton. He had quickly set plans in motion for the arrest of the weaver. He wished to leave nothing to chance. Only that afternoon he had completed yet another exhausting session with his attorney - a man steeped in the intricacies of the Common Law of England. When John finally took his case to constable and sheriff he wanted it watertight. Witnesses needed to be questioned and their statements noted. Under no circumstances did John wish a sergeant-at-law in the King's court to find glaring gaps or inconsistencies in the evidence presented by John's advocate.

Only that afternoon John, Edmund and the attorney had re-questioned Appulby in the privacy of the solar. Once again, as pen scribbled, he reported the movements of Newton and of Yonge. He added that Newton had long breathed threats against the Mentmores but was reluctant to make his charges. 'I feel terrible,' he had said over a mug of wine, 'for Newton and I are of the same mystery. Yet, by God, I'll not condone murder.' John would have liked to see the thug whom Philippa had followed more clearly linked to Newton and had said as much to Appulby who had promised to keep his ears open. When this was over the Mentmores would look favourably upon the work from Appulby's weaving shed.

It was not only these things that John was pondering whilst he listened to the soft tones of the clerk. A warm evening sun was filtering through the thick glass medallions. A fly buzzed about the room. June 1380 was turning out to be pleasant and dry. John surveyed his family. Thomas was sipping at his wine. Margaret, like Philippa, was sewing as she listened to the words falling from the lips of the clerk, but she was pale and looked ill. Philippa had remarked on this to John and he had raised the subject with his sister but she had brushed off his concern. By the trestle table Edmund was studying a roll of vellum. Beside him William leaned against the wall panels. When the clerk had finished, John went over to join his two brothers. 'Is it your new contract?' He motioned to Edmund's vellum sheet.

'Aye, so it is.' Edmund pushed it towards him.

John picked up the thick material and scanned the carefully penned words.

'This indenture made between Thomas Duke of Buckingham of the first part and Edmund Mentmore of the other part; witnesses that Edmund Mentmore is bound to the said Duke of Buckingham to serve him for the campaign which the said duke shall make to France . . .'

John flicked over the rest of the document. Every now and then a phrase caught his attention and he lingered on it. 'The said Edmund shall have with him thirty men-at-arms' . . . 'he shall take for the wages of each man-at-arms ten marks and each archer fifteen marks for the said year' . . . 'and that the said Edmund shall take wages, of himself, of sixty marks.' John glanced at his brother. 'This will be a long campaign. Does the duke intend to winter in France?'

Edmund nodded. 'The Duke of Brittany, Jean, Comte de Montfort, has given the use of the Castle of Brest to our lord the king. The French King Charles was not best pleased at that news. The bad blood between him and Montfort runs deep since Montfort repudiated his French vassalage and rejoined us as an ally. 'Tis less than two years since Charles tried Montfort in his absence and declared his dukedom confiscated, but Montfort drowned the priest sent as messenger from Charles and now stands in open rebellion against the French king. He knows full well the old hatred between the Bretons and the King of France. His Breton lords will not desert him in a conflict with Charles, and this conflict suits us well. Going to de Montfort's aid gives us a gate and entrance against the French. This matter of the Breton forts opens up a way into France and we'll not let the opportunity go by. And Charles knows it – and would deny us use of Brest, if he could. He knows we have to extend our bridgehead in France if we are to win the war.'

'As Gaunt tried at St Malo,' William said with contempt. Edmund eyed his brother. He did not take offence at the words. He had no time for Gaunt's military ability.

'Aye, as Gaunt tried and failed to do.'

William sniggered.

'How think you Woodstock will do as commander? Does the Duke of Buckingham exceed the Duke of Lancaster in martial skill?' John raised a querying eyebrow at Edmund as he asked his question. The women continued to sew.

'By St John,' Edmund said, 'it would be hard to do less well! But to be serious: he goes in earnest and his commanders are men to be trusted. He has given commands to Sir Hugh Calvely, Sir Thomas Percy and to Sir Robert Knollys. The French will not rest easy in their beds while the like of Knollys are abroad.' Edmund looked forward to serving under Knollys again. The bluff Cheshireman was a legend in his own time.

William twisted in his seat. 'If all goes well, why have you not sailed this month as planned? It sounds as if Woodstock is quite as inept as the fool Gaunt.'

'William!' Thomas snapped. 'You will not speak so in my house. I shall not hear you talk of the Duke of Lancaster in such a fashion.'

No doubt Thomas was thinking of tapestry commissions for both dukes hanging from his looms.

'It does not become you, father, to be the defender of Gaunt. Not in this city.'

'By Our Lady, Will,' Edmund said teasingly, 'this is a sea change. 'Twas but a little while ago and you were at Godfrey de Avalon's throat on Gaunt's behalf.'

William could hardly deny his brother's jibe. He had once been an unashamed partisan of the Duke of Lancaster. Now that had changed. This year Wyclif had published his most radical document so far. Entitled 'The Eucharist', it had rejected the doctrine of transubstantiation, the selling of indulgences and the cults of saints. As the sharp-tongued Yorkshireman had sailed closer to heresy so he had been dropped by his royal patron. Gaunt had warned him of his danger but had been ignored. Wyclif marched to the beat of a different drum. Now he marched without Gaunt.

William rose to his feet. He was unsteady. His goblet tipped over and wine splashed on to the thick rushes. He opened his mouth as if to dismiss Edmund's reminder but no words came. The women raised their heads and studied his turmoil with detached glances. It was too much. He stormed out of the room.

For a while there was silence. The room was darker now. The sun was setting. A servant brought candles.

'He's right, of course,' Edmund said. 'We should have sailed this month. Woodstock has not yet completed his preparations so we'll not embark until July. God knows what we'd have done without Philipot. He's supplying the fleet to Woodstock's specifications.'

'He's a grocer who deals in a wide range of merchandise,' Thomas grunted.

'He is that,' Edmund agreed. 'Not many grocers can boast of having captured a pirate fleet.'

Edmund was remembering Philipot's triumph in destroying the fleet of the Scottish pirate whilst Gaunt was holed up in the failing siege of St Malo. That success had made Philipot many friends, but it had also earned him the jealousy of the aristocratic faction about Gaunt.

'Gaunt hates him for it,' John said with a wry smile. 'I can still remember with what relish the good duke removed Philipot from the post of treasurer of the poll tax at the Gloucester parliament.'

'But Philipot bounces back,' Edmund said. 'I'm told that the new parliament has made him one of the commissioners to review government spending. Which, of course, means reviewing Gaunt's spending.'

John laughed. He had no great love for Gaunt and had never adopted his father's stance of good will towards him. John was too suspicious a character. Even when Thomas made attempts to distance himself from the duke it did not greatly alter his friendly disposition towards his new customer and patron.

Seeking to steer the talk back to safer ground, Thomas broke in with: 'Philipot is certainly a good friend of this city. Only last year when the city set up the defence chain across the river, 'twas

Philipot who paid for one entire tower himself. He deserves gratitude for that if for nothing else.'

Edmund nodded. 'And more than that. With this delay in our start, many of the poorer knights have been forced to pledge their armour for cash. Philipot has redeemed a thousand jacks of armour himself. He's quite a man!'

Philippa was daydreaming. She was thinking of that far-off day when she had supervised the feast for this guildsman; the day she had finally turned on Margaret.

Margaret, too, looked distant. Was she also thinking of that bitter encounter? Or was her mind on other things? It was impossible to tell.

Soon Edmund was ready to join his soldiers at Southampton. He left on a showery morning along with Sir Robert Knollys and his personal knights. The following evening a muffled courier came seeking the warrior Mentmore. It was with disappointment that he learned of the man's departure only twelve hours previous. He would not deliver his message to John, claiming that his lady had sworn him to pass the message only to Edmund Mentmore. Seeing the bird had flown, and noting his destination, he left the hall and vanished into the rainy evening. John was full of curiosity but guessed the letter carried references to some amorous adventure of his brother.

Out in the street the courier remounted his horse. The city gates were not yet shut. With hard riding he could get well on to the Southampton road by dark. By nightfall he was beyond Southwark and riding for Guildford. He decided to keep going through the night. The rain had cleared and a moon lit his road.

At one point the track led down to a narrow ford. The place was deep and dark. The wet earth smelt of mugwort and the fragrant perfume of bog myrtle.

Footpads rose, as leaping patches of darkness. The courier's horse shied and the courier fell. Floundering in the water, he knew his arm was broken. A ragged bone broke the surface of the skin. His horse, on its feet again, had bolted.

A voice yelled coarsely: 'I've got him! I've got the . . . damn him, he's stabbed me. Catch the bastard. Stick the pig . . .'

Gasping for breath, the courier stumbled along the river bank seeking shelter. The footpads cascaded behind. Hands clutched at his cloak. His boots filled with water. A blade hammered into his back. Water filled his mouth as he was pummelled and pushed under.

One of the footpads jerked at the courier's leather pouch. Ripping it open, he tore at the letter with grimed hands. He stared – illiterate – at the jumble of squiggles on the vellum.

'My dear Edmund. I write to warn you. You have no idea of the danger facing your family. Death stalks you, and all for the price of . . .'

'Any money in it?' The illiterate shook his head. 'Then chuck it.'

The words and thoughts were swept away into darkness. Downstream a rat splashed in the river. For a moment its nose touched the waterlogged form which bobbed along in the current. Then it dived and was gone.

The same night a second visitor came to the Mentmore hall. It was the jaundiced Nicholas Smalecombe.

John had retired to his solar and was called by one of the servants. Since Smalecombe asked for him by name, he came directly down into the hall. He remembered the weaver's insolent attitude and was puzzled at this appearance. The weaver was waiting in the hallway which ran the width of the house and had an uneasy look about him. He clearly felt he was on enemy territory.

'Yes?' John enquired briskly. 'What do you want?'

Smalecombe glanced at the hovering servant. John took his drift and dismissed the man. Now he was alone with the weaver. From behind the screen came the sounds of the servants in the hall.

Smalecombe held out a small package to John. It was the size of a man's hand and wrapped in cloth.

John undid the package. The cloth fell to the passage floor. In his trembling hands he held a purse. An acanthus flower decorated one panel of the supple calfskin. He felt his mouth go dry. His stomach churned.

'Where did you get this?' His voice was suddenly hoarse.

'It is yours, then? Dick thought it must be.'

'Where did you get it, man?' John was urgent. He gripped Smalecombe's arm.

The yellow skin on the weaver's face twitched.

John remembered buying the purse on London Bridge. More importantly, he remembered where and when he had lost it. Once more he was in the lane with his reins cut. He could almost see the faces of the murderous 'lepers'.

Smalecombe shook his arm loose. 'Appulby's cousin is apprenticed to Robert Newton. He is working on his piece for consideration by the guild. 'Tis his masterpiece. If 'tis accepted to be of sufficient quality he will be a master himself...'

'For God's sake, man, what has this to do with the purse?'

'He was working late on his piece,' Smalecombe continued, 'and sought to compare it with the samples which Newton keeps at the back of his shed. In a stout box he keeps them. The box is locked. Appulby's cousin knows where the key is kept. He searched the box to find the right sample of cloth. God alone knows why Newton locks the box and hides the key. At least till now. For now we know. At the bottom of the box he found a store of silver pennies and this. It was hid like. The boy thought 'twas odd. He'd heard your purse was stolen, so he took it to Appulby. He told me to bring it directly to you.'

'So. So this at last is the proof I have been seeking. Tell Appulby he has the gratitude of the house of Mentmore. But where is Newton now?'

Smalecombe shrugged. 'He's in the city, that much I know. Where I cannot tell. He may be at his tenement above the weaving shed. You'll know where that is?' John nodded. 'But if he's not there, ask your sister.'

John froze. He stared at the man without any comprehension. 'What?'

'Ask your sister. She regularly meets him. At the Church of St Magnus they meet. Didn't you know?'

The question was malicious. Smalecombe knew that John could not possibly know. The mercer's face was a deathly mask.

'You jest, man, and 'tis not funny. Do not think this small service gives you the right to slander my sister.' John was rigid with fury.

''Tis no slander,' Smalecombe replied defensively. 'I can vouch for it myself. I have seen them there. I carry the witness of my own eyes. You'll not deny a man his own sight! Besides, Appulby's nephew found this.' He handed John a folded piece of vellum. On it was writing in Margaret's bold hand. Her name lay at the bottom of the script.

John dismissed him and ran back through the hall. In the solar, Margaret and the women were sewing. Thomas was checking accounts with a clerk. John burst in like a man demented.

'Get up, Margaret. And you – out!' The clerk vanished and Thomas gaped at his son. 'What do you know of Robert Newton?' John demanded of his sister.

Margaret was on her feet. Her face was scarlet. Her freckles glowed.

'How dare you? I hardly know the man ... I ...'

John held out the letter. Margaret's mouth dropped. 'Oh my God!'

John began to read: 'My darling Rob, I ache for you and cannot live without you. I will come away with you. But you must be careful. My brother makes plans to – '

'No, no, no! Stop it. Stop it!' Margaret's voice was hysterical. She snatched at the letter and thrust it into the candle flame.

John hit her. She reeled. He seized the flaming material and, striking it on the trestle, he put out the flame.

'So you have whored with the dog who murdered Adam!'

'Sweet Jesus, Margaret, is this so?' said Thomas.

Margaret, by a superhuman effort, took hold of herself and faced her accusers with deadly defiance.

'We are lovers ...'

Thomas struck her a blow which sent her flying. Blood spurted from her mouth. She crashed against a bench.

Philippa stood up. 'No, no – '

'Be silent, girl.' Thomas was in a wild fury. His daughter had shamed him beyond measure.

John stood over Margaret. 'Get to your room. We will deal with you later.'

Like his father he was doubly shamed. Not content with squandering her marital value, Margaret had done so with the enemy of the house. Soon it would be common knowledge. The house of Mentmore would be humiliated before the whole city.

Weeping bitterly, Margaret left the solar.

'And you can pray for your damn lover,' Thomas shouted after her. 'We shall have that impudent dog imprisoned for rape.

As God's my judge he shall be in prison before the end of tomorrow.'

Margaret stood at the door, her eyes wide with horror. She shook her head. Blood splattered her dress.

'No. He never took me by force. I loved him. I still love him. Never would he dishonour me.'

'Good God, woman,' Thomas spat back, 'who gives a damn what you think? A man has taken my daughter out of wedlock. It is your family shall decide if you were raped or not. No one shall give a groat for your views.'

Margaret turned into the darkness of the passage, totally destroyed.

For long hours Philippa was silent witness to the furious agony of her husband and her father-in-law. Together the two men, in shocked indignation, planned the swift destruction of Robert Newton.

At dawn they went to see Margaret. They needed more information. Almost at once, John was back in Philippa's room.

'She's gone!'

'What do you mean?' Philippa shrank against the wall, fearing some terrible outburst.

John gritted his teeth. 'She has forced open her window and has escaped. By God, she will learn to regret what she has done!'

Within the hour the journeymen and apprentices were up and horsed. In armed force they descended on Newton's weaving shed. He was not there. His weavers were at a loss as to his whereabouts. It did not take long to solve the mystery. The watchmen at Moorgate reported a man and a woman who left the city at first light. They shared a horse.

The day was glorious and the previous night's rain had passed on. The few puddles on the road were scattered beneath the galloping hooves of the pursuing Mentmores.

Margaret and Robert had no hope of outdistancing their pursuers. They were overtaken before they had made ten miles from the city. By mid-morning, before even they had reached Waltham Abbey, they had been seized.

By nightfall Robert Newton was in the ward lockup, prior to remand in Fleet Prison. Margaret was beaten and a prisoner in her own room.

Chapter Twelve

St Swithun's day, 15 July, was dry. To those who had watched the approach of the day with trepidation the sunshine came as a relief, for forty days of good weather could be counted on. To the troops encamped at Southampton it was a good omen.

Cogs and other merchantmen jostled at the wharves or lay at anchor in the estuaries of the rivers Test and Itchen. Philipot had worked hard to arrange sufficient transport for the Duke of Buckingham's army. The fleet assembled was testimony to his efforts. Nevertheless, the transports were insufficient for the task. It soon began to dawn on the officers charged with embarkation that this invasion was not beginning as planned.

Edmund and Stephen de Knolton watched the loading of yet another contingent of foot soldiers. The sun was hot. Sweat streaked the faces of soldiers carrying their bills and quilted jackets. Stephen was excited by the movement and the kaleidoscope of colours and standards.

'There are thousands of them.' He looked with amazement at the winding lines of English soldiery along the quayside. 'By Our Lady, I cannot count them!'

Edmund smiled indulgently. 'Knollys says the duke has gathered over five thousand. There are just a fraction here. The taverns – aye and the wastes beyond the city gates – are jammed with them.'

Stephen remembered riding through the pitched camp of part of the army. 'Is it true the king has pawned his jewels?' he asked.

Edmund pulled a face. ''Tis true enough, though God alone knows how Buckingham could have miscalculated the cost so. The word is that Richard raised ten thousand pounds by pawning his crown. And mark you this, Stephen: that sum of money will not see us through the next year. Not by a long way.'

Stephen whistled. To him ten thousand pounds seemed a sum beyond mortal comprehension. 'And if that money runs out . . .?'

'Not *if* Stephen, when! It will merely start the campaign. 'Twill be plunder and ransoms that will end it. And the wise towns making it worth our while to keep our soldiers off their fields of corn.'

Edmund thought of Philipot saving a thousand pawned jacks and a fleet not up to the task. Even his natural jauntiness could not accept such matters as cause for celebration. The parliament at Northampton with its poll tax, aiming to raise sixty-six thousand pounds, had from what John told him, sparked revolt in the countryside and even so it had not yielded sufficient cash to start the campaign. A deep twist of unease turned in his stomach. Such a cost and still the army was not ready for war. It did not bode well. The graduated poll tax of 1379 had been similarly squandered. Invested in an invasion fleet led by Sir John Arundel, twenty thousand pounds had been frittered away. Arundel had let his men rape nuns and despoil the countryside. And that before he sailed for France! Gossip said he had spent seven thousand on his own needs. Then, when at last he sailed, storms had wrecked his fleet. Arundel had drowned.

Such concerns did not come naturally to Edmund for he had a rare capacity for dismissing them. This spring, though, he had had his own taste of unrest on Giles's Essex manor. In no way did it compare to John's experience, but it gave him the uneasy feeling that the countryside was mined beneath his feet. Men openly said God had judged Arundel. Others said He would likewise judge those who taxed the poor in 1380. It was disquieting.

Stephen had not detected the change in his knight's mood; he had embarked on the futile task of counting the foot soldiers. Edmund watched him as he mouthed numbers, twitching his fingers as an abacus. He wondered if his lack of concern simply arose from being unable to read the situation. That was a dangerous weakness in a soldier. Sometime, he told himself, I must warn him about it.

Not now, though. The sun was high and the sky was summer

blue. The air was fresh with salt. Gulls cried on the faint breeze. Now there was hope of victory and exultation. There would be plenty of days ahead for warnings and for fears.

Thomas of Woodstock, Duke of Buckingham, sailed on 17 July and landed at Calais on 19 July. With him sailed the great English captains Sir Thomas Percy, Sir Hugh Calvely and Sir Robert Knollys. Edmund and Stephen took ship five days later on 22 July, the feast day of Mary Magdalene. Their crossing was uneventful. Their cog, in keeping with the makeup of the army, was almost exactly divided in its passengers between men-at-arms and archers. Despite frequent summer raids on the south coast by French and Spanish fleets no attempt was made to dispute the crossing.

It took two weeks for Philipot's navy to complete the great transportation. By the time the task was finished it had carried five thousand and sixty men to Calais. Paymasters juggled tally sticks and winced at the cost.

The movement of so many men and so much material turned Calais into a vast, sprawling armed camp. It was one of the few remaining English bridgeheads in France. Now Brest had been added to the English toeholds of Bordeaux and the Breton forts and Cherbourg had been acquired by treaty in 1378, there was a desperate need to extend and deepen this slender hold on France. If these forward bases could be advanced, King Charles V of France might be brought to heel.

Gaunt had tried at St Malo. Now it was the turn of his brutal and pugnacious brother. Could he do any better? All England was watching. France was waiting. The likes of William Mentmore had little faith in his ability; the likes of John Mentmore were paying for the attempt; the likes of Edmund Mentmore were chancing life and limb to make the venture a triumph.

Thomas of Woodstock was aggressive and ruthless. In his late twenties, his temperament was overbearing and he had the restless arrogance and love of violence of his dead brother the Black Prince. Yet Thomas was insecure. As he watched the twinkling lights of his great army, he felt a curious restlessness. He was not a reflective man. He dealt in the concrete not the abstract. As such, he did not possess the ability to analyse his own motives and weaknesses. Indeed, he would have been singularly incapable of admitting even the possibility of the latter.

Nevertheless he was a man driven by the need to prove himself. He had been passed over by his father in favour of his elder brother. It was only three months since he had been invested with the Order of the Garter, and men had begun to wonder whether he would ever aspire to that honour. Even Gaunt's son Henry had been honoured before him. It still rankled to recall how the dying Edward had acceded to Gaunt's desires for Edward's grandson before considering the needs of his own son.

Within the confines of his chamber his captains were planning the details of the forthcoming campaign. Once more, Thomas looked down from the castellated defences of the town of Calais. Then, with a shrug, he returned to the company of his commanders.

Percy, Calvely and Knollys were seated around a dark oak table. Its pitted surface was covered by a profusion of wine jars and pewter plates, a leg of cold mutton lying among them. Dogs fought and snarled over discarded bones on the rush-strewn floor. About the chamber, the personal knights of Buckingham's household were serving the commanders. When unemployed they diced in a corner.

Thomas stood at the doorway. The draught caused the candles to gutter. Eyes lifted towards him. One of his household knights brought him a cup of wine. He took it without acknowledgement and with one swift movement he drained it. The knight refilled the cup from a green glazed flagon.

Knollys rose from the table. A subdued smile played across his weatherbeaten face. 'We've good news, my lord.'

Even his flat accent could not efface the note of quiet pleasure. Buckingham raised an eyebrow in query. He took the brimming cup once again from his household knight.

'De Guesclin is dead, my lord.'

Knollys's French was fluent but still the hint of Cheshire strayed about its edges.

Buckingham was frozen for one moment. Then he roared with laughter. The wine spilt over his hand. It poured on to the sour rushes. Startled, the dogs leapt up. They whined and howled. Buckingham slammed the goblet down on to the table. Wine flew.

'When? When did the whoreson die?' He laughed again.

'A courier came while you were upon the wall walk. It seems

he died shortly after we landed. At Auvergne.'

'So he died rather than face me, did he? Well, well! How . . . convenient for him.'

De Guesclin had been Constable of France. He was the premier knight of French chivalry. His death was an unexpected piece of good news to the English duke.

'It seems he was reluctant to fight his Breton neighbours.' The speaker was Calvely. He had a high nasal voice. It was an irritating contrast to Knollys's accent. 'Our good ally, de Montfort, is not making life easy for the French. It seems that de Guesclin was not the only man unhappy at making war on the Bretons. Others still hope to win Montfort back to his allegiance to the French king.'

'Fat chance!' Buckingham was in a good mood. The news of the constable's death had improved his humour greatly. 'Between us – Montfort's Bretons and my army – we shall squeeze the French king dry.' His eyes sparkled at the thought of booty and loot.

'There's more good news.' Knollys was enjoying himself.

'By Christ, but you know how to cheer a man, Rob. You'll tell me you've a gaggle of whores warming my bed next!'

'This will keep you happy for longer than a bitch on her back, I can assure you. They cannot replace the constable.'

'What?' Thomas bellowed his laughter. '*What?*'

'It seems there's no great rush to fill de Guesclin's position. 'Tis common knowledge that the French king is dying.'

'By God, that's true enough. Why else are we here?'

'True enough, my lord. But meat for one man is poison to another. With Charles of France rushing to his maker there are few who crave so sensitive a post as Constable of France. There's no love lost between the king's brothers, as you well know, my lord.'

Thomas chuckled. The news was getting better and better. Too long had English chivalry been held back from tasting triumphs akin to the old days of the war. Arundel's disaster of December last was still on everyone's lips. Now the wind had changed. Thomas could feel it. He knew a benevolent providence was smiling on his fortunes.

By God, he thought, 'tis long enough in the coming. He signalled with his cup. It was swiftly filled.

'No love lost?' Thomas echoed Knollys's statement. 'That litter of wildcats would tenderly scratch each other's eyes out for us. Hell will freeze over ere Louis, John and Philip bury the hatchet.'

Knollys nodded sagely. 'The Dukes of Anjou, Berry and Burgundy would sooner bury it in each other's heads. And to our good advantage. Let Cain kill Abel all over France.' The assembled knights hooted. 'But see, my lord, how this works together to our common good? Since the king's brothers are such bitter rivals 'tis likely a constable might find himself the enemy of all. 'Tis too exposed a post at such a time. 'Tis plague tainted.'

Calvely put down his plate of meat. 'Enguerrand de Coucy and Marshal Sancerre have both declined the offer so far. Mayhap the whole story will be cast as a pantomime this time next year.'

'A pantomime in English, though, not French,' Knollys chipped in.

Thomas stretched and leaned against the plastered wall. 'So de Coucy turned it down, did he? That must have stuck in his craw. To have such a post within his grasp and to fear to take it.' Thomas was thoughtful. De Coucy was the most renowned knight in France.

'De Coucy has not turned down all offers though, my lord,' Knollys said. 'It seems that the day we landed Charles made him Captain General of Picardy and raised him to the Regency Council. He has summoned the knights and squires of Artois and Picardy to host against us.'

Thomas was in too good a mood to be daunted by the might of French chivalry. He dreamed of another Crécy, another Poitiers. Glory and honour beckoned to him. He could almost feel his fortune rising.

'And it will avail him nought, Rob, for we will crush him like a fly.' He was not going to let de Coucy's preparations cloud his horizon.

Once more he raised his cup. This time a different knight filled it. Thomas studied the young man. He was not one of his personal attendants, yet the face was familiar.

'What is your name, sir knight?' Thomas asked, mildly interested.

He was met by the frank and open gaze of blue-grey eyes. 'I

am Edmund Mentmore, my lord, heir to Giles de Brewoster, Lord of Woodlands, Knolton and Upton.'

Edmund only mentioned the more prominent of Giles's manors. It was enough. He saw enlightenment dawn on the Duke.

'Were you with the Duke of Lancaster at St Malo?' The hard eyes held him fast.

Before Edmund could answer, Knollys broke in. 'Indeed he was, my lord. This is the knight who captured the Castilian vessel from the *Gabriel*.'

The Duke of Buckingham nodded. 'I have heard of it. A chivalrous deed. And is your father not Thomas Mentmore, the mercer of London?'

Edmund was aware of tapestry commissions from Buckingham but he hardly expected to be discussing them in the personal chamber of the duke himself.

'He is the same, my lord. And honoured to serve you – as I am.'

Edmund knew how keenly he was being watched. The appraisal by the duke was unusual. He had clearly been taken by both the reputation and the bearing of this young man.

'Good,' Thomas said. 'I trust our ride through France will give you many opportunities to repeat the triumph off Bayonne.'

Then the spell was broken. Thomas turned back to his captains and Edmund retired. Now was the time for detailed discussions. The duke dismissed all but his closest esquires to serve him and his commanders.

As Edmund Mentmore left, Knollys spoke quietly to the duke: 'He interests you?'

Thomas raised one corner of his mouth in half a smile. Had anyone else dared to intrude on his motives he would have withered them. However, Robert Knollys was not anyone. 'He fought well at Bayonne?'

'He has a lion's heart, my lord, but a quick mind also. He is a capable and ambitious knight.'

'My brother hopes much from these Mentmores. He is not universally popular, you know.'

'Really, my lord?' Knollys's voice was expressionless. He was aware of Gaunt's standing in England.

Thomas laughed. It was good, once in a while, to dwell upon

the unpopularity of his brother. 'Yet there are men in London who have proved amenable to him. These Mentmores are such. If your Edmund Mentmore acquits himself well on this campaign mayhap I shall make him a knight of my household.'

Buckingham found satisfaction in the idea of securing control over one of his brother's camp. It could be a useful move. London was a volatile city. The ambitious could do worse than gain allies there. Thomas was too bluff and violent to truly outplay his brother, but he knew the value of spies within a city like London. That much he had learnt from Gaunt.

'Then I hope he does not overplay his valour and die,' Knollys said, 'for 'twould be a shame for such promise to feed worms in France.'

Thomas looked at him without comprehension. 'These young knights have everything to thank me for. Until this year they had been cheated of a goodly war. I tell you, Rob, they can live better in war than in peace. In lying still at home they will find no advantage.'

Knollys had seen countless knights form a feeding ground for carrion, but for those who survived there was booty undreamed of. Had not he himself, leading his Great Company, made a fortune? For the surviving victors, war was the most lucrative enterprise known to man.

August 1380 was good campaigning weather. The English army left Calais and began a plundering progress across Artois. French knights shadowed the English advance but made no attempt to halt it.

Riding at the head of their contingent, Edmund and Stephen de Knolton surveyed the rolling countryside of Picardy. Here and there the green spires of poplars pointed to heaven in bucolic supplication. Or was it accusation? For the villages were burning in the wake of the English advance. Dark fingers smudged trails of smoke across the vast canvas of the summer sky. Herds of lowing beasts were driven along with the marching ranks. Those that could not be so used were butchered and burnt. The handiwork of men at war was everywhere to be seen. On the horizon, parties of French knights followed the English march.

Edmund drew up his horse on a lightly swelling rise. About him the spreading arable fields were alive with the scarlet of poppies and the yellow glow of charlock and corn marigold. On the rough grassland beside the rutted, dry track pale blue speedwell and shy wild pansies hunched their tiny petals against hooves and boots.

Below him lay the gutted ruins of a small village. A herd of captured cattle were grazing in the meadowland of the ruined settlement.

'How many beasts would you say? One hundred? One hundred and fifty?' Stephen de Knolton asked with youthful glee. He stood in his stirrups to get a better view.

Edmund watched the herd with grim detachment. 'What would your father say to have those beasts in his meadow?' Edmund was thinking of the tiny villages nestled along the banks of the Stour.

'He'd hang the hayward for letting such a disaster occur! No one could claim herbage rights in the common meadow this time of year. At Knolton it is in defence from Candlemas; no beast may be let loose there till after Lammas Day, at least. Sometimes the hay is not mown until the end of August and only then may the beasts forage on the meadow aftermath.' Stephen laughed at the absurdity of Edmund's question. No one but a man out of his mind would let beasts at the meadow before it was mown.

Edmund was not laughing. For a moment he turned in his saddle. His palfrey sneezed and shook its mane. Columns of men-at-arms moved past, chattering coarsely. Then he turned back to survey the blackened wreckage of thatch and timber, turned to ash.

'But what if such an event happened, Stephen? What would be the end of the misfortune?'

'Why, 'twould be a disaster for the manor. The animals would not overwinter without the hay. The cattle and oxen would die in the stock pens and crew yards; the sheep would never find enough forage in the pasture come February – if not before!'

Edmund cast him a sideways glance. 'Laugh not, Stephen de Knolton, to see a manor destroyed before your eyes. Lest providence work similar deeds upon your own.'

Then Mentmore spurred his horse forward, kicking up dust. Startled, Stephen watched him go. He had in no way expected a rebuke. He was not used to such talk from his knight.

Behind him the mounted archers and mounted men-at-arms were watching him impatiently. The packhorses, laden with armour and gear, munched at the grass. The destriers snorted with their usual foul temper. Stephen felt foolish and slightly vulnerable. With a sharp movement of his hand he signalled the advance to continue. Down they rode into the vale; down past the slogging foot soldiers with their leather jerkins and bills; down past the shattered village.

Stephen soon caught up with Edmund. For a couple of miles they rode together in silence until Stephen could stand it no longer. In an attempt to break the ice he asked: 'Why do the French offer no resistance?'

Edmund grunted. He was already feeling remorseful at the way he had choked off his enthusiastic squire. To tell the truth, he had surprised himself as well as de Knolton. It was only as he spoke that he realised how much he had tired of this looting, without chivalry to accompany it. For as Stephen had indicated, the French had made no attempt at forcing a decision by battle.

Stephen tried again. 'Do you think de Coucy is afraid? I know Hugh Calvely says de Coucy is the chief mummer in the French king's pantomime. What think you?'

'Enguerrand de Coucy is no coward, Stephen. He has the courage of any of our captains. He has campaigned in France, Italy, Alsace and Switzerland. His dynasty is a legend of power and martial might. He married the eldest daughter of our late King Edward – God rest his soul – and was a fitting match for so royal a bride. Do not listen to slanders, Stephen. It is not fear which holds him back.'

The palfreys had slowed to a gentle walk. Skylarks were singing. The mounted soldiery were joking and laughing.

'So why does he not fight us?' asked Stephen, puzzled.

'Because his king forbids him to. Charles is dying but he has his wits yet. He thinks to draw us ever deeper into France and yet deny us a crushing triumph.'

'But his land burns!'

'Indeed it does and we plunder as we go. But do you think Thomas Woodstock brought five thousand men to France to do this? Did the Duke of Buckingham land at Calais to burn countless villages and rustle cattle and – ' Edmund fixed a glance on his squire – 'and despoil a hay crop or two?'

Stephen blushed and began to stammer out a reply.

Edmund broke in on him. 'If you were going to the aid of Jean de Montfort, Duke of Brittany, where would you proceed to from Calais?'

Stephen tugged at his reins to bring his horse's head up. 'To Brittany, I suppose.' He frowned. He knew this vast progress across France was not the way to Brittany. The road to Jean de Montfort did not lead across Artois, Picardy and Champagne.

'Quite so,' Edmund replied, 'but you may have noticed that we are taking the "scenic route" to Brittany.' Stephen had to smile at the dry humour. 'And why? Because this is the way to honour and glory. A triumphant campaign across France will give ample opportunity to bring the French to heel. With towns captured and knights seized in battle we shall all make our fortune. And minstrels will sing of our exploits to children not yet born. Do you not know that Sir Robert Knollys took ten thousand crowns from ransoms whilst campaigning in Normandy?' Stephen shook his head. 'But we have a problem Stephen, my lad. The French are refusing to play. We march, they retire. We attack, they fall away. It is hard to ransom a knight when you cannot catch one.'

'So what shall we do?' Stephen was beginning to grasp something of the problems attending this campaign. 'What shall we do if the French king continues to forbid Enguerrand de Coucy to fight?'

'We shall push yet harder at him. We shall burn more villages and destroy more crops. We shall fill his nostrils with the stink of his own land afire. We shall strike at him at every turn, then sooner or later he will have to act. The opportunity will present itself and he will be unable to hold back. And until that time we will advance and attack and strike at every man and beast we can reach. Then we shall rile him beyond reason. He will have to give us what we demand – a contest of arms.'

Stephen was very serious. 'But – if you were Charles – would you do that? Would you give us what we demanded?'

Edmund smiled a cold cynical smile. 'Of course not! Would you?'

By nightfall they had reached Robert Knollys's encampment to the west of Reims. As they rode the last few miles they were once more aware of shadowing columns of French knights.

It was 9 August, the eve of St Laurence's day. Knollys had encamped in a captured village and set up his headquarters in a substantial manor house on the edge of the settlement. Over the gated entrance he had hung his personal standard. It fluttered in the light evening breeze and declared to those who passed beneath it: "Whosoever captures Robert Knollys, Shall win one hundred thousand sheep", in boastful reference to Knollys's evaluation of his own worth in ransom money and also to the price on his head offered by an affronted French monarch.

Around the manor house campfires were twinkling like stars. Hurdle fences and outhouses had been broken down to provide fuel.

Knollys himself was not in a good humour. He was growing tired of the French refusal to face the invading army. He had also had to endure the mounting frustration of his commander-in-chief. Thomas Woodstock was becoming impatient with a procession across France which did not involve martial glory. Angrily the duke had struck ahead for Troyes.

The 'old brigand' seemed pleased at the arrival of Edmund and his contingent. They had been apart for a day or two as Edmund mounted guard over the English foraging parties.

Knollys was seated, with his cronies, around a log fire. Although it was summer the clear nights brought chilling temperatures. The logs spat and crackled on their fire dogs. The little panelled hall was full of smoke. Knollys poured wine from a chipped flagon for Edmund and his squire. Men-at-arms from Knollys's personal troop carried in platters of steaming meat to the squires, who in turn served their knights.

'What news of de Coucy?' Edmund asked while cutting at a thick slice of mutton. 'Have you seen him?'

The old warrior shook his head. 'Our scouts say he is holding reviews and deploying units for the defence of towns. He's on the move almost daily. He's moved from Peronne with our advance. He's been to Hesdin, Arras, Abbeville and St Quentin. But he makes no attempt to halt us.'

Edmund chewed on his meat. 'You say he has fortified the larger towns?' Knollys nodded. 'And we've little enough preparation for a successful siege.'

'Besides which,' Knollys interrupted, 'It is too early in the campaign to bog ourselves down in a siege. And what for? Towns of no consequence. Like it or not, his refusal to face us is like rain on the whole campaign. Everything depends on our forcing a confrontation with the French chivalry.'

Knollys had made a career out of pitched battles and lightning campaigns. This dull start was dampening his enthusiasm. He poured out another bowl of wine. Its splashes sat on the table, like drops of blood. Changing the subject, he enquired: 'What news of the French as you rode in? Did your scouts make contact with our shadows?'

Edmund pulled a face. 'Our shadows have matched us pace for pace. They always keep close to the line of march. They make no attempt to stop us, but they hamper the foraging parties. Some of our scouts skirmished with them – we killed two – but they refused further battle and broke off the fight. It is like wrestling ghosts.'

Both men sat silent for a while. The green logs spat and hissed on the fire.

'De Coucy has promised his knights that they shall have battle before they finish their march. Yet we've seen nothing of such intentions. How do you read this puzzle, Master Mentmore?'

Edmund had the feeling he was being tested. He thought very carefully before he replied.

'Their new constable, de Clisson "the butcher", has said, I believe, that we are so proud we think we cannot lose. Charles, on the other hand, takes a more interesting view. He has seen so many defeats that he believes the French chivalry cannot win. He seems to have decided that a clash of arms is too risky a business to be used to decide a war. He will wait, and wait . . . and trust that we will make mistakes. For he knows that, denied a major triumph, our glorious progress will come to nought. Mayhap this caution is the most dangerous strategy for us to face. 'Twould be a most terrible event should English courage starve to death for want of ought to feed it.'

At that moment Knollys knew beyond doubt that he had not misjudged or overestimated the intelligence of this knight.

'I have a task for you, which will not bring glory but will require a steady nerve.' Edmund raised a quizzical eyebrow. 'We have stripped the countryside of food. The land is as unyielding now as a Jew's purse. The foragers must go further each day and the French, who will not face my knights, are not averse to spitting my foragers like pigs! The good burghers of Reims will not part with a pennyworth of provisions though, God knows, we've burnt enough villages this past week to make their eyes water with the smoke.

'Now my spies bring word that the citizens of Reims have crowded several thousand head of sheep into corrals built in the city ditch. They think their walls will protect what's outside of them as well as what's in. I need a cool-headed knight to lead a party into those ditches and seize those sheep. I think you are that knight.'

Edmund, who could never say no to a wild deed, looked reassuringly impressed with the challenge.

That very night, he and Stephen de Knolton picked out the cream of Knollys's finest archers. By dawn they had approached the sleeping town and were contemplating its grey curtain wall in the dew-wet stillness. From a deeper darkness at the foot of the wall drifted the bleating of their quarry.

Edmund had brought his own mounted archers and men-at-arms. Their horses snorted and jostled in the pre-dawn darkness. Ahead of these he had laid out a screen of archers on foot. Both Edmund and his squire were in full armour.

Outside the city wall a straggle of poor cottages had been set afire and Edmund made his camp in the black-ashed shelter of these victims of war. From the shouted commands from the wall walk it was evident that his movements had already been detected. He was not unduly concerned. Surprise was not his main tactic today.

At dawn a flurry of crossbow bolts signalled that the defenders of Reims were aware of their company. Edmund's forward line of archers, behind shields set up on wattle hurdles, returned the fire. Soon the Welsh archers in their distinctive green and white livery were sweeping the battlements with goose-feathered death. Their sheer numbers and accuracy made it suicide for any defender to raise a head.

Along the edge of the ditch, to left and right, foot archers advanced to give additional covering fire. Their presence prevented French archers further down the wall from opening up an enfilading fire. Under cover of the storm of arrows the mounted men-at-arms swept down upon the stockpiled sheep. They were accompanied by mounted archers who provided back-up cover.

So keen was the shooting that no defender of the city dared to venture out, or even appear, on the bulwark. Within half an hour the frantically bleating flock had been driven up out of the ditch and back towards the English lines. As they moved, the archers slowly withdrew. It had been a perfect success. Away across the fields of standing corn more villages were burning. Knollys was not standing idle whilst Edmund worked.

When Edmund returned to Knollys's camp it was to hear that English knights, out with the foragers, had clashed with a party of French knights. The news of the skirmish brought a string of oaths from Edmund. Compared to such action, his adventure before the walls of Reims was but a game for common soldiery.

It came as some relief to learn that the French had withdrawn, although some of the knights claimed to have seen the arms of de Clisson the butcher. These English knights were disappointed. 'Soul of Mary,' they moaned as they calmed their excited destriers, 'if we'd caught him they would have paid us forty thousand francs in ransom.'

Stephen listened with awe as the returning knights recounted how a fortune had slipped through their fingers. He was intrigued by the name of the man who so vexed the English chivalry. As he assisted Edmund in the removal of his jupon and breastplate he could conceal his curiosity no longer.

'My lord, this Clisson who men say is, or will be, the new constable of France: why is it he is termed "the butcher"?'

Edmund grinned. 'Now there's a story to chill your blood,' he began with mock horror. 'Olivier de Clisson is a one-eyed monster who would as like eat you, Stephen.'

'Holy Mary, what has this monster done?' Like any young squire Stephen lived on knightly gossip.

'Olivier has been bred on hate. He is a Breton like our ally de Montfort, but the two are sworn enemies. Clisson's father dealt with our late king against the King of France. For his double dealing he was seized in the middle of a tournament, conducted naked to his place of execution and his head cut off.

'But there's more: Clisson's mother carried her husband's head home to Brittany and made her son swear vengeance on the King of France. Then, in an open boat, they fled to England. There Edward, our young king's father, showed them every courtesy. As now, we were then ever mindful of how useful Breton loyalty could be. Clisson was brought up at Edward's court, where he was called "the churl", so foul were his manners. His hatred of the French took him to the battles of Auray, Cocherel and to Najera in Spain. 'Tis said that none who faced his two-handed axe stood up again . . .'

'But now he fights for the French king. I do not understand.'

'Ah, yes. Well Clisson's hatred did not diminish, it simply shifted. As a Breton his overlord was de Montfort. He and the duke hated each other. De Montfort favoured other lords above Olivier de Clisson and this fanned Clisson's dislike to revolt. Besides which the old French king had died. His son, the present King Charles V, wooed Clisson back with gifts of land and other favours. So the hatred Clisson reserved for the French he now directed toward the English and their Breton ally de Montfort.

'It was and is a terrible hate that the man can sustain. When his squire was killed by the English he captured fifteen English knights. With his own axe he cut off their heads. 'Tis said he called them, one by one, out of a locked room and as they stepped through the door he . . .'

Stephen would have to wait to hear the end of the tale of Olivier de Clisson, aptly bynamed 'the butcher'. At that moment one of Knollys's esquires came to summon Edmund to dinner at the senior knight's battered command post.

It was hot and stuffy in the requisitioned hall. The noonday heat was penned in. The presence of so many banneret knights and lesser knight bachelors, and their squires, only added to the heat. Even the dogs seemed subdued.

Knollys had news. 'The good citizens of Reims have observed the burning villages and noted the loss of their sheep.' There was laughter at his flat tones. 'They have agreed to deliver sixteen carts of bread and wine to us if we hold back from burning the standing crops.' There were mutters; some had been looking forward to directing further acts of arson. 'But of more moment is news from the Duke of Buckingham.'

Swiftly Knollys related how Woodstock, with the vanguard of the English army, had penetrated as far east as Troyes in Burgundy. Here he had been met by the cream of the French chivalry. According to Woodstock's courier, the English heralds had counted the assembled arms of the Duc de Bourbon, Enguerrand de Coucy, the Duc de Bar, the Comte d'Eu – all under the command of Philip the Bold, Duke of Burgundy, the French king's brother.

Edmund bit his lip in disappointment at the battle which he had missed. Yet Knollys amazed his audience by saying that the dying French king had forbidden the assembled army to cross swords with the English host. All that had ensued was an inconclusive half battle, which had fallen far short of the hoped-for contest.

In disgust, Woodstock was now swinging westward towards Brittany. He ordered Knollys to make speed to move southwestward from Reims and meet him on the Loire. Here he was convinced that, at last, the French would face him in full battle. If they failed to do so, he would cross the Loire and Sarthe and enter the Breton territory of the English king's ally, Jean, Comte de Montfort.

During the first week of September Knollys and his company met the English duke on the banks of the sandy-bedded Loire above Tours. The countryside was burgeoning in a mellow autumn. The land was rich and fertile. Men-at-arms foraged in the orchards and picked pears and medlars.

Buckingham had so far failed in his attempt to induce a battle. His humour was not improved by news of the good fortune which had favoured Knollys and his company.

Moving across the rolling countryside west of Vendôme a party of Knollys's foragers had been ambushed whilst looting a village. The French knights had been led by a wealthy aristocrat, the Sire de Mauvoisin. Mauvoisin and his men had misjudged the proximity of the vulnerable foragers to their screen of mounted archers and glory-hungry knights.

What had begun as a tip-and-run attack had, in consequence, developed into a major skirmish. Knollys had taken the surrender of Mauvoisin himself. He was not the only one to have profited by the encounter: Edmund's men-at-arms had unhorsed two French knights in a mêlée. As their captain, Mentmore was entitled to a third of their captives' ransom money. He estimated that his prisoners would be worth some fifteen hundred pounds. He was no longer troubled by the fortunes of the English enterprise. His buoyant spirits had returned.

Denied similar success, the Duke of Buckingham now led his straggling host to the west of Tours. Despite the presence of large companies of French knights, his advance was unimpeded. At the end of the first week of September 1380 the English host crossed the river Sarthe into Brittany. It was the feast of the Nativity of the Blessed Virgin.

On 16 September King Charles V died. Four days later the news reached the English host camped amidst the hedged bocage countryside of Brittany. It was received with celebration.

A week later Buckingham ate the Michaelmas goose at Carquefou on the lower Loire. Frustrated over his longed-for repetition of Poitiers or Crécy he had turned his attention to the Atlantic coast. He had resolved, in a council of war, to lay siege to Nantes.

Nantes, with its towering castle and crenellated walls, dominated the estuary of the Loire and controlled much of the trade of the northern sweep of the Bay of Biscay. It was the key to Brittany and a valuable prize – if it could be won.

The city was no stranger to warfare and sieges. It was only forty years since the father of the present Duke of Brittany, also named Jean de Montfort, had contested control of the city with the rival claimant to the dukedom, Charles de Blois. On that occasion, de Blois – whom many had considered a saint – had used his siege engines to hurl into the city the severed heads of partisans of de Montfort.

Now the city was once more a bone of contention. This time, though, it had not stood by its duke. Wooed with gifts and promises by the late French king, it had swapped allegiance like Olivier de Clisson. Its gates were shut against both the English *and* the Breton duke.

Edmund settled to the siege without enthusiasm. He knew how little chance the English had of taking the city. Buckingham had not much siege equipment and could not hope to make a decisive attack on the walls. Whilst English engineers and carpenters cut down trees to fashion mangonels, trebuchets and rams, the divisions of the army encamped about the fortress like a legion of locusts.

Neither did Buckingham have much hope of blockading the city from the sea. French and Castilian vessels held supremacy in the Channel and news had even reached Edmund that in August a Castilian fleet had sailed up the Thames and burnt Gravesend. It was with relief that Edmund recalled the great defensive chain erected across the river by Philipot. That, at least, shielded London from assault.

As October gave way to a wet and windy November, only cartloads of supplies, dispatched to the besiegers by de Montfort, kept spirits up. Knollys sent Edmund and Stephen away towards the coast, to escort a convoy of provisions back to Nantes. It was a blustery day and both men, and their escort of mounted men-at-arms, were cloaked against the damp and chill. Above them seagulls wheeled and called mournfully.

As they rode they talked. It was a relief to be away from the ramshackle encampment with its overflowing latrines and earth closets. Stephen was particularly curious about the whereabouts of their Breton allies.

'I'll not deny I'm grateful for the provisions,' he conceded, 'but I'd like better to see a siege tower or a company of knights bachelor.'

'Would not we all?' Edmund said. 'It's no secret that Woodstock himself is not pleased at the tardiness of our allies. 'Tis a wonder he still calls them such. God knows, de Montfort swore a thousand sacred oaths to support the siege but, damn him, he's been slow enough to back up his promises with swords.'

'Mayhap he tires of the alliance? Did not Clisson change sides like a straw in the wind?'

Edmund gestured to his squire to lower his voice. They had been talking in French to shield their conversation from the English-speaking men-at-arms. Nevertheless, Edmund had no wish to impart his squire's fears to the soldiery.

'Hst, man, 'tis not a matter for gossip.'

Stephen coloured at the mild rebuke. If he knew the gossip then every soldier must know it too, but he followed his master's order and dropped his voice.

Edmund pulled up the hood of his cloak. He was bored of the siege. More than that, Knollys considered it a waste of time and Robert Knollys's opinion counted for much with Edmund Mentmore.

Riding ahead of the wide-wheeled ox waggons was a tedious business. In order to relieve his boredom, Edmund spurred his palfrey ahead to where a manor house was burning fiercely. Edmund was curious to see the cause of the conflagration.

As he suspected, the culprits were English soldiers looting for sport. Technically their actions were reprehensible since the Breton locals were allies of the English, but as Arundel's now-drowned soldiers had so plainly displayed there were no civilians who were not considered fair game by the common soldiers.

The gates of the manor were smashed and burnt. Two bodies lay tumbled in the wreckage. As Edmund rode into the smoky courtyard, he became aware of shrieking above the crackling flames. Laughing soldiers were chasing squawking hens in feather clouds of chaos. Amidst the confusion, three men-at-arms were engaged in the noisy and energetic rape of a middle-aged serving woman.

Stephen de Knolton rode up. He had a look of utter distaste on his face. He had not seen as much of an army's activities as Edmund and was clearly disgusted. Edmund adopted a more pragmatic stance. This was how soldiers behaved. He could do little to stop it. Many were convicted criminals who had been saved from the gallows by their willingness to turn their lust for murder and rapine on the King's enemies.

'Whoresons. These dogs sicken me.' Stephen's voice was thick with contempt. 'They're a disgrace to their companies!'

Edmund did not move. Arundel's men had raped and kidnapped nuns – and that was in England. When their fleet had faced its final, awful gale, they had tossed them overboard like so much ballast.

The same memory must have stirred in Stephen's mind. 'By God, these are no better than Arundel's scum. God knows that heaven itself was sickened by what they did.'

He was looking at Edmund with intense concentration. The knight was aware of the stare of his squire. My God, Edmund thought, is he the same man who counted off the companies at Southampton? He probably included this merry crew. What did he think he was counting – scholars at a choir school? And yet Stephen's indignation was having its effect. Despite his realistic appreciation that this situation was beyond his control, Edmund was drawing his sword from its scabbard.

He had already urged his mount forward when he saw the girl. She was young, perhaps sixteen. Her flowing pelisse of grass-green finespun marked her out as a woman of gentle breeding. Her circled plaits of auburn hair were trailing behind her.

Two raucous men-at-arms were dragging her across the

muddy yard. One of the men carried a wide purple birthmark on his cheek. Behind them the manor house sent sparks high into the sky. Edmund's palfrey collided with the foremost soldier. He lost his grip on his prize and was sent sprawling. The other man swore foully. He jerked at a dagger in his belt but with one arm around the struggling girl he was handicapped. Edmund pulled up his mount. Turning in the saddle, he struck the man a sweeping blow with the flat of his sword blade. As he fell, the soldier dragged the girl down.

Edmund swung from his horse. Grabbing the girl, he lifted her up and across his saddle pommel. She was light and fragile. As Stephen steadied the nervous horse, Edmund hauled himself back up. The men-at-arms were swearing and jeering but none interfered. They had caught sight of Edmund's mounted troops moving up from the roadside.

Then Edmund and Stephen were out of the smoke; out through the smashed gates; out into the fresh, wet air.

The river Loire, at Nantes, flowed below rising bluffs in a maze of channels amidst scattered islands. Beyond the city its irregular course left islands and sandbanks behind and opened out into a widening tidal estuary. Here too, tributaries poured their waters into its flow.

Edmund's encampment lay to the west of the city. From slightly rising ground, he commanded views both across the river and into the town. Below the camp, and on the river bank, lay the gutted ruins of the trading centre of the Quay de la Fosse. Out beyond this victim of warfare, the river flowed steadily around the low islands of Ile Gloriette and Ile Ste Anne. In better days these channels had seen a regular traffic in vessels carrying the city's famed delicacies of Atlantic salmon and estuarine lampreys.

Edmund had commandeered an outlying section of the city's extra-mural settlement. Its citizens had long since fled inside. Now the comfortable bourgeois tenements and timber artisan accommodation were littered with the booty and the debris of an army at war. There was a desolate feel about these wrecked houses, now the squatting places of careless soldiery.

A squall of rain blew in from the coast. Edmund ignored it as he watched a group of soldiers manhandle an awkward trebuchet. They had set it up, out of arrow range, between the encircling siege camp and the grey, rising walls.

Stephen de Knolton and another knight of Edmund's party also watched the proceedings with interest. They had finished an inspection of the stabled destriers and were now bored.

'See how the city will capitulate before this attack!' Edmund said softly.

Stephen grinned. He had got used to his knight's irreverent humour. It had become a tonic against the squalor and overcrowding of the siege camp. Even the rain had not diminished it, and Stephen knew the reason for his master's refound bonhomie.

At last the siege weapon was ready. With enormous energy, its great catapult arm rose and threw its projectile against the city with terrible force. The clutch of rocks crashed down upon the burghal tenement roofs between the St Nicholas gate and the stout tower of a well-built church. 'There, Stephen. We have ruined the dinner of a rich merchant. 'Tis the stuff of tales of chivalry, think you not?'

Stephen laughed. 'I feel it will take more than that siege engine to reduce the city. Had we a dozen more then, by God, we could have sport with their defences.'

He gazed wistfully down across the towers of St Nicholas and St Croix to where the castle occupied the south-eastern quarter of the city. Scarred but unbowed, the mighty tower of Vieux Donjon stared back at him. 'Aye,' he said with a note of disappointment. 'If we had more, but we do not.'

'And if we had a Breton army,' Edmund quipped. It was now clear that Jean de Montfort was not going to send his promised knights to support the siege. Too many Breton nobles had baulked at the thought of reducing a Breton city, albeit when that city was in alliance with the new French king. De Montfort's promises had come to nought.

Stephen and Edmund's conversation was interrupted by the unseen approach of a young woman. Adèle d'Auray came upon them quietly on cat's feet. The breeze caught at her auburn hair and flapped the edges of the man's cloak wrapped around her slight form. Without a trace of nervousness she stood beside Edmund. As the trebuchet fired again she watched the scattering flight of its projectiles, then turned her sea-green eyes on the knight and asked:

'Have you news of my father?' She held him with those clear, bright eyes. The tilt of her small chin conveyed a sense of amused curiosity. She was a woman used to getting her own way.

Edmund shook his head. Since he had rescued the girl, he had made half-hearted attempts to send her to her father but had failed.

Guichard D'Auray was a lesser knight of the Duke of Brittany. The day before the French king died he had received the feudal summons to attend upon his liege lord at Rennes. He had not returned. Jean, Comte de Montfort, had gathered his host but had declined to deploy it. With winter on the way, he would soon have to scatter it again. Obviously the Duke of Brittany could not make up his mind which side to adhere to. Whilst he deliberated, D'Auray's manor had been despoiled by his supposed allies – the English. Had Edmund and Stephen not intervened, his daughter would have been deflowered as well. Adèle's brothers were with their father and de Montfort.

'Are you still trying, sir?' The sea-green eyes sparkled.

Edmund blushed. It was not a habit with him but the girl's insinuation was obvious. She knew men desired her.

Stephen watched impotently. He had carried a torch for the lithe young lady since the rescue. She, on the other hand, had scarcely recognised the existence of his rather awkward suit. Instead she had outrageously flirted with the knight, his social superior.

Edmund, who was no stranger to flirting himself, was oddly ill at ease in the presence of Adèle. This was strange. Edmund had graciously paid court to more ladies and bedded more serving wenches than he could remember. The two types of women were chalk and cheese to him. For one was reserved the rough and tumble in the hay loft; for the other the arts of 'gentillesse' were practised. Edmund, unlike his more fastidious brother John, knew no restraints when it came to an available lower-class woman. The girls at Giles's manor knew all about that!

True to his nature he had paid careful attention to his young guest. He had turned three of his cheaper knights out of their accommodation and given it to her. He had been the model of courtly virtue. He had also kept a careful eye on her. Her presence had excited considerable interest amongst the soldiery and

Edmund had not rescued her to have her gang raped in his camp.

He could not deny that he found her very desirable. She, on the other hand, had a disconcerting confidence which belied her youth. There was something worryingly reminiscent of Anne Glanville in the young Breton girl's self-assuredness. She seemed well aware that her rescuer would bed her if he could. She also seemed to be quite unassailable. In the meantime she just enjoyed his attentions and added fuel to the fire. Edmund had the feeling that the young woman liked the thought of men fighting over her. Edmund was less happy with that idea!

'You should not stand here,' Edmund scolded her. 'It is coming on to rain. You will take a chill and our physicians will have their work cut out to save you.'

He refrained from escorting her back himself and instead signalled to the attentive Stephen de Knolton. The squire's eyes lit up. Adèle frowned slightly.

The rain was heavier now. It was not long after noon but the sky was darkening. The short November day was assailed by storm clouds and mist.

For a few moments Edmund continued to stare out over the city. Away to the east, facing the St Pierre Gate and the castle, he could make out the encampment of the Duke of Buckingham. Accompanied by his household knights, his chaplains, secretaries, pages, valets, esquires, wardrobe men and cooks, the camp resembled a sprawling – if muddy and now rather squalid – village. The heavy banners flapped in the wind.

Around the trebuchet the soldiers, cursing, were abandoning their bombardment. The rain had ruined the tension of their rope mechanisms. Edmund went to enquire after his charge. He had finally resolved to send her away to her father.

She sat before a log fire, the cloak about her shoulders. Edmund felt a dryness in his throat. The strength of his desires shook him. For a few moments they talked of trifles, then something within Edmund was fanned to a leaping flame. Adèle reached out her foot and warmed it by the fire. The slim white calf shone in the firelight.

Edmund grasped her shoulders. He turned her. She gasped. Her small hands came up in a gesture of unenthusiastic defence. He stifled her gasp with his mouth. Suddenly his passion exploded. He crushed her body against his own. His lips and tongue took the tiny fortress of her mouth with irresistible force. Her hair fell loose against his cheek. With one experienced hand he swept the smooth skin of her thigh.

Suddenly, Stephen was in the room.

'The French, the French . . . oh God – '

Edmund turned in fury. Adèle fumbled with the cloak. Her naked, white body silenced Stephen's words.

'What the bloody hell do you want, Stephen?' Edmund rose in wrath.

Stephen found his voice. 'The French . . . the French have sallied forth from the St Nicholas gate. Sir Robert has sounded the alarm. The camp is on fire!'

The night of 12-13 November passed in a whirl of confusion. The French had indeed broken out. When Edmund and his men stumbled into the darkness they could clearly make out the extent of the chaos.

The trebuchet had been doused with some inflammable substance and was ablaze. Men-at-arms were rushing to and fro in panic. Horses broke loose and stampeded through the throng. French soldiers were pressing up from the city gates. Steel rang on steel. The English quartered along the Quay de la Fosse had been trapped with their backs to the river. Those who could swim were beating about in the dark waters of the Loire. The siege line was fracturing.

There was no time to fetch the horses. Already French soldiers could be seen, silhouetted against the flames. They pressed towards the spot where Edmund stood surveying the chaos and carnage.

Never before had Edmund's skill in the mêlée been so fatefully tested. 'Two men to a lance,' he thundered, 'then back to back in the mêlée. Archers to the flanks. Move for God's sake. *Move!*'

Desperate men-at-arms planted their lances in the mud and angled them towards the surging French line. Archers scrambled to left and right. Soon the first French knights were crashing against Edmund's hedgehog phalanx. Horses screamed. The valets, with the lance-wielding men-at-arms, dashed forward to jab at equine bellies.

On the flanks the archers began to shower arrows into the

faces of the French. Behind the dismounted men-at-arms, Edmund and a party of knights stood: a solid core of half-armoured chivalry. When the storm burst on and over them, they fought back to back, with desperate ferocity.

The French attack faltered. From the left Sir Robert Knollys – mounted and in full armour – was leading his household knights in a determined counterattack. His boastful banner was flung out against the night sky. With fierce cries the knights, on destriers, scattered the infantry. The snorting beasts raked fleeing men with great teeth. The air was wild with screams and when eventually the hesitant grey light of morning filtered through the darkness it was clear that the French breakout had failed.

Edmund and Stephen had fought their way down to the river to relieve the English troops there. The gutted buildings and muddy roadways were scattered with bodies. More corpses bobbed out amongst the grey sandbanks in the Loire. Dying men lay amongst the stiffening dead. Here and there was a dead horse in the tangled mess of its own entrails. The few chaplains available moved about hearing gasped confessions, but many of the common soldiers were dying unshriven. It made Edmund shudder to think of them going unprepared to meet their maker.

Bending over a wounded man, Edmund found his wrist grasped in a vice-like grip.

'Confess me. For God's sake, confess me . . .'

Edmund knew that in extreme cases a layman could hear a deathbed confession in the absence of a priest. William had once informed him that in the plague year of 1349 even women had been allowed to hear confession in the overwhelmed diocese of Bath and Wells. Even so, Edmund was discomforted by his predicament. He looked around for one of the chaplains. He could see none.

At last he planted his sword-guard before the bloodshot eyes of the wheezing man. Blade pointing to the ground, it took on the appearance of a crucifix without a figure. Dying fingers grasped it. A torrent of muttered words tumbled from the blood-caked lips. Edmund listened intently to the almost incoherent stream of sins, then the man was dead. It was sudden. One moment he was gasping out a confession of a life spent in licence and lust. The next his death rattle filled his throat.

Edmund prised off the fingers clutching the sword handle. As he turned away, more hands grasped at his cloak.

Oh my God, he thought. Not more. Not more.

This man had been run through by a lance. The blow had broken the weapon. A ragged stump of splintered wood protruded from his quilted gambeson. The mail of his hauberk was drenched in blood. The rotten, blackened teeth were gritted together in agony.

'Confess me, confess me . . .'

Wearily Edmund raised his sword again. The man's face, a mask of blood and filth, twitched uncontrollably as he gasped out his sins. Edmund scarcely listened to this flood of words. Suddenly he was immensely tired. His plate armour felt heavy and his eyes ached. It was all he could do to hold the sword upright as a makeshift cross.

Then a shaft of light pierced his tiredness. He jerked awake and bent low over the whispering man. The soldier's breath stank of garlic and beer.

'What was that you said?' Edmund's voice was urgent. 'Repeat it. What you just said!'

'The man-at-arms was scarcely conscious now and paid no heed to the knight's request. Instead he just rambled on. Edmund let go of the sword. It fell across the man's gory chest. The knight clutched at the ragged gambeson. Broken circles of mail dug into his palms. He ignored them and pulled the man towards him. The bloody head flopped forward. The eyes were wide – all whites – as the pupils swivelled up.

'The mercer's clerk. For God's sake. The clerk . . . repeat it.'

The man coughed horribly. Edmund felt gobbets of spit and blood on his face but no revulsion or pity. He shook the man brutally. 'The clerk. Repeat it!'

At last his demand hit home. 'Killed a clerk. We killed a clerk, we . . .'

'We? We? Who were you with? Who?'

'Killed a clerk.' He groaned. 'Killed a mercer's clerk. Did it with the lads.'

Edmund was desperate now. 'When, when? How long ago?'

'Years . . . don't know. Killed him . . . bales of cloth. Three, four years. Christ, I can't tell . . . Who cares? Just a god-damned clerk . . . did the job and away . . .'

The man retched. Edmund scooped water from a bloody puddle and dribbled it over the parched lips. It ran between the blackened teeth.

'What was the clerk's name?'

'God's sake ... I don't know. It was just a job ... did it for the money. Good money. Silver pennies.'

Edmund could not believe what was happening. He could feel the man's life trickling through his hands. How could such a coincidence occur? The hairs stood up on Edmund's neck. Was this juxtaposition of lives an act of God? Then Edmund thought of Newton.

'Was it Newton? Did Newton pay you? Newton the weaver?'

The dark teeth parted. A swollen tongue flapped like a beached fish. 'Never heard of ... never heard of Newton ... paid silver. Paid by ...' He coughed again and his train of thought was lost. 'Killed a clerk ... under cover of a riot ... Gaunt at cathedral ... family wedding.'

'But who paid you, man? If it wasn't Newton, who was it?'

Now the man was incomprehensible. The words were half formed, the syllables slurred. 'Drink ... water ... give me ... horn ... horn ... water ...'

Edmund cast about for the man's drinking horn or leather water bottle. Neither could be seen. Once more he scooped up handfuls of puddle water and splashed them over the contorted face.

The shock seemed to clear the man's mind. 'Confess me, confess me,' he gasped. 'For pity's sake, confess me.'

'I'll give you water if you'll tell me who paid you.'

Edmund let the man fall back. A tarred rain barrel lay up against one ruined building. The water was green slimed. Edmund scooped it up in his bascinet. Hurrying back to the man he splashed it over his face.

'Who paid you?' Edmund shouted, but the man was already dead. Staring eyes were fixed on the lightening November sky.

Edmund sank to his knees. He knew the dead face. It was one of the men who had tried to rape Adèle, one of the pardoned criminals. Edmund recognised the birthmark on his cheek. Oh my God, he thought as the truth dawned on him. A mark on the face. Edmund reached out bloodstained hands and touched the purple skin the colour of raspberry juice. Half-remembered words of his brother flooded back to him with utter clarity.

'Sweet Mary,' he muttered incredulously, 'what fate has thrown us together?'

The terrible realisation dawned on him. He now had to tell John. Someone – not Newton – had paid to kill Yonge, and John thought the killer was Newton. But how could he warn his brother? John was in London and Edmund was in the filth and death of the siege camp at Nantes.

'Sweet Mother of God,' he hissed, 'what in God's name is happening to us?'

And that was how Stephen de Knolton found him: kneeling beside a stiffening corpse, a corpse with a ragged lance protruding from its chest and a raspberry-stained birthmark on the cheek.

PART FOUR

Nine Men's Morris
1380-81

Chapter Thirteen

Margaret Mentmore sat in the semidarkness of her chamber. The shutters were fastened tight. She was a prisoner in her room. Dawn had come in cloud and mist this November morning and awoken her. Pale fingers of light ventured cautiously through cracks in the window cover.

The room was cold and smelled of damp. In the middle a brazier had been set up on a plinth but its fire was now mostly glowing ash and afforded little heat. Margaret was wearing a thick woollen pelisse over her faded cotte and surcoat. She wrapped her numb fingers in the flowing, loose sleeves of her pelisse. She was cold to the very marrow. Cold and crushed.

Once more, from a need to find solace, she turned the waxy pages of the *Book of Hours*. Although she could write in English she could not read the Latin words of the prayers. In better days she had sat and heard them read during an hour of devotion, but she took some solace from knowing that within these familiar forms lay supplications to God. She felt as if she could make the prayers her own simply by touching the words. Her fingers caressed the Latin script in an unspoken 'Amen' to the prayers locked within.

She moved her position on the edge of the box bed. Sitting for hours, without motion, was an agony and yet too much movement brought back the spinning in her head and the ache in her shoulders and neck.

Bitterly she recalled how she had been beaten on her recapture. Beaten! She who had been Thomas Mentmore's proud 'swan'. She could still recall with startling clarity the pain and the terrible humiliation. Never before had her father taken a stick to her. Absent-mindedly she ran her finger along the thin white lines which seamed her forehead where the stick had left its mark of bloody vengeance. For days she had been scarcely able to move, so great was the pain from her cracked head and aching limbs. Even now, five months into her house arrest, she moved stiffly and awkwardly.

She turned the leaves of the book. She went through this ritual every day. It was for her a purgatory and a salvation. It tore her apart but it was the only means by which she could hold on to sanity now that Rob was destroyed. She was in agony over what she would see, yet see it she must. At last she recognised the final page before her intended prayer. Slowly she lifted the page. Her stomach turned. The vellum dropped heavily open.

On the page before her a beautifully painted panel illustrated the capital. Lordly knights and ladies paraded in mute pageantry, a chivalrous procession captured in inks of sapphire and vermilion. In the centre of the page lay a tiny bouquet of forget-me-nots. They had been carefully pressed and dried. The blue petals were thin as silk, the yellow centres still bright. Margaret could see them as they had been on that April morning when Robert Newton gave them to her. A simple gift of love. Not without reason did the country folk call the flower 'scorpion grass', from tales of distant lands and beasts of mythology. The very presence of these fragile flowers stabbed agony into Margaret's heart. She wept and wept . . .

In the yard between the hall and the warehouses, a furious argument was developing. Tom, the Mentmores' journeyman, was engaged in a fierce altercation with the clerk of the nearby burghal plot.

Listening, Philippa could catch the gist of the disagreement.

'. ... three and a half feet from my master's land. It should be three and a half feet – and that's common knowledge.'

'No!' the neighbour's clerk answered Tom hotly. ''Tis but two feet that is prescribed in the statute. Two feet and this is no closer. You may measure yourself!'

'Hah – two feet if it were stone lined. Is it stone lined?'

'No, it is an earth . . .'

'Then your master is in the wrong. For an earth-lined cesspool, three and a half feet is the stipulation.'

Philippa was no stranger to the debate. It had been raging off and on for months. It was over a year since the disagreement between neighbours had started.

When the Mentmores' draper neighbour had lost much of his house in the blaze which wrecked the tapestry workshop, he had rebuilt on a slightly different plan. As part of his rebuilding he had set up a new private latrine. Most of the lesser citizens were forced to use the public latrines; some had one attached to their block of tenement houses. From here the scavengers would haul their awful cargoes to the lay stalls of Dowgate and Puddledock. From thence it passed to farmers' fields out at rural Pimlico and beyond.

Wealthy guildsmen did not suffer such inconvenience. They built their own. It was a cesspool which was causing the current controversy. Seepage from the draper's new construction was now contaminating one of the Mentmore wells. It had consequently been designated the well used by the servants, but Thomas Mentmore was not content to allow such fouling of his property. With the draper protesting his innocence, it seemed likely that the row would go to litigation.

Philippa listened a little while longer to the argument then retired to the house. She was feeling tired. After a truly miserable summer, she had miscarried in September. All in all it had been a tragic time, what with Margaret's disgrace and William's death.

The death of William Mentmore had followed hot on the heels of his sister's failed elopement. The night after Margaret's humiliation he had gone to bed with a racking headache and a high temperature. Feverfew in hot wine had failed to reduce the heat in his face and head and he had woken with aching limbs and agonising knots in his groins and armpits. Within a week of the start of these terrible symptoms of pestilence, William Mentmore was dead.

Philippa had scarcely known the mouse-haired scholar with his passionate espousal of Wyclif's cause. For much of her marriage he had been at Oxford but despite her distance from him his death hit her because it had hit John.

John Mentmore had taken William's death hard. As a result he had thrown himself more heavily into his rural venture. It was as if he sought a triumph to set in the scales against the summer's tally of disasters. Edmund, of course, did not even know of his brother's end. He was away in France. The city was full of rumours that that venture, too, was turning into a dismal failure.

Philippa found her husband in the hall warming himself by the fire. It cheered her when he was home. For a moment she stood by the screen. It gave her pleasure to watch him unobserved. Sometimes as she sewed in the solar of an evening she would secretly watch him as he did the accounts with his father or planned out a new trade venture. She would let her eyes linger on his bobbed hair, the long sweep of his nose, the sparkling depths of his blue eyes and she would know herself truly blessed: a woman who had come to love her husband.

Little Ann came careering down from the dais, hotly pursued by Emma. The tiny feet scattered rushes and dogs. John turned and crouched to receive the blonde tornado. Sweeping her up in his arms, he found himself smothered with jammy kisses. Little arms strained to get round his neck in a toddler hug.

Emma was breathless. 'I . . . I'm truly sorry, sir. I do not know how she got away from me.' She brushed back a trailing lock of black hair, which had become dislodged in the pursuit.

John laughed. 'By St John, girl, don't go on so. I'll not scold you. Is it not a joy to hold my own daughter?'

Emma smiled diplomatically. She knew many fathers would not have responded so favourably to a toddler's enthusiasm. She knew that the older household servants and the wet nurse disapproved of John's interest in his child. That a father should play with a child and welcome her advances was quite enough to cope with. That he insisted on the child joining the family in the solar when there were adequate servants to mind the little scrap was surely excessive. 'No good will come of it,' the wet nurse would whisper. 'She'll be ruined,' a maid jibed. 'All that fuss for pestilence to steal away,' was the cruel comment of others.

Emma took a resolute stand against these commentators. She knew her mistress loved Ann and John, which was enough to make John sacrosanct to Emma. More than that, it was plain to see that John loved both Philippa and Ann. For the loyal Emma, this was a wonder to be treasured. When snide remarks were made about John Mentmore's lack of extramarital sexual activity, Emma would fiercely defend his fidelity to his wife. When other servants would offer the wisdom of 'a wife for children, a lover for romance', Emma would grow icily cold in her indignation.

Philippa had seen enough. It pleased her. She crossed the hall to kiss her husband and her squirming daughter.

Laughing, John gave Ann back to the willing Emma. 'She'll wear me out. I feel like a grain between the grindstones. Take her, Emma, before I faint from exhaustion.'

Emma took Ann in her arms. The toddler made no complaint. She loved Emma. It was difficult to think of a greater contrast than that of the dark-eyed, black-haired, still-shy serving girl and the rumbustious toddler with eyes of August blue and hair the colour of white gold.

With Ann chattering like a jay, Emma made off in the direction of the yard. There she would find sights and sounds in abundance to occupy her charge.

The hall was fairly quiet once more. Only the scurrying of the kitchen servants and the snarling of the dogs could be heard. In the absence of Ann Mentmore this seemed to be almost silence.

'Did you get any news?' Philippa asked her husband.

Soon after dawn he had ridden over to John Philipot's house. The energetic grocer had recently returned from parliament in Northampton. John had been keen to learn what had passed at the assembly. He had obviously discovered information, for he had not returned in time for dinner. It was now well past noon.

John looked about the hall. The nearest servants were stacking rushes in a corner. Another group was clearing soiled plates from the trestle table on the raised dais. He spoke in a hushed voice.

'They've executed Kirkby.'

His voice betrayed his emotion. He had no affection for the dead merchant, but his life had become curiously intertwined with that of the risk-taking guildsman.

Philippa put out a hand and touched his arm reassuringly. 'But that does not affect you?'

She was not sure whether her question was rhetorical. She could not stifle the raised intonation at the end of the sentence. She required reassurance.

John shrugged. 'Mayhap it does not.' His frown belied the casual lift of his shoulders.

Philippa moved closer. She had not long remained ignorant of her husband's whereabouts on the night of the ill-fated escape of the two squires. It was a measure of her relationship with John that he had poured out the full details to her.

'Surely,' she insisted, 'there is nothing in this to be tracked back to you, my heart?'

'No. You are right. No one can link me to his actions, but . . .' His voice trailed away.

'But what?' Philippa's brown eyes narrowed.

John shook his head. 'I cannot but worry that some may hazard a guess at why I went to the Gloucester parliament.'

It was a fear which had haunted him since the news of Kirkby's arrest had reached the city. No matter how the blame for the killing at Westminster was laid at the door of the constable of the Tower and his knights all agreed that Gaunt's hand lay behind it. And Gaunt would not rest easy until he had punished those behind the insult to his dignity.

'But the parliament was in Northampton.'

'Yes, as was the January assembly. Why?'

'Well, that is far away. No one there can know of the existence of John Mentmore.'

'Had they held parliament in Cathay there would be those there who have an interest in destroying the house of Mentmore. Mark my words: distance is no defence.

'But there's worse. Kirkby's death will cause the usual surge of feeling against Gaunt. We'll not be safe from that, no matter how artfully my father plays the part of the skilful juggler. There will be men who see the Mentmores as of Lancaster's party. That might become a very dangerous position to be in.'

'You mean the weavers . . . ?'

Philippa's brow was furrowed with concern for her husband. Newton's humiliation had done nothing to defuse the problem. Instead the situation with regard to the weavers had deteriorated since the summer. A series of strikes and wage disputes had marred September and October. It was as if harder men than Newton now had the ear of their fellow weavers. Philippa guessed that, for all his crimes against the Mentmores, Newton had not been the most extreme of the craftsmen. It was a curious thought indeed.

John pulled a bitter face as he considered his wife's question.

'Yes. The damned weavers. God's Mother, but they are as slippery as eels, with teeth like lampreys. They will jump at the chance to turn men's minds against us. And do not think they will be unsuccessful. There are many who would take a bite at us in such a dog fight.'

His metaphors mixed hopelessly as he sought to channel his mounting rage and frustration.

'And,' he continued, 'they have shown how much they can be trusted – damn them.'

He was thinking of how Appulby and Smalecombe had retracted their accusations against Newton. Appulby's cousin now insisted that he had found John's purse in the weaving shed where any worker might have dropped it. It was as if they did not want to be seen as the hangmen of a fellow weaver, now that their accusations had precipitated his flight with Margaret and both their destructions. But Newton had a charge of rape over him, even if affidavits were being sworn by other weavers as to his presence at well-attended places during the day of Yonge's death.

Mentmore money had been spent in sufficient quantities to ensure that Robert Newton would wait a good while before his trial took place. It was not for nothing that Thomas Mentmore held a position of power in the city. Let the craft guilds clamour to the Common Council. Newton would rot for months in the Fleet Prison before he could plead innocence of murder at a trial. His public elopement with Margaret and his public apprehension had destroyed him.

Philippa longed to comfort her husband but could think of nothing. Besides which, she did not approve of the denial of a swift trial. Philippa was convinced that the longer the issue was in doubt the greater would be the ensuing bitterness. She did not dare voice this opinion to her husband, though. He was bent on the fullest destruction possible for Newton. Both John and Thomas were aware of the damage that the elopement had done to the public standing of the house. While John could not fully condone the savage beating of his sister, he could understand it.

Philippa said softly: 'Your father is in the solar. Richard Lyons is with him.'

John nodded. He had seen the escort in the passageway and had recognised Lyons's badge. He crossed the hall to the stairs. To Philippa it seemed an age since she had watched him lift the laughing toddler. How she wished that she could drown the cares that beset them in such brief pools of happiness.

In the solar, Thomas and Lyons were engaged in a low conversation. As John entered they both looked up. The talk died. When Thomas saw the figure was that of his son and not one of his retainers he relaxed. Clearly the two had been discussing private matters. Richard Lyons greeted Thomas's heir in a relaxed way. He was leaning back against the panelled wall. A goblet was held in one bejewelled hand.

Accused of profiteering at the 'Good Parliament' of 1376, Lyons had not only survived but prospered. He had proved amenable to Gaunt and this was clearly the key to his success. Against him were ranged such powerful London anti-Lancastrians as John Philipot and William Walworth. Nevertheless, Lyons had a knack of surviving. Only recently he had purchased a new manor at Overhall in Suffolk. Money seemed to be attracted to this shrewd vintner.

John poured himself a goblet of wine. He did not trust Lyons and did not fully approve of any alliance between Thomas and this man. There was a superciliousness about his manner which John disliked.

'And what word does our friend Philipot bring back from Northampton?'

John drank deeply then gave his father and their visitor the same outline which he had just given to his wife.

Lyons grunted at the news of Kirkby's demise. John bit down on a hot retort. But Lyons had seen the look in John's eyes.

'Men will blame the Duke of Lancaster, of course, but it was parliament which decided this issue. Men would do well to recall that.'

'Aye,' John replied, with mock sincerity, 'the duke is away on the Scottish border. He can have had nothing to do with the death of a man who so affronted him.'

Lyons smiled and did not take the bait. 'Affronted the king, I believe. The charge was treason. A crime against his majesty.' He scratched at his thick black hair, streaked with grey. His dark eyes betrayed no secrets. He was right, too. Although it was common knowledge that Gaunt had encouraged the idea of a shift of trade from London, Kirkby's actual crime had been treason. That was a blow against the king's authority, not that of Gaunt.

John flushed. It was not like him to sound too open a critic of

Gaunt. He normally played the pragmatist more carefully. However there was something about Lyons's assurance which irritated him. He had spoken before he had fully thought out the implications of his rejoinder. The ghost of William Mentmore stalked the room.

'On the streets there is less doubt. Few are shy of seeing the Duke of Lancaster's hand in this.'

'On the streets?' Lyons raised his voice. 'What does it matter what is spoken by apprentices and the rough? Surely you have not joined John of Northampton in the desire to make the mayor and aldermen answerable to the minor guilds?' Lyons was aware of John's manoeuvrings with regard to the weavers and Northampton's campaign against the fishmongers. ''Twould be a strange stance for a liveried guildsman. A dangerous and an isolated stand.'

Lyons's words were cold. His long, ringed fingers played over his half-full goblet. He raised it and, with practised care, sniffed the wine breath.

Thomas frowned at his son. He would not have been surprised at such comments from William. John was usually more sensible.

'I'm sure you mistake my son's comments. For whilst we must accept Northampton's Common Council, while it lasts' (he emphasised the last three words), 'there is no great guildsman of the trade guilds who would encourage fetters on the mayor and aldermen. By Our Lady, that would be a fetter on ourselves!'

He exuded bonhomie, but his balding head was red. It betrayed his embarrassment. John recovered from his momentary weakness. His father's interjection had given him time to think.

'My father is right. We have no use for the Common Council. It is but a talking shop for the minor guilds and for the least significant of the great guilds. The mayor and aldermen have always protected our interests. It is only shrewdness that has caused us to cast our weight behind the campaign against the fishmongers. Surely you'll not gainsay such adroit actions? I'll wager that your heart does not go in the same direction as those who oppose Northampton and curse Gaunt!'

It was a clever move and John knew it. He had more than made up for his earlier blunder. There were many guild masters who were as antagonistic to the idea of popular government as Lyons and the Mentmores. Only some of these were also vehemently anti-Gaunt and in favour of the fishmongers. John had put his finger on one of the complex divisions with which the guilds – even the major guilds – were riven. The council meetings at Guildhall were fraught with complex antagonisms. The likes of this year's mayor, Walworth the fishmonger, could count on the support of the great guilds when opposing demands of lesser guildsmen; however, he could not withstand Northampton's popular demand for the abolition of the fishmongers' monopoly.

Lyons was not pleased. 'Little the duke's opponents do finds favour with me! And I'll not dispute that the fishmongers need a lesson in humility. Not that that makes me favour Northampton. He's a man who marries a good cause to a bad!'

'Still, that does not concern us here.' Thomas was conciliatory. 'We have common goals and projects of mutual benefit.'

'Aye,' Lyons concluded, glad to be off the hook. He was clearly not happy to find that John had turned the tables on him. John smiled inwardly.

Thomas continued: 'Richard is pleased to invest in our expansion. There's not only the tapestry work of Charles de Gouarec; there is our expansion into the rural cloth industry to consider also.'

He smiled at his son in a concentrated way, willing him to adopt a sunnier disposition.

'Your father has given me good cause to think such an investment will pay handsomely. For whilst the royal tapestry makers grind their teeth, there is every likelihood that the king himself will commission pieces from your workshops. De Roos may complain of breach of mystery but he'll do no good against the court should it decide to look elsewhere.

'More than this. I've heard of your enterprise on de Brewoster's estates. Your father has outlined your future plans. I, for one, believe you are right. There is an opportunity here that will not repeat itself. But, as you know, sufficient wealth is needed to establish such an enterprise on the right footing. Your Cotswold venture, it seems, will now have your East Anglian plans added to it. You do have plans there? And both plans would benefit from more money?'

John had listened carefully to Lyons's speech. The great Italian bankers dealt with Lyons and when the man who had become the English agent for the great house of the Bardi invested in his enterprise, John could not help but feel proud. Nevertheless he was still cautious. Richard Lyons was to be utilised but never trusted.

'The plans are set in the Cotswolds. Both the lords who run the sheep and the lords who have the fulling mills and weaving villages are in our confidence. We have already negotiated for next year's cloth and have contracted for a full third of next year's clip at Northleach fair. It will be our wool which will feed the spinning distaffs and weaving frames of the Cotswolds. It will be Mentmore cloth produced at Stroud and Castle Combe! And it will be our cloth which will be shipped out of Bristol and sold in our hall here in London, though we will have to fight the weavers to secure that last point. But theirs is a lost cause, anyway. 'Tis long since that they lost their monopoly.

'We aim to capture the home cloth trade in middle-grade cloth, while still supplying the court and the nobility with imported silks and velvet. By working in finished cloth for export we'll escape the export subsidy of the Calais Staple and undercut our competitors in finished cloth in Flanders. I know you've tried often enough to escape exporting through Calais, so you will see our advantage.

'We have high hopes of driving aliens out of the contract for the Damerham flocks of Glastonbury Abbey too. We have secured the flow of fine quality woollen cloth in the West Country. Now I aim to gain a stake in the medium cloth of Suffolk and the new worsteads appearing about Norwich. Your money will be well spent. I think you'll agree?'

Richard Lyons smiled and nodded. He never let money go unless he could see a good return. 'You'll be travelling this winter again. St Christopher must be your patron; you've crossed many streams in winter spate and traversed many miles of mud roads.'

John took the compliment to his endurance as the olive branch it was meant to be, and returned Lyons's smile. Leaning forward, he refilled the guest's goblet.

'I'm away to the Cotswolds before Christmas, then home for the feast and away to Norwich with the first thaw. Though, God help me, I might make better speed if I travel while the highways are frozen.'

Thomas raised his own goblet. 'To our mutual enterprise.'

John and Richard Lyons solemnly raised their own.

'To your journeys,' Lyons toasted the younger Mentmore. 'May your road be clear and the verges cut back. May footpads be blind and St Christopher vigilant.'

'And may our poll tax assessment stay at one shilling a head!' Thomas quipped with unusual merriment, for he was not a man given to off-the-cuff repartee.

All three laughed at that. They loathed the frequent taxes as much as everyone but the flat-rate tax of 1380 was more acceptable to the wealthy than the graduated tax of 1379.

Enjoying their unity, the three livery guildsmen raised their brimming goblets in mutual salute and hopes of high profits.

John left London for Giles's caput of Upton on St Andrew's day, 30 November 1380. Before he left, he and Philippa attended mass and prayed for the success of the new venture.

John rode out towards Newgate in the company of four of the apprentices. A journey on a dark winter's day was not one for a lone man. Richard Lyons may have wished for cleared verges and blind footpads but John knew that he was more likely to find dark roads and vigilant cutthroats. The news from the countryside was not good. The harvest had been poor and cattle murrain was once more evident. However this was not the main grievance in a depopulated rural scene no longer as desperate to feed itself as it had been in the years before the 1348 pestilence. This winter it was news of the new, flat-rate poll tax which was fuelling the fires of dissatisfaction. Travellers in from the country brought tales of hedge priests out amongst the resentful peasantry, and clandestine meetings of labourers who met by night and seemed to possess an organisation beyond their local village, or even shire.

It was an unsettled season. John, for one, had vivid memories of his last excursion to Upton. Edmund had shared similar stories of peasant surliness in Essex. It did not bode well. With the new royal Chancellor, Archbishop Simon Sudbury, being pressed to justify royal expenditure and the Treasurer, Sir Robert Hales, being condemned as the mind behind the new poll tax and its 'oppression of the poor', the city was rife with rumours of plots and rebellion in the countryside.

As John and the apprentices crossed the stinking, turgid waters of the river Fleet and rode out through Holburne they carried swords beneath their cloaks of Mentmore cloth. The day was cold; they rode with their hoods drawn up and in silence.

Philippa did not find it easy to watch her husband leave. The news of unrest did nothing to calm her feelings. Seeking to overcome her worries she buried herself in the care of the house. She scolded the servants, tasted the soup and questioned Agnes Bakwell concerning the salt fish cooked in flat loaves. The house keys hung at Philippa's slim hips.

As it was the feast day of the great fisherman's brother, they took fish in some quantity at dinner. The fact that it was Friday only served to provide more reason for the banishment of meat.

Without John the noon-time repast was a rather dull affair. Thomas and Philippa sat at the high table, Margaret being confined to her room in continued disgrace.

In the afternoon Philippa went shopping in Grasschurch Street market, accompanied by Emma and an apprentice chaperon. While Philippa and Emma handled and discussed the dried bunches of thyme, parsley and rosemary, the chaperon lolled about in ill-concealed boredom.

The meat in the house was rare and salted. Already it was past its best and by February it would be difficult to make it appetising. Thomas liked his meat made palatable by spiced 'sharp sauces'. It was the only way to disguise old meat through the winter.

Philippa sniffed at the fragrant herbs. 'I love rosemary. 'Tis said it's for remembrance,' She smiled. In her room a sprig of dried rosemary lay amongst her treasured books. John had given it to her.

While Margaret stroked her forget-me-nots, Philippa caressed her rosemary sprig. And neither woman spoke of her loneliness and anxiety.

Emma noticed the distant look in her mistress's eyes. She could read that look easily. Seeking to cheer up her mistress, she said, 'We will need to stop at the grocer's shop for spices for the cameline sauce and the mortrewes.'

She knew how much Philippa liked the highly spiced interior of the grocer's hall. The mention of it helped her shake off her melancholy.

'Yes, Emma,' she said more cheerfully, 'and we must hurry, for it's getting dark.' Signalling to the chaperon, they set off.

Philippa's favourite grocer's hall lay just north of The Poultry on the edge of Old Jewry. No Jew had lived here, to the west of the Walbrook, since Edward I's cynical expulsion of the Jews from his realm in 1290. The name lingered like candle smoke after the bright flame has been snuffed out in darkness.

The grocer's shop, which fronted his hall, was piled high with richly aromatic spices and delicacies. Philippa purchased cloves, cinnamon and ginger to make a 'sharp' cameline sauce.

'Vinegar, mistress?' Emma asked. Philippa nodded and the grocer went to fetch a tightly stoppered bottle. Philippa and Emma browsed amongst the exotic spices. The shop was crammed with varied merchandise.

'Think, Emma, of this place, when others accuse the Mentmores of a breach of mystery!'

It was over a generation since the spicers, pepperers and canvas sellers had united as the Guild of Grocers. The shop by Old Jewry bore vivid testimony to the rich diversity of that amalgamation.

'Mistress, is it not true that the other guilds tried to force the grocers to deal in but one ware?'

'Tried and failed. The clamour from the other guilds brought such an act into force, but 'twas repealed within a year. I was ten at the time. I can still recall the talk between my father and my brothers.'

Then the elderly grocer returned with the packaged goods in the hands of an apprentice.

'And the mortrewes, madam?' Emma was enjoying herself.

The grocer watched the peculiar intimacy between mistress and maid with interest. He half expected the older woman to scold the dark-haired servant. Instead she gave her agreement and ordered pepper, saffron and precious sugar. When their shopping was complete, the two women and their sleepy attendant made their way home. They lingered a while in The Poultry then, as the brief afternoon faded, they made their way down Walbrook Street to Thomas Mentmore's house.

The next day, Philippa had Agnes Bakwell prepare the meat and spices for a supper meal. Thomas was talking accounts with

Tom the journeyman. Their conversation soon turned to the neighbour's earth closet and Philippa took the opportunity to take a bowl of food to Margaret in her room. Ever since the virtual imprisonment had begun, Philippa had felt a growing pity for the other woman. It was like watching a wild song bird imprisoned in a wicker cage. As the weeks turned to months, this song thrush was pining and dying.

Philippa tapped lightly on the oak door. There was no reply. She entered the tiny, bare room. A candle guttered in the draught. Margaret lay on the bed. Her *Book of Hours* was clutched to her bosom. She looked as if she had been crying.

As Philippa entered a flash of life crossed Margaret's face, then it was gone. Dead eyes, sunk behind tight cheek bones, followed her movement. Was it despair or just plain hatred which stirred there? In the shadows, the blue seemed to have darkened to ebony. The whole room was hung with despair like malignant spiders' webs. Philippa shivered and, feeling herself to be an unwelcome intruder, walked softly, almost on tiptoe. She placed the bowl on the plank floor and hovered awkwardly. Margaret continued to stare at her coldly.

'I ... I've had Agnes cook you up some mortrewes.' No response. 'I – I know how much you like it. She's ground up salt pork with breadcrumbs, egg yolks and pepper. Emma and I purchased ginger, saffron and – '

'Thank you.' Margaret spoke at last. Her voice was frosty. 'I am familiar with the ingredients of the dish.'

Philippa bit her lip. Why was it that Margaret unnerved her so? No one else would have made her cover up her confusion in such a torrent of superfluous conversation. Still, she refused to flee from this abode of darkness. She sat on the edge of Margaret's small wooden trunk.

'I expect you'll want to know the gossip.' Philippa did not wait for a reply. 'John has gone. He hopes to be home for Christmas. Do you remember that knight who went with the constable of the Tower and killed the squire at Westminster Abbey?' Margaret made no answer. It was possible that she nodded. 'Well, he was not charged with that, of course. The Duke of Lancaster saw to it. But what do you think? Mayor Walworth has accused him of treasonable correspondence with the French!' Margaret looked almost interested. Her brother was in France. 'The charge was brought before the parliament at Northampton but he has been acquitted. Everyone is outraged. They say Gaunt would not have him tried; and he with a brother fighting the French at this very moment! They're saying Gaunt cares more for his creatures than for his own brother.'

Margaret leant down and picked up the bowl of steaming stew. She spooned out the contents carefully.

'Of course,' Philippa continued undaunted, 'all the city is interested. They say Shakell and Hawley's Spanish hostage had run up massive debts with the likes of Kirkby and Lyons. Everyone seems to have an interest in this affair!

'Talking of interest: Walworth and Philipot are still watching over the spending of the royal household. Gaunt is off in Scotland but everyone says he is furious about it. And guess what! Anne Glanville – the one whose favour Edmund carried at Smithfield – is going to marry Ralph Horne next August. They've set a date. 'Twill be in the fishmongers' Church of St Michael down by the river. Whatever will Edmund think? Mayhap he will return from France and carry her off . . .'

Her voice trailed off. Oh my God, she thought. What have I just said? Margaret's eyes burned with a curious, brimming light. The bowl trembled in her hands.

Philippa stood up like a startled game bird. 'There, I have gone on. You'll be tired. I'll see you tomorrow, after church.'

Then she was out of the room. Behind her, Margaret sat in the semidarkness, alone with her memories.

Philippa made many sallies into Margaret's chamber that winter. Each time she brought snippets of gossip: the unwelcome visit of poll tax officials, enquiring into personal circumstances; Agnes Bakwell scalding herself on the arm; bad news from Brittany; a fight outside the Bishop of London's house caused by a mob demanding that the clergy should be taxed. Each time she refused to be rebuffed by the indifference of her sister-in-law. It was a painful business but Philippa did not abandon it.

Christmas brought heavy snow. It was not until after Epiphany that John could return to London. By the time he returned the streets were streams of brown slush. The holly and ivy which had decorated the hall had been taken down and burnt lest witches hide in them over the coming year. John was not best pleased at having missed yet another season with his wife and child.

He stayed home for less than a month. The work in East Anglia required his attention. Worstead cloth needed purchasing and shipping back to London. Soon it could be shipped to the Low Countries.

Winter saw many of the rural weavers occupied with their craft. Many were yeoman smallholders. In the spring they would once more be occupied with subsidiary agricultural pursuits. If John was to make the most of his opportunities he must not long delay in London.

The money provided by Lyons would purchase large quantities of cloth at Norwich and at the royal fair held at Lynn. A return to London by way of Bury St Edmunds, Lavenham and Hadleigh would secure contracts with the wool producers and small-scale weavers of southern Suffolk and northern Essex. Back in London the cloth could be sold at a good profit and still undercut the city weaving guilds.

'And next season,' John assured his wife and father, 'we shall begin shipping finished cloth abroad, avoiding the Staple taxes on raw wool.'

He was not pleased by Thomas's accounts of delays in cloth supplied by the city guilds. Led by Appulby, who had rapidly replaced the disgraced Newton, the craftsmen were pushing for higher wages. Small guildsmen, who had taken on nightwork to fulfil Mentmore demands, had been penalised by their guilds. Hidden looms had been discovered and smashed. Appulby was welding the weavers together and applying well-established sanctions against any who did not toe the line.

All these factors only served to convince John that the future of the family rested on his securing an out-of-city source for medium-grade cloth. More than this, the capture of such contracts – and the elbowing aside of foreign traders anxious to purchase wool for weaving abroad – offered the chance of an enormous expansion beyond London.

'Just wait,' he confided at dinner, 'this year we're buying cloth at markets and selling it at a profit in London. But the Cotswold venture points the way forward: buy the wool at source, supply the weavers, fullers and dyers ourselves, then sell it where we want, at local markets and here . . . And then, who knows? The possibilities open up before us. We shall soon repay our debt to Lyons, mark my words!'

'But what of the countryside?' Philippa asked. John's enthusiasm had not dismissed her fears, or dispelled the rumours of unrest. 'Is it safe to travel so far?'

John frowned. He had no wish to worry his wife but he would not lie to her either. He had heard more rumours of unrest than he could count: hay crops spoilt, boon work disrupted or denied; mob rescues of fugitive villeins who were being returned to their lord's manor.

''Tis a hard time and no doubt. The poll tax collectors are out and none welcome them! And it's not helped by lords who pay above the legal wage. For, by St John, they know full well 'tis an offence to pay more than five pennies a day for mowing or over threepence for reaping corn. Yet they pay to suit themselves and soon the whole rural populace will not take the legal pay from anyone. The Statute of Labourers may as well not exist!

'Come spring, and get the tax away, mayhap the country will settle down. There's naught to fret over.'

What he chose not to mention was the violent attacks on landlords who kept to the labour laws and demanded boon work; and the killing of justices who enforced the hated, crumbling laws. Nor did he make mention of the armed assemblies poaching in the woods at night, or hedge priests carrying the seeds of revolt from parish to parish.

'Fret not,' he assured his wife. 'There's nothing to fear.'

She did not look convinced.

When John finally left for Norwich he took Tom the journeyman and three apprentices. It was a cold, clear day. Philippa, though, felt as if she were under a storm cloud.

Ann wriggled to run after her father. Emma caught the excited child and returned her to her mother's arms. As Philippa took the blonde imp, she could not help but notice that her maid looked uncommonly fatigued. Perhaps she was carrying some of the strain of her mistress. Then John was out of sight and the responsibilities of the day beckoned to his abandoned wife.

The week following John's departure was not particularly eventful. Charles de Gouarec and his craftsmen completed a tapestry for Thomas of Woodstock. Thomas Mentmore celebrated with a more than usually lavish dinner, but the joy was tempered by the ongoing dispute with the weavers.

The only noteworthy event was the outbreak of illness in the house of the Mentmores' draper neighbour. It had troubled his servants for a week or two. Now it struck the guildsman himself. Since there was bad blood between the two families, little concern was shown at the news. Amongst some of the apprentices there were even muttered references to God's judgement on a sinner.

At the beginning of the second week two events occurred of some moment. Two Mentmore apprentices were assaulted near Old Jewry by a mob looking for substitutes for Lancaster. That was disquieting enough. More worrying, however, was the sickness afflicting some of the Mentmore household servants. People ceased to talk of it as God's judgement.

It was a Tuesday evening when Emma complained of feeling unwell. Philippa had watched her for a while but had not been able to coax out any comment from the girl. Now the maid could disguise her feelings no longer.

'I feel such a fever, mistress,' she moaned softly. 'It is burning me up.'

'You do not surprise me, girl. You looked so pale at mass this morning.'

The family usually attended church each morning. Philippa had noticed how Emma's attention tended to drift during the celebration. That was unusual. Emma was as devout as her mistress.

'Aye, mistress. I could not keep my mind still. It raced and jumped like a March hare, God forgive me.'

Philippa smiled. 'On that you may count, Emma.' The God whom Philippa worshipped would be keen to forgive the frailty of an eager serving girl. 'But I shall pray for you tomorrow. Now to your bed. I do not need you any more. Hurry, to bed!'

Emma did not improve. Her fever worsened and was accompanied by a severe headache. She would have continued to rise at dawn to help her mistress dress, but Philippa forbade it. She was beginning to feel a real fear for her maid. Some of the draper's servants had died. Had Emma breathed their polluted air? Philippa could not tell.

Two kitchen maids who had fallen ill before Emma were being eaten up with fever. Emma slowly followed the same course.

Philippa sent Agnes Bakwell to the apothecary for a measure of feverfew. Taken in mulled wine, it possessed a wonderful power to reduce temperature in the sick.

On the third day of her fever Emma began to suffer bleeding from the nose. She lay on her damp pallet in a desperate, sweaty heat.

'Oh mistress,' she groaned, 'my head is cloven with an axe. I do not know what I shall do.'

Philippa held her hand to the hot forehead of her maid. A slow drum beat of a pulse throbbed in Emma's temple. Her dark eyes rolled, and she wept. Thomas ordered Emma's pallet moved into the hall. He feared the power of the miasma in the confined space of Philippa's room.

Philippa scarcely slept. For hours she knelt beside the sick girl. Around her bustled the business of the house. At last Thomas relented and the girl was moved back to her mistress's room. Thomas's clients – the wealthy examining ells of cloth, and weavers en route to the warehouse store – had begun to cast doubtful glances at the sick girl in the hall.

A conference with Agnes produced a suggestion of powdered eel skins for the nose bleeds. Late into the night Philippa watched Agnes burning the skins over a small brazier. Carefully she blew the dark ashes into Emma's nostrils. Emma gagged and choked. Margaret stood silently in the doorway. Before her, Philippa and Agnes held the retching girl.

No end of fetching and carrying of water could assuage the sick girl's thirst. Nor could Philippa ignore the hot, distended stomach, which was painful to the touch.

Agnes – who seemed quite fearless – rubbed Emma's skin with mutton fat and lanolin ointment.

'Oh Jesus, Jesus!' Emma moaned. Her once glossy hair hung lank and greasy. Philippa could hardly hold the writhing girl. Suddenly she was aware of other hands about Emma. Margaret Mentmore did not speak. She simply knelt with Agnes and Philippa.

On the Sunday, Emma's skin was blotched with an angry red rash.

''Tis as the others, madam,' Agnes muttered. 'And . . . and him of the draper's guild. 'Tis spotted fever, I swear it.' She was scared.

Philippa did not reply. The draper had died after two weeks of fevered pain. That day Philippa prayed earnestly for the life of her maid. As she bowed her head towards the candle-bright nave she could feel the tears on her cheeks.

The other servants were terrified of their sick comrades. Only goading and hectoring would produce a willingness to approach the agonised victims of the fever. One night Philippa sat beside her restless companion. A low mutton-fat candle burnt with a smoky flame. Margaret stood in one corner watching.

'By Our Lady, I have tried all I know.' Philippa shook her head in frustration. 'God knows how she suffered last week, so I gave her licorice root to open her bowels. But now she is too loose and soils herself hourly. And she burns yet hotter with fever. What can I do?'

She stared at Margaret. Never had the two women shared in such a need. Emma had become a bond between them. A common thread linked them. Both now knew a little of the other's agony. They were still strangers, but the frost between them was thawing.

'You've given her henbane, for the pain?'

'Henbane, feverfew, poppy seeds ... Agnes has scoured the apothecaries and grocers' shops, but her belly swells hot and torments her. If only ... if only a doctor of physic could examine her.'

Both women knew the impossibility of such a dream. Thomas would never pay the five pounds fee of even the least practised physician. Not for a servant. The more eminent would demand perhaps twenty pounds and that before the cure was even begun.

'God's pity, Philippa, I've known of such doctors who have charged a man forty pounds and rich robes, and five pounds a year for life, to open a swollen belly. And then the man died because the planetary patterns were not right for the treatment.'

Philippa sighed.

'You can only pray,' Margaret said quietly, 'as I have prayed.'

Emma drifted into delirium in the second week of her fever; a low muttering state. It haunted Philippa.

One of Agnes Bakwell's assistants died. For the first time, Philippa began to doubt. She and Margaret continued to bathe the girl on a soiled linen mat but the fever would not subside.

On the eve of St David's day a storm drenched the city in wind and rain. Its violence shook the gables and threw lightning across the cloud-billowed sky. Emma's pulse was rapid and soft. It fluttered like a dove against Philippa's fingers. Emma rambled on incoherently. Only once was she lucid. As Philippa moistened the cracked, parched lips, she muttered: 'I love you, mistress. Pray for me . . . do not fear for me.'

At midnight the thunder was directly overhead. It seemed to tear at the very pillars of the world. Sheets of lightning cast wild illuminations through cracks in the shutters. The candle flickered.

In the early hours, Emma died. She simply slipped away. Philippa was holding her hand.

In utter desolation Philippa wept on Margaret's shoulder then, together, they sat in silence. It was a long, deep silence within a wild, dark night. Tears coursed down Philippa Mentmore's cheeks.

At last she turned to her sister-in-law. 'Is this how you felt?' The question hung, naked.

Margaret nodded. 'As if my life had been drawn out on a rack and all my hope beaten from me. But you . . . you have John, and Ann. I have nothing. In my dark days it has only been God and His angels who have carried me through.'

Then, because she had to know, Philippa blurted out: 'For God's sake, Margaret, did he do it?'

Their eyes met. 'No, he did not do it,' Margaret said. 'He did not kill Adam Yonge.'

'Then who? Who?'

Margaret smiled – a thin, agonised smile. 'I asked Rob that. The night before we threw our lives away.'

'And?' Philippa ran a hand over her tear-smudged face.

'He does not know either. Truly he does not know. We have no secrets.' Tears glistened in her eyes. 'We *had* no secrets. 'Tis true he saw much of Yonge. Adam was chief clerk. He believed – though only God knows why – that there were those amongst the weavers who wanted more than longer holidays and another penny for cloth. He believed that there were those who wished destruction on the house of Mentmore.'

Philippa was shocked. 'But why? Who? For what reason?'

Margaret shook her head. 'Adam did not know. Nor would he

tell Rob all. He did not fully trust Rob, you see, for he too was a weaver. And yet Adam deemed him an honourable man, and so he is.'

'So Adam confided in him?'

'To an extent. For he believed there were forces behind our discomfort which cared as little for Rob Newton as for the Mentmores. And Adam Yonge wanted peace. He was a peaceable man.'

'Yes they quarrelled?'

'They did. That much is true. Adam came to the weaving sheds one night in a towering rage. Said he'd discovered things that would disgrace a cutthroat. He said Rob must know of it too and he would never trust him again. Hot words passed – for Rob knew nothing, you see. That night he resolved to go to Yonge but Adam would not see him. Instead, Rob spoke to me in secret – but not of weaving! The next day Wyclif appeared before the Bishop of London. You know the rest.'

Philippa's cheeks were gull white. 'So he never told Rob?'

'He would not speak with him. The door was shut to him. The next day Adam was dead.'

There was a silence. Both were lost in their dark thoughts.

'Why did you not tell John?'

Margaret laughed bitterly. 'Because he had willed to kill Rob. I tried – too late – and got this for my pains.' She touched a facial scar. 'My father called me "liar" and "whore".'

Outside the wind howled. In one corner Emma lay silent on her pallet. The angel of death beat his wings upon the house.

The cog *The Annunciation* rose and fell into the towering wall of black water. Sheets of spray drenched the decks. Then the wave had pased. The vessel wallowed in a rolling trough before the next mountain of white-crested darkness hammered on her aching timbers. The wind screamed in the taut rigging. Ragged sails flapped and cracked like whips.

Stephen de Knolton stumbled against the glistening canvas of the deck shelter. Inside the men-at-arms were crouching. He could hear their retching. Sliding on the streaming, pitching deck he staggered after the captain who was desperately trying to save what remained of his sails. Stephen fell heavily. Another wave swept the ship. He was drenched to the skin. One hand, inside his cloak, hung on to the precious leather despatch pouch entrusted to him by Edmund Mentmore.

Good God, he thought bitterly, what a homecoming! Before he rose again, he muttered one, desperate prayer to the patron of travellers. The storm was getting worse.

All day *The Annunciation*, out of Southampton, had battled up the Channel. With darkness the storm had intensified. Each sheet of white lightning revealed mountainous seas on every side. The land was lost in the darkness.

The siege of Nantes was over. Jean de Montfort had thrown in his lot with the king of France. The English had been betrayed. Starving and friendless in a hostile land Buckingham had been forced to scatter his army about the southern Breton ports. All were miserable.

Edmund had resolved to send word to his brother. He had thought long and hard since that dawn on the Quay de la Fosse. Now he was convinced that he understood. Stephen carried a sealed despatch for the eyes of John Mentmore only.

The Annunciation was on her way home from Italy. Her hold was heavy with spices and Mediterranean cloth and wine. For a handful of silver pennies the captain was willing to carry a squire and his escort of men-at-arms.

'Will you put in at Poole? She'll not take much more of this!'

'No, I'll not chance her in the tidal race at the harbour mouth.' The captain swept his hand through the air. 'Like a mill leat it runs, by God. Like a mill leat.'

'We'll not ride out this storm.'

'Damn you, man, I'm the captain. I know what I'm doing.' He seized Stephen's arm. The two were only inches apart, but screaming to be heard. 'Do you know Old Harry and his wives?'

'Aye,' he shouted. The great chalk stacks at the tip of Dorset's Ballard Down were familiar to him.

'When we see them we're safe.' A wave hit the vessel. The captain swore. 'We'll put into Studland Bay. Ride out the storm in the lee of the point. You know it?'

Stephen nodded. His capuchon was swept back by the wind. His hair was matted with salt water.

'Then get down on your knees and pray we'll see Old Harry before the mast goes!'

Around the vessel the sea rose and fell in unimaginable power.

As Stephen struggled back along the pitching deck he wished with all his heart that the captain had put in at Melcombe Regis. By now, he thought, I could be abed in a pot house in the town. Another wave surged black water across the forecastle.

As the shivering squire reached the shelter of the castle, he looked back along the deck. The prow tipped down into a fearsome trough. As it did so, another sheet of lightning burst behind the arrow shafts of rain. On the port bow a dark shoulder of shadow rose from the tormented sea. It was more solid, more permanent than the heaving darkness about it. Even over the roar of the storm, Stephen could hear the explosion of breakers on the foot of the headland.

'Oh God!' His lips trembled. For he was a Dorset man. He knew the towering darkness was St Alban's Head. He also knew of the great, pitted black slabs of rock which spread out from the foot of the cliffs.

The captain was nearby, dragging on a rope.

'God's mercy, man, look!' Stephen screamed. 'We're on to the Kimmeridge ledges.'

The captain gazed at him without comprehension. Stephen pointed. The panic was carved on his corpse-grey face. The mask of sheer horror shook the captain.

He turned as lightning lit up the misshapen snout of Hounstout Cliff; behind it the surf cannoned into Chapman's Pool. He returned Stephen's look of horror.

Then a wave smashed into the starboard planking. The ship swung away from the blow and the ballast of bricks shifted. Both men felt it go.

For a moment the cog yawed wildly.

'Sweet Lord!' Stephen's voice rose in desperate resignation. 'To come home. Oh, to come home and to end like this!'

Then the sea rose. With a teeth-shattering jolt *The Annunciation* was flung on to its side. Hungry waves snatched at ship and crew.

Like a maniacal giant, the roused sea hurled the disintegrating vessel on to the clawing ledges of rock.

Chapter Fourteen

The Cluniac house of Castle Acre seemed to slumber in the golden light of a late April evening. From the monastic church, the rising chant of vespers signalled the slow drawing in of the day. The waves of sound rose and fell like the surges of a distant tide. The damask rays of the failing sun lingered on the great west front and cast startling shadows on the majestic blind arcades. Norfolk drifted into night.

Since its foundation this mighty house of prayer had watched the seasons of three long centuries. Now the very founder's line had died out; ashes to ashes and dust to dust. Yet the prayers continued for souls long passed away. A steadily rising incense of worship. Mortals faded, like field grass, but the church endured.

John Mentmore leant against the open shutters of the abbey guest house. He yawned slowly and carefully. A niggling toothache had been troubling him for days. He had applied oil of cloves to the offending molar but had not succeeded in eradicating the pain. Considering the cost of cloves, he was not best pleased. As a result he took care to keep the cool air away from the back of his mouth and breathed slowly through his nose.

Away towards South Acre a poor cow-herd in short brown cotte was wading with his cattle through the deep ford of the river Nar. John watched him with the detachment of one who has other things on his mind. With one hand he rubbed at his swollen jaw.

In the still evening he could hear the clatter of horses' hooves from the castle atop the swelling rise. As the sun sank, the castle gate's flanking towers dipped into darkness. Soon only the battlements of the great shell-keep were washed with pink light.

A deep and deliberate cough reminded John that he was keeping someone waiting.

'Your move.' The voice was thick and the language was heavily accented French.

John picked up a counter on the board of Nine Men's Morris. After a moment's consideration he made his move. The bearded man grunted with annoyance.

'You're blocked,' John commented. 'Hemmed in on every side; no room for manoeuvre.'

His companion studied the counters intently. It was as if he hoped that force of concentration might shift the pegs from their rough-drilled holes. Then he grunted again and a tanned hand lifted a clipped silver penny and laid it on John's side of the pitted trestle table.

'Play again?' John had begun to forget his toothache.

His dark companion scratched at his swarthy chin and shook his head. Nine Men's Morris was a pleasant diversion on a spring evening, but this was getting expensive. John nodded to Tom, the journeyman, who gathered up the coins and secreted them in his leather purse.

Nicholas Kempe of Bruges shrugged and poured himself another beaker of wine. There would be other games in other guest houses and inns. For a merchant such hostelries were more familiar than home. He would win back his money at another board.

The guest house had its usual array of visitors: pilgrims en route to the shrine of Our Lady of Walsingham, merchants and travellers heading for Norwich or King's Lynn. Sitting astride the ancient track of the Peddars Way the castle and monastery were no strangers to travellers. The guest house stables contained an odd assortment of packhorses, donkeys and mules. The guest house itself held no less wide a spectrum of humanity.

John, along with his escort, had arrived only that day from Swaffham in west Norfolk whilst the monks were celebrating the service of nones at three in the afternoon. He had taken the opportunity to stretch his legs in the cobbled courtyard and there he had met the garrulous Flemish merchant. Nicholas Kempe was a heavyweight barrel of a man. A thick red beard, of startling shade, adorned his weatherbeaten face. In an age which praised the pristine pale, that face would have done service on a ploughman, open to wind and weather. However, anyone who mistook the station in life of the face would have soon been set right by the jewelled fingers and the fine cloth of the surcoat and hose. He wore his capuchon twisted up as an elaborate head piece. The waving coxcomb put John in mind of Roger Starre.

John soon discovered that Kempe was on his way to Boston on the Wash. He too travelled in cloth. For all the rivalry between an alien and a native mercer, this common livelihood had created an affinity between the two.

The fact had been noted, and disapproved of, by Tom and the apprentices. Their xenophobic suspicions found no room or charity for outsiders. Busy, bustling Flemings found no warmth there. To Tom and his cronies the red-bearded foreigner meant only competition and trouble. They eyed him with suspicion, if not downright hostility.

John ignored the dark looks of his servants. He had often dealt with Flemish weavers in London. Since the late King's marriage to Philippa of Hainault, there had been an influx of cloth workers from Flanders. The native weavers hated them; the uneducated loathed them as 'outpersons'. John Mentmore was more pragmatic. In the communities of Flemish weavers he saw a source of cloth which could supplement his reliance on the London craft guilds.

Settled in the candlelit hall of the guest house, Flemish merchant and London mercer were swapping tales of travel and were reaping a bountiful harvest of rumour and gossip.

'Pour us more wine, Tom,' John said and signalled to one of the apprentices to close the shutters.

Tom emptied the leather bag of wine into the two wooden beakers on the table. John read the disdain in his face as he filled Kempe's drinking vessel. He chose to ignore it, but made a mental note that, when he had a private moment, he would tell the journeyman to keep his hostility to himself. John could not afford to let such sentiments get in the way of business.

'So, where were you before the fair at Ely?' John asked as he settled back on the bench.

Kempe drained his beaker. 'We stayed at the priory of St John by Burwell Castle. There's good business there. Do you know it?'

John did. Burwell and Reach were the principal ports for Cambridge. An ancient cut – the Reach Lode – connected the settlements to the Cam at Upware. From there merchandise could be sailed down to the Wash. It had been a while since John had ridden through Reach but he could recall the maze of canals and basins behind the merchants' houses. He could also recall the awkward bulk of Burwell's unfinished castle.

'And you? You came through Essex and Suffolk, no? What news is there from those parts? More tales of unrest?'

Kempe had an insatiable appetite for rumour and speculation. The state of the countryside gave him ample opportunity to indulge such an appetite.

'We rode north through Chelmsford,' John replied. 'I had business with the weavers there.' He did not give too much away although he guessed that Kempe was familiar with the area.

'There are communities of my countrymen there. You visited them, no doubt, at Dedham and Lavenham?'

Kempe's casual question indicated how familiar he was with the communities of aliens in Suffolk and Essex. Yet unlike John he could not enjoy freedom on the home market.

John had no real reason to cloak his movements but he did so nevertheless. He always played a close game in the presence of even a peripheral rival. 'Yes, about there. They produce good cloth. I like their blue cloth best. It sells well on the London market.'

'Yes,' Kempe replied deviously. 'They live peaceful lives under your King's peace.'

John smiled slightly. Kempe too must have been aware of the antipathy felt towards these alien craftsmen.

'But what news of the jacques?'

Kempe's contemptuous reference to the peasantry shifted the conversation. John was content to see the direction altered and did not demur.

'The royal council's decision to renew efforts to extract the poll tax is not exactly popular.'

'Ah,' grunted Kempe with a grin, 'I have heard similar tales. Your King has not gained all the silver that he hoped for. Is that not so?'

'He's short, by St John. So short that the collectors have been charged with gross negligence and a new commission has been appointed to pursue those who evaded the tax collectors. It's headed by John Legg, a sergeant-at-law. But the mind behind the new commission is the royal Treasurer, Sir Robert Hales.'

'The one the jacques call "Hobb the Robber", no?' Kempe

asked his question with a thin smile. That name was gaining currency at every village fair and meeting place.

'Hobb the Robber – the very same. God knows the first tax was unpopular enough, but now the people fear a new tax is intended. 'Tis nonsense, of course, but the ignorant pass on the fear like plague. There's talk of it at every pot house and tavern.'

Kempe pushed ringed fingers through his bushy beard and leaned towards his drinking partner. 'Never dismiss fears of the jacques, my friend, for it breeds like vermin and erupts like a plague of Egypt. And the black hearts of the ignorant shield demons.'

His statement would have sounded melodramatic had not John seen the battered body of the bailiff of Upton. The events at Todenham and Wolford were too fresh in his mind. He loathed the royal tax, like every other Englishman, but there was something in the Fleming's words which put roots down into a deep pit of disquiet within himself. For a brief moment he stood once again before the body of Adam Yonge, caked dark with blood.

'There's unrest abroad. The country is unsettled. There's scarce a villein but will try his luck with his master. Will go for day wages, despite the law. Will turn his back on boon work on the demesne. And there are plenty who seek to profit from such acts: heretic hedge priests and lords who see their own advancement in the destruction of law-abiding neighbours . . .'

John wanted to add, 'And there are weavers who will butcher a clerk for a lark, and footpads who will hurl a pregnant woman from her horse.' But he did not say the words. He could feel the emotion rising in his voice and had no wish to betray his feelings to this stranger.

Nevertheless, the foreign merchant must have caught the inflection in the younger man's voice. He recognised a kindred loathing of the rebellion which ran, like a deep dark current, within the mob.

'I was twenty-two when you English captured the King of France at Poitiers.' Kempe's voice took on the rhythmic cadence of a practised teller of tales. 'And I travelled through Picardy in the spring of 1358 with my father. We had business in the dioceses of Laon and Soissons. Have you heard of "The Jacquerie", my young friend?'

John nodded.

'Well, by Christ, whatever you have heard 'tis only a half for you heard tales from afar. I saw it with my own eyes.' Kempe crossed himself. 'The jacques rose up against their lords. I saw them. With these eyes I saw those ravening dogs. I saw the mob, with pitchforks and scythes.

'They burnt and destroyed manors. They violated women like heathens or Saracens. With one knight, they roasted him on a spit before his wife and children and forced the lady to eat the flesh of her husband. Then they killed her without pity. Christ, they were like demons . . .'

'God, man, did you witness that?' John's face paled. His knuckles were white. Even Tom the journeyman paused from his game of dice. The room was dark. The candle threw up wild, high shadows.

'No, but I spoke to a man who saw it all. And churches were looted and castles burnt before the fury abated. Such things were done as would make a brute beast weep. But the jacques did not weep. No! They were lower than beasts and fouler than the pits of hell.'

John had heard the stories of horror as a young child. He had seen fellow Londoners laugh at the terror which was sweeping the enemy land. However, Thomas Mentmore had not laughed; nor had his son. They saw little profit to be gained in any sense, from a world run wild with blood. It was with disgust that they had heard of guildsmen in the French towns making common cause with the rebels against the nobility. Perhaps Thomas Mentmore's kinship to Giles de Brewoster made him more than ordinarily sensitive to the traditional animosity between the bourgeois of the towns and the landed gentry. John, too, was not free from that ambiguity of attitudes. It was one more tension within the Mentmore family.

Kempe was studying his companion. He read the revulsion on the mercer's face.

'And you escaped?' John's question was pitched low.

Kempe paused before he answered. This had ceased to be a mere traveller's tale. Now he was chronicling his own feelings. The room was quiet. Others were listening too. Kempe was suddenly aware of a wider audience. He noted the inquisitive yet hostile eyes of John's companions.

'I escaped, but my father did not. He was taken at Beauvais.

The mayor and magistrates had opened the town gates to the mob. It was a chance for them to even old scores. To settle debts. To write off losses permanently. My father had done much business with the guildsmen of the town and many owed him money. They handed him over to the mob. The jacques killed him in the main square. He was an outsider, you see. A Fleming. Such a man may be hounded and destroyed at will. At one stroke, his debtors settled their debts and came out of it at a profit.'

Kempe's voice had a note of intense bitterness about it. A throbbing hatred rose within his throat. For a moment he broke off, then he concluded: 'And when, at last, the nobility organised themselves, they crushed the rebels like vermin. They hung them from their cottage doors and burnt their hovels with fire. But I did not weep, for I had seen their deeds . . .'

John rose from the table. 'It's late,' he said, 'I must bid you good night.' He turned and left the room. The Fleming watched him go then with a grim smile he poured himself another beaker of wine.

John slept badly that night. The box bed in the draughty cubicle of the guest hall dormitory brought him little comfort. The straw paliasse sagged on its support of criss-crossed ropes. When he did sleep, his dreams were haunted by curious, shifting nightmares. Threatening shapes – drawn from his own and the Fleming's experiences – cast long shadows on his imagination. He woke well before dawn. His tooth was aching and he felt weary.

High mass was at ten o'clock. The monks had scarcely vacated the church for their chapter meeting when John took sanctuary in the building. The echoes of the psalms of terce still lingered amongst the columns and arches.

The arm of St Philip was held at Castle Acre. From its reliquary by the high altar it assured the faithful of the particular care of the apostle and it was to St Philip that John prayed this morning. He prayed not only for the commercial success of the venture but also for the safety of his family. John Mentmore had ceased to disguise his concerns. He felt distinctly uneasy. Whilst he had told Kempe of the unrest in Essex, he had not been able to communicate fully the sense of disease. It was difficult to do justice to the feelings of anger and suspicion that flooded conversations at fairs and taverns by the roadside.

After mass, the Mentmore party left the abbey and took the

wide dusty road north towards Walsingham. The baulks at the edges of the open fields were already ablaze with cowslips and ragged robin. The winter had been mild and spring had arrived early and in force.

John would have ridden in silence for his gregarious tendencies were at a low ebb. Tom, however, was more talkative. As ever he was clarifying the situation, making sure he understood it just right. It was, perhaps, a natural extension of his role as journeyman but John found it irritating at times.

'I'm right to say that the cloth contracted for in Essex will be collected in the autumn?'

John grunted. He had gone over this before. Tom knew what had been arranged.

'That's for the weavers at Coggeshall and Clare?' Tom could turn any statement into a question.

Since John took the question as rhetorical, he made no reply. Instead he hummed tunelessly to himself.

Starved of assurance, the journeyman tried again: 'I'll ride up into Essex after Michaelmas to collect the rolls on packhorses? But what of the Suffolk villages? Will you have me deal with them at the same time?'

'Of course!' John's answer was noticeably testy. 'You heard the agreements made in Essex. When we ride south again we shall finalise arrangements at Kersey, Lavenham and Long Melford. I made provisional arrangements with the Flemings last summer. 'Tis only the final dates of delivery that now need fixing. Mayhap they will haggle but I'll wager on Michaelmas for all the cloth – of Essex and of Suffolk. Fret not, Tom; there's little that can go wrong with this enterprise.'

With that the journeyman had to be content. He reined back his mount and let his master ride on ahead. Clearly he did not relish company.

The decision to go north to Walsingham had been made by John once the enterprise had started. Originally he had planned to go direct from Suffolk to Norwich, but on the way he had changed his mind. A visit to the shrine at Walsingham could only succeed in securing additional blessings on the venture.

As with all pilgrims approaching Little Walsingham from the south, the Mentmore party made their first stop at the tiny Slipper Chapel at Houghton St Giles. Here they left their boots. The last mile was to be travelled barefoot. As they walked, John's devotions were disturbed by a bickering amongst the accompanying apprentices.

' – 'twas an angel that placed the shrine here. Do you know nothing?'

'Huh! Who heard the like? It was Our Lady herself who built the house and revealed its place to – '

'Enough!'

The irritated voice of their master silenced them. Even Tom had begun to tire of the fractious dialogue. He took the opportunity both to assert himself over the quarrelling apprentices and ingratiate himself with the guildsman.

'Set them right, sir! They'll only accept it if you tell it.'

John could well believe it. ''Tis common knowledge', he began, 'that the widow de Faverches was directed by Our Lady to build a replica of the house of the Holy Family here in Norfolk. The widow saw the house in a vision. It was as if she stood in Nazareth herself, so 'tis told – '

'But the angel, master? What of . . .?'

John gave the apprentice a withering glance before continuing: 'The site for the shrine was in a dew-wet field. Dry patches revealed where it should stand. At first the wrong place was chosen and the house would not rest on its foundations until it was moved to another dry patch.'

The company were awed at their master's knowledge.

'But since then,' John concluded, 'Our Lady has further hallowed the shrine. For when the infidel overran the holy places, the spirit of Mary did leave Jerusalem and settled here.'

The heir to the house of Mentmore had spoken and none dared contradict him.

John stayed for a week at the shrine. The guest house at the priory was full and the travellers found shelter at the Franciscan Friary. It was a newer building, scarcely more than thirty years old, and the party was more than satisfied. On each day John attended high mass in the morning and vespers towards sunset. After weeks of riding and bargaining, this quiet time came as a refreshment to the soul.

When it was time to leave he felt as if a veil had been lifted from before his eyes. Where once he had seen only gloom and destruction, now he saw hope and opportunity. As they followed the track south-eastward towards the coast, he could not help but notice that the wild places were alive with daffodils and primroses.

At the infirmary at Walsingham the herbalist had supplied John with a stoppered bottle of powdered tormentil. Taken with wine, the astringent root had relieved the worst of his toothache. Life seemed indeed to be brighter.

This optimism was soon to be severely tested. Seeking shelter at North Elmham, the travellers were once more accosted with the cares of the world. The talk was of tax evasion and of a profligate court. The peace of Walsingham would have to be resilient indeed to survive within the tales of unrest and rank insubordination. When John took his party out past the tumbled ruins of the Saxon cathedral his mind was again busy with the cares of a troubled world.

Their destination was Worstead. Situated on the coastal plain between Norwich and the sea this growing community had given its name to the cloth made from closely twisted woollen yarn. John had been to the settlement twelve months before and his return was expected. During his previous visit he had conducted detailed negotiations with the manorial overlord of the village community and this second one was concerned with the more prosaic matter of decisions regarding ells of cloth. This needed careful fixing, since the ell of Flanders was shorter than the English measure. The arrangements for collection of the finished cloth went smoothly. What occupied most of the conversation was news of conflict and dissatisfaction.

Once the deal had been clinched, John and the leading Flemish weaver took a stroll before the midday meal of bread, meat and ale. In the centre of the village the church of St Mary was being rebuilt. Great blocks of stone lay amidst the wooden scaffolds.

For a few idle minutes the two men watched the masons at work.

'What's this I hear of trouble in Norwich?' John asked casually. 'It sounds more than a grievance to the king's tax.'

His companion, a heavy jowled saturnine man, nodded. 'Oh the tax. It is always the tax! Who does not grumble at the tax? They say it was intended that a rich man should help his poorer neighbour.' He laughed sourly. 'But do you think he does?'

John, who had no urge to subsidise the tax bills of his less affluent neighbours, shook his head. 'What man would?'

The Fleming grunted. 'The poor are burdened by this tax. They say why should they break beneath it when the rich carry so light a load? They talk of the graduated tax and say it is the doing of the wealthy and the lords that this present tax weighs so heavy on their backs.'

'But it is more than the tax. I heard talk of trouble between the guilds. Is it so?'

The Fleming eyed him. 'Overload a donkey and his back breaks – no? Who can tell which piece of cargo did it? Some point to this, others to that. It is together that they snap the spine. It is always the last load which men notice. They ignore what has gone before.'

John began to catch the man's drift. 'And what loads do you see on the back of this donkey?'

The Fleming was thoughtful. For a moment there was a profound silence between the two men. In the background the masons hammered and chiselled.

'In the countryside the villeins flex their muscles. They will not work as their grandfathers did. "Let the lord pay us to work his demesne," they say. "Let us work for what a lord can afford." And if the law demands otherwise? What care they for the law, or the king's justices? And behind these cries you may hear others, if you listen carefully: "Give us land at a groat an acre rent"; "let us trade with who we want and be free of the lord's mill and the abbot's fair"; "give us more common rights and divide the land of the church among us".'

'Good God, man!' John said, shocked.

'Do you not listen?' The weaver raised one bushy eyebrow. 'Or is it that an alien's ears hear more keenly? For come what may, they will name us among their enemies.'

'You have your enemies,' John admitted.

'But sir – so do you!' The weaver's face was grim. 'For as the poor parish priest loathes the rich clergy and cries for freedom from royal tax and papal tax and a stipend to live on, so the lower guilds seek vengeance on the rich master. Is this not so in London? For it is in Norwich!'

John's eyes glittered. He made no reply.

'You asked me what ails Norwich. In the city there is a man

named Geoffrey Litster. Do you know him?'

John shook his head and the Fleming continued: 'He leads the lower guilds against the monopolies of the great guild masters. But his influence does not end there, for the tax is a load to break the donkey's back. Men search for a leader against the whole range of their enemies.

'The bishop and the merchants fear Litster. You may look aghast, but they fear him nevertheless. And why? Because they know that a single man may seize all complaints and mould them into one.'

'This Litster. Who supports him?'

'Surely sir . . . those who have complaints. Who see their own good in the toppling of God's order of society. Such men see courts living in luxury and foreign wars ending in disaster and grow tired of the state of things. And they count amongst their number knights of the shire. Men who would raise themselves on the backs of popular anger. Men who would be leaders of revolt to secure their own ends.'

John remembered the Compworths and shuddered.

The Fleming had almost finished, but not quite. 'Do you not know, sir, that there are those who thank God for this sea of discomfort? As every new wave rises they thank God, for they see in such an ocean opportunities without number. Men who seem far distant from the complaints of the poor have a hand in their actions. They move half seen and play their part from afar but, mark me sir, they play their part. As they seek to block their enemies, they will lay hand to any weapon left lying about. They are not squeamish about the company they keep. All things may work together for their good.'

For an instant John had a glimpse of the Nine Men's Morris board at Castle Acre. He could see his opponent's pegs hemmed in with no way out. Then a terrible, cold thought came to him. It was like the first shaft of sunlight on a morning of frost, when the air is crisp like unleavened bread and seems to crackle at the touch. He knew what was happening to his family. A clammy sweat broke out beneath his shirt. He felt the pumping of his heart. Blood beat in his temples.

'Oh, sweet Jesus!'

'Master, what ails you? Are you taken sick?'

John took a grip on himself. He was shocked at how he had

betrayed his feelings.

'Nothing . . . it is nothing.' He rose from his seat, a block of rough-hewn stone. 'Let's eat. I'm hungry.'

He was lying. He had never felt less inclined to dine. The Fleming seemed far from convinced, but he held his peace. It was not his station in life to question a merchant clothier.

Tom and the apprentices could not fail to notice the change in their master. They had thought to stay at Worstead for a day or two, but John informed Tom that he intended to be back in London by the first week of June at the latest. This new itinerary left scarcely three weeks for the completion of John's plans. Tom was surprised but, like the Fleming, kept his peace.

The next morning the party left for Norwich. It was a magnificent city of over six thousand souls. With its twenty churches and forty-three chapels it dominated the Norfolk landscape. John had intended to spend a week there but now he was more urgent. By Wednesday 15 May he had finished his business and agreements had been made for the bulk delivery of cloth. Three days had been expended but to John it seemed it had taken a lifetime. He would have left that evening but knew the futility of travelling so soon before sunset in strange country.

They rode out soon after breakfast and two days later reached Bury St Edmunds. One of the apprentices had a fever. John would have continued the journey the next day, but even his impatience was tempered by the cauldron of the man's forehead.

Whilst the infirmaver plied the man with feverfew and herbal draughts, John was forced to kick his heels at the guest house of the monastery. About him the daily office was celebrated with prayer and psalms. Its quiet regularity acted as a brake on his urgency. At parish mass and at vespers he gathered his thoughts together and laid them out before God.

In the abbey gardens after prime and in the cool cloisters before compline, he could be seen walking deep in thought. If anyone came close to him they would see his lips moving, though whether in silent prayer or in troubled, half-spoken thoughts it was difficult to tell. John himself would have been hard pressed to say where one ended and the other began.

During these perambulations he thought often of Philippa and baby Ann. He wondered what they were doing. As he thought of them he became acutely aware of the miles which separated them. At such times his belly ached with homesickness.

One particularly warm evening, between vespers and compline, John was walking in the shadowed cloisters. Out beyond the walkway the abbey buildings were sinking from gold to deep blue in the afterglow of sunset. A star twinkled shyly in the eastern sky.

John recognised the monk who casually crossed his path. As the abbey's land agent and the manager of the guest house, the holder of the rank of 'Terrar and Hostillar' was a man of importance in the monastic community. He was tall and big-boned and moved with a rolling gait which threw his arms in an ape-like motion. It was a distinct characteristic. John knew who spproached long before he could recognise the aquiline nose and high cheek bones beneath the tonsure.

The brother hostillar seemed bent on conversation. That was unusual since he should have been at collations in the chapter house. John had a suspicion that the man was on a mission. Only that afternoon before vespers Tom had remarked on the hostillar's interest in their journeying.

It came as little surprise to find that his questions now addressed to John were of the same ilk.

'Brother infirmaver tells me your apprentice improves. His fever subsides, praise God.'

John leant against a ribbed column. 'Yes. We have prayed for him and our prayers are answered. In a day or two we shall continue our journey.'

The deep eyes behind the hooked nose moved quickly. 'You travel to London?' John nodded. 'But through other villages?'

'We have business with the Fleming weavers.'

'Ah!' the hostillar said. 'Ah, yes. And have you come far?'

John smiled inwardly. It was clear the man was gathering information. It was also clear that he possessed little art as a spy. It was difficult to take offence at his questions poorly disguised as casual conversation.

John briefly explained his business. The hostillar seemed interested in what John thought of the state of the countryside and apparently regarded his guest as a useful source of information. John wondered if every traveller was interrogated in a like fashion.

The bell for compline rang. The hostillar, all smiles, excused himself. John watched him until he vanished into the darkness.

Well, well, he muttered to himself. Who wants this information? He sucked in his breath and chewed at his cheek in determined thought.

John had not been idle in Bury. He too could gather information when he desired. The town was alive with talk of trouble at the abbey. The chapter meeting of monks was divided over the election of a new abbot. Many of the senior merchants had involved themselves in support for rival candidates. Whilst the interregnum lasted the timid prior, John of Cambridge, was left with the task of administering the divided house. It was some consolation to John to learn that others also had their problems.

On Wednesday 22 May John announced that the Mentmore party would leave after prime the next day. The apprentice, though tired, seemed sufficiently recovered. That afternoon, the hostillar brought a message to the mercer. Would he dine with the prior before he left? This new arrangement would put off his leaving until noon. Nevertheless he agreed. He rightly assumed that the invitation was connected with the information-gathering of the hostillar. Besides which, the better provisioned table of the prior would make a welcome change from the monkish fare of soup, cheese and vegetables in the guest hall.

The next morning, Tom oversaw the packing of the horses. After high mass the sub-prior escorted John to the prior's chambers. The suite of rooms was well apportioned. There were medallions of glass in the windows, carved wooden ceilings and rich red hangings on the panelled walls.

Prior John took dinner, this May morning, in his cosy parlour. The trestle table was laden with cold meats and vegetables. Salt, in a silver gilt cellar, sat in pride of place amidst the pewter plates and bread trenchers. John was not disappointed by the repast.

John of Cambridge was in his fifties but looked ten years older. The worries of his rank had etched themselves on his thin, mousy face. The haur round his tonsure was grey and his thin, ringed fingers played constantly with the crucifix on his chest. With him were his chaplain, lay steward and his cellarer. With John and the sub-prior, the number of diners was complete.

After grace they ate and exchanged pleasantries. It was not

unusual for a prior or abbot to entertain guests. The talk was light and uncomplicated. John helped himself to oysters and salmon. He tasted cloves and mace in the meat dishes and smiled wryly. At three shillings a pound, such spices did not come cheap. The prior did not stint himself!

The prior took a handful of dates and currants. 'We hear talk of unrest in Norwich. Have you news?'

So, at last, the conversation was fixing on the events which had so interested the hostillar. John was prepared for the question and repeated the story he had heard from the weaver at Worstead.

'And the lower clergy,' he concluded carefully, 'do not preach against the sin of rebellion. Indeed, some say there are those amongst the parish priests who fuel the flames.'

The prior's face twitched. He put down his stale trencher and motioned to his lay steward. The steward plunged one hand deep inside the breast of his cotte and brought forth a scrap of grimy vellum and handed it to the prior, who passed it to the sub-prior.

'Read it for our guest.'

The sub-prior's voice was deep and mellow. It offered a contrast to the rather nasal tones of the prior.

'John Shepherd, now of Colchester, greets John Nameless and John the Miller and John Carter and bids them tell Piers Ploughman to go to his work and chastise well Hobb the Robber. And take with you John Trueman and all his fellows . . .

'John the Miller, grind small, small, small, the king's son of heaven shall pay for all . . .'

'Enough!' The prior's voice was agitated. He turned to John Mentmore. 'This was taken from one of the lay brothers. He has been beaten and thrown out of this house.' The prior's hands drummed on the table. 'The steward tells me these evil and mysterious missives have appeared in many of the villages. You have travelled far this spring. Have you heard ought of such secret letters?' He signalled the sub-prior to hand the letter to John.

John studied the untidy script and the words cloaked in allegory. He shook his head. 'I have not seen the like of this, but, by God, I have heard talk enough of common cause amongst the peasantry and of knights who would act as leaders. One such could have written this, or a hedge priest. God knows there are enough heretics and seducers of the ignorant and foolish.'

'Yes,' the prior said steadily, 'we are aware of such renegades. One has incited tenants of this house against God's holy order.'

'And are there not guildsmen in Bury itself who would exert pressure on this house to grant a charter to the town? Have they not interfered in the very election of your new abbot?'

The prior seemed unwilling to pursue that line of argument. A poorly disguised glance at the cellarer prompted a totally new discussion, centred on wine supply and the problems caused by the war. Evidently the prior had got what he wanted; or at least was satisfied that the traveller knew no more.

At noon the bell rang for celebration of the service of sext. Graciously the prior excused himself; the meal was at an end. It was a very thoughtful John Mentmore who took the road for Lavenham that afternoon.

At Lavenham, Long Melford, Kersey and Dedham, colonies of Flemish weavers had settled. Their arrival had brought a tremendous stimulation to the rural cloth industry.

At Lavenham the talk was more of politics than cloth. According to the weavers, the London merchant, Richard Lyons, had sent armed retainers to guard his manor at Overhall on the Suffolk-Essex border. It was even rumoured that the Chief Justice of England was storing his silver plate in the fortress tower of his parish church.

The talk of preparations in case of insurrection ensured that John only stayed one day at Lavenham. Arriving at the river port of Long Melford he fixed a date for the collection of cloth in the autumn and bought fresh horses at the town's horse fair.

On Sunday 26 May he left for Kersey after parish mass. Situated on a tributary of the Suffolk river Brett, the cloth produced here had given its name to a specific type of material. Riding into Kersey, John passed the stream in which the newly made cloth was soaked. It being the sabbath, the banks were deserted.

He put up at the Augustinian Priory situated at the north end of the village. The next morning he made final arrangements with the Kersey weavers over a jug of ale. The Flemings were agitated. They had heard of wandering bands of soldiers fresh back from Woodstock's campaign in France.

'They've brought to England the ways of soldiers in France,' one Fleming lamented in broken English and French.

John had no need to ask for details concerning the 'ways of soldiers in France'. He could imagine the brigandage and violence of such men. Many had been criminals in their shires before ever they had practised their skills on French towns and villages.

The news made John determined to finish business at Dedham as soon as possible. He would then make for London, via Coggeshall. By Tuesday evening he was on the banks of the Stour at Dedham. The village lay to the east of the King's highway which connected Colchester and Ipswich. The weavers welcomed the travellers and listened to their news.

At dawn John was up and to his work. The leading weaver lovingly explained how the cloth was woven, washed, fulled to remove oil and grease, dyed and shorn of loose threads. He unrolled at least an ell of the thickened cloth for John to handle.

'See how it has been beaten after washing? It makes a fine felt. It wears very well. As you can see, it will not unravel.'

John was impressed with the quality of the material. Normally he would have liked to have stopped and talked to such a master craftsman, but this day he could only think of sealing the contract and getting home.

By Wednesday night the travellers reached Colchester, and on Thursday morning they left for Coggeshall. Sited on the upper reaches of the river Blackwater, the Cistercian Abbey of Little Coggeshall was a wonder. Built in brick, it was the talk of the neighbourhood. However, it was not the building material which stunned the travellers. The town was up in arms. Hordes of people milled about the streets and documents lay strewn about the highway. Papers and books were being carried about on pitchforks.

John grabbed a hurrying man, dressed in short cotte and broken hose. 'God's sake man, what is happening?'

The man was terribly excited. 'They're sacking the sheriff's house . . . No more will we pay taxes.'

Smoke was billowing from the centre of the town. John guessed it emanated from the house of the unfortunate sheriff.

John let the man go to enjoy the riot while it lasted. He had more luck with a party of merchants, leaving the town bloody and barefoot.

'Christ on the cross!' a bruised and muddy middle-aged man sobbed as John seized him. 'They've all gone mad. They beat us for nothing. Thank God they released us...'

'Why, what happened?'

The tearful victim cast John a look of amazement. 'Haven't you heard? Good God, man! The poll tax commissioner for the shire has been driven out of Brentwood. The men of Fobbing and Corringham and Stanford-Le-Hope have risen in revolt. The king's men have fled for their lives. And it's spreading ... everywhere.' He sobbed uncontrollably. 'There are brigands in the town – Woodstock's scum – they stole our horses. Don't go into Coggeshall, for God's sake!'

Already John could see a crowd was gathering. Now they had dealt with the sheriff's house, the mob was looking for fresh victims. Tom caught at his bridle. He looked terrified.

'Yes, Tom. Yes, I know! We'll not go forward,' John assured his frightened journeyman. 'Back, back the way we've come. And for God's sake move smartly!'

With a heart torn by despair, John Mentmore tugged at his mount's reins and turned away from home.

On Sunday 2 June 1381 the Chief Justice of the Common Pleas rode to Brentwood, Essex, with a commission of enquiry and an escort of pikemen. He was attacked by a mob. His papers were burnt and three of his clerks were murdered before his eyes. On his knees, he was forced to promise the end of taxation.

That same day, in Kent, the Monastery of Lesnes at Erith was attacked. The abbot was forced to promise support for the rebels. That evening leaders of the Kentish men crossed to Essex.

Chapter Fifteen

It was the feast day of Boniface, bishop and martyr: Wednesday 5 June 1381. Edmund Mentmore was scarcely aware of this date. His body ached with fatigue. Although he had seen and experienced worse journeys, the road to Rochester had not provided him with pleasant diversions. The journey across Kent had been tedious and not a little worrying. It was almost ten at night and Edmund – usually the hell raiser – was longing for his bed. So far he saw little chance of retiring.

Across the room sat Sir John Newton, the constable of Rochester Castle. An old acquaintance of Edmund's, he had greeted the unexpected arrival of the knight with some eagerness and was keen to learn details of Edmund's journey from Sandwich.

Newton was a small man with a forked beard, but his quick, darting eyes revealed a reservoir of energy which seemed to exceed the extent of his small-boned frame. Pouring out a beaker of wine he motioned to Edmund to continue.

Edmund had already regaled him with stories of Woodstock's final withdrawal from the debacle of Brittany. Now he focussed his attention on events no less worrying.

'We'd heard of unrest in France. Woodstock returned in March. I followed him later. Knollys left me behind to . . . how shall I put it? Make one or two arrangements for him. He has hopes of more action in Brittany before the year's out.

'Having found myself amongst the rearguard, I had thought things would have settled down by the time we landed at Sandwich. To my surprise it was worse than the gossip had suggested. The roads are swarming with runaway villeins and the dregs of Woodstock's soldiery. And the towns and villages are as excited as a bitch on heat! I was glad I had my escort of men-at-arms.'

'You weren't threatened?' Newton sounded genuinely

concerned.

Edmund dismissed the worry with a wave. 'No one made an attempt to touch us. Had they tried we'd have put steel into their gizzard. No, it was not actions which concerned me, more a miasma of unrest as if the beggars and ploughboys thought they could dictate. Have you seen that look – an insolent one, without fear or respect?'

Newton sipped his wine. 'I've seen it. It's been getting worse since the last tax commission. The worms of the earth seem to have taken it into their heads to speak against the lions.'

'That's it,' Edmund said. 'You've seen the look on the faces of tavern keepers, common folk on the road, apprentices in the towns. They seem infected with a plague of insolence. And more than that: they possess a commonness of insubordinate purpose.'

'A Great Society!' Newton stood up abruptly and walked to the unshuttered window. Down in the outer bailey of the castle, sentries were talking. Their voices carried on the still summer air. No words survived the distance. Only the tone of the voices could be discerned. A newly risen moon was reflected in the widening estuary of the river Medway. Cogs and galleys lay at anchor. Their masts and rigging seemed entwined in a dark filigree. He turned back to his guest. 'How long have you been away from England?'

'About a year. Why?'

Newton gazed into the deep-red contents of his beaker. With one booted foot he stirred the rushes. The tallow candle guttered. He seemed lost in thought. 'Can you hear anything?' he asked at last.

It was an unexpected response. Edmund, puzzled, cocked an ear. 'Nothing, save some talk in the courtyard or on the wall walk. Why? What do you hear?'

Newton laughed. It was bitter and held no humour. 'I hear the landless who would be lordless. I hear them whisper of the fall of nobility and the destruction of Holy Church. I hear them snarl against their betters and those whom God has seen fit to place over them. And of late I hear other voices. I hear the artisans and the wealthier villeins. I hear the guildsmen. I hear the voices of those who would gain from unrest. I hear whispers in the dark. Can you hear them?'

Edmund felt a cold wind blowing through the room. He remembered John's tales of Upton and of the weavers. 'The whispering of the worms,' he said.

'Well, they whisper no longer. Were they whispering at Sandwich? Were they whispering on the roadside? Or were they talking openly, brazenly?' Edmund nodded. 'Aye, well that has happened in the last year. The towns and countryside are as rotten as each other. There are some who talk of a "Great Society". Runaway villeins carry messages written by others from village to village. Their "Great Society" is a company of brigands and robbers and slowly they have made common cause with one another: the heretic priest with the runaway villein; the lesser guildsman with the apprentices of a greater guild. There is a devilish force at work. Mark my words: fiends guide this union. For every hedge priest the bishop imprisons two more appear to take his place. For every villein branded two more run away from their manor. It is like holding back the sea. All about me the dykes crumble . . .'

'We are not alone,' Edmund confided. 'Before I left France I heard that there is unrest amongst the weavers of Flanders. Once more there is talk of the artisans against the nobles. I even heard talk of common men arming with pike and bill.'

Newton crossed himself. 'God forbid. God forbid the rebels should spawn another Courtrai.'

He referred to the legendary battle of Courtrai. In 1302, the workers of Bruges, in open revolt against the magnates of Flanders, had destroyed an army of French knights. It was an event which horrified the nobility of western Europe.

'Aye, God forbid. For 'tis said that then they stripped seven hundred golden spurs from the bodies of slaughtered knights.'

Newton crossed himself again. 'Jesus, have mercy,' he muttered.

'I spoke with a Franciscan before I sailed. He had travelled through southern France and carried tales of peasants in revolt who would kill a man if he lacked callouses on his hands. It is such barbarians who now seek to overthrow the knightly and gentle.'

'The gallows are heavy with them,' Newton said. 'I have such a man here in these very dungeons. He was a villein of the king's tutor.'

'Of Sir Simon Burley then?'

'The very same. Not content with the lot God chose for him, he ran away to Gravesend. There he rose to be a burgess of the town, but Burley learned of his existence. Not two days ago he sent two sergeants-at-arms to seize the man. As a result he is held here. Now there is talk of trouble at Gravesend. And this not three days since a mob of brigands attacked the monastery at Erith and forced the abbot to promise support for the ending of villeinage.'

'Good God, man! Has the king not been told? Why have these rebels not been suppressed?'

Newton spread his arms wide in a gesture of despair. 'See how fate encourages these dogs! Gaunt is away in Edinburgh. Woodstock is on the Welsh marches. Edmund of Cambridge has sailed for Portugal with an army. There is no one in the south-east with force enough to disperse the rebels.'

'Holy Mother!' Edmund could begin to see why Newton was so concerned. Events were running away from them. He had no intention of losing his spurs to another Courtrai.

'You have scarce heard half of my bad news. Yesterday one of my captains brought me word that on Sunday last a Commission of Enquiry was massacred in Essex. He heard it from a fisherman. This man had left Tilbury the night before and reported that all Essex was ablaze.'

'Good God!'

'Only this morning I had two more fishermen brought to me. One of my sergeants heard them relaying gossip in an ale house in Rochester. They reckon to have heard that an Essex mob has burnt Treasurer Hales's house at Temple Cressing. It seems the manor was rich in wine. Three tuns! You know how such things impress the simple. I have no reason to think these fishermen were lying. God knows, they were frightened enough when I questioned them. They claimed to have picked up the tale at Stanford-Le-Hope. There too, it seems, fishermen and fowlers had driven out tax commissioners with violence. They boasted of it, so my informants claimed.'

'Treasurer Hales's house burnt? This is sour news indeed. God knows we have all spoken hard words against taxes and against the king's ministers, but this talk of peasantry in arms is another matter. I'll not be ruled by fishermen and fowlers.'

'This Hales the common folk call "Hobb the Robber", on

account of the tax – ' Newton was interrupted by a rap on the door. 'Enter.'

The visitor was one of Newton's sergeants. He wore a short-sleeved mail hauberk over a quilted gambeson. A narrow-bladed misericord hung at his waist. He and the constable conferred for a few moments. The sergeant appeared breathless.

Edmund watched the two men and wondered what the problem was. For by the look on Newton's face, there clearly was a problem. His eyes were narrowed in concern. When the soldier had been dismissed, Newton cast a sharp glance at his guest. 'When had you intended to go on to London?'

Edmund noted the emphasis on the word 'had'. 'I had thought to push on after morning mass. I have some business to attend to in the city. My brother will be expecting me after the despatch I sent with my squire. Why?'

'The news is not good, I fear. The men of Erith and Gravesend have risen in revolt.'

'Erith and Gravesend? Are these the men who attacked the monastery of Lesnes on Sunday? The ones who harboured Burley's runaway villein in defiance of the Statute of Labourers?'

'The same.' Newton stroked at his forked beard with long, pale fingers. 'It seems almost one hundred men from Essex have crossed the Thames to join these rebels. I told you there is a common purpose behind the unrest. Does this not reveal it at work? The cunning dogs, the architects of this "Great Society", are pulling together all the strands of rebellion. By God, if I had but a hundred archers . . .'

'You think this means I cannot go to London?'

'Yes. The men of the Kent marshes have risen in response to the tax collectors of John Legge. But they are not content with the flight of that sergeant-at-law and his commissioners. Now they are up in arms, they will not easily be quieted again.

'The abbot of Lesnes, at great personal risk, has sent one of the lay brothers to warn me of this turn of events. The rebels have proclaimed a list of grievances and will not disband until their complaints have been met. They have called on all to rally to their cause and to march on Rochester. They only except those living within twelve miles of the sea; these should remain at home to guard the coast against the king's enemies.'

'How loyal!' Edmund's comment was bitterly ironic.

'So you see, the road to Greenwich is no longer under the king's peace. I have but ten archers and twenty men-at-arms. Insufficient to secure your safe passage, I am afraid.'

Edmund shrugged. 'I have an escort of ten men-at-arms on good sturdy mounts. No one will dare raise a hand against me. I am no sergeant-at-law or tax commissioner.'

'But have you callouses on your hands?'

Edmund began to laugh but saw that his host was not joking.

'Believe me, Edmund,' the constable advised, 'you should remain here until the situation is clearer. By St John, you should not ride head on into these rabid dogs.'

Edmund drained his beaker and rose to his feet. ''Twill come to nothing, John, believe me. You have walls here to keep out a thousand rebellious peasants. Did not King John's men break down the entire angle of your keep but fail to take this castle?'

Newton nodded. 'In the year of grace 1215 he brought it down with a mine tunnel. 'Tis said he used the fat of forty pig carcases to fire the props.'

'Then take heart, my friend. I've seen darker days in France! And think on this: in 1264 the rebel barons seized the entire bailey of this place, but still could not take the keep.'

Newton acknowledged his friend's optimism but did not appear convinced. 'But in 1088, when the conqueror's half brother Odo rose in revolt, the army of William Rufus took this fortress by force.'

'True, true. And legend has it that the stink from the overflowing latrines drove the garrison to surrender. But the chronicles say that the Rufus had an army of honest men. And it was with two fortified camps that he blockaded and captured both city and castle. You, on the other hand, face a mob of churls and apprentices. You must take heart.'

Newton came close to his confident guest. It was as if he feared being overheard. The room was, however, surrounded by thick walls and his precaution was scarcely necessary. Still, it conveyed something of the constable's unease.

'Listen, Edmund.' His voice was low and husky. 'It's more than the stink of the latrines that fills my nostrils. There is a rottenness here, but not the rottenness of garderobes.' Newton glanced at the closed door. 'I do not trust all of my men. And the whole city is suspect. The apprentices and journeymen are corrupt to the core – '

'But surely – '

'Hush. Let me finish. I told you I could not spare men to escort you. Well, it's worse than that. I do not possess enough men to defend the donjon.' He slapped one hand against the mighty, whitewashed walls. 'The king's uncles have stripped my garrison to further their own adventures in Wales and Portugal. Believe me, Edmund, I fear I cannot hold the castle for Richard.'

Then a thought seemed to strike the constable. He clicked his tongue softly. It was as if he was no longer aware of his guest.

Edmund was suddenly conscious, once more, of his aching tiredness. It seemed to eat at his very bones. 'John?'

Newton came back to earth. 'God forgive me. You must be exhausted. I have an urgent matter to attend to. Wait here, my friend. I'll have the sergeant escort you to your chamber.'

With that, Edmund had to be content. Left alone in the room he could hear voices from the great hall below but could not pick out words. Bored, he returned his beaker to the cupboard, or aumbry, built into the thickness of the wall. He was not used to being unattended. The solitude irritated him.

At last the sergeant appeared. He was an affable fellow. Leading the knight up the spiral staircase, he gave him a running commentary on the revolt. If the man was to be believed, the rebels would be at Rochester before dawn.

Newton's household servants had prepared a small chamber in the north-west tower. Unlike the other commanding towers, it was circular. When King John had brought down the corner of the keep, the ruined tower had eventually been replaced by this one. No longer was there a corner to undermine. Edmund noted the oddity. He hoped it was a good omen.

Edmund was grateful not to be bedded down in the hall with his men. Before he slept, he went out on to the wall walk. His talk with the constable had not banished tiredness; it had, however, banished sleep.

The night was cool but not cold. Shielded from the river breeze by the overhanging timber platform of the hourding, Edmund watched shadows cross the face of the moon.

Newton's fear was like a canker. It seemed without substance, yet of daunting, crippling power. Edmund pondered the view from the massive tower keep and wondered whether the constable's fears were justified.

Rochester Castle guarded the crossing of the river Medway. It was of breathtaking power that its stones spoke eloquently. When William of Corbeil had laid the plans for its soaring four-storey keep, he had conceived of both a palace and a fortress. Placed commandingly at the top end of the bailey, it soared one hundred and thirteen feet from the chalk cliff on which the castle stood. Far below, the great plinth foundation was lost in darkness. Invigorated by the cool air, Edmund made a circuit of the summit. He had passed the square bulk of the north-east tower when he paused once more.

A movement caught his attention. A dark group of half-seen figures were descending the approach ramp which led up to the first floor entrance. The shadow of the guard turret at the top of the slope almost enveloped them. Edmund moved further out on to the plank floor of the hourding platform.

The figures were directly below him now. They came out from the shadow of the forework and hurried down into the bailey. Horses were waiting in the silent courtyard and the figures mounted them. Some were carrying small bundles. Swiftly they were led away towards the twin towers of the outer gatehouse. Soon they were lost in the dark. A cloud obscured the moon.

Edmund turned back to his chamber very thoughtful. Rochester Castle was a fortress of the king; from its forework the three leopards of England hung listless against the flagpole. It was built to withstand assault by mangonel and trebuchet. So why was its constable sending his wife and children away by night, under cover of a cloaked moon?

At dawn the disaffected apprentices of Rochester opened the city gates to their fellows from Gravesend and Dartford. Sir John Newton had been proved right: there was a rottenness in his city which did not emanate from the latrines only!

Shortly after prime, the rebels, in their hundreds, began a disorderly assault on the castle. The tide of humanity fell back before a shower of arrows. The castle's handful of archers were earning their six pence a day.

Newton took mass with his lieutenants in the spacious chapel of the donjon. After the celebration, he assembled his sergeants in the two-storey Great Hall. Here he laid out plans for the defence of the fortress. Light fell through the long, narrow windows on a scene of frenzied activity.

The day was hot and clear. Gulls wheeled outside. With the castle under siege, the constable had few options. Edmund listened to his nervous tones. The man seemed to be deflated by the energy displayed in the early morning assault. For all its failure it had deeply shocked him.

It's as if he hoped that when it came to it the rebels would not dare touch him, Edmund thought as he watched the military preparations. He has given up already. God! He had given up last night!

Edmund was right. Newton was bemused and astounded by the sheer turbulent fury of the Kentish mob. He had heard the tales of the revolt but only now was it sweeping around him like a raging flood. He could scarcely believe that the populace was capable of such sustained fury. Each passing day had sapped his resolve with its rumours of widespread revolt. Now the dawn assault had brought him face to face with the incongruous picture of the commons in spate. It was as if the animals in the stables had revolted. He was paralysed with shock and fear.

Shortly before noon, another chaotic assault crashed against the walls. Once more it was beaten off. Then the mob beyond the gate-house parted. A delegation of the Gravesend citizens asked for parley. In their midst, securely guarded, were the white faces of Newton's wife and children. His midnight attempt to spirit them off to Maidstone had failed.

Grimly, he heard the terms of their survival: the surrender of the castle and the release of Simon Burley's serf. Gravesend had refused to pay the three hundred pounds for the manumission of the fugitive. Instead, it had paid with coin of a different stamp. Defiantly and confident, the triumphant citizens faced the constable with their ultimatum.

That afternoon – Thursday 6 June – Sir John Newton, constable of King Richard II's castle of Rochester, surrendered his charge to the rebellious citizens of Kent and their allies from Essex.

That night the constable, his family, the castle sergeants and Edmund Mentmore were held prisoner in the chamber above the Great Hall. Whilst they spent a sleepless night the castle was looted. At dawn, the exultant leaders of the rebels announced their sentence on their high-ranking prisoners: Newton and his knightly guest would be taken with the rebels when they left the city; Newton's family would remain under guard – hostages for Newton's compliance.

The streets were crowded as the victorious rebels led their prisoners out into the city. Sunshine dappled St Andrew's cathedral, but Newton and Mentmore saw little beauty in the jeering faces of the mob.

'They'll not harm us,' Edmund hissed to his fellow. 'We are of use to them. Mark what I say. They'll seek to use us when they make demands of their betters. I know the minds of these such . . .' He nodded towards the more substantial leaders of the rag-tag rebel army. 'Peasants may slaughter a man for want of a callous or two, but not these. They'll have their own personal betterment on their minds. Why else would they throw in their lot with the mob? Mark my words: they at least will use us. It's those we should fear.'

Edmund glanced towards the mass of peasants in their threadbare hose and cottes and the surly apprentices. Newton took in the looks of hatred and the colour faded from his cheeks.

'By God, I hope you're right. Holy Mary, I pray these burghers can control the storm they've loosed.'

From Rochester the rebel army, growing in numbers by the hour, marched up the Medway valley to Maidstone. On their arrival the populace rose in solidarity with their neighbours from the north. A town guildsman who tried to oppose the uprising was kicked to death by his fellow citizens of the lesser guilds.

Edmund and Newton were jostled on all sides by the citizens. A wild euphoria had gripped the town. Sheaves of documents were burnt in the market square. Frightened tradesmen and their families watched, helplessly, as the poor of the town ransacked their homes, halls and shops. The sun beat down from a huge dome of blue.

The killing of the resisting guildsman had been led by a group of soldiers who had joined the Rochester men as they moved south. Now the mob acclaimed one of these soldiers as their captain.

Edmund was watching the chaotic scenes. Men drifted amongst the crowd whispering and pointing and it was these who, from dispersed positions, led the baying for the selection of the captain. Edmund had no doubt that these were the partisans of the stocky figure now elevated to leadership by 'popular' acclaim. Some of the better-off guildsmen of Gravesend were less than happy with this turn of events. Clearly, they could see power slipping from their hands, but there was little they could do to arrest the process.

Edmund and Sir John, still mounted, were pressed close together by the mighty throng. The armed apprentices of Rochester, who guarded them, jostled to get a better view of the man being propelled towards the steps of Maidstone church. Nearby two men in padded gambesons were leading a 'spontaneous' chorus of 'Tyler, Tyler, Tyler!' The crowd took up the chant.

'This man. Do you know him?' Edmund whispered to Sir John Newton. Newton turned glazed eyes on him. He was as white as a shroud. 'This Tyler. Do you know him?'

Edmund spoke in French to shield his words from the crowd. When Newton replied, he too avoided using the vernacular.

'Never seen him. Heard of him. Just a brigand, a preyer on travellers on the highway. He has fought with a company in France, they say. I've heard he is an unruly cadet of the family of Culpepper. They hold land along the Medway.'

'Then he has education and an experience of fighting. No wonder the good burghers of Gravesend look displeased. They'll not hold the mob against such as him. But tell me, if – '

Then the apprentices took notice of the whispering. Jeering, they hauled the two men apart and rough hands pulled them down from their horses. For a moment Edmund thought he was about to join the murdered guildsman of Maidstone. Instead, he found himself pushed through the mob. The movement was directed by one of Tyler's men: a scar-faced tough wearing a kettle helmet and in possession of a sword.

The unseemly progress halted before the steps of All Saints' church. Here the two knights were unceremoniously forced to crouch near the feet of Tyler's henchmen. The newly promoted captain studied the battered noblemen, then turned his attention back to the thousands of expectant faces.

'We will admit,' he called out in a commanding and surprisingly melodic voice, 'no allegiance, save to King Richard and the true commons!' The crowd roared. Sparrows rose in surprised flocks from the soaring perpendicular of the church. 'We will have no king named John!' The reference to the Duke of Lancaster brought hoots of approval. 'And no poll tax shall be levied on the true commons.' Wild applause. 'We shall sweep away the traitors who hem in our king. We will destroy the lawyers and officials who have corrupted the realm. Death to Sudbury!' The mention of the royal chancellor's name produced howls of hatred. 'Death to Hobb the Robber and his minions! Death to them all!'

The mob, its grievances and hatreds so adroitly focussed, screamed their delight.

From within the heart of that heaving sea movement stirred. A tight knot of men were pushing their way through the crowd, squeezing between the jostling peasants with their black flags on hoe handles. The newcomers were Tyler's men. They were shepherding forward a man in his fifties. His head was crudely shaven but within his weathered face hazel eyes were kindled in triumph.

The crowd recognised the newcomer and welcomed him with fresh cheers. When he reached the church Tyler stepped forward and welcomed him. Hurried words passed between them. Tyler was grinning and nodding. The two men stood but a couple of paces away from the crouching Edmund; he could see the shaven man wore the patched habit of a priest. His fingertips were raw and seared by fire. The mark of a heretic.

Their conference over, the men signalled for the crowd to be silent. The turbulent sea died down.

Sir John wriggled closer to Edmund. ''Tis John Ball,' he whispered hoarsely. 'A hedge priest and a heretic. Only a week or two ago the good archbishop clapped him in Maidstone gaol. The man has made it his life's work to mislead the ignorant and the foolish, damn him.'

Judging the crowd receptive now, the excommunicated priest began to speak. His voice carried over the upturned heads. It possessed the measured cadence of a natural orator.

'My dear friends, nothing shall go well in England until all is held in common; when there will be no longer villeins and lords. For by what right do they hold us in bondage? Are we not all descended from our father Adam and our mother Eve? And yet they have clothes of velvet and of fur while we wear rags! They have wine and fine white manchet bread, while we have water and rye bread! They sit in palaces and manors while we brave wind and rain in winter fields! But it is our labour which supports their pomp! Ours is the work and theirs the luxury! Let us go, then, to the king. We will remonstrate with him. He is young and from him we may receive a favourable answer.' He paused. His brown eyes scanned the crowd. 'And if not, then we shall seek a remedy by our own blood and toil!'

Once more the crowd erupted in a storm of approval. Tyler and Ball went up into the church and Tyler gestured to his men to bring the two hostages.

The interior of the church was cool, despite the summer sunshine falling through the windows. Tyler and Ball sat down in the chancel and laid their plans. Edmund and the constable were held some distance away. When the captain and the preacher had finished, the former approached the now grubby hostages.

'Forgive us for so inconveniencing you, good sirs!' His voice was slightly mocking. 'But you must grace us with your company a little longer. And ere we have finished our travels, you shall, I trust, give full allegiance to King Richard and the true commons.'

A bushy red beard contrasted with his sandy hair. His green eyes danced with the delight born of triumph. The beard quivered with laughter.

'Come, Wat, we've work to do.'

Ball was not laughing. His brown eyes held not a hint of merriment. Tyler signalled to his men to keep the hostages well guarded. Before he left the church he reminded the constable: 'Forget not your family, Sir John. Forget them not. With them ever before your eyes you will not waver in your loyalty to King Richard and the true commons!'

Edmund and the constable spent a wretched night in the church. Newton was lost in despair, Mentmore in thought. At prime they were forced to take mass from the hands of the heretic priest. The crowd received it as if they had taken the cross and were on their way to expel the infidel from the Holy Places. Then the mob burnt down the residence of the absent archbishop.

Simon Thebaud of Sudbury was of similar stock to Edmund. His family had long traded out of Suffolk. Some of the weaving communities now contracted to the Mentmores supplied cloth to the Sudburys. It was with mixed feelings that Edmund watched the newly constructed building being put to the torch.

God knows, he reflected, I've cursed the king's ministers with the rest, but never thought I'd come to this.

As if reading his thoughts, Sir John Newton muttered, 'Such a kind and gentle man. Sudbury is without malice and devoid of martial instinct. God help him.'

'God help *us*!' Edmund said.

It was late afternoon when Tyler and Ball, now mounted, led their army out of Maidstone. It was a glorious summer Saturday. From horizon to horizon a clear vault of azure was unmarked by even a hint of cloud. They followed the Pilgrims' Way to Hollingbourne, then crossed the ridge of the North Downs to Faversham.

From Maidstone the leaders of the revolt had sent out emissaries to the surrounding villages. At least one group had ridden down the Medway Valley with messages to the Essex men. Edmund, a captive audience, watched as the shaven priest dictated his cryptic missives to 'John Nameless', 'John Trueman', 'John Miller' and a host of other secret by-names.

On Monday 10 June the horde reached the cathedral city of Canterbury. A fine and prosperous settlement, it was situated where the river Stour left the chalk of the North Downs and entered a gap in the low hills which finally fell away into the Thames and the sea. Entering through the freshly built west gate they were met with enthusiasm. Since the death of Thomas Becket in 1170 the shrine had attracted pilgrims from far afield. Many of these now flocked to join the rebels.

Amidst the carnival crowds, Tyler enquired if there were any 'traitors' in the town. Eagerly the crowds led the way to the houses of prominent Lancastrians. Three were dragged into the street and executed on the spot. Edmund watched the twitching, decapitated corpses with disgust.

The sheriff, who had wisely made no attempt to defend the city, was beaten up before the cheering people. His life was spared. Forced to vow allegiance to 'King Richard and the true commons', he was compelled to lead the mob into Henry II's mighty castle keep. With a hangman's noose about his neck, he was forced to watch the partisans of Tyler drag heaps of judicial and financial records away for burning. All the time, he had to repeat his allegiance to the commons. Tears flowed down his cheeks. Insolent apprentices spat at him.

Sensing the mood of the moment, the wealthy leaders of the trade guilds came forward to swear fealty to the new cause. The mayor and corporation made their obeisance. Away to one side, now forgotten, the summer flies gathered on three limp corpses.

Then it was the turn of the monks. John Ball led the exultant crowds into the great cathedral. Pilgrims, too shy to join in, moved silently away with suitable displays of deference. The celebration of mass ended in chaos. The choir of William of Sens echoed to raucous cries and the beating of running feet. Down the nave – still being rebuilt at Sudbury's command – Ball led his army. Beneath the glittering vertical mullions of soaring splendour, the terrified clerics swore the oath of loyalty.

'And,' cried Ball, 'elect a new archbishop, for Sudbury is a rogue and a traitor and will soon be beheaded for his iniquity!'

That night, while Ball and his more ardent followers kept vigil before Becket's tomb in the Trinity Chapel, Edmund and Rochester's constable were held in the circular apse called Becket's Crown. Neither slept. The constable seemed on the point of total collapse. He complained of a heavy belly and of a looseness in his bowels. With coarse comments, his gaolers led him to the monks' reredorter latrine.

At midnight Ball came, a shadow amongst shadows. For long minutes he watched the stiff, cold prisoners.

'What do you mean to do with us?' Edmund's voice was uncowed.

Ball surveyed him. He was a shrewd judge of men. He had no doubt about the mettle of this knight.

'You, too, will serve King Richard and the true commons.'

'When we reach London?' Edmund's assertion was defiant.

Ball laughed. 'The more knights who ride with us, the more will join us. Have no doubt of that!'

'Any who know us will know we have no truck with heretics.'

'For God's sake, Edmund.' John Newton's voice was almost pleading. 'Forget not my children!'

Ball waved back an ex-soldier who would have struck the assertive prisoner. 'Heretic? Haven't they crushed with iron and fire every voice, in every generation, which cries down the anger of God upon the wicked of the world?'

Edmund noted the eloquence of his enemy. For this truly was

his enemy. Ball was no mere disgruntled parish priest ejected for having a concubine. The fires of prophecy burnt in his eyes and on his raw fingertips.

'Listen to me, sir knight. Listen to the voice of Piers Ploughman! The poor are bowed down to the ground. Listen to the lot of the poor man: he pays tax and tithe; he pays fine if his daughter marries; he must grind grain at the lord's mill; bake bread at the lord's oven; press apples at the lord's cider press; at death his best beast is seized by the lord.

'Listen, knight. Listen to the voice of the poor man: he must labour on the lord's land; he must save the lord's hay, the lord's harvest, before his own; he must drive his beasts to pasture and home again over the lord's fields rather than his own. Even the dung must first serve the lord and his land.

'But God's justice will no longer tarry. The voice of the poor has come before God. As the Israelites cried out in the bondage of Egypt, so has their cry come before God. It is a righteous army whom you call "heretic". Be mindful of these things, sir knight, before you open your mouth again!'

He turned and was gone.

'Holy Mary,' the guard murmured in awe, 'you must tire of life to speak so to the new archbishop!'

Edmund fixed him with a steely stare of cold anger, but wisely held his peace.

On Tuesday morning, after despatching messengers to raise the peasantry of east Kent, the 'righteous army' decamped. By nightfall it was back in Maidstone.

After scarcely six hours' sleep, the host was roused again. Before dawn – while agitators sped away to Sussex and the western counties – the main force, of perhaps twenty thousand, marched on London. On the way they were intercepted by emissaries from the king at Windsor. To his demand of why they were in rebellion, Tyler sent the answer that they were in arms until 'the head of Gaunt and every other traitor around the throne is delivered to the Great Society of the true commons'.

That very evening the young monarch left hastily for London and the security of the Tower. By nightfall, the rebel army was encamped at Blackheath, in sight of London. Before midnight news arrived that the Essex rebels, led by the Londoner Thomas Faringdon, were at Mile End and camped outside the eastern suburb of Whitechapel.

For Edmund Mentmore the night brought no rest. A group of Kentish men were sent on ahead to secure the passage of London Bridge. The knightly hostage was forced to attend, to assist in the parley. Frustrated by Mayor Walworth's raising of the drawbridge they vented their fury on Southwark. They sacked Lambeth Palace and opened the gates of the prisons of the Marshalsea and the King's Bench. The citizens of Southwark appeared in droves to cheer on the mayhem.

'And the Flemish brothel. Burn the Flemish brothel!' chanted the xenophobic mob.

Soon the building had been found and torched. Sparks shot into the night sky and fleeing Flemings were hunted by the mob. Escaping whores were forced to give, for gratis, what had previously cost a half silver penny.

Edmund's escorts were jostled by the crowd. Chaos reigned. A fleeing prostitute was brought to the ground. One of Tyler's soldiers allowed his lust to overcome his discretion and went to grab the girl. Edmund slammed his fist into the face of his other guard and was off into the night.

On Blackheath, Wat Tyler and John Ball received a delegation from the city. They had risked the dark waters in a boat and came with the authority of the mayor, aldermen and Common Council to beg the rebels to disperse.

When early in the morning they made ready to leave, one hung back. Asking for a private interview with Tyler and Ball, he carried news to cheer their hearts.

'There are many thousands who long for your entry. The mayor knows this well. That was why he shut the city gates before dark and entrusted their security to the aldermen of the city wards. But you have friends amongst the aldermen. Good friends. And I am one of them.'

In the light of the spluttering torches, Ball appraised this eager guildsman.

'We know we have friends: labourers, apprentices and journeymen seek justice as we do. They seek the overthrow of the sleek and fat. But what of *you*? Why do *you* seek to aid us? Why may we trust you?'

John Horne flushed. He was not used to being addressed in

such a tone by a nobody like Ball. He fought his anger. He was too close to victory now to lose his gamble.

'You are right, of course,' he said in a flattering tone which seemed lost on the sceptical cleric. 'I am no journeyman or apprentice, but I too have my grievances.'

For a brief moment he wanted to pour out all his fury: his hatred for the merchants, drapers and mercers; his humiliation at the Gloucester parliament; the loss of the monopoly in fish. Checking the tide of murderous fury, he said: 'We are in alliance with the wage-earners and small craftsmen. The great trade guilds are their enemies and ours. They hate their overweening power, as we do.' He did not add that only the hatred was common, not the class or status of this confederation of malcontents. 'Their enemies are our enemies *and* your enemies, too. Mayor Walworth is weak. He is a fishmonger, but lacks the vision to seize this opportunity. We are not all so lily-livered.

'As proof of my good faith, send three of your men across the river to the steps by St Magnus Martyr east of the bridge. Send them! The alderman of Billingsgate will not arrest them. Send them and spread your message within the city to your friends. As further proof of my good faith, I will meet you below the bridge with two royal banners after prime tomorrow.' He checked himself. 'Rather today, Thursday. And the bridge will be opened to you.'

'And what do you ask for in return?' Ball's question was crisp.

'Simply to deal with the enemies of the fishmongers.'

'So be it,' Tyler agreed.

'So be it,' echoed Ball, with a faint smile.

At first light, a dripping Edmund Mentmore clambered from the spray-drenched supports of London Bridge on to the rough-hewn stone. Below him a small boat vanished into a maelstrom of white water. Slowly, with bleeding fingers, he inched his way higher. His movements were noted from above.

Voices summoned someone in authority. Edmund recognised the face of the burly guildsman.

'Thank God. You know me? You do!' He saw a light of response in the man's eyes.

A smile crossed the moon features. 'Oh yes, young sir, I know who you are.' He paused for a moment, then turned to his guards. 'Seize him. Seize him and lock him up!'

Protesting in indignation Edmund Mentmore was dragged away.

Meanwhile, the army at Blackheath was stirring. Today was the planned day of betrayal and of triumph. Under banners of St George, John Ball celebrated mass. It was Corpus Christi, Thursday 13 June 1381.

The indefatigable priest faced the expectant faces turned towards him. For years he had worked for this. In winter mud and summer heat he had tramped the country urging the flicker of revolt into a flame. Never had he lost faith in the rightness of the cause of the poor of the earth. Now at last, at long last, his hour had come. Something like excitement beat in his pulse. Slowly he raised his hands. The morning sun fell in golden shafts between his widespread fingers; his seared, mutilated, fingers.

Finally he spoke. For a moment he was halting, then the flame rose. He found the words. He forged them on the anvil of his suffering and these people's revolt.

'Oh my brothers, listen to me: when Adam dug and Eve span, who was then a gentleman?'

Chapter Sixteen

The Common Council of the city of London met before dawn. They heard the results of the visit of the emissaries to Tyler at Blackheath and found little in the report to give them good cheer. Mayor Walworth – a steady and calming influence – argued for a resolute refusal to negotiate with the rebels. The young king, Walworth informed the meeting, was as they talked going by barge to Greenwich. He would undoubtedly order the army there to disperse.

It was noticeable that the lesser guilds were vociferous in their support for the peasants. Wealthy guildsmen – whether for or against the Duke of Lancaster – made it clear they would have no truck with the insurgents. There was consternation amongst this group when it was learnt that agitators from Blackheath were already in the city. From the jeering of the craftsmen it soon became obvious to whom the agents of Tyler and Ball had directed their messages of revolt.

'Where is Horne? Where is John Horne?' Lyons demanded angrily. 'Why is it we hear he talked with that dog Tyler on his own? And is it true he brought agitators back with him? Where is he?'

Mayor Walworth jumped to the defence of his fellow guildsman. 'Horne must answer for himself whether these scurrilous accusations are true or not. For myself, I cannot believe them. No fishmonger would have such dealings with the enemies of the king.'

Lyons glanced at Thomas Mentmore. Neither was reassured by Walworth's confidence.

'Then where is he?' The wealthy vintner was clearly angry. 'Why is he not here himself?'

To that question, Mayor Walworth could find no suitable reply. Had he known what Horne was doing at that moment he would not have been so quick to come to his defence.

For whilst the mayor and Common Council argued John Horne was with Tyler at Southwark. He had kept his bargain. With him he had a heavy royal standard which was seized eagerly by the red-bearded rebel. He reminded the leader of the peasant host of the other side of the bargain.

'Yes, yes,' Tyler answered without reserve. 'You may do what you wish with your enemies. You may do with them as you please.'

A little after dawn the council meeting at Guildhall broke up in confusion. A breathless messenger had brought startling news: the alderman of Billingsgate had lowered the London Bridge drawbridge for the rebels. Tyler's furious host was, at that very minute, pouring into the city.

Thomas and Lyons hurried from the cat calls of the craft guilds. Appulby and Smalecombe had already slipped away. Outside the hall the mighty tradesmen were mounting their horses or making for their halls with something akin to panic. Armed and liveried retainers were milling about. Already some of the craftsmen were kicking over the traces. A portly mercer was surrounded by a crowd of insolent weavers. His retainers were hemmed in by the jeering mass.

Lyons was pale. Thomas Mentmore was shocked at the fear etched on to the other man's face. The vintner ran agitated, ringed fingers through his full head of black hair.

'For God's sake, Thomas, we are undone! This lout Tyler has worked for me. I know him, do you hear me? He smuggled goods for me to avoid the Calais Staple. The dog is a ruthless son of hell. He'll do for the lot of us.'

Lyons looked old and frightened. In a few moments the worldly pomp of the great monopolist had fallen away. He was a terrified man.

'What shall we do?' Thomas tried to remain calm, though he was thinking of the murderous mob pouring across London Bridge. 'What shall we do?'

'We must get out of the city. Forget your family, Thomas. Run. These whoresons will soon have the scum of the city up in arms. Did you not see the weavers' faces? Like devils who have won a licence to sin. For God's sake, Thomas, we must get away.'

Waving a hand to his attendants, Lyons swung up into the saddle of a skittish mare.

'God go with you, Thomas.'

'And you, Richard.'

It was the last time they would see each other alive.

One of the Mentmore apprentices tugged at his master's arm. 'Sir, sir. They say the Essex mob have been let in through Aldgate. What shall we do, sir? The weavers are dangerous!'

Numb with shock, the head of the House of Mentmore said, 'Back to the hall. We must get back to the hall. Now!'

It was a short distance but it was far too late. The news of the penetration of the city had aroused every labourer and disgruntled apprentice. The streets were beginning to fill with a riotous assembly of the poor and powerless. The agitators from Blackheath had not been idle during the hours of darkness. As Thomas Mentmore rode, he was assailed by vicious, uncouth cries and soon he was making little headway. His retainers pushed and shoved. One had drawn his dagger.

At the southern end of Old Jewry, the overhung street gave way to The Poultry. Philippa's favourite grocer's hall was shuttered and locked. The whitewashed walls were suffused with dawn light of palest rose.

Thomas had no time to reflect on the significance of the shuttered shop or the beauty of the dawn. Before his horrified gaze, hordes of armed men were pouring down Lombard Street. Black flags flapped like carrion crows above their sharpened scythes and hooks. Thomas Mentmore was trapped.

The ranks of the Kentishmen had been swelled by hundreds of London's and Southwark's poorer citizens. Journeymen, apprentices and labourers had flocked to join the invaders of the capital. Already they had tasted blood. A group of fleeing Flemings had been hunted like hares. Caught in a narrow alley near the Mentmores' hall they had been savagely slaughtered. Their blood adorned the rough blades of Tyler's army in primitive initiation.

The killings had whipped the crowd up into a blood lust. Sensibilities and pity had been drowned beneath a tide of hatred and racial loathing.

'To the Savoy . . . to the Savoy!' hundreds of rough voices clamoured in agitated cry. The apprentices of the city had old scores to settle. They had not wasted a moment in inciting the newcomers to acts of violence.

Along The Poultry the hungry Kentishmen were overturning tables and breaking into shops. Barrels of ale were being breached in the very centre of the thoroughfare.

Amid the scene of debauchery stood the handsome, square-jawed Dick Appulby with Smalecombe. The jaundiced weaver was passing on Appulby's instructions to a group of Kentishmen. Guided by the weaver's advice, they began to smash the shuttered windows of selected houses. Smalecombe urged them on with his usual irascibility. Appulby surveyed the whirlwind of destruction with detached approval. A slight smile played around the corners of his mouth.

Nearby, under a royal standard, stood Horne with a bodyguard of burly fish handlers. Gutting knives hung from their leather belts.

It was difficult to tell exactly who it was that recognised Thomas Mentmore. It was probably one of the weavers with Appulby. A shout went up and was caught in a hundred throats. Horne shouted something to Appulby who pointed menacingly at the startled, elderly mercer.

Like hounds off the leash the mob turned on the balding Thomas. Vainly some of his apprentices drew their daggers. They were clubbed down and hacked to death. Thomas's horse shied. He lost control. His mount swung him into a building, stumbled and panicked. One last apprentice stood by his master. The remainder had fled or were dead.

'Back, you bastards. Back, you whoresons!' he screamed at the weavers who gleefully egged on the snarling peasants.

A pike caught him under the chin. He jerked up and then backward. He landed in the gutter in a sitting position. Blood gushed from his throat. His mouth dropped. His head lolled. A rain of kicks hurled him sideways into the filth and slime. His body vanished beneath the pitiless boots of the mob.

Thomas punched wildly at his attackers. Hostile hands grasped his bridle, greedy fingers tore at the Lincoln Scarlet of his surcoat. For an instant he hung in the saddle, then he plunged down. He was hauled to his feet. His face was black with filth, his coat torn and muddied. Blood oozed from a dark, ragged wound on his temple. He was stunned. His eyes could scarcely focus.

One of Appulby's henchmen struck him. He would have fallen but his reeling body was caught and held upright. Another weaver hit him. Blood streamed from a split lip and nose. He fell back and was caught again. The crowd parted. Dimly Thomas recognised the satisfied face of John Horne.

'For God's sake, man ...' Thomas panted. His chest was pierced with agony. Ribs were broken. 'Have mercy. For God's sake ...'

Then he saw Appulby within the crowd. For a dazed moment he shifted his blurred gaze from weaver to fishmonger. He shook his head. Desperately he wanted to understand what was going on.

'Appulby, Horne,' he muttered incoherently. 'Appulby ... Horne ... ' Blood dribbled on to his linen shirt.

Then a terrible realisation dawned on him. For a moment his clouded mind was clear. The mist was blown away by the awful understanding.

'You! Horne! All along! It was you, and that dog ...' He gestured towards Appulby. 'That dog is ... your creature – '

Smalecombe hit the elderly mercer. Horne had tired of his triumph. He had other scores to settle.

'Finish him.' The fishmonger gesticulated towards the sobbing mercer. 'Finish the fat swine. He'll say no more about the price of fish.'

The fishmongers moved forward. Sunlight glinted on their long-bladed knives.

When the job was done, Horne signalled to Appulby. 'On to the Savoy. Tyler will be there soon. I'm away to the Essex men. They'll be through Aldgate by now.'

Appulby waved his men back. Some of the Kentishmen scrabbled about in the muddy street. Eagerly they stripped the soiled but costly cloth from the body of the crumpled mercer. They shouted coarse jokes at one another. As they worked, they wiped their bloody hands on their patched and grubby tunics. When they had finished, they hauled the naked corpse out into the wrecked market place. To cheers and hurrahs, they hurled it on to the littered trestles and debris. Then, their tasks only just started, they turned westwards towards Gaunt's Palace of the

Savoy.

Even while Thomas Mentmore's fish-pale body was being so cruelly displayed, the vanguard of the insurgents had swept as far as the Ludgate. As they progressed, their numbers were swollen by the addition of excited apprentices carrying flaming torches.

Whilst the Kentishmen hurried with eager expectation towards the Duke of Lancaster's palace, others of their party broke into the Fleet prison. With whoops of joy they battered any who stood in their way. Criminals flooded out on to streets. Amongst the liberated prisoners was Robert Newton. Caught up in the tide, he was swept westward. Away, on the bend of the river, the Palace of the Savoy was already in flames.

On Fleet Street the mob, led by Londoners, tore down a chandler's shop which intruded on the street and put it to the torch. Dancing and cheering they watched as it burnt. The hapless shopkeeper had fled at the sight of the mob.

'But why? Why this shop?' Rob asked one of the capering looters.

The man laughed. 'Why? This was where no shop should ever be. This is where we walk of a Sunday afternoon. We'll not have such monsters built on our street.'

Rob shook his head in amazement. Was it possible? Could it truly be that the city had degenerated to such a degree; a state in which a man's livelihood could be destroyed on a whim?

Jubilant at their experience of arson, the torch-bearers stopped long enough to burn a blacksmith's premises. Then it was on to the palace! By the time Rob reached the Savoy it was burning fiercely. The London commons had attacked it before the arrival of the mob from the country. Now both were happily united in an orgy of destruction.

Fabulously expensive coverlets and furniture lay smashed and jumbled in the courtyard. Up against the hall a massive bonfire was fiercely burning and eager men and women ran to and fro adding to the pyre. John of Gaunt's wardrobe was carried out of the looted building. Ermine, silk and velvet fed the hungry flames. Nothing was stolen. All was destroyed. Plate, jewels and furnishings were systematically broken up and cast into the Thames. In one corner of the courtyard a shaven-headed priest supervised the destruction of gems and jewellery. With cold fury, the precious stones were smashed to smithereens.

Newton stared in wonderment at the savage energy of the mob. Never had hate been so perfectly worked out in actions. He watched in disbelief as a magnificent tapestry was dragged out of the smoking buildings. Those carrying it held it up before the scrutiny of a red-bearded man wearing mail. He called to the priest. Together they peered at the intricate masterpiece of an angel slaying a coiled serpent. Satisfied as to its high quality, they consigned it to the fire with obvious delight.

Newton walked quietly away. For a moment he stood at the smashed gates. To the west lay the Palace of Westminster and the countryside, to the east the road back to the city. He hesitated. His choice seemed an obvious one. Escape beckoned him away into the country yet still he hesitated. His mahogany eyes were troubled. He ran a hand through his beard – now untidy and bushy. For an instant he turned towards Westminster.

'Damn it, Maggie!' he muttered to no obvious hearer. 'Haven't I paid enough for our love?'

Torn by indecision he halted his escape. Then, with an oath, he turned about and with loping strides swung back towards the city. Behind him muffled explosions signalled that the fire had reached the Duke of Lancaster's gunpowder store. Without a backward glance he continued on his course. A small scar pulled at his mouth in a wry smile.

Edmund Mentmore spent the Thursday incarcerated in the store cupboard of a shop on London Bridge. It was dark, he was hungry and in a foul temper. When at first he had been seized by the alderman of Billingsgate he had been incredulous. Soon his amazement had turned to fury. He had pummelled on the door of his prison for hours, but the thick oak planking gave no heed to his assault. At last he had tired of this futile attempt. Reconciled to his imprisonment, he had settled in a corner of his cramped dungeon. About him, rats scampered.

His waiting turned to hours. He seemed to be quite forgotten. His world was reduced to a small patch of gloom. Outside voices were raised in angry chorus. It was as if thousands of revellers were crossing the bridge and Edmund felt a twist in his belly. He had a good idea what the noise indicated. Down below the river thundered in pent-up force.

One wall of the prison faced the outside world. From the sound of water, Edmund guessed it overhung the eastern side of the arched bridge. Through the stout planking light fell in tiny gobbets of gold. Edmund tried to force the wood apart.

'Damn . . . damn!' he exclaimed as splinters sheered off into his fingers. Cursing, he sucked at his bleeding hand. He tasted the saltiness of blood and sweat against his lips. There was no way he would ever force open the wall. Inactivity was an agony to Edmund. He sprawled in festering fury.

Outside the afternoon gave way to a June evening. Evening, in turn, faded into a sunset-streaked dusk. Edmund Mentmore finally slept . . .

It was a bright day. Smithfield was alive with banners and heraldry. The great helm echoed to the dull rhythm of his own breathing. Sweat poured into his eyes. A heavy pulse beat in his temples. The cries of the crowd echoed strangely within the confines of the helmet. The hoof beats of the destrier sent vibrations through his spine.

Above the noise of the tournament arose a softer, gentler sound. It was like rain on an early spring morning.

Through veil on veil of unconsciousness the voice rang. With each new utterance it came a little clearer.

'Edmund . . . Edmund . . . Edmund . . .'

The darkness was absolute. Edmund's eyes could make out nothing in the smothering night. He groped at the straps of his helmet. His fingers clawed at his face. Sweat streaked his cheeks. He rolled over, trying to free himself from the horse which had collapsed upon him. The horse which was blocking out the light. He struck his head and jerked awake. A voice was calling.

'Edmund, Edmund!'

The voice was urgent, insistent. It was also familiar; firm but edged in softness. Edmund scrabbled in the dark. Sacks fell about him. Dust stirred beneath his knees and hands. He coughed as it rose.

'Here. I'm here. Mother of God, I'm here!'

Outside the door there was the movement of heavy, booted feet. Fragments of light broke through the tiny knots and cracks between the planks. Hands fiddled with a lock. The door creaked as more pressure was applied. It groaned and moaned like a living thing. A shoulder heaved against the wood. Planks splintered. Boots drove hard against the door. Hinges whined and gave way. With a tremendous crash it was flung inward. The person exerting the final force almost followed it in.

Edmund shielded his eyes from the flaring torches. The pitch crackled and spat. He was drawn to his feet and was aware of being surrounded by a group of cloaked men. Their woollen garments brushed against his face. For an instant he felt utter puzzlement. What was going on?

A torch was held up. He drew his head back from the sudden heat.

'Is this the man, madam?'

'Yes, Jacob. It is the man.'

The wall of cloaked humanity parted. Edmund found himself face to face with Anne Glanville. Her black eyes flashed in the leaping torchlight.

'Yes, Jacob. This is Edmund Mentmore.'

Edmund had not seen the alabaster-skinned beauty since the tournament at Smithfield. That was not to say she had been far from his thoughts! For a moment his power of speech deserted him. Then he laughed. He laughed and laughed.

Anne Glanville looked serious. 'You could at least say "Thank you", Edmund.' Her eyes shimmered like starlight on moving waves.

'Thank you?' Then Edmund understood. 'Yes, thank you. Thank you for freeing me. But how? And more to the point – why?'

Anne smiled. 'Not just yet. And not here. Come with us. We will find a place to talk.'

The ground floor shop was deserted. Leading the way along a narrow corridor, Anne took Edmund out to the room which faced the street. From the boxes of ribbon and lace, Edmund guessed he was in a shop of the guild of haberdashers. How and why it had been chosen as his prison he could not fathom. Indeed, he was never to know the reason behind the choice.

A heavy box was on one side of the room. Edmund sat down. Anne dragged over a stool and did likewise. She pulled off her heavy black cloak. Beneath it she wore a surcoat of blushing damask. It was as if a dark, gloved hand had opened to reveal a wild rose. She smoothed out the creases in the flowing material.

'Jacob – ' She spoke warmly to a boyish-faced young man.

'Take the men outside, will you? Keep watch.'

Whoever Jacob was, he possessed authority. At a sharp word, the four other men followed him without a murmur. As he turned to shut the door, he cast a kindling look at his mistress.

Edmund tumbled out his questions: 'What is going on? I heard a mob cross the bridge. Is it the Kentish men? Did the fishmongers let them in? And how did you know? And why did – '

Anne laughed. She had a light laugh, like a morning breeze through frosted trees. 'I'll answer one question at a time!'

'Was it the fishmongers?'

'Yes, it was. The alderman of Billingsgate lowered the drawbridge to them. He'll say the London mob forced him. That's a lie! He let them in willingly. They carried loyal flags. John Horne gave them to the leader, a man called Tyler.'

'Yes, I know Tyler.'

She nodded, remembering something. 'Of course. You came with them from Blackheath.'

Edmund was amazed. 'How do you know?'

Again, the light laughter. She cast him a teasing look. 'Be patient. I'll tell all.' Then she was proud and haughty again. Fire and ice!

'Go on. I'm your prisoner. You are, after all, daughter of a fishmonger's child.'

'Well parried, Master Mentmore.' She smiled approvingly. 'But to continue: the fishmongers let them in. At first they just looted bakers and vintners, then the London rough advised them of who were Lancaster's men and the killing began.' She looked at Edmund. 'That does not shock you?'

'It does not surprise me. I was with them when they kicked a Maidstone guildsman to death.'

Anne frowned. 'I fear many Londoners and Flemings have met their end today. They killed Flemings on Chepeside. My heart went out to them, even though they were foreigners. Was it their fault that King Edward brought them here to work as weavers?'

Edmund shook his head. 'I know the London weavers do not see it so kindly.'

'It was they who led the killing,' Anne said. 'The weavers and the Kentishmen slaughtered some who had taken sanctuary at

St John's Hospital at Clerkenwell. They burnt the hospital and the priory together. They have destroyed the Savoy, though most of Gaunt's servants saved their lives by flight.'

'The Savoy destroyed? You mean attacked?'

'I mean destroyed! Tyler led the destruction. It is burnt to ashes, but nothing has been stolen. Tyler had a man burnt who pocketed a silver piece, for they are not thieves or robbers!'

Edmund caught the irony in her voice. He guessed that, however Tyler saw himself, this day's actions would have cloaked theft beyond count.

'So they burnt the Savoy,' Anne continued, 'and Treasurer Hales's house and Chester's Inn and the Bishop of Lichfield's palace – '

'Good God!'

'And this is but the start of the list. They have broken open every prison and attacked the Inns of Court; they burnt the books and murdered every lawyer who was slow to flee.'

'You are well informed, Anne! How do you know this? And how came you to be my rescuer?'

'I know it because men do not think about whether to speak in the company of a mere woman.'

Edmund laughed. 'Only a fool would treat you so.'

'My intended husband treats me so, as does his father.'

Edmund sobered. His eyes narrowed. 'You speak of that cur Horne.'

'My intended father-in-law.'

'That cur!'

'The very same.' She stood and stared down at her rescued knight. 'You know I am to marry Horne's son?'

'I had heard.' His voice betrayed no emotion. His heart pounded.

Anne raised one quizzical eyebrow. 'Why did your family not heed my letter?' Edmund's blank face told her what she needed to know. 'You never received it, did you?'

'I know nothing of a letter.'

'When he did not return I was afraid. What if they had stopped him? But I hoped – hoped against hope – that you had received it. You did not?'

'Anne, you speak in riddles.'

'I think then that I must tell you all.'

'I think you had better.'

She paused. Then, slowly, she unravelled the mystery to Edmund. As she spoke, his face grew dark with anger.

'When I came that day to Smithfield I was already affianced to Ralph Horne.'

'I did not know that then. I only heard later, before I went to France.'

Anne tossed her head. 'I think my father and John Horne would have preferred it that way! They did not – how shall I put it gently? – "approve" of your attentions. When you took my favour on your lance my father was furious and Horne was beside himself, too. He had lost out once to the Mentmores, when Starre's daughter married your elder brother instead of Horne's son. He had no intention of seeing you humiliate him.'

'So that was why you vanished from London?'

'Quite. My father had me shipped out like baggage. It is a woman's lot.' She spoke without conviction. 'He also noticed that I spoke to your family at the tournament. He thought I passed some message to you. He would have beaten me but feared to harm my looks. This marriage to Ralph Horne is useful to both sides. My father would not scar me. It could jeopardise the match.'

'But you warned John. Why?'

'Because I had already heard what was passing between my father and John Horne. You cannot believe how Horne hates your family. First you stole his son's bride, then you attacked the monopoly in fish. When you supported Northampton his rage knew no bounds. You have not seen such hate, believe me.'

'He had Yonge killed?'

'You know! So why did you accuse the poor weaver who loves your sister?' Edmund stared at her, perplexed. Suddenly it dawned on her: he had been in France when Margaret and Rob Newton had been exposed. She explained the terrible news to Edmund, but he was less shocked than she had expected. He was the closest to Margaret in the family and perhaps he had suspected something. Clearly he did not approve but he did not react with the expected fury.

Heartened, Anne repeated her question: 'So why did you accuse that poor weaver?'

Edmund let out a hiss of breath. 'We did not know then. I only began to understand when I was in France. I took confession from a dying man. He did not, could not, tell all — I doubt he knew it — but I heard enough. I had a lot of time to think, sitting out the siege at Nantes. The more I thought, the more I was convinced that it was more than a weaving dispute . . . So, Horne had Yonge killed. Why?'

'I don't fully understand. He knew something. I only heard things in snatches. Horne spoke of "silver well spent" and "weavers doing fishmongers' work". That seemed to amuse him greatly. Once he spoke of a "meddlesome clerk who knew more than he ought". You see why I had to warn you?'

'Indeed I do. It was Horne's silver which fed the weavers' demands, though I doubt they ever knew of their leaders' motives. There has been such a division between weavers and mercers for so long, who would question a campaign against the Mentmores?' He ground his teeth. 'So who did Horne pay to stir the weavers? It was not Newton, then?'

'Horne never said. He once referred to "faithful Dick". Does that mean anything to you? His last name may be Appulby.'

'John would know,' Edmund said. 'He deals with the weavers closely, he and my father. When we tell them, we will find out more about this Dick Appulby.'

'So I wrote to you. But my messenger vanished. I feared I had been betrayed. For days I waited in terror. Had my father or Horne read my letter they would have destroyed me. Then, as weeks turned to months, I dared to hope I had been spared, yet I could not begin to think what had become of my messenger.

'When my brother brought me up to London for my wedding in August I was shocked to discover your father had taken no steps to defend himself. Then I knew that, whatever had befallen my rider, the warning had been lost before it reached you.'

'Do not fret. I wrote to him from France. I did not have half of your information but I had my guesses. In fact, I wrote to John. They have been warned. Do not fear.'

The colour drained from Anne's face. 'No, Edmund. They cannot have been warned. If they had been, then it would not have happened.'

Edmund was on his feet. 'It will be good to see Stephen again. He's quiet but is a good lad. A man could not wish for a more devoted squire. He's as serious as William! But a good man. Mind you – so is Will, for all his talk of Wyclif. I shall be pleased to see both of them . . .'

He caught the meaning in her words. 'What is it? What do you mean?'

Anne bit her lip. 'I was at Horne's house for dinner. It was arranged long since. My brother escorted me from our town house in Tower Street. Oh, Edmund, I could not believe it. Horne seemed to crow about it. He was so pleased. He said he had not done it. He would blame it on the mob. But, Edmund, he exulted in his crime . . .'

'Mother of God! What is it? What has he done?'

'Your father is dead.'

Edmund was utterly stunned. 'No. No, I'll not believe it.'

Anne took his hand. 'Dear heart,' she said softly, ''tis true,' and she related the story of Thomas Mentmore's death.

The fishmongers had delighted to announce it and had also celebrated the capture of his warrior son.

'I could not bear it, Edmund, but I had to sit through it. I had to smile and nod lest they read my thoughts. They watched me to see how I would react. I satisfied them, for I am cleverer than they. And as I sat I made my plan. By evening I was back in our town house. My brother is out with Horne – God rot him – and I was left guarded by our household servants. Jacob, my father's steward, loves me. Nay, do not bridle so! He loves me and I do not love him. He knows this but would walk on fire if I asked him. I did not do so! All I asked was that we find the haberdasher's shop at the far end of London Bridge. That much they had let slip at table. So here we are, but I wish I could have brought news to cheer you. I fear I have none.'

Edmund wept bitterly.

At last he mastered his distress. When he spoke, the passion lay just below the surface. Eddies of fury swirled beneath the steady flow of his words.

'We must go to my father's house. I must know what fate has befallen my family. Did the fishmonger speak of them? Of Philippa, John and Margaret?' Anne shook her head. 'Then there's hope. They at least will have had time to defend themselves.' He paused as he thought out his strategy. 'How is it on the street?'

'The Essex men have returned to their camp out on the

Brentwood Road.'

'At Mile End?'

'So Horne said. Beyond Whitechapel.'

'And Tyler's rabble?'

'The Kentishmen are camped around Tower Hill and St Katherine's Dock. The king addressed them from the ramparts of the Tower as it was getting dark. We were able to slip away while the mob listened. My men say the streets may be ventured on but are not truly safe. Some of the leaders of the mob are still hunting out those they call enemies. They took a tailor from the high altar at St Martin Le Grand and beheaded him at Chepeside.'

'I'll risk it, but what of you?'

'Why, we'll come with you,' Anne said, affronted. 'I can hardly return home. My brother is not likely to believe I went out for a stroll. He'll hand me over to Horne.'

'But how will your father react when he discovers what you have done? You are contracted to Ralph Horne. I cannot allow you to do harm to yourself. I'd die ere I – '

'Hush, my brave knight! My father is not a hero, nor is he a traitor. He was content to hide Horne's killings and mischief making, I'll grant you, but he was never privy to this letting in of the mob. Truth be told, I doubt Horne himself thought of it before Tuesday. He's a fly one. He saw an opportunity to back his enemies into a corner and wipe them out. My father will be none too pleased to find he's set himself against the king.'

'But your brother?'

'He is a fool! Mark my words, my father will soon be wriggling to disassociate himself from Horne. When he comes up to London next month I'll wager the marriage is called off. Do not fear for me. We will come with you. You'll need my men and Jacob will do as I command.'

Edmund grinned at the pluck of the woman. 'So be it. We're in this together.'

Then suddenly, impulsively, he took her hand and kissed the palm. As a lover would.

'Really Edmund – I am affianced!' But she did not look particularly outraged.

The way to Walbrook Street was dark and dangerous. Drunken

apprentices roamed the lanes. The city watch was nowhere to be seen. The curfew was without force. No one challenged the determined band with their spitting torches. Here and there, shopfronts were broken in. Elsewhere the shutters turned houses and halls into fortresses against the predatory dark.

When Edmund stood before his home, the stink of smoke caught at his nostrils. He was late; far too late.

The weaving shed was a gutted wreck. The body of Charles de Gouarec was just recognisable in the alley which led to the street. He had been savagely beaten. The doors to the hall were smashed in and the place had been ransacked. Cloth and screens lay in chaos about the hall and the upper storey had been fired. As the ceiling of the hall collapsed, vast mounds of burnt wood and plaster had crashed on to the dais. Here and there fragments of Thomas's precious glass windows crunched under foot.

Bodies lay amidst the ruination. Charred and broken, they were impossible to identify. Tears ran in streams down Edmund's face. Anne wept beside him.

'There is a chance that these are not your family. You had many servants. These could be some of those.'

'Yes,' Edmund said. 'There is a chance...'

Jacob whispered to his mistress: 'We should not stay here, madam. There are men in the street. We were seen. We should go away.' He was frightened for her.

'We'll go to Knollys's house.' Edmund wiped a soot-blackened hand across his tear-wet cheek. He had thought to go to Starre's house by Newgate, but the glow in the sky had signalled violence north of the cathedral.

Without checking to see if he was being followed, Edmund Mentmore left the burnt ruin of his home. To the north-west, flames licked at the dark sky. Houses were burning in the night. Cries could be heard. It was shortly after midnight, Friday 14 June.

Edmund's resolve to go to Robert Knollys proved to be wise. The old brigand had gathered a force of over one hundred men-at-arms in his house and garden. His preparations for another Breton expedition had turned the residence into an armed camp.

No prowlers stirred in the alleys about the house. Patrols of Knollys's men enforced their own curfew on the neighbourhood and it was one of these, armed to the teeth, which intercepted Edmund and Anne and led them back to the house.

Knollys was pleased to see the newcomers and captivated by Anne Glanville's good looks. Despite the late hour, he was not in bed when they arrived. Summoning his sleepy cook, he ordered an impromptu meal.

'You'll excuse the plain food of an old man's table,' he said to Anne in his flat accent. He winked at Edmund.

It seemed an age since the bull-necked Knollys had clambered aboard the *Gabriel* and ordered Edmund to the sea battle off Bayonne.

The hall was crowded with dicing, or snoring soldiery. Weapons and mail lay in heaps. The obligatory dogs sniffed about the rush floor. Brusquely the old warrior cleared room around the head trestle table. Scurrying servants carried in plates of beef and sweetmeats. With an affable wave, he signalled to Anne's men to take off their cloaks. Flagons of ale appeared to assuage their thirsts.

Edmund could conceal his curiosity no longer. 'What is going on? Do you intend to sweep this scum out of the city?'

Knollys pulled a face. 'We could but we won't! Sit down, I'll explain it to you. This isn't the *Gabriel*, you know! More like Nantes.' Edmund frowned. This did not sound encouraging.

Knollys poured wine for Anne and Edmund. 'The king is in the Tower. You know that? Right, well you'll also know the state of the city. It's only my men who keep the rebels out of this ward. Elsewhere they go where they please, kill who they please. All the dregs of London are with them.'

'How many men have you got?' Edmund interrupted.

'I've over one hundred here. Mostly men-at-arms, some knights bachelor. In the Tower there are perhaps six hundred men-at-arms and six hundred archers.'

'Then act now! Attack the rabble while they sleep. I'll wager not one in a hundred of them has armour. They'll panic before your men. Attack now in the dark!'

'Boldly said, boldly said. So speaks Mayor Walworth. He's with the king. He too counselled action now. Whatever one says about members of his guild, no disgrace rests on Walworth.'

'So why is there no attack?' Edmund's voice was ragged with impatience. He could still smell the stink of the smoke in

Thomas's hall.

'The Earl of Salisbury counselled the king not to.'

'Why ever not? Has the man no nerve?'

Knollys tutted with annoyance. 'Steady, man. You forget that Salisbury fought at Crécy and at Poitiers. The man is no coward. I was there that Monday morning on the ridge at Poitiers when the constable of France drove through our line. It was Salisbury who held the breach.'

'Then why does he urge caution now?'

'Because he fears that if we strike we cannot afford to blunder. There are thousands camped about the Tower. Should we err in the slightest, they could swamp us and all would be lost. The Earl has advised the king to meet with the rebels at Mile End at seven this morning. There he will agree to their promises in order to disperse them. Once they have left for home he can repudiate the promises as being obtained under duress.'

'So, the king will meet them?'

'He's arranged to go after breakfast, as I said; he will be accompanied by Walworth and some of the nobles. While he is away, Chancellor Sudbury and Treasurer Hales can be smuggled out by boat. It is them the crowd hate. With them gone, it may be easier to induce the mob to disperse.'

'And what of you and your fighting men?'

Knollys chewed on a sweetmeat. He nodded in sympathy with Edmund's impatience. 'We are to remain here. The king himself sent Walworth with that message. 'Tis the Earl of Salisbury's advice. He fears that for us to escort the king would act as provocation to the mob. We are to wait. Walworth will send a messenger for us if we are needed.'

The old knight was as dissatisfied with these arrangements as his young guest. Nevertheless he had sufficient experience of combat to provide him with the discipline to swallow the unpalatable. If his face showed his displeasure for a moment, the look had soon vanished. However, Edmund had seen it. It gave him some consolation to discover he was not alone in his desire to see bloody action.

It was therefore difficult for Edmund Mentmore to retire to bed. Nervous energy was coursing through every muscle and fibre, but he too knew the advantages to be accrued from a personal discipline. If he was to be effective the next day he must snatch at least a few hours of sleep.

Knollys cleared out a small robing room for Anne Glanville. The men-at-arms fell silent when she passed. Even in chaos, she could exude a cool fascination. Nothing seemed to disturb her immaculate poise.

For Edmund, accommodation was found in Knollys's personal chamber. Here, about the screened bed, his squires slept on mattresses of flock. One was moved out in favour of the surprise guest.

At last, in the darkness, Edmund had time to collect his racing thoughts. It did not seem possible that it was only twenty-four hours since his capture on London Bridge. As he drifted into a shallow, restless sleep, he tried to take stock of the day's events and its news of betrayal and murder. What started as a tired assessment ended in a welter of nightmare-ridden dreams.

Dawn came early and glorious. The sun rose over the roofs and steeples like a great flare. It was a superb June day. The span of blue was untouched by even a wisp of pale summer clouds.

Edmund and Anne breakfasted with Knollys. The sop in wine was ill equipped to tempt palates thick and dry with anticipation. Edmund and Anne only picked at the damp contents of their wooden bowls. Knollys, on the other hand, ate heartily.

Edmund remained in the house until seven of the clock. Knollys had warned him that whilst the Essex mob would be moving out of the city, many of the London rough would be crossing the metropolis to join them.

'Let them pass through,' he had advised his impatient guest. 'For there are those among them who wish your family nought but harm.'

Given the fate of Thomas, Edmund could not but agree with this counsel. It would be an act of foolishness to rush into the arms of the craft guild apprentices.

Knollys had also advised Edmund to wait until news came back from Mile End. This Edmund would not do. He was desperate to gain any news concerning the fate of his family. In this he was aided and abetted by the redoubtable Anne Glanville. She spurned any suggestion of remaining secure at Knollys's house. Where Edmund was going, so was she. Knollys could scarcely disguise his opinion of this madcap courage.

So it was that, shortly after seven, Edmund, Anne and the handful of Glanville retainers left the house. Finally accepting that he could not restrain them, Knollys had strengthened their escort with ten of his men-at-arms.

Knollys's house lay between the Priory of St Helen's, Bishopgate, and the city wall facing Shoreditch. To get from there to Starre's house, by Newgate, was no great matter. At any other time it would have involved a pleasant stroll down Threadneedle Street to Old Jewry, and thence along Chepeside to Greyfriars on Newgate Street. This day, the stroll was far from pleasant.

Smoke was still rising from the Priory of St John beyond the western wall of the city. From the direction of the Guildhall more smoke besmirched the clear air. Obviously some other 'enemy of King Richard and the true commons' had had his home fired in the night.

There were more people about than Edmund had expected. Indeed, the mob seemed to be on the streets in force. From their rude accents, he recognised them as Kentishmen. This was not as he had expected. What had happened to the gathering at Mile End?

By the time the armed group reached Philippa's grocer, by Old Jewry, the air was full of menace. Crowds were moving towards Chepeside. Once more there was blood on their scythes and bills. Edmund knew the grocer well. Although it took a welter of blows, the iron-studded door was finally opened. A timid servant appeared. A mere glance dismissed fears as to the identity of the visitors. They were hastily taken in. While Edmund listened to the terrified tales of horror and outrage, one of Anne's servants - the trusty Jacob – was sent to gather intelligence.

He was not long in returning. The paleness of his countenance betokened bad news. He reported to his mistress, ignoring Edmund.

'The dogs have broken into the Tower, my lady!'

Anne was astonished. 'But what of Mile End? Surely it was agreed they would go to speak with the king at Whitechapel?'

Jacob sighed. ''Tis true. But it was the Essex men who went there, with but some of the Kentishmen. The rest – and many of the city apprentices – kept watch on the Tower. How they gained entry I cannot tell. It must have been by guile or treachery, for I'll warrant they did not storm it.'

'Entry? *Entry?*' Edmund's voice rose in astonishment. 'You are telling us they have gained entry to the Tower?'

Jacob turned his boyish glance on his interrogator. It was clear he resented the knight, but he could do nothing about it. In social station he lay as far below Anne as Rob Newton did below Margaret Mentmore.

'Aye, my lord,' he said reluctantly, 'They have entered the Tower. There they took Chancellor Sudbury and Treasurer Hales and John Legge, the commissioner of review for the poll tax.'

'Took them, you say? And what did they do to them?' Edmund asked.

'The Kentishmen make no secret of that, sir. They carried them to Tower Hill. There they were beheaded over a log of wood. The London apprentices, led by a weaver, have taken the heads to London Bridge to display on the gate.'

Edmund had no need to ask the name of the weaver. Appulby had become a very busy man.

'But that is not all.' Jacob pursed his lips. 'They sacked the king's privy wardrobe and distributed the weapons stored there to the multitude. The Princess of Wales has been carried safely away by her chamber knights, but not before the mob attempted familiarities with her. 'Tis said she was taken away in a swoon. And the Kentishmen killed a friar who was physician to Gaunt.'

'William Apilton . . .' Edmund's voice was soft.

'I do not know his name, only that he was physician to the Duke of Lancaster. Now he is dead; his head struck off, along with the others.'

For a moment Edmund was lost in thought. Gaunt had once sent his physician to tend Thomas Mentmore's son, after the attack in the alley. Now both Thomas and the friar were dead. Bloody treachery had not been content with those knife thrusts in the dark. The hatred which lay behind those far-off blows was still unsated.

Absent-mindedly, Edmund fingered the coat of mail beneath his jerkin. It was time for recompense.

'What is the mob doing now?' The questioner was Anne.

'They are hunting down those who escaped them yesterday. Tyler himself is in the city. He is heading the hunt.'

'Then we have no time to delay.' Edmund's fierce anger had

crystallised. He was ready for action. 'We must avoid Chepeside, for that is their favourite execution ground. We'll drop down to the river. By God's grace there will be less activity there. Come . . . follow me!'

Leaving the quivering grocer, they once more took to the streets. Ducking into Walbrook Street, they watched a cheering mob on its way to Chepeside.

'The leader – see him?' Edmund whispered into Anne's delicate ear.

'With the red beard and sandy hair?'

'Aye, and dressed as a soldier but carrying himself like a king. That's Tyler. Keep back lest he sees us. We're carrion if he recognises my face.'

However, Tyler had other things on his mind. Behind him a group of armed men were leading a pathetic, broken figure. Bloody and bruised, the man had a rope round his neck. His captors led him as if he was a heifer. Others in the marching company delighted to trip him with their spear shafts.

'Holy Mary! That is Richard Lyons!' Edmund's hiss froze the hearts of his small band. In horror and mute fascination, they watched as the fabulously wealthy vintner was dragged away to his destruction.

Edmund motioned for their progress to continue. Walbrook Street was quiet. Walking swiftly, they passed the gutted remains of the Mentmores' hall. A dark crowd of kites and crows hung about the blackened roof timbers. The heat was stifling in the narrow street. The odour of death hung heavy on the fly-blown air. Anne paled to think of the awful presence within the house. Edmund squeezed her arm. They hurried on.

At the bottom of the street they paused. In the lane opposite a pitched battle was in progress. Bodies lay sprawled in the central sewer. Steel clashed on steel. Savage cries gave vent to primeval emotions of fear and hate.

Jacob could not understand why Edmund had stopped. This was nothing to do with them. To their right, a broad thoroughfare – Candlewick Street – led towards Baynard Castle and St Paul's. That was their intended route, away from this primitive mêlée being fought out in Dowgate Lane. Still, Edmund hesitated.

'Hansers,' Jacob commented impatiently and with a shrug.

'No business of ours!'

His tone was bordering on the insolent. He felt it was justified. What concern was it to them if the mob slaughtered a few foreigners? In fact the battle could cover their escape. Jacob frowned when Edmund seemed unmoved by his comment. The other Glanville retainers were restless too. Only Knollys's men-at-arms and Anne stood patiently in the bright sunshine. They seemed possessed by a curious calm.

Edmund's face was set, carved from stone. It was in Dowgate Lane that he had nearly lost his life four years before. He watched as the German guards fought for their very existence.

The mob surged about the foreign soldiery. Clearly the guards had been escorting some German merchants back to the Steel Yard when they had been ambushed. Amongst the battling guards Edmund could make out civilians, also fighting hard.

'This is not our business!' Jacob's voice was insistent. His youthful face was contorted in a grimace. 'We must get my mistress away!'

Edmund made up his mind. A debt was, after all, a debt. Now it would be repaid.

'Guard your mistress, man,' he ordered curtly. 'First I shall clear away these curs.'

Edmund shouted to the men-at-arms to join him. They looked only too pleased to oblige. For too long they had sweated under the tunics hiding their mail. With ill-concealed relief, they stripped off the disguise, drew steel and waded into the fracas. The mob was taken by surprise. The first some knew of the assault was when they were cut down. A furious apprentice jabbed a dagger at Edmund. It sliced through his tunic and glanced off his mail. Puzzlement flashed across the apprentice's face. Edmund slashed with his own blade. The surprised look dissolved into agony.

All around, the mob was giving way. They had not banked on so determined a resistance from the Hansers and this assault from the rear was the last straw. Knollys's men had hardly got into their stride when the battle finished and the mob fled in disarray. Behind them they left many of their number contorted in death.

Edmund wiped sweat from his brow as the Hansers thanked him. Did they recognise him? Perhaps not, but someone did.

Someone was calling his name. It was one of the 'German merchants'. It took Edmund a moment to grasp reality.

'Edmund! Praise God that it should be you!'

'John? John! For the love of God, what are you doing here?'

The two brothers embraced in the blood-splattered lane. Knollys's men and the German guards looked on in amazement.

'What are you doing here? In this battle?' Edmund was laughing.

'I came back to the city only this morning. I've been away in East Anglia, but, God, I've been to the hall! What has happened to Philippa and my daughter?'

Edmund stopped laughing. 'I don't know. I'm looking for them too. We're on our way to Starre's house.'

'I'd only just left the hall when I ran into this.' John gestured about him. 'The apprentices recognised me. Weavers, you know. They were already setting about the guards and if you had not arrived I fear we would have been overwhelmed. How did you know it was me?'

'I didn't!' Edmund grinned at his brother's confusion. 'Never mind, I'll explain later. I've got a lot to tell you.'

Tom, the Mentmore journeyman, came panting up. He had taken a cut on the cheek. Apart from that, he was none the worse for his dice with death.

'Well done, Tom,' John said with real gratitude, 'you did well. Get our men together. We're going with my brother.'

At that moment, John saw Anne Glanville. His mouth visibly dropped. He turned to Edmund.

'Later,' Edmund said, anticipating the host of questions. 'I've got tales to fill an evening or two, but not now.'

Flushed with their triumph the two brothers led the way westward. At the church of St Martin in the Vintry they paused for a moment. Dozens of headless corpses lay scattered about the roadway and side gutters. The street was awash with blood. Flies rose in dark clouds from the blackened corpses.

'Flemings.' John's voice was thick. 'Dragged from sanctuary and murdered.'

Jacob shook his head at the obvious Mentmore partiality for aliens. John ignored him and crossed himself.

At St Paul's the yard about the cathedral was thronged. Passers-by were hurrying towards Chepeside. From that direction came the sound of barbaric entertainment. Screams rent the air.

From the great square-towered cathedral, it was but a short distance to the house and hall of Roger Starre. The street outside was full of jostling people, who seemed to be heading towards West Chepe. Some were dragging reluctant prisoners. Slogans of 'King Richard and the true commons!' filled the summer air.

John hammered on the closed door of Starre's house. All the windows were shuttered. A gruff voice came from within and John announced his identity. After a while one of the first storey windows was opened and Starre himself leant out. His red face was twisted in suspicion. At the sight of the Mentmores and their escort, the choleric features dissolved into relief. He vanished back inside and soon iron bolts rattled on their runners. The heavy door was swung open, and armed retainers almost dragged John and his party inside. The door was slammed shut behind and the bolts slid home.

Starre's hall was a hive of activity. Armed servants were sharpening swords and daggers. Children were crying. Dogs were barking. The heat was overpowering.

John saw none of this. His eyes were drawn instantly to the slight figure standing by the dais. A slim oval face opened like a flower before rain. In a moment, husband and wife were in one another's arms.

'Oh sweet Jesu, I thought I had lost you!' John was almost sobbing. He clutched at Philippa as if he would never let her go. 'Oh my God, I thought you were dead. My heart. Oh, my own dear heart.'

Philippa was weeping. Little Ann Mentmore scrabbled between them. John lifted the toddler and all three were locked in a laughing, crying, desperate embrace. Roger Starre watched the reunion with ill-concealed exasperation. He had no time for such emotion!

Margaret Mentmore threw herself into Edmund's arms. She too was weeping. Still clutching wife and child, John threw out a hand to his sister.

Close by stood Robert Newton.

Margaret disentangled herself from Edmund. She took John's hand and kissed it. John was staring at Newton. Edmund, too, had his eyes fixed on the weaver. He appraised the man with unfeigned, if superior, curiosity. An impish smile played about the corner of the knight's mouth. John seemed more troubled.

'John, John, take no affront that Rob is here. He has done us no harm. Never has he done the family of Mentmore harm, save in that he loved me. Nay – he *loves* me.' Margaret emphasised the present tense.

Philippa pleaded with her husband. ''Tis true, John, I swear it. He has done us no hurt. Margaret has told me all. Believe me, my heart, his only crime was loving her. No other hurt has come from him. When the mob came, he was already with us. God knows what had become of your father! It was Rob Newton who led our clerks in resisting them. He struck down the insolent weaver with his own hand . . .'

'Smalecombe,' Margaret interjected. 'He would have butchered us, but Rob killed the dog.' She paused, thinking of household servants abandoned to the mob.

'Yes, my love.' Philippa was awash with tears. 'It was Rob Newton who carried us away. It was he who saved us.'

Anne Glanville stepped forward. She had watched the unfolding drama with keen interest. Now it was her turn.

'In time I can tell you all, John Mentmore, and a bloody tale it is. Suffice it to say that this man Newton did not kill Adam Yonge.'

John had harboured doubts throughout, but his hatred and outrage had exiled them. Now he knew. Perhaps he had always known somewhere deep inside his heart. Rob Newton had not been the source of his troubles. Since the sombre conversation with the Fleming at Worstead he had begun to guess something of the enormity of his error.

Edmund laid a hand on his shoulder. 'I can assure you of the truth of what Anne has said. Newton was not, and is not, the architect of our troubles. For that, look to Horne and Appulby.'

'Where is my father?' John's voice was cracked.

'Our father is dead, John. Dead at the hands of Horne and Appulby.'

For a brief moment there was silence as those present absorbed the awful news. Edmund slowly realised that the family was incomplete.

'Where's William?' he asked.

Now it was John's turn to break bitter news. His voice husky with grief, he related William's death from plague. Margaret bowed her head, touched by the grief of her brothers.

Robert Newton came forward. He put strong arms about Margaret's shoulders. Through streaming eyes, John saw the determined movement. He nodded at Newton. Some things could not be resisted any more. Newton returned the gaze. For a few seconds the two faced each other. Man stared at man. Between them surged the tidal race of their tempestuous relationship. Then the weaver also nodded. He turned and kissed Margaret on the forehead.

Soon after nightfall the Mentmore survivors with their armed escort returned to the town house of Sir Robert Knollys. The city was in the hands of its most brutal and criminal elements. In the darkened alleys apprentices and country radicals killed all who refused to swear an oath of allegiance to the 'true commons'. Whilst it was dangerous on the streets, Edmund and John had decided that the safest place of refuge lay in Knollys's armed camp. The packs of killers would steer clear of a party with an escort of men-at-arms in mail.

Knollys's house, by St Helens, Bishopgate, was seized with frenzied preparation. Clearly some action was planned for the morrow. Pleased at the safe arrival of the Mentmores and their escort, the Cheshire knight ordered a Friday supper of bread, fish and wine. Crowded into Knollys's solar, the two Mentmore sons were soon pumping the world-weary knight for news of the events at Mile End.

'So the king agreed to their demands? Can this be true?' John was incredulous.

'He did,' Knollys replied. 'He agreed to abolish villeinage and the work on the lords' demesnes; he agreed that labourers may work on free contract for whatever they can get as pay; he acceded to their demands that land should be rented at fourpence an acre. The king has promised the liberation of all prisoners and conceded that the "true commons" may seize traitors wherever they find them. You will understand that the mob will decide for itself who are "traitors" and who are not!'

John whistled. 'Holy Mary!'

'And on that note, the Essex men broke up and returned to their homes.' Knollys smiled cynically. 'I told your brother that the king intends to keep to none of these agreements. Even now, he has appointed Arundel to replace the murdered Sudbury. He has thirty clerks writing out charters enshrining these rights, but by Monday they'll not be worth a penny piece for the lot.'

John's eyes widened in understanding.

'As of now,' Knollys continued, 'the king – God bless the lad – is all that stands between us and destruction. But by this day's work he has halved Tyler's army. So far the Earl of Salisbury's counsel has held good.'

John raised a quizzical eyebrow.

'I'll explain later,' Edmund whispered, 'along with much else.' John had much to catch up on.

'And what will happen tomorrow?' Edmund had not failed to notice Knollys's martial preparations.

Knollys grinned. 'Ah, yes ... tomorrow. Tonight the mob holds the city. You heard they sacked Treasurer Hales's house at Highbury?'

'Yes, but what of tomorrow?' Edmund persisted.

Knollys scratched his short bull neck. He was obviously amused by Edmund's impatience.

'Sir Robert, what of the Kentishmen?' Anne Glanville's voice was cool and crisp. It demanded attention. Both Philippa and Margaret viewed her with respect.

'You must not fear for tomorrow, good lady.' Even the hardened warrior had no defence against Anne Glanville. 'Tonight King Richard is safe at Baynard Castle. Tomorrow he will go to meet this Tyler and his rabble at Smithfield.'

'Tyler is dangerous. The king must beware,' Edmund said.

Knollys sniffed. 'We know. This Wat Tyler would make himself king if he could. He has abused the common people. Sheeplike, they truly believe they are rooting out traitors and serving the king. The simple are easily led. But this Tyler is neither simple nor humble. His appetite for insolence knows no bounds. For this reason, Mayor Walworth has ordered me to prepare my knights and men-at-arms. He in turn has warned all loyal guildsmen to hold their armed retainers ready for his instructions.'

'What means he to do?' Philippa said, shaking off her shyness.

Knollys smiled at the pretty face creased with concern. 'The king will ride to Smithfield with two hundred men as escort. Mayor Walworth will meet him at Smithfield market – the place arranged with Tyler. The king's escort shall wear armour beneath their robes – '

'But you will not be there?' Edmund had a knowing look.

'No. But I shall be mounted and ready in full armour. Walworth intends to arrest Tyler; to kill him if necessary. He believes that without its head this beast of rebellion will collapse. As he acts, we will ride out and face the mob with visors down and weapons drawn.'

'By St Anthony, that is a gamble!'

'Yes, John Mentmore, it is that. Tomorrow we shall gamble for the future of the realm. But take heart. I believe Walworth is right. We shall seize the day, have no fear.' Knollys rose from the table. 'Edmund, a word before I leave you with your family and . . . friends.' His eyes lingered on Anne Glanville as he said the last word. At the door he spoke softly: 'The Duke of Buckingham has not forgotten your gallantry in France. He would have you become a knight of his chamber. He asked my opinion. I said I knew of none better.'

'Sir Robert, I owe you – '

'Quiet, Edmund. You owe me nothing. It was your gallantry that won you this honour. It is a door that opens into the court, my friend. Tread carefully and you may profit greatly.' Knollys cast another glance at Anne Glanville. 'It would be a favourable marriage bargain, you know. Were I a country knight, I would leap at the chance to marry my daughter to a chamber knight of the king's uncle. Especially if I had dallied too close to the king's enemies. It would be an act of sheer loyalty to agree to such an advantageous match.'

The incorrigible old brigand gave Edmund a wink.

'Thank you, Sir Robert. As always, your strategy is faultless.'

'Of course, of course. Now eat, for I would have you ride with me tomorrow. You are owed a moment of triumph over the king's enemies – and your own!'

Back at table, the meal was tense. It would be a long time before John and Robert Newton would relax in one another's company. Neither could fully fathom the future, save that some things once thought impossible could now scarcely be resisted. Margaret moved between them pouring wine into their cups as Anne Glanville retold her story. Edmund filled in a gap here and there.

'Tomorrow Appulby will pay the price, if God wills us victory, and Horne will not escape destruction.' Edmund's voice was choked with righteous anger. 'Have no fear, John, there will be opportunity enough and I have the necessary skill.'

'But what of us?' Philippa was tearful.

'Aye, what of us, John?' Margaret looked to the new head of the House of Mentmore. 'Father is dead, the cloth store is destroyed, the tapestries are reduced to ashes. What will we do?' It was rare for Margaret to show herself so dependent on anyone. John swilled his wine about his goblet.

'Giles will receive us at Upton,' Edmund said to his sister. 'John has done great work in the Cotswolds. Isn't that so, John?' Edmund also thought: There's worse to fear than a Mentmore married to a weaver. However, he held his peace.

But before John could reply, Margaret laughed bitterly. 'But all we own has been destroyed.'

'It seems we are destroyed, Maggie, but we are not,' John said. 'We own hundreds of marks' worth of cloth in East Anglia and the Cotswolds.' He looked at Newton, who seemed resigned to the inevitability of what John was signalling for the cloth industry. 'We bought it with Lyons's money but he is dead and his records destroyed. It is now our cloth. The destiny I pointed out to father has been thrust upon us. We own almost nothing here, but our wealth is in this venture. This autumn, the contracts I made will be fulfilled and Mentmore cloth will be in our hands again.'

Philippa touched her husband's hand. 'I must lay the child down.' The golden-headed toddler was sprawled in her lap. 'And I too must rest, but before I do I will thank God for this deliverance; for we have been delivered, as surely as anyone ever was.' She paused and her eyes were soft, like shy leverets. 'Too often we make requests and then either forget to look for the hand of God or neglect to give thanks for His kindnesses. This time, I shall not be so remiss.'

She smiled at her husband. He returned her look of open, vulnerable love. She rose quietly and John kissed her.

The other women also rose to leave and bade the menfolk good night.

John poured a goblet of wine for Newton. Warily Rob took the olive branch and sipped the wine.

'We must talk, Rob Newton,' John said.

'Yes, John Mentmore. That we must!'

Edmund leaned back against the wall panel. 'So, brother, did we win or did we lose? And all for the price of fish!'

John regarded his younger brother. 'Win? Lose? The game is still in play, Edmund. The dice are still in flight.'

He raised his goblet of wine. Robert Newton and Edmund did likewise. In the flickering glow of the tallow candle, the goblets met in cautious but mutual salutation.

Afterword

The medieval chronicles record that on the morning of Saturday 15 June 1381 the fourteen-year-old King Richard and his escort rode to meet the Kentishmen assembled at Smithfield.

Wat Tyler met him insolently with many demands. At the height of an angry altercation, Mayor Walworth arrested the rebel leader. Tyler, in fury, stabbed the mayor. Walworth was wearing armour and took no harm. Drawing his own sword, he cut down Tyler and killed him.

In the resulting confusion, Walworth summoned up his reserve force of armoured knights and armed citizens. Leaderless and confused, the insurgents were soon outflanked by Knollys's men. A band of heavily armoured knights pushed through the crowd and rescued the king.

At the eleventh hour the revolt collapsed. It was an appalling gamble by the city authorities, which succeeded. Urged by Knollys to show mercy, the king allowed the now-leaderless Kentishmen to return to their homes. For the instigators of the rebellion (both in London and outside the city) the only recourse was flight from the fury of the king's officers and the landed classes. For these rebels, there was no pity. John Ball was betrayed at Coventry and executed, as were other radical priests. The French chronicler, Froissart, estimated that fifteen hundred died at this time.

One week later, a group of peasants from Essex reminded the king of his promises to give them their freedom. To their plea, he replied: 'Villeins you are, and villeins you shall remain.'

The rural cloth industry continued to grow apace, to the detriment of the city-based guilds. In the west country and East

Anglia the weaving communities began an expansion which would carry them into the fifteenth century and beyond. Fortunes were made by the new class of merchant clothiers, men and women who had anticipated the rising commercial tide and backed their business acumen with money, time and vision.

More compulsive fiction from Headline

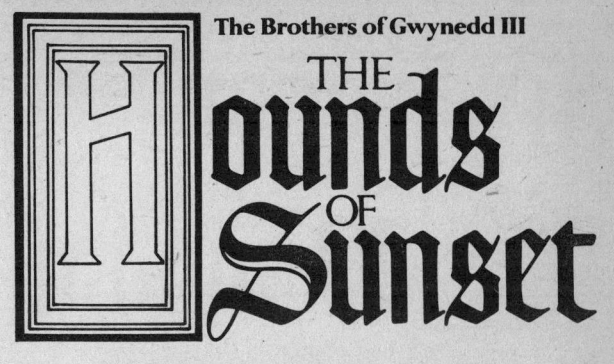

The Brothers of Gwynedd III

THE Hounds OF Sunset

EDITH PARGETER
WHO ALSO WRITES AS ELLIS PETERS

BROTHERS IN LOVE...AND WAR.

The third chronicle traces the destiny of the warring brothers of Gwynedd.

Powerful Prince Llewelyn still treasures his vision – Wales as one, united against the threat of the English kings. The dream seems near fulfilment, until Edward, vigorous, ambitious and arrogant, takes old Henry's place on the English throne – and more than his share of power.

Troubles loom nearer home, too, where the youngest of the Welsh brothers – David, blue-eyed, charming and deadly – is plotting his downfall.

Threatened on all sides, Llewelyn looks for comfort from the beautiful Eleanor de Montfort, the jewel in his crown and the only shining star as night falls on his dreams of power.

Also by Edith Pargeter from Headline
SUNRISE IN THE WEST
THE DRAGON AT NOONDAY

Historical Fiction   0 7472 3029 3

More compulsive fiction from Headline:

THE Dragon AT Noonday

The Brothers of Gwynedd II

EDITH PARGETER
WHO ALSO WRITES AS ELLIS PETERS

BROTHER AGAINST BROTHER

The gripping sequel to *Sunrise in the West* sees Wales gloriously united and England torn in two by bloody strife. Llewelyn seizes the opportunity to force recognition of his title and right as Prince of Wales, refusing to be deflected from his goal, even by the tragic deaths of his mother and sister, or by his brothers' treachery. But in allying himself with the mighty Earl of Leicester, he stands to win everything . . . or lose all.

'The complexities of medieval life are excellently presented' *Sunday Times*

'A powerful drama . . . a vivid and imaginative storyteller' *South Wales Argus*

Also by Edith Pargeter from Headline
SUNRISE IN THE WEST

Historical Fiction   0 7472 3017 X

More Historical Fiction from Headline:

THE BROTHERS OF GWYNEDD QUARTET

EDITH PARGETER
WHO ALSO WRITES AS ELLIS PETERS

'A richly textured tapestry of medieval Wales'
Sunday Telegraph

The story of Llewelyn, first true Prince of Wales, is the history of medieval Wales in dramatic and epic form.

Llewelyn's burning vision is of one Wales, united against the threat of the English. But before he can achieve his dream, he must first tackle enemies nearer home. All three of his brothers hamper his efforts to create an independent state. The best-loved of the three, David, brought up throughout his childhood at the English court, restless, charming, torn between two loyalties, is fated to be his brother's undoing. Despite the support of his beloved wife Eleanor, Llewelyn finds himself trapped in a situation where the only solution is his own downfall and a tragic death . . .

Edith Pargeter writes:
'I have previously written historical novels in which Llewelyn the Great and Owen Glendower appeared, and it struck me as a great pity that virtually nothing had been written about the second Llewelyn, who came between the two, and seems to me a greater and more attractive personality than either, and a fitting national hero.'

Here, for the first time in one volume, is the entire saga of The Brothers of Gwynedd, including:
Sunrise in the West
The Dragon at Noonday
The Hounds of Sunset
Afterglow and Nightfall

'Strong in atmosphere and plot, grim yet hopeful . . . carved in weathered stone rather than in the sands of current fashion' *Daily Telegraph*

HISTORICAL FICTION 0 7472 3267 9

More Historical Fiction from Headline:

WISE WOMAN'S TELLING

Daughter of Tintagel
FAY SAMPSON

You couldn't mistake the shape of big Uther Pendragon striding into my lady's chamber. We saw his shadow huge across the curtain. He was like a giant bending over the bed. Over his wife and son, that should have been the wife and son of Gorlois, Morgan's father. We saw him lift that golden child into his arms before the door slammed shut.

A boy. And Gorlois's little maid was left outside in the dark and the storm. He never even noticed her.

'Morgan!' I cried.

She'd gone beyond my help now. The darkness had taken her. And we may all suffer for that.

Uther Pendragon, with the aid of the Cornish warlord Gorlois, united the scattered kingdoms to defeat the invading Saxons. To celebrate his victory he summoned his chieftains — and their ladies — to a feast in London.

The bards have sung that tale the length and breadth of Britain: how the Pendragon fell in love with the beautiful Ygerne; how she and her husband Gorlois fled to Cornwall, pursued by Uther's warriors; how Ygerne and her daughters took refuge in Tintagel; how the Pendragon came to her bed disguised by Merlyn's craft as Gorlois, even as her husband lay dying on the field of battle; how she bore him a son, Arthur.

But the bards do not sing of the grief Morgan felt for her father; of her bitter enmity for Uther; of her mistrust of Merlyn, who tricked her family. They do not sing of her feelings for Arthur, the brother she should have hated . . .

FICTION/HISTORICAL   0 7472 3263 6

More Historical Fiction from Headline:

GRETTA CURRAN BROWNE

An epic novel from Ireland's past

TREAD SOFTLY ON MY DREAMS

The Emmets were Protestants, belonging to the elite society of Ireland's ruling class. Robert Emmet, the gentle, diffident youngest son of the State Physician of Ireland, developed a deep love of his country and a devotion to justice that took entire possession of his soul.

In the historic year of 1798 his life changed from its charted course to one of rebellion. A brilliant student at Trinity, he cast aside all hopes of a scientific career, all the privileges of his class, to join the United Irishmen – a society dedicated to the unity of Protestant and Catholic.

After the '98 Rebellion, Robert was forced to flee to France. But as his boat sailed away, he watched the sun rising over the Wicklow Mountains, like a phoenix from the embers, and knew he would return – to the cause of his country, and to the beautiful girl he had fallen in love with, Sarah Curran, daughter of Ireland's most talented lawyer.

He returned – and met Anne Devlin, a Catholic country girl, who became his most devoted and bravest companion.

Set against the background of a world in turmoil, a country at war, this is the vivid and powerful story of three young people, Robert Emmet, Sarah Curran and Anne Devlin, drawn together in love, in hope, in tragedy.

'Well and simply written, with feeling and humour, and the meticulous research illuminates the scene without ever intruding upon it' *Sunday Telegraph*

'A very fine achievement' *Irish Sunday Press*

'I can't recommend [it] highly enough' *Irish World*

'A vivid and moving story' *Irish Post*

FICTION/HISTORICAL   0 7472 3612 7

More Historical Fiction from Headline:

VALERIE ANAND

Crown of Roses

'A warmly detailed and credible picture of the Middle Ages. One of the best Richard III books that I have read' Rosemary Sutcliff

England is at war, the houses of York and Lancaster locked in bitter conflict. King Edward has married commoner Bess Woodville, incensing even the most loyal of his supporters. Then events take a dramatic turn when his brother Richard is brought to power and the court grows diseased with treacherous intrigue . . .

'A well-written novel that has plenty of action . . . Valerie Anand writes with considerable understanding of the period' *Best*

HISTORICAL FICTION   0 7472 3344 6

More Historical Fiction from Headline:

DAUGHTER OF LIR

DIANA NORMAN

author of TERRIBLE BEAUTY

Although she's been raised in the richest, most sophisticated convent in twelfth-century France, Finola is Irish, and because of that the Pope sends her to take charge of the powerful Abbey of Kildare.

But her French upbringing is in opposition to the complex, political power struggle of the clans around her, and one prince especially becomes her enemy – Dermot of Leinster. Within months she is an outcast – to be rid of her, Dermot has had her raped, and she has been publicly humiliated by her Church.

All she has left is the desire for revenge. With the help of an English knight, she finds her way to her birthplace in western Ireland where an academy of warrior women teaches her to fight. In the process she gains friends and a love of her country; though Ireland is in danger of invasion by the Normans.

By building her own network of spies Finola opposes Dermot, the Normans and the machinations of King Henry II's spymaster. But one of the lords she's fighting is the man she loves . . .

"A fast-paced read." *Best Magazine*

"Rich and entertaining." *The Times*

"A ripping historical yarn with much authentic detail."
Publishers Weekly

FICTION/HISTORICAL 0 7472 3282 2

A selection of bestsellers from Headline

FICTION		
HUNG PARLIAMENT	Julian Critchley	£4.50 ☐
SEE JANE RUN	Joy Fielding	£4.99 ☐
MARY MADDISON	Sheila Jansen	£4.99 ☐
ACTS OF CONTRITION	John Cooney	£4.99 ☐
A TALE OF THE WIND	Kay Nolte Smith	£5.99 ☐
CANNONBERRY CHASE	Roberta Latow	£4.99 ☐
PRIDE	Philip Boast	£5.99 ☐
THE EYES OF DARKNESS	Dean Koontz	£4.99 ☐

NON-FICTION		
A CHANCE TO LIVE	Marchioness of Tavistock and Angela Levin	£4.99 ☐
THE GREAT DONKEY TREK	Sophie Thurnham	£4.99 ☐
THE JACK THE RIPPER A TO Z	Paul Begg, Martin Fido, Keith Skinner	£6.99 ☐
HITTING ACROSS THE LINE	Viv Richards	£5.99 ☐

SCIENCE FICTION AND FANTASY		
BUDDY HOLLY IS ALIVE AND WELL ON GANYMEDE	Bradley Denton	£4.99 ☐
BRAINCHILD	George Turner	£4.99 ☐
A BAD DAY FOR ALI BABA	Craig Shaw Gardner	£4.99 ☐
DESTROYING ANGEL	Richard Paul Russo	£4.99 ☐
ALBION	John Grant	£4.99 ☐

All Headline books are available at your local bookshop or newsagent, or can be ordered direct from the publisher. Just tick the titles you want and fill in the form below. Prices and availability subject to change without notice.

Headline Book Publishing PLC, Cash Sales Department, PO Box 11, Falmouth, Cornwall, TR10 9EN, England.

Please enclose a cheque or postal order to the value of the cover price and allow the following for postage and packing:
UK & BFPO: £1.00 for the first book, 50p for the second book and 30p for each additional book ordered up to a maximum charge of £3.00.
OVERSEAS & EIRE: £2.00 for the first book, £1.00 for the second book and 50p for each additional book.

Name ....

Address ....

....

....